The Wind From The South

THE WIND
FROM THE SOUTH

Son So-hui

translated by
Suzanne C. Han
Kim Mi-za

Si-sa-yong-o-sa, Inc., Korea
Pace International Research, Inc., U.S.A.

Published simultaneously in KOREA and the UNITED STATES

KOREA EDITION
First printing 1988
Si-sa-yong-o-sa, Inc.
55-1 Chongno 2-ga, Chongno-gu
Seoul 110-122, Korea

U.S. EDITION
First printing 1988
Pace International Research, Inc.
Tide Avenue, Falcon Cove
P.O. Box 51, Arch Cape
Oregon 97102, U.S.A.

ISBN: 0-87296-031-5

This book is a co-publication by Si-sa-yong-o-sa, Inc.
and The International Communication Foundation.

About the Author

Son So-hŭi was born in 1936 in Hamgyŏngbuk-do Province (now in North Korea). After graduating from high school, she went to Tokyo to attend college but soon returned home because of poor health. She later passed an examination for teacher certification.

In 1939 she went to Harbin, Manchuria and worked for the *Mansan Ilbo*, a newspaper for Koreans living in Manchuria. In 1942 some of her peotry was included in a collection of poetry by Korean residents in Manchuria.

She moved to South Korea in 1949. From then she wrote many short stories and poems that were published in literary journals. She enrolled in the English Department of Hankook University of Foreign Studies in 1957 and graduated in 1962. During that time she won the Seoul City Culture Award for *Ku Nalŭi Haetpitch'ŭn* (*The Sunshine of That Day*) in 1961. Her literary career peaked in 1963 with the publication of *Namp'ung* (*The Wind From The South*). She died after a long illness in 1986.

Most of her works focus on emotional conflicts between the characters and conflicts within the characters themelves resulting from environmental influences.

Translator's Note

Koreans rarely use names or pronouns, relying instead on titles of respect or honorific verb endings that indicate relationship or familiarity. Thus, for the convenience of readers, we have used names and pronouns while retaining some titles where necessary. At the same time, some of the text has been interpreted in an attempt to evoke the same emotional reactions in readers as is evoked by the Korean. This is because such responses are not always achieved with literal translations due to cultural differences that are manifested in idioms and choices of words.

Terms for food, clothing, units of measurement, monetary units and other words for which there are no English equivalents have been transliterated and explained either in the text or in footnotes. The McCune-Reischauer system has been used for the Romanizing of such words as well as for the names of the characters and place names.

As for the geography, it should be remembered that this is a fictional work and thus the places and geographical descriptions may not conform to maps. The author did not spell out some place names; for example, giving only "N Hospital" or "C Port." However, for the convenience of readers, we gave them names.

While we received help from many sources, we would like to acknowledge Mr. Dave Loeding and his wife Choi Young-sook for their help in preparing the manuscript.

K.M.
S.C.H.

CONTENTS

CHAPTER I

1

Already they were at the outskirts of the white poplar woods at the village school. A few more steps, they would be at the lotus pond in front of the school. Chin Se-yŏng and Ch'oe Nam-hi had passed the railroad crossing without knowing it. On the other side of the crossing the road ran along a rambling hill to the right. The pond was to their left beside the road.

The night was dark. Frogs croaked loudly in the rice paddies on the hillside and in the pond. Without saying a word, Se-yŏng and Nam-hi soon found themselves in front of the school. After it would come the village so they knew better than to go farther and risk being seen together.

A bridge spanned the pond in front of the school. They sat by the pond, a safe distance from the bridge. Silence continued between them as they gazed into the pond. Nothing was visible in the opaque stagnancy except an occasional flash of darkness. The water was much too muddy and most of it was covered by lotus leaves.

Sometimes the frogs stopped croaking, and strange noises like bubbles floating up to the air from the water sneaked into the quietness. Perhaps tiny creatures such as leeches, snails

and young fish were diving and sputtering in the water. These
frail sounds would soon be drowned out by the full blast of the
legions of frogs.

"It seems like we're in a country of frogs," Se-yŏng muttered. Nam-hi kept looking into the dark pond without so much
as turning toward him. A certain desire slowly filled Se-yŏng
and made him blush. The way Nam-hi curled up made her look
fragile like she would fall down with one light touch of his
hand. Se-yŏng's eyes followed her profile emerging more
clearly from the darkness. She looked unreal.

Se-yŏng pulled his hands from his pockets and then thrust
them back in. He felt for cigarettes and pulled one out.

"When will you go to Changchun?"

Nam-hi's gentle murmur awakened Se-yŏng from his
thoughts.

"I don't know. When do you think I should go?" He exhaled
smoke, his hand cupped over the cigarette. The night was submerged in the persistent croaking of the frogs. "I want to have
it all settled before I leave, but with you so clammed up on the
subject...."

His voice was low and hoarse. She felt it vibrate through her
body as if it were coming from a deep cavern. He always talked
as if it were up to her to decide, Nam-hi thought. But she had
absolutely nothing to do with making decisions for herself.

"Won't you see my father? I'm sure he's expecting you.
Regardless of what the outcome may be please come to talk
with him."

"If he's expecting me, it's only out of curiosity. I can't
imagine any other reason, for I know he doesn't like my being
here."

"That's what you think. Father's not like that. Why are you
so prejudiced towards him?" Asked Nam-hi in a clear soft
voice, turning her face towards Se-yŏng for the first time.

"From what cousin U-yŏng tells me, he seems to be quite
leery of me."

Nam-hi too was aware of that. Only the day after she had

been to U-yŏng's with her younger brother Tong-shik to deliver her elder brother Tong-jun's letter to him, her father, Ch'oe Ch'i-man, repeated quite deliberately that her betrothal to Yi Sang-jun was almost finalized and admonished her to behave accordingly. There was no mention of Se-yŏng.

"Chin Saengwon* told you so?" Nam-hi asked timidly. The Ch'oe family called Chin U-yŏng, Chin Saengwon. Even ten-year-old Tong-shik and eight-year-old Tong-su called him that, for they could not think of any other polite title.

Se-yŏng nodded and said, "It wouldn't surprise me, since I'm my mother's son." He groped for Nam-hi's hand with the hand that had shaded the cigarette, but he could not get it.

"People might see your cigarette from the road." Nam-hi curled up even smaller, wary of the glowing cigarette. While she truly worried that someone would see the cigarette, she always turned the conversation to something else whenever Se-yŏng mentioned his mother. From afar came the sound of a train whistle. The locomotive was probably coming out of the Changyŏn tunnel to the south. The croaking of the frogs jolted to a stop and the locomotive's heavy breath tore through the ensuing silence as it passed behind the school.

"It's the eleven o'clock train. We're late."

"Yeah."

"It's much too late for me to be out."

"I know. Nam-hi.... Well, I'll come to see your father tomorrow. Actually, I should have gone to see him right after I came home, but I just kept putting it off and now it's too late. I guess I was just wrestling with my inferiority complex. Anyway, it seems the people here are still a meddlesome lot. The older people have been complaining to U-yŏng that I haven't called on them to report my homecoming, but greeting them in person would be too embarrassing. Should I thank them for flog-

---

* Saengwon was originally a title given to a person who passed a lower civil service examination but was later adopted as a polite way to address a man.

ging my mother's coffin, Nam-hi....?

"Anyway, I'll visit your father tomorrow and ask him face to face for your hand. But I can see his response even now. Showing up so unceremoniously after having kept silent so long since my return, he'll think I'm trying to pick a fight by proposing to you on my first visit. I won't have anything to lose, though. Obviously, he doesn't think very highly of me."

"You don't understand my father. He's never done wrong to you, has he?"

Se-yŏng nodded. Perhaps he was too hardened by the resentment and shame he had carried with him ever since that unforgettable day. It was a day of shame and punishment brought about by his mother's infidelity. It was because of the unerasable shame of that day that he still resented and avoided facing the people of Pukch'on, especially Ch'oe Ch'i-man. It was because he was the son of his mother, because his neighbors were not tolerant towards her, and because they had betrayed his trust. There were other reasons too, Se-yŏng told himself, shaking his head again.

"Whether they were right or not, I just can't forgive the elders of Pukch'on. I wish you weren't a Pukch'on resident. Nor Tong-jun, either."

"You've been in my thoughts continuously because of that day. It's been impossible to forget you." Nam-hi blushed and was thankful for the darkness of the night.

"Yes, I knew how you felt from reading Tong-jun's letter. I think it was when Tong-jun was in teacher's school that he wrote the two of you were waiting for me to come home when school was out. I tore the letter into shreds, fighting back tears the whole time. I went to a restaurant and downed some three pots of liquor, too."

"My brother waited so long for your letter. That was when I finished public school and was staying at home doing nothing."

"Why didn't you write me?"

"I might have if you had answered his letter."

"Even if you had written, I wouldn't have written back. I was trying to become successful so I could surprise the people of Pukch'on someday. The simple vanity of a boy. A wretched childish dream."

"I kept thinking how truly wonderful and great it would be if you were to become a glorious success and return."

"Nam-hi."

"Yes?"

"We always thought the same way when we were growing up, didn't we?"

"I'm so happy I've had a chance to tell you my thoughts like this. I used to think that if you never came back, I'd hide somewhere in a deep mountain or at a remote seashore and make myself sick missing you. The idea of a pale, delicate existence was so popular among the girls at school that I must have caught it, too."

Se-yŏng looked down into the dark pond, repeating Nam-hi's name silently. The circular silhouettes of the lotus leaves blurred as tears sneaked into his eyes. He pinched his nose hard to force them back. The frogs that had become silent because of the train whistle began croaking with a full vengeance.

"What if your father turns down my proposal? Of course, he'll refuse me. And I know I'll just jump up and get out of the place as fast as I can. What will you do if things turn out that way?"

"You're not being fair. What'll happen to us if you behave so rudely in front of my father?"

"But that's what I'll do."

Nam-hi stifled a sigh. Her nose tingled at the tip and her lips trembled, but she did not move a finger.

"What will you do in that case?"

"I guess Father will decide."

"But he'll refuse me, he will."

"Do you think he'll decide right on the spot.?"

"What if he never says yes? What if he never gives us his

permission?"

Ņam-hi pulled her shoulders together and lifted her face. He was asking her far too much, she thought. Tears welled in her eyes. "I'll have to think about it."

Se-yŏng grabbed her hand. "You're the only person in my life, Nam-hi."

Tears began to stream down her face. She did not know why she was crying so much. She wiped them off with a stealthy hand and stood up. Se-yŏng got up, too. He wanted to take Nam-hi in his arms but refrained, remembering his mother's shameful conduct. They crossed the bridge to the wïder road. The frogs were quiet at last for the night was now very deep. They walked up the road silently. After a while, Se-yŏng got very close to Nam-hi and called to her, "Nam-hi?"

"Yes?"

"What are you thinking about?"

She turned to him with a smile and said, "I was thinking of ghosts."

"Ghosts!"

"Yes, ghosts." Saying the word made her shudder for she remembered suddenly that part of the road was rumored to be haunted by ghosts. Se-yŏng too remembered vaguely of hearing such stories when he was little.

"I don't believe there are ghosts these days."

"But there are. They say they're a mother and daughter."

"A mother and daughter?" Asked Se-yŏng a bit louder. The child they took out of his mother's body was a boy, he told himself.

With a shriek, Nam-hi threw herself into Se-yŏng's arms. Se-yŏng hugged her. In his arms, she was like a little bird, light as air. His strong arms held the little bird tightly. His arms that had stayed away from her snapped out of control and he could not control himself any longer. His lips sought Nam-hi's. As if she were truly a weary bird, she did not resist him.

When at last Se-yŏng released her, Nam-hi wanted to die then and there. How could she have let him kiss her? She almost fainted with shame and guilt. She could feel sweat running down her back and also on her forehead. It was not so much the fear of ghosts but the awful way she had just behaved.

"Do you regret it...? I must be worse than a ghost. Anyway, why did you suddenly think of that? I mean the ghosts."

"I was scared."

"Oh?"

"I heard footsteps. Rustling footsteps." Nam-hi shuddered again. She thought something was following them.

"You're not well. Is that why you look so pale? Have you been ill?"

"No."

"Then it's just nerves."

"But there are people who have really seen the ghosts."

"Then they're weak-minded people."

"You think so?"

"Nam-hi, look at the sky. Do you see the stars?"

"Yes, I do."

"Do you see my face?"

"Yes."

"Do you see my eyes? Come nearer and look. Do you see them?"

"Yes, I see them."

"Good. Now you'll understand what you see. Do you know what I mean?"

"No, I don't."

Se-yŏng came very close to Nam-hi and clasped her shoulders with his hands. "Then look at my eyes again. Look very carefully until you see the pupils. Do you see them?"

"No, I can't see them."

"You can, if you keep looking hard. You must see them." Se-yŏng's eyes blazed in the darkness, but Nam-hi could not see his pupils.

"Even if you can't see them now because it is too dark, you will see them soon. Do you see? Do you understand what I mean? We're going to get married. We're destined to marry each other. Just remember that, Nam-hi. Do you understand me? Do you?"

Se-yŏng repeated the same words again and again before he told her the time and place to meet him the next day and left her in front of the rice mill from which a shaft of light was leaking out.

As on previous nights, they were seen by no one.

Nam-hi walked home with a heavy heart. In her numbed mind she knew she was passing Sun-shil's house. Some insects were chirping under the wall of the house. Did they already feel that morning was near? Some dogs barked half-heartedly somewhere and soon stopped altogether.

"Is that you, Nam-hi?"

Nam-hi jolted to a stop as if someone had grabbed hold of her hair. Her legs wobbled. For a crazy moment she thought her stepmother had learned her secret.

"Where have you been?"

"Over there, "Nam-hi softly answered.

"Over there where?"

"To Sun-shil's house."

"You've been to Sun-shil's house?"

Nam-hi walked to the well, drew up some water with the dangling bucket and drank it.

"I came out here to wait for you because your father's so worried about you. Why do you have to stay out so late? Try to come home earlier."

She was Ch'oe Ch'i-man's second wife. She bore him two sons, Tong-shik and Tong-su, and was only a couple of years past thirty. Knowing her husband dearly loved Nam-hi, she always tried to be very nice to her. The only thing Nam-hi could complain about her was that she told her father everything she did as she did not want to be blamed if something unfortunate happened.

"What if I go and ask Sun-shil tomorrow? Are you sure you've been there?" She asked again as they passed through the gate and stepped into the house. She seemed to sense something was wrong.

"That's what I said," Nam-hi retorted and dashed into her room.

2

Chin Se-yŏng had gotten off the eleven o'clock train at Pukch'on station about ten days ago. Since it was quite late and he was visiting the place for the first time in ten years, he had not expected to see anybody he knew. Besides, he had already made up his mind to ignore any familiar faces he might encounter. But the first people he saw on the platform that night were Tong-jun and his sister. He was taken by surprise at the strange coincidence. The brother and sister represented all the yearning he harbored for his hometown, for Tong-jun had been his closest friend in childhood and Nam-hi, who was so cute tagging along after them, had been like a sister to him. They had been both brother and sister to him as well as friends. It was quite natural that the memory of them always tugged at his heart whenever he thought of his home.

Pukch'on was a small place, but even express trains stopped here as its station had a water tank filled with water from the Yongch'ŏn Stream. Another reason they stopped was the long tunnel between here and the next station. Every train had to stop and wait until a train coming from the opposite direction made it through the tunnel before it could go through.

Chin Se-yŏng was the only person that got off the north-bound train that night. Though it was dark, there was something about him that caught the eye of the local people. He started forward before he noticed a young couple standing side by side. They stopped talking to look at him. He pulled his hat down over his face, lifted his bag, and called to a passing attendant. If his memory was correct, there had been a short cut to the bridge along the slope of the hill and he wanted to know if it was still there. The attendant shook his head, gesturing broadly. The path was blocked when the water tank was built.

Se-yŏng walked forward reluctantly. The distance between the two parties shortened step by step. He had no choice but to go past them. He could feel the insistent scrutiny of the man and woman. Like hunting dogs sniffing after their game, he thought disgusted. How insolent of them. Yet they looked quite refined for people of this remote place. He was almost in front of them. Their eyes were still locked on him, they were the eyes of hungry predators eyeing their prey. He slightly turned his face away from them to express his disgust and walked past them. He could still feel their eyes on· his back when the man called after him.

"Excuse me?"

Se-yŏng looked over his shoulder.

"Excuse me, but aren't you Chin Se-yŏng? Forgive me if I am mistaken."

Se-yŏng turned around and put down his bag.

"Yes, I'm Chin Se-yŏng." He knew instantly it was Tong-jun, but he gave his name anyway just in case.

"Yes, it's you! I knew it must be you. It's me, Tong-jun. Didn't you recognize me?" Se-yŏng and Tong-jun shook hands vigorously.

"I'm sorry, but a favorite son I'm not. It's not like I'm return-ing home in a silk robe." Se-yŏng said in a husky voice.

"Don't say that. I'm on my way to Chuŭl. I'm teaching there. You must come visit one of these days, and we'll take in a hot spring. We'll get bloody drunk the whole night and you can tell me all about your life in Tokyo. Wrestling with snotty nosed brats day in and day out is driving me crazy." After the long handshake, he turned to Nam-hi. "Nam-hi, you know Se-yŏng, don't you? Well, this is Nam-hi. Can you recognize her? The kid who pestered us so much by tagging along after us all the time?" Then he added gaily, "But she's now known as a beauty around here."

Nam-hi and Se-yŏng bowed to each other at the same time. Nam-hi's face was red.

"You've really changed." Se-yŏng looked at her admiringly and back at Tong-jun.

"You've changed, too. But you couldn't slip by my sharp eyes." Tong-jun slapped Se-yŏng's back and laughed.

"Thanks." His laconic answer was full of emotion. Nam-hi lowered her eyes as something hot welled up behind her eyelids. Her thick eyelashes hid her eyes. Her lashes were so thick that they almost looked heavy.

A whistle sounded from a train coming over the crossing.

"It looks like my train is coming. Be sure to come visit. My wife will be glad to see you. We keep talking about you and thinking we need to change our way of life. Nam-hi, why don't you come with Se-yŏng too?"

Se-yŏng and Tong-jun shook hands again and the train pulled into the station. Seated in the car, Tong-jun repeated his invitation again and again until the train started. Se-yŏng and Nam-hi stood there watching till they could no longer see Tong-jun's face.

"I've always thought of you as a little girl." Se-yŏng smiled at Nam-hi, turning his eyes from the darkness left by the train. She looked shyly at him and bowed her head quickly. Her clear, luminous eyes glittered with untold emotions. Her eyes seemed to say that she was not the only one who had grown up but that Se-yŏng had, too. Nam-hi lifted her eyes again and she and Se-yŏng looked into each other's eyes for a long moment. Then, bowing their heads, they walked toward the ticket collector. Outside the station, they looked at each other again. They knew they had to go different ways.

There had been a memorial service for Nam-hi's mother the previous night, and Tong-jun had come home for the service as it conveniently fell on a weekend. He had to come alone as his wife was still recuperating from having a baby. Afraid that he would not be able to make his father's birthday later in the month, he had taken the chance to bring a birthday gift.

That night she had been at the platform seeing her brother off with some food for his wife. Since the train was delayed, she had taken the chance to ask his advice about getting married. More than seeking advice, she had poured out her heart to him. She was unhappy with the man to whom her father was so anxious for her to marry. He was a Meiji University student named Yi Sang-jun. She had seen him a couple of times at some student meetings and had received letters from him. They were so full of outrageous words that they made her blush. Once he enclosed a photograph of himself in nothing but swimming trunks at a beach. Shocked at the indecent display that showed he was so skinny his ribs could be counted, she thrust it back into the envelop immediately. She could not bring herself to tell Tong-jun all these details. She just said that there was something about him that made her want to turn her face away whenever she set eyes on him.

"Well, father knows best. And he's the kind of man that no matter what you or I say, he will not change his mind. We'll just have to wait and see."

Tong-jun tried to placate her and reasoned that her aversion toward San-jun was an impulsive feeling that could not be considered a just assessment of him. Nam-hi smiled sadly as she listened halfheartedly to her brother's advice. 'You don't know anything. You really don't know anything,' she shouted silently to herself as she looked at the brightly lit windows of the northbound train pulling into the station. As it was not very often that she could talk intimately about herself with Tong-jun, she was happy and sad and lonely at the same time. Perhaps she felt sadder and lonelier because of the overwhelming bleakness of the small deserted country station.

Se-yŏng's appearance in front of them on such a night and at such a place was certainly a big event for the brother and sister. Especially for Nam-hi who, looking at the bright windows of the night train, had been praying fervently for a miracle to happen then and there. It did not have to be the return of Se-yŏng, but here he was in front of her, the most wondrous of miracles. From the moment he appeared her eyes became lustrous pools of rapture and her feet kept missing steps as if she were walking on air.

Nam-hi came out the exit turnstile with Se-yŏng. Outside, drowsy lights were blinking in the pleasant warmth of the night. Se-yŏng seemed to want to tell her something. Or perhaps she was more eager to pour out her heart to him. There had not been a day in the past ten years that she had not thought of him. When she was a little girl, she had thought of him because she felt sorry for him, but as she grew up he had become the one and only man in her life. There was no room in her heart for any other man to slip in. Sometimes she thought he might be thinking of her like she thought of him. Her heart thumped wildly. She gathered strands of stray hair and pulled them behind her ear quietly. She noticed that Se-yŏng had stopped walking and was trying to say something.

"I want to see you alone. Maybe tomorrow?"

She blushed and lowered her eyes. What he wanted was her wish as well. The flames in her eyes were veiled by her delicate eyelids and heavy eyelashes. Se-yŏng was reminded of an old incident involving those lashes. Nam-hi had snipped them with scissors when she was about ten years old. She had countless blood stains around her eyes as though she had been stabbed by lots of needles. She had been upset because she had heard thick eyelashes brought misfortunes to women. The fact that her girlfriends said that her lashes looked false or ominous did nothing to assuage her anxiety. So one day, she took the scissors and, looking in the mirror, snipped off the horrid things down to the root, believing that because she did so she would not have to die young like her mother. She went about weeping for some time thereafter as the stubby lashes pricked her skin so painfully that she could not open her eyes which were constantly watery anyway. Naturally, she was the object of grown-ups' laughter and pity.

Se-yŏng's lips twitched with a smile as he remembered the incident he had long forgotten.

"Where?"

Nam-hi looked up at him from beneath her thick eyelashes.

Se-yŏng was captivated by her eyes that opened like some mysterious windows when their shutters were taken away. He suggested a place near the bridge. They had met there almost every night since then.

3

The village sat like a hen brooding over its chickens under a mountain that branched off from the T'aebaek Range at the General's Rock. It was called Pukch'on, "North Village," because it was located at the northern tip of Changyŏn, an elongated basin as its name, "Long Lake," indicated. The shape of the basin was similar to a writhing snake. It was said that it had been a waterway streaming down the T'aebaek Mountains in ancient times. The other end of the basin was blocked by a mountain which looked like an island, without a head or a tail to connect it to the main range, and in front of it flowed Yongch'ŏn Stream, separating Sŏch'on, "West Village," from Yongdam. About 5 ri* from Pukch'on was Tongch'on, "East Village."

A long time ago, the villages were about 10 ri from each other. Except for mules and ox carts, the only means of transportation was walking, but nobody felt any inconvenience as it was just accepted as a normal way of life.

One thing that was not natural to outsiders was the villagers' bickering about their ancestors. The question of whose ancestors were more prestigious was pursued fanatically among neighbors and between villagers. Some would create a very dubious book of genealogy for their clan and boast about it to other clans. Marriages were arranged only after a thorough scrutiny of the genealogies of the parties involved. More intriguing was that these people, isolated in this remote area of the mountainous Hamgyŏng-do Province with virtually no

---

* "*Ri*" is a traditional unit of measurement; 10 *ri* equals approximately 4 kilometers.

chance of getting an honorable public position, valued their genealogies more than anything else.

In such a place, Ch'oe Ch'i-man, the elder of the local Confucian shrine and the head of the Ch'oe clan, was Pukch'on's respected patriarch. His estate included some 10,000 *p'yŏng** of fertile land in Pukch'on, over 20,000 *p'yŏng* near Tongch'on, and over 4,000 *p'yŏng* in Yongdam. He also owned a large pond between Pukch'on and Tongch' on, which was a source of considerable income because lotus roots and seeds from it were valuable herbal medicine ingredients. When his wife died after a prolonged illness, leaving him with two sons and a daughter, he put on mourning clothes and spent most of his days secluded in the *sarangch'ae*** with his little daughter and an old earth colored chest in which his clan's genealogy was kept. After a half year of mourning, he had the memorial altar to his wife removed from the house. He reasoned that, by leaving this world prematurely and thereby deserting a husband she should serve and children she should marry off, she had sinned in this life as well as in her previous one, this one being the direct result of the previous one. Six months after the removal of the altar he married a maiden of the Hyŏn clan of Tongch'on. At that time he built his oldest son a house identical in size and style to his own.

Ch'oe Ch'i-man was a handsome man of sturdy build, made even more handsome by a luxurious beard. He was revered by all villagers and none ever complained about him dominating them. In the countryside, living harmoniously according to ancient traditions was the most plausible law, and when there was some doubt or a conflict of interests, people would go to a revered person to pass judgement. Ch'oe judged fairly in such cases and his opinions were highly respected.

What made his name most well known in that part of the

* A unit of measure equal to 3.3 square meters.
** A separate part of the house used by men as a study and a place to entertain guests.

country, however, was the punishment he imposed on the dead Widow Chŏng, even though it was not his idea alone. Another thing for which he was known was his donation to the local school of over 10,000 *p'yŏng* of land near Tongch'on. It was due to his donation that a school had been built in Tongch'on.

When the railway was laid in the area, the school was upgraded to a public one, and Ch'oe was given a letter of appreciation by the county chief. The presentation of the citation was held at the town office on the occasion of the dedication of its new building. Of course, many of the guests who were invited to the dedication saw him being honored and some of them touted that it was through his efforts that the township office was moved to their area, even though it was actually because of the new railroad station that it was moved here together with the police station.

Ch'oe had the letter of appreciation framed and put it on the southern wall of his room in a place where he could see it when he sat with his back against the chest where his genealogy was kept. The chest was made of mulberry wood coated with an earth color paint and decorated with white brass. Beside it was a low book case shaped like a desk, on top of which were a large ink stone, a purple circular water dropper for grinding ink, and a bamboo brush holder. Well-thumbed Chinese books were stacked on a narrow reading desk. A large hat box papered with pale mulberry paper hung high at the west corner of the wall, and a folded up two-meter-high, ten-panel folding screen was propped underneath the box. These were some of Ch'oe Ch'i-man's most treasured possessions. He bought the screen to celebrate his appointment to elder of the Confucian shrine. He also had two more screens. A calligraphy scroll hung by the southern window. The calligraphy was done by Tong-ho, his eldest son. So that he would have something to do, recently Mr. Ch'oe had been having him do most of the necessary writing, including the signs to be put on the doorways to welcome the spring.

About twenty or thirty houses were clustered behind Mr. Ch'oe's. With the exception of an occasional tin roof, most of them were thatched with rice stalks. The timber and style indicated that they were all built within ten years.

There was a little vegetable patch that looked like an island between these new houses and the road behind it. The road had been recently constructed as a main road. A stone mound in the vegetable patch, which looked like a tiny hill covered with lush pumpkin vines in summer, could be seen from it. The land around the mound and that on which the new house stood was originally owned by Chin Sŏk-jae, Se-yŏng's father. He sold all of it but 100 *p'yŏng* for his house to Ch'oe Ch'i-man at a reasonable price during his long illness.

Ch'oe Ch'i-man turned the land into housing plots and sold them at a considerable profit after the railroad was laid and invested the proceeds in building waterways from the Yongch'ŏn Stream to develop rice paddies near the vegetable patch and in planting fruit trees on the slope by the roadside. The hill was transformed into an orchard and the arid field into valuable rice paddies. It was said that Mr. Ch'oe was indebted for this innovation to Hwang Chin-su, the foreman of the Yongch'ŏn railroad bridge construction crew, who had suggested the idea to him and had undertaken all of the work himself. Still, he was never allowed inside Mr. Ch'oe's house for Mr. Ch'oe was of the opinion that a man who drifted from one construction site to another was of the lowly class and no better than a seaman who lived by gutting fish. He prided himself on having never let a vagrant cross the threshold of his house.

For some time strange rumors were heard throughout Pukch'on about the stone mound in the vegetable patch a few hundred meters from Ch'oe's house. The tenant of the patch was Chin U-yŏng, Se-yŏng's cousin. One early spring day after Ch'oe Ch'i-man had turned his field into rice paddies, Chin Saengwon was working to remove the stone mound so he could turn the vegetable patch into a rice paddy. When the A-frame was full of stones and he was readying himself to carry the frame on his back, he was seized by a sudden pain in the stomach that caused him to turn over the stones. It was said that his head ached and his stomach hurt terribly. Nonetheless, a few days later he returned to the patch to remove the stones. All went smoothly until when he lifted the loaded A-frame to his back, the supporting stick broke under the weight and he fell forward with the A-frame and all and one of the stones struck his head. He had to stay in bed over a month. A shaman called in to determine the cause of the disaster, announced that a vindictive ghost abided in the stone mound and that anyone who attempted to do so much as lift a stone from it would be harmed. Chin promptly abandoned his efforts to develop the land into a rice paddy.

Following the incident, dubious stories began to be heard not only in Pukch'on but also all over the Changyŏn basin. Some said that a woman was seen nightly sewing something or nursing a child on the mound, others said that the mound turned into a house at night and light could be seen coming from it, and some even said they heard a woman's wailing near it.

When his neighbors greeted him by saying, "Hey, Chin Saengwon, I see you've survived a curse," Chin would shake his head vehemently and answer with a wry face, "Yeah. I was spared because I prayed to the ghost lady and offered her a fat pig and tasty cakes made with the best rice powder." But it was only Chin U-yŏng himself who could tell how much truth there was in his story about the ghost and his illness.

Ch'oe Ch'i-man first heard the story from his young wife one morning after breakfast when he was in the main room fondling their first child Tong-shik. He turned pale for a second but, calmly removing the baby's hands from his beard, he knitted his brows and denounced the ghost. "What a wicked woman! Obviously she was not punished enough! The job had to be left unfinished because her son burst in. Perhaps that's why her ghost has not been able to enter the hall of ghosts and keeps haunting and causing trouble."

Carrying the breakfast table towards the door, Mrs. Hyŏn*
murmured deferentially to her handsome husband, "Who
knows she didn't become a vindictive ghost? I'm sure she must
have."

Ch'oe Ch'i-man, who was talking to the baby in a low voice
and tenderly nibbling its small hands, clucked his tongue and
said, "What an absurd idea! She may have turned into a ghost
but she has nobody to blame but herself. How dare she resent
anybody when she took her life with her own hands?"

"But we'll never know for sure. The dead cannot say. And
the circumstances of her death were strange. She didn't leave
a note or anything."

"What are you trying to tell me, woman, by saying that the
circumstances were strange?"

"I can't help pitying the poor woman. As the saying goes,
there is no tree that won't fall down if axed time and again. We
never know if she fell at the first try or after many. Whatever
the case, it was awful to treat the dead that way. She didn't
deserve it. Death was more than enough punishment."

"Damn the wagging tongues of harebrained females! Are you
in your right mind? What do you mean by her being tried or
fallen down? Are you saying that the Widow Chŏng was killed
by somebody?"

"You know that's not what I mean. I mean somebody could
have sneaked into her house with wicked intentions, and
maybe she was too weak to help herself."

"What a dangerous idea! A woman should always keep her
doors securely locked when she is alone. Even if she had been
assaulted, she should have fought to her death to preserve her
virtue. If the woman had resisted with her life, she could have
been spared such a wretched consequence."

"But such is not the way with ordinary mortals. She was just

* Women in Korea retain their maiden name after marriage. Thus
Ch'oe's wife is called Mrs. Hyŏn.

a helpless woman with a son to raise. How could you expect so much of her?"

"That's exactly what I'm saying. If she was a good mother and remembered she had a son to raise, she should have done everything to avoid such an unfortunate disgrace for her son's sake if for nothing else."

Putting aside the little boy who was still clutching at his beard, Ch'oe stood up and brushed his trousers with his sleeves. As usual, he was wearing the gentleman's pointed hat he was never seen without. There were a few streaks of white in his well tended beard and brows.

"A good mother certainly wouldn't abandon life when she has a little child. Even in the most dire situation, I would never think of leaving my little Tong-shik alone by dying so easily. Maybe it couldn't have been avoided even by fighting to her death." Mrs. Hyŏn was not her usual meek self in obstinately defending the dead woman.

"Are you saying that I was wrong and unjust?"

"Please don't ever do such a thing again. Leave the punishment of the dead to other people, I beg you." She blinked her tearful eyes and turned towards her child who, making a game of wrecking the breakfast table, had his hands in the kimch'i bowl. After sucking the spicy sauce off the child's hands, she said, "Come, Tong-shik, get up on mommy's back." Placing his hand on her shoulder, she lifted the child to her back and wrapped a blanket around the two of them, securing it with a wide band.

With a dignified cough Ch'oe Ch'i-man said, "Be sure not to mention that senseless gossip around Nam-hi. She would become afraid of the dark."

"I'm scared of going out at night myself these days. I wish the village people would hold a memorial ritual at the stone mound."

4

After seven or eight years the eerie story about the stone

mound had become a legend. And no attempt had been made to remove the mound.

Mrs. Hyŏn became a seasoned matron. A woman of generous nature and honesty even when young, she was always a dedicated wife who respected her husband as her superior and was a good stepmother to Nam-hi. She would go out of her way to choose dresses that best became her stepdaughter and tried to meet all her whims and wishes whenever possible. She was also the mother of two young boys. Tong-shik, the oldest one, was now ten years old and Tong-su, the youngest, was eight.

Ch'oe Ch'i-man had five children in all from his two marriages. His oldest grandson T'ae-yŏn, his eldest son's son, was eleven years old, a year older than Tong-shik. There were also the ten-year-old Yŏng-ae and two more grandchildren by that son. Tong-jun gave his father a grandson and a granddaughter. Mr. Ch'oe's most serious concern these days was Nam-hi, for she had reached marriageable age. He doted on his only daughter as she had lost her mother when she was very young.

Aside from his donation of over 10,000 *p'yŏng* of land to the school, there was another thing that earned Ch'oe the name of a man ahead of his time in the Changyŏn Basin—his sending his only daughter away to Seoul for higher education. Nam-hi was not only a beauty but the first girl in the Changyŏn area who was educated in Seoul. There was no need to say that Mr. Ch'oe was immensely proud of her. It would have been preposterous a few years before to even think of sending a girl as far away as Seoul for a higher education, but time had changed his way of thinking as it had done his village. What remained unchanged was Mr. Ch'oe's handsome house with a tiled roof whose furrows were mortared white, though there too time had begun to leave its marks in the lichens that covered the old tiles.

This particular day found Mr. Ch'oe, wearing his usual pointed hat and a pale beige summer outfit made with the finest linen, in his wooden floored hall. He spent most of his summer days in the hall because it was cooler there than in the *sarangch'ae.* He had added the hall to the southwest corner of the main building several years ago. The elevated floor was his favorite sitting area and where he met guests. The space under the floor served as a storage.

The day was pleasantly warm, and Mr. Ch'oe was cleaning his long bamboo pipe with a thin wire and swab. Next to him was a low table on which was a blue glass bowl of sweet fermented drink sprinkled with lotus seeds. Oblivious to the tiny flies buzzing over his drink and lighting on the bowl, he sat on the well-used grass mat, routinely sucking at his pipe and poking it with the wire.

As the next day was his birthday, the smells of greasy cooking drifted out from the kitchen along with the voices of women and the clatter of dishes and pans.

"So the birthday of my younger sister-in-law's new baby falls in the same month with its grandfather's, doesn't it?" Abruptly muttered Nam-hi's older sister-in-law who was removing bones from a dried fish. "Why, so it does." Her stepmother was busy breaking dry branches of wood and feeding them into the cooking fire. As the fire blazed and crackled, thick steam rose from the rice cake steamer securely placed on top of the oven. A rooster was crowing and flapping its wings in the back yard. Squatting near the back door of the kitchen, Nam-hi was cooking colored rice pastries.

"This kind of pastry should be sealed along the edge. Press the edges with your fingers." Her stepmother looked into the tray filled with cooked pastries between feeding the fire.

"It's about time you learn cooking from your good mother since you're going to get married this fall. Why, you're a late beginner, as it is. You'll have to keep yourself pretty busy to learn all the things you'll need to know if you're not going to shame yourself in your husband's house," her sister-in-law said.

"But Nam-hi's an educated girl of the new times. It's all right if she doesn't know how to cook. We do it because it's about the only thing we know how to do, being no better than a blind person in our ignorance," her stepmother said in a tired voice.

Nam-hi had only been helping in the kitchen since spring when she returned home after finishing school in Seoul.

"But you should really begin to train her in earnest. They will blame you if she doesn't know how to cook properly."

Cock-a-doodle-do, the rooster croaked again. "About what time is it now? Why, the stone by the well is already shaded. It's about time for the children to come home from school."

At that moment Nurŏngi, the dog that had been eagerly peeping into the kitchen a few minutes ago, barked. Nam-hi's stepmother craned her neck toward the gate. "I wonder who's coming? Seems we have a visitor." Even as she was muttering to herself, a tall, solidly built young man stepped into the gate. He wore a western outfit of white pants and a dark jacket. A straw hat covered part of his face. Nam-hi peeped out to see who it was. It was Se-yŏng. She was not surprised. Her throat had been burning with anxiousness as she had been waiting for him since morning.

"That's Mr. Chin Se-yŏng." Nam-hi murmured softly and stretched up to stand.

"You mean the Widow Chŏng's son who they say is back from Japan?" Her stepmother whispered to make sure she understood. Nam-hi nodded.

"My, my, how could he...?" Her sister-in-law's eyes grew as large as burning lamps.

"Excuse me?" The visitor was already in front of the main room and asking for the master of the house.

"Oh, please wait a minute." Tucking her hands under her white apron, Nam-hi's stepmother rushed through the front veranda and the spare room to the wooden floored hall. "Do we have a visitor?" Mr. Ch'oe asked without lifting his head.

"Er, yes, er, the Widow Chŏng's son is here." Her tongue did not work as she wished, and her heart thumped unreasonably.

"Huh! The Widow Chŏng's son's come to my house? Why don't you show him in. I thought he would never show up." Mr. Ch'oe stood up slowly and put on his linen frockcoat. Mrs.

Hyŏn stepped out onto the veranda and guided Se-yŏng into the hall. "Please come this way. You've changed so much I couldn't tell who you were at first. That saying is really true that as long as we are alive, there are always chances of meeting each other again...."

Removing his shoes, Se-yŏng stepped up past Mrs. Hyŏn into the hall and prostrated himself in a deep bow in front of Mr. Ch'oe.

"Why, you don't have to..." Mr. Ch'oe acknowledged his greeting, sitting cross-legged and shifting the open hems of his coat over either side of his knees. "You've endured the difficulties of living away from home very well. I can see you've changed a lot. I respect your strong will and effort to achieve so much," he said, caressing his beard.

"I'm glad to see that life has treated you well, sir," answered Se-yŏng politely, sitting in a kneeling position.

"Yes, time's been kind to us. You've been away from your hometown too long. We thought you'd forgotten us altogether." Though polite, his words of greeting implied that Se-yŏng's visit was long overdue. Se-yŏng smiled quite solemnly and said, "I've kept myself out of sight in a way befitting the sinner's son that I am."

"Hmm, is that so?" Mr. Ch'oe nodded, and putting tobacco into the pipe he had been cleaning, nodded again and said, "Anyway, it's nice to see you turned out so successful. I congratulate you. I'm sure your late father can now rest in peace. Hmm, hmm," to which Se-yŏng responded with a bow. "So you are staying at Chin Saengwon's house, I guess?"

"Yes, sir. That's where I'm staying now."

"Incidentally, what happened to all your land? If I remember correctly, there should be a family mountain left, I think."

"I understand it's all gone for debts."

"U-yŏng told you so?"

"Yes, sir."

"Well, that's a shame. But then it's understandable since he gambles every winter. It's a bad habit he picked up when he worked in the gold mines in Siberia, I hear. Still, I think your late father had not been idle in the other world, considering how you have succeeded and how U-yŏng works like a bull during the summer."

Se-yŏng was not listening to him. He did not know very much about his cousin U-yŏng, nor was he interested in knowing. He was anxious to turn the conversation to the subject for which he had come.

"Please enjoy this," Mrs. Hyŏn brought Se-yŏng a tray with bowls of honey and a sweet fermented rice drink and made a hasty exit. There were some lotus seeds floating in the drink. Se-yŏng felt impatient and told himself he should press on to what he had come for. He pushed the tray aside after taking a sip of the honey water at Mr. Ch'oe's urging.

"Drink some more. It will cool you. I hear you will go to Changchun soon."

Silently cursing his cousin for his big mouth, Se-yŏng said he was and, after much hesitation and wavering, began by saying that he had a favor to ask. "I would like to ask for your permission to marry Nam-hi. I'll not make her regret it." It took all his courage to finally say it. He looked at Mr. Ch'oe, whose face abruptly turned as rigid as a stone. Shaking his stony face, he stared at Se-yŏng hard.

"Your eyebrows are too high. But then so are mine. I don't just mean that you have very high standards. You've really got your eye on something too good for you." Indeed, Se-yŏng's brows were quite high. "You're a handsome man and maybe a very good one too, but that's a favor I can never grant. In fact, my daughter has already been promised to someone whose parents are both living, though he is far inferior to you, considering. I wonder if you know Yi Sang-jun from Hadong? He too has been studying in Tokyo...."

"There's no reason for you to feel humiliated since I had already promised her to someone else. If anyone should feel humiliated, I should. Huh! To think that you're actually asking for my daughter's hand in marriage!"

Mr. Ch'oe kept staring at Se-yŏng, shaking his topknotted head. Se-yŏng's face turned crimson as if it were on fire. It actually burned. Even his high, clear forehead gradually became dark red. At last, Mr. Ch'oe turned his eyes away. He filled his pipe again and, after taking several draws, said, "I advise you to behave yourself until you leave this place. Don't bring trouble on yourself. People would love to see you disgrace yourself, but they wouldn't stand for me disgracing myself. I wouldn't forgive myself either. Do you think I went to all the trouble of sending my daughter to Seoul for an education so that I could become your father-in-law? You've got some nerve!"

Se-yŏng's eyes were blazing with a strange luster and tiny blood vessels shot into the whites. He stood up. Mrs. Hyŏn bid him good-by from the veranda but he did not hear her.

"Whatever Father said must have upset the young man very much," said Nam-hi's sister-in-law who, though older than her stepmother, was too shy and polite to let the visitor see her and thus watched from behind the door as he put his shoes on and walked out. Nam-hi also watched his receding back through the kitchen door. She sensed there had been some conflict between her father and Se-yŏng.

Returning from the hall with Se-yŏng's tray, Mrs. Hyŏn told Nam-hi that her father wanted to see her. Nam-hi hastily washed dry paste and grease off her hands and went to the hall. Her father looked at her seriously and told her to sit in front of him. She knelt with a sinking heart. After a dry cough, he said, "I'm not like the mother of Mencius who moved her house three times to give her son the best education, but you know I've done my best to raise you well. I even sent you to Seoul. You're the only girl in the Changyŏn Basin to be educated in Seoul. When I first sent you to Seoul years ago all our neighbors thought I was becoming senile or demented. We know now who was thinking ahead, though." Nodding his head vigorously, Mr. Ch'oe went on. "After all, it was because I gave you the best education in Seoul that your betrothal with Sang-jun, the heir of the Kongju Yi clan of Hadong, was possible. It was finalized yesterday, but I didn't tell you last night because a dark night isn't a propitious time to break good news. I was told that he will be back from Tokyo in about ten days. The wedding ceremony will take place as soon as he comes home. Remember who you are and don't be going out and around. Women are always compared to fruits or fish, meaning that they are apt to go stale with the slightest neglect. So be very careful of your demeanor and stay in the house, do you understand?"

Nam-hi thought she was going to pieces. She stared at her father with disbelieving eyes, refusing to believe what she heard. Hadn't Se-yŏng come home and proposed to her? His proposal was an overwhelming joy for her and she was not going to lose it like this.

"I'm not going to marry him, Father. I told you the other time that I didn't want to marry him." Her voice was low but clear. Mr. Ch'oe cocked his head and glared at her.

"What did you say?"

"I said I'm not going to marry him."

Mr. Ch'oe kept glaring at her and leaned closer to her.

"I'm not going to marry him."

"Why?"

"I don't like him."

"What?"

"I said I don't like him."

"Hmm, so you think a daughter can talk to her father like that! You should remember that the wedding has already been agreed to, and your father is not a person to go back on his word. This time I'll forgive you because I know you're behaving this way because I've always pampered you. But don't you ever try to plot something under my nose, and don't go out of this house. Is that clear?"

5

The last glimmer of the evening light trailed away and darkness settled in the room. Nam-hi sat listlessly in front of her desk. She had sat like that for a long time. Except for an occasional flicker of her eyes, she sat so still it seemed she was arrested by eternity. She had decided that she would follow Se-yŏng. In her mind she could see clearly how disappointed her father would be, but she told herself she could not throw herself into the abyss of desperation for his sake.

It became darker in the room, but her eyes grew used to it. A vivid scene was replayed in the familiar darkness, a scene that was branded in her memory and would never go away. She thought perhaps it was due to the sorrowfulness of the unforgettable scene she had witnessed so early in her life. And perhaps Se-yŏng had held a special place in her heart since that day.

That was the day the coffin of Se-yŏng's mother was flogged. Nam-hi pitied Se-yŏng. She was so sorry for him she felt she would die. The whole village was aswirl with activity as if it were the eve of a festival, but the faces of the women were overshadowed with worry. The sky was dark with ominous clouds as if reflecting their troubled hearts.

The village women, humbly clad, gathered in the yard of the Widow Chŏng's house. The menfolk also gathered. Dogs prowled around wagging their tails. As it was Sunday, runny nosed schoolchildren contributed to the bustle by playing by the stone fence or stampeding through the yard.

The yard, which was not spacious to begin with, was already packed with people by the time Nam-hi stepped in with her stepmother. Men were standing in groups near the house and women near the gate. At the center of the yard was a coarsely woven grass mat and a coffin covered with a sheet of cloth stood on it. There were no chief mourners or relatives in hemp mourning clothes to be seen. And no lamenting chant could be heard. The coffin covered with a white cloth held the body of the Widow Chŏng. Yun Sŏbang* was the only person

* Sŏbang is a way to address a man of low birth.

standing close to the coffin. He wore a netted band on his head and gaiters on his legs, but his attempt at decent attire ended there as he wore no over garment or vest to cover his soiled clothes. With a bemused face and holding a long staff, he stood waiting. His topknot above the head band trembled like a tiny animal from time to time, betraying his inner tenseness. His greasy, purplish face looked menacing. In fact, he looked capable of destroying anything if he set his mind to it as he stood firmly beside the coffin with the point of his staff planted in the grass mat. Nam-hi was afraid of him. It was more out of fear of him than fear of the coffin that she clung to her stepmother's skirts with all her might. He was the only butcher in Pukch'on and Yongdam and he did all the slaughtering in the area. Mr. Ch'oe would send for him not only to slaughter a hog but also to slaughter even a simple hen, insisting that slaughtering was a job befitting only a butcher.

At the higher part of the yard, some men standing around Nam-hi's father noisily discussed something. Someone hollered at the top of his voice, and another clicked his tongue in disgust. There seemed to be a lot of accusations and differences of opinion. Finally they seemed to reach an agreement. Several men stepped up to the coffin and told Yun Sŏbang to remove the cloth sheet. Still clutching the staff, he stooped and removed the sheet. As if to play some kind of game, the men separated into groups of three at both sides of the coffin, lifted it easily from the grass mat and placed it on the bare earth.

Nam-hi clung even tighter to her mother's skirt, unable to take her eyes off the fearful but fascinating sight in front of her. She heard Sun-shil's grandmother clucking her tongue beside her mother. "Ah, poor soul," she said.

Ae-sun's mother whispered, "I heard it was one of the vagabond musicians that came to the village last spring."

"So they say, but who knows what really happened?" Sun-shil's grandmother spat the words with a bleak face. Her eyes were wet with tears. Nam-hi felt her nose tingle and tears welled up in her eyes. She buried her face in her mother's skirt until she heard someone clearing his throat. It sounded like her father, and lifting her face, she found him in front of the villagers. Wiping her eyes and nose on her mother's skirt, Nam-hi stared at her father. In his white coat of bleached cotton and familiar pointed hat, he looked very distinguished, much more so when seen from afar like this than at home. She blinked her eyes and watched him through her thick lashes. He read aloud something written on a piece of mulberry paper. Some of the women stiffened as if paralyzed, but some nodded in silent agreement. Nam-hi did not understand what her father was reading at the time, but she was deeply disturbed. Perhaps it was because she saw tears oozing out of the reddened eyes of Sun-shil's grandmother. Her mother too was weeping profusely.

Mr. Ch'oe finished reading, rolled up the paper and stepped back a few paces. Then a village officer stepped forward and hollered, "Nine flogs it shall be!"

Yun Sŏbang shuffled a few steps away from the coffin and lifted his staff high above his head. The village officer hollered again. "One!"

Yun Sŏbang's staff hit the coffin with a resounding thud. Everyone gasped.

"Two!"

"Three!"

"Four!"

"Five!"

"Six!"

Each time the village officer yelled, Yun Sŏbang's staff smacked the coffin mercilessly. Each time the staff landed on the coffin, Nam-hi buried herself in her mother's skirt. Sun-shil's grandmother, whose eyes and nose were red, shuddered. "Dear god, the wretch will break the coffin!" Her mother turned her head away.

"Seven!"

It was when the village officer called for the seventh flog that a boy, clad in ordinary clothes, pushed his way through the

crowd and looked around bewilderedly. His eyes were bloodshot and his lids were swollen from crying. At the sight of Yun
Sŏbang's staff striking the coffin, he charged forward like an
angry bull. Screaming "Mommy, mommy!" he toppled over the
coffin. The people around it gasped.

"Oh, mommy, mommy!" The boy wailed writhing over the
coffin.

"Why, isn't that Se-yŏng? Yeah, it's Se-yŏng."

"Tut, tut.... Poor child! His mom treasured him so, but now
there's nobody to dress him in decent mourning clothes."

"Really, at least somebody could have clad him in hemp
clothes." The women whispered among themselves. Nam-hi
sobbed hard into her mother's skirt. By now her mother was
crying openly, blowing her nose into her skirt.

"Get away, brat! Somebody, get rid of the wretch!" Mr.
Ch'oe thundered angrily. The village officer rushed to Se-yŏng
and coaxed, "Come on, boy You shouldn't be here."

The boy's mouth gaped open like a cave. Blood vessels stood
out on his neck as he gurgled in a muted wail.

"What're you doing here, kid? It's no place for you." Chin
Saengwon plodded forward and dragged the boy by the arm.
Because he was jostled as he moved through the packed crowd,
his oddly shaped gray hat hung on his head precariously.
Under the dirty blue cotton coat one could see he wore gaiters.

The boy's name was Chin Se-yŏng and it was his mother's
coffin being flogged. Which meant that he, not his cousin, was
the chief mourner and should have been wearing hemp clothes
and a hemp cap. However, there was no chief mourner and no
mourning relatives at this funeral. Wearing gaiters was all U-
yŏng could do to pay respect to the dead. The gaiters would be
needed later anyway since he would be one of the bier bearers.

"Come on, kid. Behave yourself. You don't want to be flogged too, do you?" Chin Saengwon mumbled to Se-yŏng but did
not try to force him away from the coffin. On the contrary, he
seemed to be taking his time on purpose, enjoying all the
attention he was getting. The last flogging of the coffin was held

back in the commotion. The people became noisier with remorseful remarks of pity, heated accusations and all kinds of advice.

Somebody in the group shouted, "Get rid of the boy. Get rid of him right away."

Kim Sŏndal* darted out and grabbed Se-yŏng up by his waist, and Chin Saengwon reluctantly lifted the boy's legs. Se-yŏng cried and pounded his head against the adobe wall surrounding the yard of his house. Tears swelled again in Nam-hi's eyes. She left her stepmother to follow Se-yŏng.

"Go to my house in Yongdam and wait there. Crying·like this won't do any good to anybody. Would it help the dead come back to life? Or would it undo the flogging they did? What's done is done. I'll be with you after the burial." Chin Saengwon consoled Se-yŏng in a loud voice.

Nam-hi ran to her house, sobbing all the way. She found Tong-jun sitting on the veranda. He was whistling with a sad face. "Brother Se-yŏng's over there crying." Reporting to her brother, Nam-hi was filled with sadness again and she sobbed even harder.

"Where? Where is he?" Tong-jun sprang up from the floor of the veranda. he had been staying home because he thought Se-yŏng was at Chin Saengwon's house. By the time Nam-hi went back to the adobe wall with her brother, Se-yŏng was not anywhere to be seen. He had probably run away to some back alleys between the houses. Tong-jun started to run blindly along the lane that led toward Yongdam.

When he came home at dusk, Tong-jun's eyes were swollen from crying. Nam-hi knew that he had been crying with Se-yŏng in the small room in Chin Saengwon's house. Nam-hi became tearful again at the sight of Tong-jun's swollen eyes. She threw herself over her little desk and sobbed silently lest anybody hear her. Crying brought back the memory of her

---

* Sŏndal is a form of a dress for a person who passed a state civil or military examination but has not been given a post.

mother who had died a couple of years before, and she cried harder. That was in the spring when she was eleven years old.

About ten days after the funeral, Chin Saengwon visited Mr. Ch'oe. He sat on the wooden floor outside the center room. A tray was brought to him bearing a bowl of wine, some slices of bean curd and kimch'i.

"Help yourself. The weather is not very promising today, is it? Have you finished fertilizing the fields?" Mr. Ch'oe addressed the visitor from his room through a small opening in the window.

"Fertilizing or not, I've missed two days work already because of Se-yŏng."

Gulping down his wine, Chin Saengwon coughed and stuffed the bean curd into his mouth. "Because of Se-yŏng? How is that?"

Mr. Ch'oe looked down at the man's averted eyes, suspecting a dubious scheme behind them. The villagers called him Saengwon because he was over thirty and it was rather awkward to call him by his name only. He took a piece of kimch'i and chewing it slowly, mumbled, "Well, the wretched kid ran away. You see, he's always been a wild and daring sort."

Mr. Ch'oe threw the window wide open. When he had visitors he thought were not good enough to invite into his room, he usually seated them on the wooden floor outside and did business through the window which was only about thirty centimeters wide.

"So what happened?" He asked, peeping out the window. His face looked like a framed photograph.

"He has a relative on his mother's side in Chuch'on. By the time I got there, he had been there and left."

"So he has a relative somewhere, huh?"

"I was told that he headed across the Manchurian border to Kando. His mother's family lives there somewhere. But I'd say wherever he ends up, the best he could hope for is not to starve to death."

Mr. Ch'oe studied Chin's face. The angular eyes drooped at

the corner and the dark thin lips curled in discontent. But then, it was no better in happier moments, for he believed he looked more dignified peering at the world from under lowered eyelids.

"Poor boy!" sighed Mr. Ch'oe.

"Well, I guess he did well by leaving this place. He had no reason to stay here. He'd just be hungry, that's all."

"Are you hungry?"

"Of course, sir. No one wants to entrust me with land to farm because I've been a vagrant for a long time. And, as much as I would like to, how can I farm without land? Of course, it didn't help me one little bit when Cousin Sŏk-jae, Se-yŏng's father, that is, died poor, leaving nothing. His widow had a hard time herself."

Mr. Ch'oe smoked his long bamboo pipe for sometime and said, "How many days' ploughing do you think you could do?"

"A land of two days' ploughing would be as easy as eating cold porridge."

"Huh? You think you can manage that much by yourself?"

"I've a large family, you know."

Mr. Ch'oe nodded and commented, "I thought Sŏk-jae's widow had some fields left for her."

"Yes, but it's only a hill, a house and a couple of hundred *p'yŏng* of barley fields."

Several days after this conversation, Mr. Ch'oe gave U-yŏng half of his 4,000 *p'yŏng* in Yongdam to tenant farm.

The next spring Se-yŏng's house was torn down completely because nobody wanted to buy it. Nam-hi used to go to the vacant lot from time to time, but stopped after hearing that a ghost abided in the stone mound on the ruins.

Around that time, railroad tracks were laid near the village and the barley fields were turned into more valuable rice paddies. As was the trend, some families in the Changyŏn Basin began sending their sons to Tokyo to study. Of the three students that went, only Yi Sang-jun of Hadong was financed by his family. The other two earned their way through college. It was from them that the village learned that Se-yŏng was studying in Tokyo.

Nam-hi was in her third year in high school in Seoul. She was the only girl in Changyŏn to study in Seoul. She was an honor student excelling in painting and calligraphy, which made Mr. Ch'oe immensely proud and pleased.

What he did not know was that every time this daughter he was so proud of returned home for vacation she was aflutter with anticipation in the hope that Se-yŏng might have come back to his birthplace. It had become almost a blind obsession with her, even though Se-yŏng had not even sent so much as a simple postcard to his best friend Tong-jun and it was said that he went out of his way to avoid anyone from his hometown. There was certainly no reason for her to harbor even a tiny hope that such a man would have returned home and be waiting for her. Yet there were moments when she blushed at the image of Se-yŏng appearing in the gateway any minute calling her brother's name.

Holidays dragged for the girl who languished in the house in the countryside. Her best friend to talk with to pass the time was her younger brother Tong-shik who was only in the first grade of elementary school. Perhaps that was another reason she awaited the return of Se-yŏng.

One day Nam-hi took on the task of cleaning the house. She dusted every corner of the main part which took her the whole morning. After lunch she started to clean the *sarangch'ae*, the outer house where Tong-shik's study and her father's room were. After tidying up Tong-shik's desk, she went into her father's room. It smelled of must and tobacco. As if to dust off the smell, Nam-hi swished her duster over the chest in which her father stored handy items. The nickel carp-shaped lock on the chest rattled. To Nam-hi it seemed to rattle in indignation. 'Sorry, lock. Sorry to surprise you.' Nam-hi caressed the lock and polished it with a rag. She also polished the nickel ornaments on the chest. Now it was time for the yellowish Chinese books. As the waxy gloss of the covers had disappeared with age, they looked more dusty than they actually were. After dusting them one by one, she tried to wipe off the bug and fly specks with a wet cloth and found that it soiled the books more.

The citation her father received from the county chief was also blemished with fly specks. She took it down from the wall, cleaned the glass and placed it back carefully. Then she began to clean the hat box. Of all the things in the room, she thought it had the thickest covering of dust. Deep in the corner where it hung on the wall, were even several spider webs. She stood on her tiptoes to reach out and pluck them away, then stopped her hand midway, remembering the story of the flat spider and how it made the king abolish the Koryŏ custom of discarding aged people. Ever since she was told the story, she somehow appreciated the meager creature.

One time a Chinese emperor sent his envoy to Koryŏ to inquire about what peacocks feed on. As there were no sages left in Koryŏ because of the custom of abandoning old people in deep mountains to die, nobody knew the answer. The king announced throughout the country that anybody who knew what peacocks feed on should come forward and that he would be awarded with whatever he wished. A young man came to the king and told him that peacocks ate flat spiders. When the king was to award him, however, the young man prostrated himself and begged for his life because he had not deserted his old mother in the mountains to die.

He said that he had taken her on his A-frame backpack to the mountains when she reached the appropriate age. It was snowing that day, and as they went deeper into the mountains, the snow fell even heavier. The young man noticed that his mother kept breaking branches from the pine trees they passed and dropping them on the road. He was annoyed because every time she broke a branch he about lost his balance under her weight, and told her not to break them. His mother said, "I want to leave some marks so you won't get lost on your way back after you throw me away. How else will you be able to find your way back in this snow-covered mountain?"

The young man's eyes became hot with tears as he forced his way through the snow. But he never could bring himself to leave his mother alone in the mountain to die. Finally, he put her back on his A-frame and headed home. The pine trees his mother broke were actually very helpful in finding his way home in the snow. And it was his old mother who told him that peacocks feed on flat spiders. The king not only forgave him for breaking the law and allowed him to live with his mother, but also abolished the custom of abandoning elderly people.

Nam-hi's mother had told her the story. Before she died, she used to tell her many stories, like the one about fishing for dragons with a golden hook. 'Ah, if only my mother were with me now!' Thoughts about her mother rushed to Nam-hi. The flat spiders brought back memories of her mother whom she had almost forgotten, and she suddenly missed her sorely.

"On the night of the full moon, a water bird cries by the shore looking for its mother...." Humming softly, Nam-hi resumed her work on the hat box. She opened the cover and took out the large hats, the inner caps and other head gear, placing them one by one on the chest. She counted three large hats, two inner caps and two head bands, all made of horse hair, and then her eyes fell on a scroll of mulberry paper that had been lying under them. She tucked her duster under her arm and unrolled the scroll curiously. It was some kind of letter written in her father's handwriting. She remembered him taking a whole day to write such a thing. She began to read it. There were a lot of Chinese ideographs that she did not understand but she kept reading anyway.

From ancient times a woman whose spouse departed has been called "one who has not yet died" and has been pitied for the karma that denied her the honor of departing this life at the same hour as her husband. The Widow Chǒng, the not-yet-dead of the late Mr. Chin Sǒk-jae, not only aggravated her sin of failing to accompany her spouse by committing despicable misdemeanor, but also furher tripled her already abominable sin by willfully hastening her own preordained time of death upon learning that she was pregnant, the evidence of her misdemeanor, thus incurring the wrath of the gods of heaven and earth and bringing disgrace on all the villagers of Pukch'on.

Alas, we fear her shameful soul will not be allowed to enter the hall of ghosts, being shunned by all the ghosts because of her grave sins, and thus will be destined to float in vacuous space indefinitely. It will be equally forlorn to wish her carnal body, hardened with sin, to return to dust. Have mercy on the sinful soul! The villagers of Pukch'on have thus decided to punish the body of the Widow Chŏng to show that the morals that bind us all are not to be easily ignored and thereby appease the angered ghosts of the other world and beg that her poor soul be admitted into their hall. As we hereby direct the coffin containing the body of the Widow Chŏng be struck nine times, we sincerely ask that the soul of the deceased appreciate the flogging by the shamed and saddened villagers and, after gaining the pardon of the multitude of ghosts, launch its long flight into the hall of the ghosts.

> On behalf of the villagers of Pukch'on,
> Ch'oe Ch'i-man writes this on this, the
> second day of the third month of the
> year of the rabbit.

Nam-hi finished reading. She knew it was the scroll her father had read before the flogging of Se-yŏng's mother's coffin. She became cold and shuddered involuntarily at the revelation that her own father had not only wrote and read such a thing but also had kept it in his hat box to this day.

She had been very fond of Se-yŏng when she was little. He and her brother Tong-jun would catch dragonflies for her and take her with them when they went to catch sparrows or bats.

One time when they crossed a log bridge hanging across a stream they had to cross one by one with her between them because it was so narrow. Halfway over the bridge, she looked into the water and felt the bridge was floating down the stream. Overcome by sudden dizziness and fright, she flopped down and, clinging tightly to the bridge, bawled. While her brother who was behind her complained that she was a nuisance, Se-yŏng carried her piggyback across the stream. She decided at that moment she liked Se-yŏng much better than her brother.

In the spring when he went to pick wild azaleas that bloomed on the hills, Se-yŏng would take her along even though Tong-jun was against it. He would also pluck berries for her from the willow trees along the bank of the stream. When she began to go to the village school, he protected her from the mischievous boys. When the village school became a private primary school and she became a second grader, Tong-jun and Se-yŏng were transferred to the public school about 8 kilometers away. Many times Se-yŏng brought her ground cherries he picked up on his way home from school. Like a miser, she would hoard them in the back yard under the garden wall and play with only one a day. Carefully removing the fleshy inside, she would blow and suck on the bladder-like husk to make a clacking sound. Sometimes when she felt generous, she would give one or two to her friends Sun-shil and Ae-sun.

It was Se-yŏng, not her brother Tong-jun, that would gladly bind sheets of paper into a neat notebook when she asked him to. In the winter he did not mind pushing her sled on the ice until she got tired. He was also the one who fixed her snowman's face with pieces of charcoal.

Nam-hi's thoughts returned to the funeral of the Widow Chŏng. The scene she watched that day remained too vivid in her mind. The sight of Se-yŏng sobbing into the adobe wall came back vividly and made her heart ache. To think the paper that ordered the flogging of his mother's coffin has been kept in father's hat box!'

'Who could have proposed such a cruel and horrible act? Was it my father? No, it couldn't have been my father. He would never have suggested doing such a thing to a poor woman who had to kill herself in despair. But then who? Could it have been Ae-sun's father? Or Sun-shil's? Not my father, anyway. He always says we shouldn't disgrace dead people by gossiping.'

Nam-hi rolled the scroll with trembling hands. Se-yŏng's mother had been not only a neighbor but also a close friend of her late mother. She remembered the two women sewing together and going on picnics to get flowers for cakes in the spring. Se-yŏng's mother had been a bit younger than hers. Nam-hi kept thinking about her while cleaning the rest of the room.

She could not help thinking of Se-yŏng even after she returned to her room. She buried her face in her knees and twitched with the pain of the memories that tormented her like a reopened wound.

Since that day, most of her days had been spent brooding over Se-yŏng. And as the days passed, she became more and more obsessed with him.

6

Nam-hi stood up quietly from her desk. It was time for her to go to Se-yŏng. She listened to the muffled clatter of dishes coming from the kitchen where her stepmother was still working. She turned past the chimney in the backyard and reached the side gate. Her father was in the wooden floored hall with two village elders playing dominoes.

She stole her way through another side gate between the wooden hall and the outer house. Outside was all thick layers of darkness. She chose the darker side of the darkness. Dim lights shone through the windows of some houses. Even though they should look familiar to her, they made her feel even more forlorn.

'I wish Tong-jun were with me now!' Nam-hi faltered as she looked for some moments into the darkness that enfolded her eldest brother's house and then went on her way. Her eldest brother was a man of profound indifference, showing no interest whatsoever in anything in the world. No closer to the family than a total stranger, he did not show up in his father's house no matter what noisy and illustrious event took place. Villagers whispered behind his back that his brain was messed up from studying the Chinese classics too much, but Nam-hi thought he was just an extraordinarily silent person. He liked to write and recite poetry, and made small tables and wooden rain shoes as a hobby. Keeping to himself, he did not have friends nor any reason to go out. However, he took it upon himself to write nameplates and talismans for the villagers to hang on their gates in spring. Other times he pored over newspapers and books. Mr. Ch'oe had been anxious at first to have him tend his estate, but now he seemed relieved that his son showed even that much interest in daily life.

'And I can't expect much of my eldest brother!' sighed Nam-hi. She headed toward the main road behind the village. To her left was a rambling hill covered with pine and walnut trees and to her other side was a dense wall of acacias that encircled her father's orchard. She found Se-yŏng sitting on a rock by the side of the road where it began to climb up toward the acacia wall.

"Have you been waiting long?" she asked as she sat down on a stone by the road.

"Oh, just a little while."

Crickets chirped mournfully in the grass. Below them the village lay immersed in quietness. With the lights of the houses blinking dreamily, it looked unreal and remote like a village from an ancient legend. The dim light of a bicycle trailed across the village like in a blurred picture. Frogs croaked in the rice paddies, but not as insistently as they had the other day. Se-yŏng gazed down at the stone mound hidden behind the darkness. It was where the house where his father died prematurely and his mother killed herself had stood. He had to admit that it was certainly a haunted place.

"What did you say to my father?" asked Nam-hi.

"I asked for his permission to marry you....He said you are betrothed. Can't you break it off?" Stubbing out his cigarette, Se-yŏng turned toward Nam-hi. She shrank imperceptibly at his warm breath on her face.

"Aren't you afraid of me? You know my mother's blood runs in me. The blood of shame."

"Don't say such a thing. My father told you that, didn't he?"

"Uh-huh, something like that, but in more illustrious words."

"I thought so."

"So?"

"I've been wondering. If you hadn't seen me that night, would you have come to my father and asked for me?"

"I guess not."

Nam-hi blushed deeply as if her face was afire.

"Perhaps I might have left this place again without letting anybody know. I think all along my homeplace was a little girl named Nam-hi. I had to come back here just to see the place for the last time. You don't have to believe me. Perhaps it would be better for you if you didn't."

Tears stole their way into Nam-hi's eyes. The sky descended in darkness upon them and Nam-hi felt that they were the only two people left alone under it.

"I don't believe you? Do you know how I've been waiting for you? Oh, you couldn't know. You'll never understand!" Stifled words cried silently in her heart.

When Se-yŏng spoke to her again after a long silence, his voice sounded as if it was tumbling out from a deep cave. "Actually, I never thought I would find you so grown up. I wasn't even sure I would find you here at all. But the moment I saw you, yes, it was right at the moment I saw you that I was struck by the revelation there was a strong bond between you and me. A bond that had grown stronger over the last twenty years. It was so deeply rooted I knew I wouldn't be able to get rid of it. And when we met again, I could tell we shared the same wishes, the same hopes. Perhaps shame bound me to you, the wish to redeem myself in your eyes. You've no doubt been pitying me for being a helpless orphan, and that has kept you thinking of me all this time. Whatever it was I knew intuitively that we had been looking for each other."

Se-yŏng's voice melted into Nam-hi's soul. Stars came out one by one, lighting the dark sky. A gentle breeze from the hill floated past them. Se-yŏng held her hand which trembled with emotion. She was amused at how big and strong his hand was compared to hers. She wished they could hold each other's hands in broad daylight and she could look into his eyes. She thought she would be able to know the meaning of happiness if only she could look clearly into his eyes. She was overwhelmed with a desire to pour out her heart to him. After a long hesitation, she just mumbled falteringly, "Everything seems so different, so changed all of a sudden. To come out after dark like this for so many nights in a row...." But there was more, much more that she wanted to tell him. She wanted to tell him how she had always waited for him and how she had been certain that he would return to her someday. She also wanted to ask why he was going to Changchun.

"At least this is the last time you will have to come out in the night. I won't be here tomorrow." Nam-hi jerked her hand from his. Her heart pounded violently.

"You're leaving tomorrow!"

"I'm going to get on the night train tomorrow."

"To Changchun?"

"I guess I'll eventually end up there."

"For good, you mean?"

"Well, I'm going there for a visit, but if I like it I might as well settle there. It depends." He said Chu Tal-ho, one of his seniors in medical school, was working at the Changchun Hospital in Changchun. Being of a gregarious and optimistic nature, Chu was well liked, which was perhaps why he had been able to get additional years at the school to finish his intern and resident courses and later the appointment at the Changchun Hospital. Se-yŏng's journey to Changchun was entirely at his invitation. Chu had persuaded Se-yŏng, who was studying to be a surgeon, that he would get good on-the-job training under favorable conditions there. Even though he had been planning to take a doctoral course since he did not have any family to support, he was much tempted by the prospect of studying and earning money at the same time.

The journey to Changchun had naturally made him think of visiting his birthplace on the way. It brought back all the memories of the people who were close to him in the past. Not only the people but the hills, the fields, the river, the bridges, the sandy shore of the river, the willow-lined riverbanks, the dirt road of the village, the village well, the dragonflies, the snowmen and the sleds they had made, the icicles, the wild azaleas, wild berries and pears, the ground berries…. Myriad small things rushed back to him with all their own stories and memories. Like a blindfolded child telling the names of things by touch, he pronounced each name slowly, hesitantly, and sometimes even in Japanese. His voice reached Nam-hi's heart and flowed in her veins. She was deeply moved. Even if he had not meant what he was telling her, it would not have changed the deep emotion those memories brought to her. Se-yŏng continued, "And most of those things had something to do with you and me and Tong-jun. How the three of us went hiking along the riverbank with you crying all the way, how you got so upset when you found worms in the wild pear you had been munching, how we ate so many wild azalea blossoms that our lips turned purple, how we rinsed our hands in salt water until they burnt after we stumbled into the poisonous lacquer bush…. In all those endless episodes you were there, Nam-hi, just like a queen bee…."

Se-yŏng lit a cigarette. It seemed to be his habit to smoke when he was tense. Nam-hi's eyes glistened with moisture, but

Se-yŏng did not notice.

"Can I really believe you?" Nam-hi asked tremulously. Se-yŏng nodded. Nam-hi could see his positive gesture, but the voice that accompanied it was quite cold.

"Well, it's up to you. Even if a person tells the truth, he can never be sure the other is accepting it as truth. So I won't insist that you believe me."

Nam-hi nodded understandingly. She realized that it would not be fair to ask for his reassurance. After all, her feelings about him were not something that had arisen all of a sudden on encountering him the other night, but a yearning that had been growing in her for a long period of time.

"And that's why, unlike Maupassant's Jeanne, I have never had a rosy outlook on life. I have always viewed the prospects of my life through a gloomy grey glass window." Nam-hi gazed down the road. "I'll believe you, even if you tell me not to. I'll wait for you, if you'll let me," she said in a low but clear voice. "But we shouldn't expect much, only disdain or contempt."

Because her voice grew very low and soft, Se-yŏng misunderstood her and said enthusiastically, "I'm sure we can get your father's consent if only we have enough time."

"No, he'll go on being as awful as ever, with the hearty approval of all the villagers."

Nam-hi tore the words out of her painfully as if she were pulling a stubborn weed from down in a hole as far as she could reach. Se-yŏng knew she was right. Mr. Ch'oe's response that afternoon and U-yŏng's ambiguous attitude were more than enough to support Nam-hi's prediction.

"But I'll persevere. I'm going to show my father that he can't live my life for me."

Se-yŏng was moved to tears and his voice caught in his throat. He said hoarsely, "I'll make it up to you. I'm going to make the happiest home in the world for us."

Nam-hi was thankful it was dark as she was overcome with embarrassment at the word "home." It also brought back to her the uneasiness, fear, yearning and the inexplicable sadness she had had about her future which, though hidden behind the rosy veil of life, was firmly related to the presence of Se-yŏng. She jerked her hand from his. The darkness of the night quivered in her misty eyes. Many times out of despair she had contemplated putting an end to her life, but each time she had overcome the temptation of death with the determination to face life.

'Do I really deserve him?' The sentiment brought new tears. Se-yŏng sat motionless. Engulfed in silence and sitting side by side without the slightest stirring, they were like two people in a black and white photograph.

There was certainly not much chance of them winning, but they had to put up a fight and, as Se-yŏng said, had to try to earn some time by delaying Nam-hi's engagement to the other man.

"Next time we'll leave Pukch'on in honor." Se-yŏng broke the silence, thinking of the night ten years ago when he had run the mountain trail by himself. He had been driven at the time by an urge to disappear without a trace. It had been an ordeal to face anybody, even his cousin. Besides he had been a mere child who wanted to shock them to remorse by vanishing altogether.

That was ten years ago. But then, counting those past years might be childish of him. Who mourned for him those hard years or rejoiced over his graduation from medical school? The reaction of his hometown people was just "Ah, that son of the Widow Chŏng, you mean?" and some stared at him on the street. "Coming home in the silk robe of success," as the saying went, was an irrelevant cliche as far as he was concerned.

He was a lone marathoner who had run the course of life with no support from anybody. The flogging to which his mother's coffin had been subjected kept hurting him as though he were being struck by an unseen hand. Every time he smarted from it, he had become even more determined and pushed himself forward through whatever hardship he had to face until he had finally returned to his hometown.

The door was open in front of him, and inside there was a spring of crystal water. An enchanting fragrance hovered over the spring. It made his throat burn with a thirst that could not be quenched by swallowing his own saliva. His head hurt and his hands trembled. His lips quivered. The water kept bubbling happily. It sparkled with a mysterious clarity.

Satisfying his thirst would not drain the spring, he was tempted to think. Yet he endured the thirst as he had endured the unseen flogger. It was not so much that he was afraid of being accused of violating the spring as it was that he was too gentle to foil its crystal pureness, at least not now.

He lit a cigarette and drew on it deeply. The smoke spread. There was a river that was his mother flowing between him and Nam-hi.

'No, I'll never commit such a transgression.'

A cooling wind swept along his spine. The cigarette smoke filled his chest. Flicking the ash in the dark, he thought with a cold calculation that had become his habit during his lonely years as an orphan, how much he had really been filled with thoughts of Nam-hi.

'In truth, I may not have been thinking of her at all. How much did I really want her? I can't possibly say that I have not wanted her.' He crushed out his cigarette. In her naivete, Nam-hi was a pomegranate that would have to split open out of its own accord. There was no crack yet but it would soon burst and spill. The fire flashing in her eyes under her thick lashes told him so. Or maybe it was her naivete that convinced him.

Se-yŏng could not deny he had been tempted by what she represented. Only his calculating mind stopped him. Yet it was also because of that same calculating mind that he awaited her proposal.

"I'll write to you from Changchun. You'll write back soon, won't you?" he said, restraining his desires.

"You'd better not use your name on the envelope."

"Yes, you're right. And don't ever doubt me or let your thoughts mislead you. You understand?"

"Yes, I do."

Se-yŏng pulled her into his arms quietly. They could each feel the wild thudding of the other's heart.

"You're my home, my hometown. I see it now. I ask nothing of life but you. I need no more." Se-yŏng's lips moved over Nam-hi's eyes and cheeks and sought her lips. He breathed in her clean fragrance. It reminded him of the wild azaleas they picked together when they were children. Overcome with shyness, Nam-hi abruptly pushed him away and stood up. Se-yŏng's face was hot. Leaves rustled softly behind them in the woods.

"I'm sorry, Nam-hi." Taking her hand gently, he stood up. Stars flickered in their eyes. They looked up at the Milky Way running askance in the dark sky.

"Ch'ilsŏk's* still more than a month away, isn't it?"

"I think so."

Both of them thought of the legendary lovers who were to join each other over the Milky Way on that day. A train whistled from afar. They could tell it was crossing the Yongch'ŏn Bridge. It was the same northbound train Se-yŏng had come on the other night.

"I'm taking that train tomorrow, after I visit my father's grave in the afternoon." Holding Nam-hi's hand firmly, Se-yŏng began to walk down the slope.

"You'll take that one?"

"Yes, that one."

"So this is the last night I will see you." Tears stung Nam-hi's eyes.

The sleeping house was submerged in darkness. Only Nurŏngi welcomed Nam-hi home by wagging his tail. Nam-hi stepped stealthily into her room. Her stepmother would surely have waited for her by the well as usual if she had not been so tired from the day's work. Thinking of the great harangue that

---

* Ch'ilsŏk is the seventh day of the seventh lunar month.

might have befallen her, Nam-hi sighed with relief as if she had just overcome a major obstacle.

She stood in front of the ochre chest with dark iron ornaments she had inherited from her mother. Its familiar smell of perilla oil still brought memories of her. She looked around. Dirty marks from Tong-shik's and Tong-su's small hands were on the white wallpaper about a meter from the floor. There was also some scribbling and scratches they had made with red, blue and black crayons. She loved her half brothers. Looking over the marks they had left in her room, she murmured softly, "Aren't you lucky to have been born boys. You won't have to suffer like I do."

The ceiling was papered with a blue patchwork filled with green flowers. Her father ordered it specially to refurbish her room when she returned after finishing her education. It was but an example of his devotion to her and was the talk of the village for some time.

The windows and the door were twofold with shutters that had three secure iron rings each, a result of another special purchase Nam-hi's father had made at the ironsmith for her. He had recently bought a new mosquito net and had quietly slipped it into her room. He was much too kind, and now she had to write a letter to him. She sat at her desk. The desk top was aquiver with the shadows of iris leaves in a small pewter vase standing in the corner. The vase was a graduation gift from her school friend Kim Ok-suk. She was from a nearby town and was now studying pharmacy in Seoul. Nam-hi had been shy at school. She had been new at school when she got a note from a senior who wanted her to be her younger sister. That was Kim Ok-suk and it was the beginning of their close friendship.

"If only Sister Ok-suk were here."

She needed someone to whom she could complain about her father's plan, but could think of no one. She would not feel completely comfortable with her brother Tong-jun becaue he was a man.

She began to write to her father with the fervent sincerity of a prayer. Tears welled up in her eyes and dropped on the sheet of writing paper. She would die if her father so wished, she wrote to him, but would he please stop planning her marriage because she simply could not marry anybody right now.

Nam-hi wrote another letter to her stepmother asking her to use her influence to convince her father to allow her to marry Se-yŏng in the future.

After reading what she had written, she almost tore the letters up before awkwardly placing them in the envelopes. She was mortified and embarrassed. Even while sealing them, she had doubts about whether she should give them to her parents or not. Leaving them on the desk, she prepared to go to sleep.

She opened her eyes to find her stepmother at her bedside. She blinked wondering how long she had been asleep.

"What do you mean by these letters? Do you want your father dead? Surely he will die when he reads this. You just wait and see. He was looking for you early in the evening, and I told him that you were at your oldest brother's helping make fluffy cookies, even though I reckoned you were out seeing that man." Mrs. Hyŏn hissed in a low voice. Her eyes looked as if they could penetrate into Nam-hi's mind. She had sent Tong-su out to every possible place in search of her. Nam-hi stared at her stepmother in a daze. Though her eyes were fixed on the woman, she did not really see her. As if her blood had stopped running and her body had become petrified, Nam-hi sat like a piece of wood.

Somewhere a cock crowed its first morning cry.

7

"Umhumhum."

Gurgling sounds kept escaping from Mr. Ch'oe's throat as he was seething. He grated his teeth cursing the fact that he ever afforded Nam-hi an education. He lamented that he was bitten at the heel by a daughter whom he gave only love.

"That girl could kill her own father in cold blood. Umhumhum." He kept groaning as he waited impatiently for daybreak. He tapped the bronze ash tray vehemently with his long stemmed pipe, coughed violently to bring up phlegm that was not there, and bellowed at his wife every once in a while. "How dare you not bring that girl to me right now. I want her in front of me right this moment. A daughter who so humiliates her own father that he can't lift his head in this world is not a daughter but the reincarnation of a vengeful enemy."

The day broke slowly. Mrs. Hyŏn brought in a tray of steaming chicken soup laced with blended eggs and sticky rice. She always prepared something special for her husband before a late breakfast.

"Will you please calm down and try this soup. I'm afraid someone will hear you and talk if you keep fussing so noisily."

Groaning again at the injustice of the situation, he glanced accusingly at his wife and, turning away from the soup tray, drew on his pipe impatiently and said in a determined voice, "Go ask Kŭn-sam to come and see me. A disaster has befallen us. It certainly isn't a simple matter."

"What on earth do you want to have Ae-sun's father here for?" Mrs. Hyŏn lowered her voice.

"Ha! What an interfering female! Just do as I tell you." Mr. Ch'oe glared at his young wife.

"Please, don't. It won't do." She guessed why her husband wanted to see Song Kŭn-sam.

"What do you mean that it won't do? I'm going to have Kŭn-sam bring me that man Chin Saengwon. I'm going to tell them how Se-yŏng violated the good discipline of our village and have them kick that wretch out without a moment's loss." He said vehemently.

"My god, you're going to do such an absurd thing. It's as bad as spitting to heaven while lying on your back. Where will the spit drop but on your own face? You know what a scheming person Chin Saengwon is. If he hears one word about this, any chance of a marriage with the Yi clan is as good as gone. And all kinds of ugly gossip will follow." Wringing her hands, Mrs. Hyŏn reasoned in a low, persuasive voice.

"Tut, that girl takes after her mother." Ch'oe gritted his teeth. Even without his wife's reasoning, he knew quite well that it was to his disadvantage to confide in Chin Saengwon. Nevertheless, he had to make such a gesture so he would not feel so much like he was going to explode.

"Then, bring that brazen girl here. I'll kill her. I'll kill her myself. A girl who humiliates her father by throwing such shit in his face doesn't deserve to live. Now I know what they mean when they say a man can put out his eyes with his own hands. Look where giving that ungrateful thing an education when everybody else was against it got me. Alas, I should have broken her legs instead."

Mr. Ch'oe kept hitting the ash tray with his pipe. Mrs. Hyŏn, who had been noting her husband's graying beard, lowered her eyes and said timidly, "Don't scold the girl too harshly. I'm afraid she might do something drastic." She was a good woman endowed with great wisdom. Knowing how her demanding husband adored his daughter of a previous marriage, she took care of Nam-hi with such devotion that even he was impressed. And to his great satisfaction she also did her best to help his two oldest sons. There was never a time when she was not generous to any of his relatives or tenants.

All of Ch'oe's tenants including Song Kŭn-sam, Chang Il-gap and Chin Saengwon listened seriously when she spoke. Song was the father of Nam-hi's friend Ae-sun and Chang was Sun-shil's father. Mrs. Hyŏn always remembered to send a bushel of glutinous rice to them for the New Year's holiday and gave them a gift of rice or some other grain whenever there was an important occasion in their households, all of which her husband found totally gratifying and laudable.

"I shouldn't scold her? I can't scold her enough as it is!"

"You had better coax her with soothing words."

"Hah! I'll be damned if I'll do that!"

He beat the bronze ash tray again noisily, but he seemed to calm down considerably.

Sometime later Nam-hi came and knelt in front of him. Although he resorted to all manner of persuasion—cajoling, coaxing, threatening and moralizing—Nam-hi kept stubbornly silent, only huge tears dropped from her eyes. She admitted to herself that unless she ran away or killed herself there was no way for her to escape the marriage.

"You stubborn little brat! I don't know with whose evil spirit you are possessed, but I'm certainly not going to break my word now at this old age of nearly sixty because of an abominable little daughter. Do you think everything will be done as you wish if only you say no? A man's word is as good as gold, and I would sooner bite my tongue than retract my words. It's because I was foolish and gave you a good education!"

After what seemed an eternity of threats and cajoling, a frustrated Mr. Ch'oe said desperately, "You will have to marry into that house. If you find you really don't like it, run away after three days. Then I will gladly accept you back. Do you understand? I don't care if you stay married three days or longer, but you have to marry him for at least three days. Is that clear?"

Insisting that the marriage should take place at all cost, he forbid Nam-hi from going out of the house. She was not allowed to send or receive any letters, the first one from Se-yŏng having turned into ash in her father's hands.

Several days later Nam-hi was in the back yard feeding the chickens. Her eyes were swollen with constant weeping. Taking a handful of feed, she threw it over the chickens. She watched them, large and small, pecking noisily with joy. She threw feed like a farmer throwing seeds over furrows. The roosters stopped pecking every so often to flap their wings, and thrust up their combs and crow.

The braying sound of an animal came from outside the wall around the house. Nam-hi stood still and listened, the sound was undoubtedly coming from a horse. It was promptly countered by the excited bark of Nurŏngi, their dog. When Nam-hi peeped out through the side door, she saw Chang Sŏndal,

Sun-shil's father, ushering in a stout middle-aged man dressed in a ramie coat. An elaborate hat string dangled over his chest from a broad rimmed hat. He had a round flat face with a double chin.

"Oh, my goodness. We have a very important visitor." Mrs. Hyŏn, who was setting a lunch table for her husband, rubbed her hands on a dishcloth.

Chang Sŏndal, having arrived in front of the master's hall, coughed dryly and said "Is the Elder home?" and coughed again.

"Why, isn't this our respected Scholar Yi! What a pleasant surprise! Please come in!"

Rushing out from his room, Mr. Ch'oe welcomed the visitor heartily. The man was Mr. Yi Yŏng-t'ae, Sang-jun's father. A brand new rush mat was laid out in the hall and the visitor was guided to there.

Nam-hi concluded that he had come by horse to formalize the marriage contract. Abandoning the gourd of chicken feed, she turned away and hid in her room.

Mrs. Hyŏn rushed into the back yard. Enticing the chickens with feed, she grabbed a fat one, wrung its neck without a sound and returned to the kitchen. Nam-hi's sister-in-law, whom she had promptly sent for, appeared at the gate.

"Here. Will you clean the caldron while I pluck this chicken?"

Nam-hi's stepmother, having already built a fire in the second kitchen, rolled up her sleeves and began to wash rice, while she waited for the water to heat up so she could pluck the bird. The daughter-in-law cleaned the caldron and began to polish silver spoons with salt.

"I hear the bridegroom came home only the day before yesterday."

"He must be terribly anxious to get married, to send his father so hastily."

"Whispering to each other, the two women busied themselves to prepare food for the guest.

That day Mr. Ch'oe received a deep ceremonial bow from the stout Yi Yŏng-t'ae, who had a face like a round rice cake, in return for agreeing to send his daughter to the Yi house. Thus the marriage contract was sealed irrevocably.

Nam-hi contemplated running away, but found there was not much chance of her succeeding. Not only was she far too timid for such a bold action, but also she was so closely watched she was not even allowed to visit her younger brother, much less leave the house. There was obviously only one way for her to attain her freedom—to kill herself. That knowledge consoled and sustained her.

She refused her supper that evening, and breakfast and dinner the next day, too. Remaining in bed, she closed her eyes and made no response whatever to Mrs. Hyŏn's entreaties and her sister-in-law's persuasions.

Mr. Ch'oe was dismayed. He wished he could force food into her. It frustrated him that the nature of the matter precluded lamenting openly to anybody. From the evening of the second day, he did not even touch his dinner. He said that he would rather starve to death than die of shame. The family was a ghast. Still, Nam-hi remained in her bed as if she were already dead.

Tong-ho, the eldest son, made a rare visit to the main house. After sitting some distance from his father for a while, he turned toward Nam-hi's room, looked at the vast sky and soon left the house. When his wife brought sesame gruel for her father-in-law, he would not so much as look at the bowl nor move from his bed.

"Miss Nam-hi, I can't for the life of me understand why you should behave this way. Look at me. I'm married to the most vapid person in the world and yet I put up with him without a complaint. What are you going to do if something terrible happens to Father?"

Gritting her teeth, Nam-hi did not respond to her sister-in-law's entreaties. Tong-jun was called home by cable, but he took Nam-hi's side. He ventured to advise his father that since

Nam-hi was the one getting married, she should be the one to choose her husband.

"What are you talking about, son! Don't you even breathe such an idea now."

Mrs. Hyŏn stopped him hastily. His sister-in-law also rebuked his thoughtlessness. In a situation already bordering on hysteria, Tong-jun's words were enough to make Mr. Ch'oe go berserk. Concluding that all his offspring were conspiring to have him die, he unknotted his topknot and, confining himself in the room where the ancestral tablets of the Ch'oe family were kept, prostrated himself and wailed. He refused the green pea gruel his daughter-in-law brought for him and the rice soup his wife made for him, reiterating his pledge that he would neither leave the ancestral tablets nor put a morsel of food in his mouth again until Nam-hi came there to ask for his forgiveness.

The entire family was agitated. They were chilled with the feeling that an evil spirit was lurking in the house. Remembering that her younger son had torn the corner of the spring greetings pasted on the gate, Mrs. Hyŏn beat the boy. When he cried from the pain, she beat him some more to make him stop crying.

The third evening after she had started fasting, Nam-hi was literally carried to the ancestral room by Tong-jun and Tong-ho's wife. At the sight of her father prostrate and with wildly unkempt hair, she realized she was defeated and said, "Forgive me, Father." The two of them then shared a meal of rice soup.

A month passed. A few days after Malbok*, when a cool breeze was rounding off the lingering heat of summer, Nam-hi, dressed in a long robe and a bejeweled wedding cap, got married. Unlike his stout father, the bridegroom was a slight man

---

* The last of three days determined by the lunar calendar to be the three hottest days of the year. They generally fall in July and August.

of medium height. His face was much too pale and his mouth was lopsided. A pointed dogtooth showed when he smiled. His hair was pitch black.

The woman who became Nam-hi's mother-in-law was as emaciated as her son. Her hard, shiny eyes were restless above a long nose and a thrusting jaw. Like her son Sang-jun, she looked to be of a weak constitution. At her husband's constant bragging about the very satisfactory marriage, she would complain under her breath to her daughter, who was not yet married, or simply leave so she would not have to listen to his eulogy. It was evident that she was not overjoyed at having a learned daughter-in-law. "An uneducated girl could make just as good a wife. For the life of me I don't understand why you keep singing the praises of education. Is that a piece of gold or what?" She glanced disgustedly at her husband before turning her face away in disdain.

"Educated ones are bound to be much better, though in what way I don't know either. You're just being a mean mother-in-law when in truth you should be grateful that we're now related to Elder Ch'oe's house."

"Grateful, my eyes! Why don't you go to that house every morning and grovel in thankfulness if you're so grateful." Her husband's enthusiasm thoroughly disgusted her. It was not so much that she held any particular grudge against her daughter-in-law as she pitied her own daughter who did not have much of an education. Even though her feelings were quite plain to see, she did try to treat Nam-hi kindly. When Nam-hi and Sang-jun went to Japan for him to continue his studies, she prepared a large package of food and sweets for them to take.

Sang-jun was quite different from the other members of Nam-hi's new family. He had a very disturbing nature. He laughed easily, but the next moment he would be sullen and somewhat angry for no apparent reason. Sometimes he disappeared from the house without a word. His strangeness became even more pronounced when he and Nam-hi began their life in Tokyo. At his worst, he hit Nam-hi and overturned his dinner table, accusing her of deliberately neglecting him. Then he would apologize with tears in his eyes.

At the end of a class, he would rush home to make sure his wife was at home, but by the time he left for the next class, he was upset for no apparent reason. He might be sweet and apologetic in the evening when he returned home, but in less than half an hour his eyebrows were morosely knit.

As he became more and more unpredictable, he also began to have fever every evening. Half a month and then a month passed, yet the fever did not go away. In fact it became worse as it was accompanied with coughing. They consulted a doctor. He suspected a chest disease. Complaining that the doctor was a quack, Sang-jun refused to visit him again.

"We'd know better what's wrong if you'd have an X-ray taken." It was the first time for Nam-hi to ever venture advising her husband, but it only angered him. For several days he would leave the house when he had fever and came home only after his temperature became normal. Eventually they had to leave Japan to return to his home.

By the time they arrived at his house, Sang-jun had to be confined to bed. His mother blamed Nam-hi for his illness. She said it was caused by the bad luck Nam-hi brought to the house and told her in no uncertain terms to go and stay sometime at her parents' house.

Nam-hi went immediately. Sang-jun came after her the same night. Though it was spring, the night was cold and the way to her house was much too long for a man in his condition to walk. He had a burning fever when he arrived. A doctor was brought. He administered some injections but to no avail. Sang-jun coughed so violently that in one outburst blood splattered Nam-hi's face. Glaring at her, he twisted his lips in a ghoulish smile. Nam-hi washed her face in the back yard and returned to her room to mop the floor but the blood soaked into the rush mat was hard to remove. After removing the last trace of it, she said, "I'll return after taking some rest here."

"All right. Is that the way it should be?" Scrambling unstead-

ily into his coat, Sang-jun stepped out of the room, insisting
that he was going home immediately. It took every member of
Nam-hi's family to dissuade him from setting forth on the journey at such a late hour. As it turned out, he did not go to his
house the next day, nor the day after that. Worried that her
young brothers Tong-shik and Tong-su might contract the disease, Nam-hi finally accompanied him to her in-law's house.

Life there was intolerable. Her mother-in-law was convinced
that Nam-hi caused her son's illness. She told her openly that
the disease was completely cured years before but returned
because Sang-jun was so engrossed with her. Sang-jun, on the
other hand, was constantly forcing himself on her and demanding her attention. She felt as if she were locked in a room of
steel and her husband, her mother-in-law and the rest of the
family were beating the walls from the outside and the metallic
clamor was shattering her nerves.

Sang-jun was sent to a nearby seaside to convalesce, and
Nam-hi returned to her parents' house to have a baby. The day
she arrived home Mr. Ch'oe took one look at her haggard
appearance and went out and bought a bunch of materials for
tonic. Mrs. Hyŏn brewed the medicine herself and watched
Nam-hi drink it with eyes brimming with pity, but she
refrained from making any inquiries. Nam-hi felt she was taking advantage of her parents' kindness since she was married
and thus a member of another family. She was ashamed of the
tenacity of her life that made her go on with her soiled existence.

Death, which had once been her consolation for its all solv-
ing possibilities, remained just a possibility she could not yet
venture to experience. She did not know her husband's love. It
was the last thing she wanted and in truth it never touched
deep down into her heart for it was always rejected unconsciously. Accepting her husband totally was something her con-
science would not let her do. She was tortured by guilt. With
Se-yŏng firmly established in her heart, life with her husband
felt impure and repulsive. Still she bore him a child. She

wanted to think that it was her child, not his.

"It's just you and me, my baby. That's enough." Lost in a whirlpool of conflicting emotions, she nursed the child and fondled its tiny fingers. With time, and the experience of raising the child, Nam-hi gradually matured.

About that time, Tong-jun was transferred to the nearby Changyŏn Public School with the beginning of a new semester. Mr. Ch'oe was very pleased, for he thought it was partly due to his contribution to the school. His friendship with the provincial school superintendents most probably had something to do with it too. He never failed to invite one of them to stay at his house when visiting Changyŏn where there was no inn. He proudly told himself that his cordial relationship with the superintendents over the past two years brought the good fortune of his son being transferred.

"I wonder if there's anything lacking in this house?" Mr. Ch'oe would ask himself. He visited his two sons every morning, dropping first by his eldest son's home and then by his youngest's. He enjoyed this morning routine immensely, especially since he had missed his younger son when he lived in the other town.

"No, I think everything is just about right," he would say to himself. He usually sat on the veranda of his second son's house to leisurely smoke his pipe. The house was modernized with glass windows, plastered walls and a tin roof.

"Didn't I arrange a good marriage for him, matching an educated girl with a school teacher." Immensely pleased with himself and his second son, he would saunter back. His thoughts then would ramble to Nam-hi. "It's a miracle that Sang-jun's cured and even secured a job." Saved from the fearful thought that Nam-he might become a pitiful widow like the Widow Chŏng, his mouth twitched with a snug smile. Sang-jun's health had improved rapidly. Some said it was because he had eaten fifty dogs in the past year. He surprised everybody by somehow getthing a position in the Sangsanbong Customs

House.

It was agreed that Sang-jun should go to his post alone because of his health, an arrangement which suited Nam-hi very well. Taking care of her child which was already nearing its second birthday, she could almost forget her yearning for Se-yŏng, not to speak of her husband. Sang-jun's family doted on the child. Not knowing what the coming days held, they basked in the sun that shined after a rainstorm.

"I knew what I was doing when I told her to go through with the marriage and live just three short days, didn't I? That's the way yin-yang works. The way she raised such a hell of a fuss not to get married, who would have thought she'd be so content, even having a baby!" Sang-jun's recovery was a constant source of satisfaction for him. Pleased with life, he swaggered home. The only thing that clouded his brows occasionally was fleeting thoughts about his eldest son who was becoming more and more a recluse and about Se-yŏng whose image kept popping into his mind without warning.

8

Every morning, children walking in groups dotted the road to the school. Tong-jun walked with them. An experienced teacher with credentials from the local teachers college, he was assigned to a class of fifth graders. He was immensely popular with his pupils, and that morning two boys jostled each other in an effort to walk beside him.

An old man rode an ox cart ahead of them. Clad in a neat bluish cotton coat and a formal horse hair hat, the man seemed to be out to make a social visit. He leisurely drove the cart himself, holding the reins casually. Clover, plantains and dandelions matted the sides of the road that ran amidst the newly ploughed rice paddies. Green patches of beds of rice seedlings dotted the water filled paddies. The old man sat on the cart with his back to the ox, eyes fondly taking in the seedbeds and the fields he had just passed. His long hat strings dangled over the hand holding the reins.

A Japanese, flourishing a club in his hand, came towards them. He wore a cap and the Japanese traditional clothes of *haori* and *hakama*. His Japanese wood sandals with unusually high supports made a loud clacking noise as he walked.

"Look at him. He's in a skirt."

"Yeah! What a silly looking Jap!"

Pointing at the man, the children giggled under their breath and passed gingerly by to avoid the club he was whirling around.

"He looks awfully scary, sir."

"Nonsense."

"He has hawk eyes."

"Have you ever seen a hawk's eyes?"

"Yes, sir. They look like this."

The boy was stretching his eyes upward with his hands when a dark flap of cloth caught their eye and they heard the club land with a dull thud on something and then a painful scream. They stared at the ox cart from which the sound came. The Japanese struck the back of the old man on the cart and he fell down with a miserable howl. The dark cloth of the *haori* and *hakama* billowed as the man beat the old man. Tong-jun's eyes met the bright young eyes of his pupils which seemed to say, "What are you doing? Are you going to let him do such a thing?" Impelled by the mute protest gleaming in the young eyes, he walked toward the cart.

"Excuse me, but will you explain what is the matter?" he said in a trembling voice. The Japanese glanced at him with an evil look in his eyes and immediately went back to beating the old man on the back and sides. His *haori* flapped like in a nightmare in front of Tong-jun's helpless eyes.

"Help me! Ouch! He's killing me. Oh, what's the matter with him? Why's he hitting me?" The old man howled, all the while trying to protect his back from the club with his hands. The club fell on his knees. His hat fell backwards, uncovering his topknot that trembled as he writhed in pain. A coral hair pin stuck in the topknot also trembled. He looked like a mouse cornered by a cat. Tong-jun threw down his book bag and, grabbing the Japanese by the neck, demanded an explanation.

"What business is it to you, bastard?"

The man shoved Tong-jun and he tumbled to the side of the road. Never having been much of an athlete, he was no match for the man who seemed to possess some mastery of martial arts. The children rushed to the cart and packed around the two men.

"You old fool, get off that cart." Rolling his eyes, the man spoke to the old man in Japanese and raised his club threateningly.

"Grandfather, he says to get off the cart." The children translated excitedly.

The old man crawled off the cart. With one hand covering his side, he tried to fix his hat. The Japanese rolled his eyes and whacked the old man on the back. A sense of helplessness choked Tong-jun and he clenched his fists. The man's violent behavior defied reason. Allowing him time to calm down, he opened warily, "Look here."

"Oh yeah. You get over here too." The man motioned with his club.

Tong-jun looked around at the children. Their eyes burned with fear and anger. He walked toward the man.

"Sŏnsaengnim?"* A girlish voice called anxiously from the children tightening the ring around them.

Tong-jun turned around. "Go to school. Come on, off you go. Now," he said, waving them away. He did not want them to witness any more of his helplessness and cowardice. He also feared that they might make matters worse by throwing stones at the man.

"Come on, bastard."

The man glared at Tong-jun, his high sandaled feet shuffling

---

* A way of addressing a teacher as well as a form of address to show respect.

impatiently.

"Look. I want you to explain why you are beating an innocent passerby and with what authority? And what right do you have to tell me to do this and do that?"

Tong-jun kept a wary eye on both the man's shifting eyes and his shuffling feet, but the man made no effort to answer him. They glared at each other. The number of children grew. They held their breath waiting for something to happen between their teacher and the Japanese standing in the middle of the road.

"I said, come here this very minute. Didn't you here me, bastard?"

Tong-jun neither moved nor answered.

"Please, it's all my fault. I'm sorry. It's all this old man's fault. That gentleman is a teacher at our school. Please let him go."

The old man appeared to be on the brink of fainting. He hunched his back even more and made an abject bow to the Japanese, who responded with another resounding whack on his back. A tremor shot through Tong-jun. He tried to swallow his anger by telling himself that there must be some legitimate reason for this outrage, that the old man must have gravely offended the other man in the past, and that he really should not meddle in other people's affairs.

"Do you know this man?" Tong-jun asked the old man who was pressing his aching back with his hands.

"Me? No, I'd never set eyes on him until today. He doesn't seem to like me riding the cart."

The triviality of the cause of such a brutal clubbing of an old man sent a fresh wave of anger through Tong-jun, but deep down he was overcome by fear and wished he could avoid an involvement.

"What has the old man done wrong?"

Before Tong-jun could finish talking, he saw the man's club flying toward him, but was not fast enough to dodge. A piercing pain stabbed him in the shoulder, almost taking his breath away. Grabbing his shoulder, he told himself to persevere, to endure the blows if only to get the thing over.

"You son of a bitch, can't you hear me? Come here right away!"

The club smacked Tong-jun again. As he fell down, his hand came upon a stone. He grabbed it and gritted his teeth. The man took a step towards him and, looking at him in the way in which a tormentor eyes its prey, taunted, "You're deaf, aren't you?" He aimed his wood sandaled foot at Tong-jun's head, but the next moment found him sprawled in the dirt as Tong-jun hit him on the shin with the stone.

"Sŏnsaengnim!"

The children cheered and rushed to his side. Tong-jun gently pushed them back, his eyes still on the Japanese. The man pulled himself up very slowly as if lifted by an invisible crane.

"You little maggots, get away from here!"

With a shout he produced something that glistened metallically in the sun.

"A gun! He's got a gun!"

The children receded like a tidal wave as a bullet cut the air with a metallic sound and lodged in a rice paddy with a thud.

"Get me up!" The Japanese shrieked and pointed the gun at Tong-jun. Tong-jun took a reluctant step toward him and lifted him up by his left arm. Dragging his leg, the man made Tong-jun walk in front of him at gun point.

"On the cart!"

After settling down on the cart with Tong-jun at his side, the man bellowed at the old man, "Turn the ox to the police station, you dummy!"

Tong-jun translated for the old man. The cart was turned toward Pukch'on. At gun point, the Japanese forced Tong-jun to turn his back toward him. The old man, leading the ox as ordered, limped beside them, his mangled hat falling down.

Something swished in front of Tong-jun. As if snatched by a hawk, he snapped backwards as a poilice loop fell around him.

With another snatch, the loop squeezed him. He was then bound with a rope.

As it turned out, the Japanese was a police detective named Kimura dispatched from the main station in the city to investigate a minor case. He was notorious for his ruthlessness and temperamental outbursts that befell Koreans that were unfortunate enough to cross his path. Koreans hated him because he wore eye-catching Japanese clothes which he felt symbolized the prestige of a Japanese.

Tong-jun had to spend a year in prison because of the incident, which was judged to be no less than an act of subversion, interfering with official duties, an act of violence and the instigation of student agitation. The old man was taken to the main police station where he was held for a week as a penalty for dangerously riding an ox cart without someone leading the ox.

CHAPTER II

1

Se-yŏng's cap was drenched with sweat. Beads of sweat stood on his eyelids and behind his ears. Nurse Oka mopped his face with a nimble hand. Head Nurse Mida glanced at her out of the corner of her eye and quickly looked back at the adroit hands of Se-yŏng who was trying to locate the abnormal lesions in a patient's opened abdomen. It had been forty minutes and the core of the trouble was yet to be found. The intestines were completely discolored as if bathed in a dark poison, making it even more difficult to operate.

"Hopeless. Just hopeless," muttered Se-yŏng. The blood he felt through his gloves was sending him an uneasy warning. "Damn!" He stuck his hand deep into the mire of the intestines and pulled them up. Blood spewed out, sprinkling his cap and mask. An artery must have broken.

"Hemostat!" Se-yŏng hissed as he held the artery between his fingers. Head Nurse Mida promptly handed him one. Her face also was moist with sweat. Se-yŏng clamped the bleeding point with the hemostat and, asking the anesthetist to start transfusing blood, eyed the dark heap of intestines pulled out from an incision more than 20 centimeters long. The patient was a middle-aged seamstress with no close relatives to attend the operation. She had blindly entrusted her life to him and now lay unconscious under anesthesia. If he failed, the woman would never regain consciousness. Somewhere in the tangled intestines was her very lifeline.

"Forceps."

Head Nurse Mida handed him the appropriate ones. Sorting the intestines with them, Se-yŏng looked for a lesion. Time was pressing. If it took longer, the woman might die. Or rather she would be killed by a doctor, a licensed killer. But the thought did not surface in Se-yŏng's consciousness as he concentrated on finding a lesion. The taut face of the anesthetist warned him that the patient was sinking fast. Having finished starting the blood, the anesthetist glanced back and forth from the oxygen inhaler to Se-yŏng's hands. Head Nurse Mida's eyes were also glued to them. The nurse who had never lost her cool for once seemed tense. Se-yŏng could feel the uneasiness that hung in the air. It made him nervous. The lesion was frustratingly elusive. He stretched his back and viewed the mess again. Exposed to the fresh air, the intestines had gained some color. With a deep sigh of relief Se-yŏng returned calmly to the task of rummaging the intestines. He located the lesion in the small intestine a long way from the stomach. An area almost 50 centimeters long was grossly infected.

He cut out the area and sutured the intestine back together. Every time a drop of sweat was about to drop off his forehead, Nurse Oka mopped it dutifully, and every time Nurse Mida's eyes followed her hands. Se-yŏng placed the intestines back in the abdomen and patiently sutured the opening layer by layer. The surgery was finally over after four full hours.

The two nurses moved the patient from the operating table to the recovery room. Se-yŏng washed his hands and took off his mask.

"Thanks, everybody. Keep her on oxygen, will you."

The anesthetist and an assistant took the oxygen inhaler to the recovery room. Taking off his cap and gown, Se-yŏng let out a big sigh of relief. He shrugged his shoulders like a freed man, and turned to the door. Nurse Oka stepped in and said, "A relative of the patient has just showed up and wants to see you, Doctor."

"A relative of the patient?"

"Yes. And, by the way, it's a woman."

"And she turned up only now?"

"She came all the way from Nanam, Korea."

"Where is she?"

"At the end of the hall."

"But I'm starved." He felt quite hungry and the prospect of a further delay annoyed him.

"Are you going to eat in the mess hall?" Nurse Oka asked and her eyes got big and round.

"Why?"

"Because I would like you to treat me to a meal," she said rapidly in a single breath. Se-yŏng cocked his head and peered at her. Her thin face was vibrating with expectation. A sudden longing he had suppressed for a long time stabbed him. He blushed and answered casually, "I could, if you give me a good reason."

"Oh, I have a very good reason, but shhh..." Oka placed a finger on her lips in a gesture of silence and rushed off to bundle up the soiled gowns and caps for the laundry.

"That relative of the patient, she's waiting out there?"

"Yes, right out there in the hall."

Head Nurse Mida came into the room and an orderly followed. She had obviously been out to find him.

"Thanks for the fine job, Nurse Mida," Se-yŏng muttered without looking at her.

"You did a great job, Doctor. I hope everything turns out well, sir." She replied, her eyes also averted, after which she quickly busied herself instructing the orderly to clean the operation room.

'Huh? She must have come under the influence of Buddha.' Se-yŏng told himself. He hid his surprise with a faltering

"thanks" and started to the door. Her voice stopped him.
"Could you spare some time for me, Doctor? I'd like to have
a talk with you."

"Me? You'd like to have a talk with me?"

"Yes, Doctor."

"Why don't we have it now?" This time he did not bother to
hide his curiosity as he stared at Mida, who was studying the
tiled floor at her feet.

"It will take a long time."

"A long time?"

"Yes."

Se-yŏng looked at his watch and said, "Well, not today, I'm
afraid. I feel so tired I might collapse any minute."

"Any time at your convenience will do, Doctor." A rather
cool, subdued voice returned.

It was the first time Nurse Mida had ever made any personal
request to him during the more than one and a half years he had
been working at the hospital. One has to live a long time, Se-
yŏng told himself and wondered if it had anything to do with
Oka's request to take her out to eat. Still staring at Mida, he
promised in an equally cool voice that he would try to find the
time.

"Thank you. I'll be waiting. By the way, there's someone in
the hall waiting for you. I'll show you, sir." Bowing her head
slightly, Mida led the way out of the operating room. Telling
himself that she must have read some books on etiquette lately,
he followed her. A young woman stood up hesitantly from a
bench and looked at him with questioning eyes.

"This is the lady who wanted to see you, Doctor." Mida
explained and left.

"I'm Doctor Chin."

"Oh, thank you very much, Doctor. I was told that you
kindly undertook the very difficult operation. The patient is my
aunt." It was a low but disturbingly resonant voice. "I'm sorry
that I couldn't make it for the operation. I wanted to start as
soon as I got the telegram but there were some preparations to

be made before leaving which put me a day behind."
"So you're from Nanam. It's quite a long way."
The woman had angular eyes and a long nose. Her pointed
chin and pouting lips made her look like a bird but Se-yŏng
could see that she was rather well educated.
"Would you say the operation was a success?"
"Well, we'll have to see. All I can say is we're doing our
best."
"Thank you very much."
"You'll have to excuse me. The patient is assigned to Ward
3, Room 11. You can wait for her there. She'll be taken there as
soon as she regains consciousness."
"Thanks again. I plan to stay here for some time to look after
her."
"Well, then, I'll be seeing you."
Walking toward the doctors' office, Se-yŏng thought of the
town of Nanam. It was a local military center. He remembered
looking out the window when his train passed through it on his
way to here. It was about 30 kilometers north of Chuŭl, where
his friend Tong-jun was teaching at the local school. And as
much south of there was Pukch'on, his hometown. Its hills and
fields came to mind and with them the image of Nam-hi. He
could almost see her staring vaguely at some distant place,
holding a child in her arms. Se-yŏng knit his brows and
trudged on.

"Doctor?" Oka Yuriko's voice stopped him near the doctors'
office. "You took a long time talking with that woman. I guess
you were being friendly because she's from Korea, weren't
you?"
Se-yŏng turned and looked at the nurse. She had put on a
coat and her hair was wrapped in a scarf.
"Going out?"
"Oh, Doctor, you've already forgotten!" She whined like a
peevish child.
"The devil!" He remembered his promise about the meal

and rushed into the office.

"Bring your coat with you."

Putting on his coat Se-yŏng muttered, "So I'm to take you out to dinner, eh?"

"That's right."

"I'll never know what mischief you're up to."

"Hush!"

She walked quickly ahead of him as if she were going out alone. Outside in the lobby Se-yŏng found her waiting for him.

"I don't understand what's going on here. Why so much secrecy?"

"What an impossible man you are, Doctor. Can't you see?"

"I don't want Nurse Mida to know."

"Why?"

"She doesn't like Koreans. Don't look at me like that."

"You'd better be careful what you say."

"But I'm not like that. I'm different from Mida."

Se-yŏng wondered why Mida wanted to see him and asked Oka, "Is that why I should take you out to dinner?"

"Oh, but didn't I tell you that I like you a lot?"

"Come on, flattery will get you nowhere. And no more talk about Mida, either."

"Oh, but she's really strange. She looks so smooth and gentle you'd think she couldn't hurt a fly but there's a dagger in her heart. She scares me stiff. Sometimes she stares at things so blindly, a wall, a window, the ceiling, whatever, without ever moving, I'm sure she's out of her mind. And then the next minute she'll look at me as if she could murder me."

"Obviously you two aren't on good terms, are you?"

"I'll say. We're always bickering. And it's all because of you. She scorns me because I told her I like you."

Se-yŏng wondered again why Mida wanted to see him. He could not get her out of his mind.

"How can you talk like that? One would think there's really something between us. You shouldn't talk so recklessly about your friend."

"But it's true. I've got to tell you. Mida's really become strange lately. I know something is bothering her. It's really serious. Maybe she caught the bug from me, I mean the love bug for you. Or maybe she realized too late what she's been missing."

"Aren't you ashamed to tell me such lies?"

"But I'm telling you the solemn truth. I sensed it a few days ago. And when that female patient clung to you for her life, Mida blushed a lot. You didn't see her, did you? And when you couldn't find the lesion during that operation today, she sweated a lot. It looks like she has fallen in love with you."

It seemed all Oka had been doing recently was watching her fellow worker. Se-yŏng's mind was in a turmoil. Oka's idea of love was too childish to take seriously but it was not easy to ignore her. Besides he realized he missed having someone to talk with.

Because his friend and senior Dr. Chu Tal-ho had been recruited to the Peking Medical School Hospital, Se-yŏng was the only Korean doctor in the Changchun Hospital. Miss Chang, the Korean nurse in internal medicine, was the only person who gave him a friendly smile, but they did not talk much to each other. He knew there were several Korean orderlies but did not bother to inquire about them. He did not feel comfortable at the hospital. Lately especially he felt as if he were being persecuted and suffered from a lack of motivation.

He wished for a lot of pressing work, but all that came his way were appendectomies at best, simple treatments or the setting of broken bones. He was disappointed that he could not perform major operations. Most of the patients were Japanese who made it clear they wanted to be under the care of the chief of the department who was also Japanese, so he could not openly complain.

Besides, Koreans who could afford to usually went all the way to Seoul for medical treatment. Most of the ones that came to the Changchun Hospital were destitute farmers who were only a little more better off than beggars. Whenever such patients arrived, Se-yŏng was embarrassed and ill at ease with his Japanese colleagues, and was also disgusted with himself for being embarrassed.

Whether to show their contempt or not, the nurses usually put on masks in front of Korean patients. At least the doctors did not scowl openly, though they treated them in an aloof manner. Se-yŏng was aware that he acted no better than the Japanese doctors. He had mixed feelings because of national sentiments. However, his national sentiments did not keep him from grimacing at their ragged and filthy clothes. All he could do was pretend he did not notice by putting on an unconcerned expression.

Though he feigned indifference, the way the Japanese doctors and nurses treated the poor Korean patients angered and depressed him. 'Conceited bitch! Your people are barbarians who still use straw ropes in the toilet!' He would curse in his mind whenever he noticed Nurse Mida scowling scornfully at one of them. He would straighten himself and look down his nose at her. Then he would curse himself for lacking a true sense of patriotism.

His attitude toward Nurse Mida was at best constrained. He was also wary of Nurse Oka's friendliness, suspecting that she might have a hidden purpose.

"That's enough. We shouldn't talk behind her back." Sensing Oka's embarrassment, Se-yŏng added, "Aren't you hungry? Let's take care of that problem first."

"I'm starved."

"Then we better hurry up."

Se-yŏng quickened his pace and Oka followed him, high heels clicking. The early October wind was already quite icy.

"Wow, it's cold." Drawing up her shoulders, Oka pressed up close to Se-yŏng and said, "May I hold to you? I'm freezing."

"Let's take a carriage if you're that cold."

They took a carriage to a Chinese restaurant famous for Russian soup. After sitting down in a quiet cubicle, Se-yŏng asked Oka what she would like to eat.

"Whatever you're going to have."

Her lips twitched as Se-yŏng looked at his watch. It was a habit that amused her.

"I'll have Russian soup and a bun."

"Then Russian soup and a bun for me too." She giggled. The soup and bread were soon on the table. Oka dipped gingerly into the soup with a round, deep Chinese spoon.

"I didn't think Japanese liked this."

"But I do."

Se-yŏng ordered another bun for himself and a dish of chicken.

"Can I ask you a question, Doctor?"

He smiled at Oka's coyness.

"Promise you'll answer truthfully."

"All right."

"What if Nurse Mida is really in love with you?"

"That again!"

"But she's really behaving strangely. I can't imagine any other reason why. I'm sure she's in love with you. You know how women are. I can definitely sense it. What will you do if she is?"

"Is that all you wanted to ask me?"

"Does that mean you don't like the idea of a nurse falling in love with a doctor?"

Se-yŏng laughed.

"I've never heard you laugh. It's nice." Oka smiled at Se-yŏng over the bun she was breaking in her hands. She had nice white teeth. It was the first time for Se-yŏng to be out with a girl since his arrival a year and a half ago. He had stayed on after a prolonged visit not only because the salary was about double what he could get in a Tokyo hospital and there were more chances to study, but also because he had been driven by a perverse desire to be alone.

"But I had to laugh. I've never heard anything so ridiculous."

"So you can be funny when you want to be. I thought you were awfully reserved."

The roast chicken arrived.

"Here. Please try some. It might be good for you after a hard day like today."

Between bites of chicken, Oka mumbled, "It really tastes good. This restaurant is very nice."

"Your name's Yuriko, isn't it?"

"Why, you even know my name! I never dreamed you would. You always look so arrogant and aloof I thought you must be a Chosŏn aristocrat."

Se-yŏng laughed. The girl's wide eyes staring at him in genuine amazement made him laugh harder.

"Does your family live in Changchun?" he asked, taking a piece of chicken.

"Yes. My father's a typesetter at the *Manchu Daily*. He's been working as a setter for twenty years, but he still hasn't made chief. Poor man. He's just impossible. Still I love him very much. And I feel sorry for him too. He's so henpecked he can't even be comfortable at home."

Se-yŏng smiled as Oka babbled on about her family and home. She went on to say that Changchun was such a romantic city it made her heart hurt.

"Then why don't I operate on your heart the first thing tomorrow?" he joked and, thinking it was time to leave, asked the waiter for their check.

"Oh, but we haven't finished yet. I mean, talking about Nurse Mida. She says she intends to have a platonic love affair with someone. That's where we're different. I've no use for such highbrow things even though I love you very much."

Se-yŏng was dumbfounded. He had never had any romantic thoughts about the two nurses, or, to be more honest, he had consciously suppressed any thoughts of women. It was not just due to the thoughts of Nam-hi. There was always his mother and the circumstances surrounding her death that swirled in him like a turbulent river. Women were untouchable beings on the other shore and the river was far too wide to cross.

"I really don't know what to say."

"I'm not surprised. I knew you had some sort of secret."

"A secret?"

The girl nodded. The waiter brought the check at that moment so Se-yŏng paid and led Oka out of the restaurant. He thought of the patient he had operated on that day, of her infected, rotten intestines, the muscles, and fat. Things. They were just things. No more.

He had been aware of Mida Akiko's stealthy glances for some time. When his eyes met hers questioningly, she did not flinch but assumed a derisive smile. Had it been a way to hide her embarrassment at being found out? Or to hide her emotions? He did not like it. Far from being pleased or proud, he was embittered and felt insulted.

"The platonic types with their holier-than-thou attitudes aren't my idea of women." He could not understand why he blurted out such silly words, but he could not help himself. Nam-hi came to mind again, and he said aloud, as if to convince himself, "I've nothing to do with that kind of woman."

"You're just like me. I hate the platonic way. I think love is something more immediate. Hugging and kissing. Don't you think so?"

"You've got it."

"Honestly?"

"Sure. Do you want to come with me, Oka?"

"To where?" Her eyes sparkled.

"Um. To where?" He dallied, suddenly wanting to back out.

"Why are you asking me? You should know."

"How about my place? Shall we go there?"

"Your place?"

"Yes, why not?"

"Okay. I'll go there if you want me to."

Se-yŏng nodded and hollered for a carriage. He noticed the coachman, wrapped in a dog hide coat and cap, was already well prepared for the wintry night.

"Aren't you scared to come with me like this?"

"Why should I? I like you as you are, the nonplatonic Dr.

Chin."

Oka nudged him with her elbow. Se-yŏng's face stiffened. The girl scared him, but then it was too late. He told himself to leave things alone and see what happened. Their carriage stopped in front of his apartment. The horse brayed and shuffled its hooves restlessly. Something was shuffling and braying in his heart too. He felt a sudden pang of remorse.

'But it's easier. I should have done it a long time ago. Why didn't I? Why have I made myself suffer so much? I've been torturing myself, and look where it's got me. Why wait? What am I waiting for? And until when?'

He groped at his jacket pockets for his wallet. "Why did I put it in my coat?" Grumbling to himself, he took out his wallet and paid the coachman.

His flat was on the southwest side on the second floor of the Pongnae Apartment which was owned by a Chinaman. Because it was steam heated, the room was quite warm when they walked in. It was about 10 meters square. It was furnished with a well stacked bookshelf, a table, a chair, a simple chest, a bed, and a wash basin.

"You've got a nice place. It's quiet."

"But it smells."

"Oh? I don't smell anything."

"No?"

"Really, I don't smell anything." Oka repeated in a high pitched voice.

Without removing his coat, Se-yŏng placed a kettle on the gas.

"Aren't you going to take off your coat?" Oka said as she removed hers and placed it on the back of the chair. Smiling flirtatiously, she inspected the room while Se-yŏng prepared tea and brought it to the table. They sipped the tea, watching the reddish liquid getting lower in the cups. At last the cups were empty. Se-yŏng stood up. Oka's eyes teased him. To his disgust, he blushed deeply.

"Why, I should have bought some fruit. I'm a terrible host,

aren't I? To have only tea to serve my guest." He grinned
sheepishly, eyes gleaming.
"I'm so full, I couldn't eat anymore anyway." Oka assured
him, trying to suppress a yawn.
'Well, there's my bed. It's cleaner than me and I'll keep it
that way,' Se-yŏng thought suddenly.
"Then how about a drink? You do drink, don't you?"
"Yes, but not much."
Se-yŏng lifted Oka's coat from the back of the chair and held
it for her to put on.
"Let's go to a bar for a drink."
"To a bar?"
Nodding silently, Se-yŏng set out of the apartment holding
Oka by the arm. He let out a sigh as if he had just rescued
something sacred from an act of sacrilege. They took a carriage again and drove to Chimaro Street.
"Why don't we go to the Chinese street in the old town? I
don't like bars." Oka suggested as their carriage was about to
turn the corner to Chimaro. They did as she suggested. Se-yŏng
felt relieved, for even though he suggested going to a bar, he
did not like the idea either.
They found the old town already quite dark. The original
part of the city, it was inhabited mostly by Manchurians. The
hoofs of the horse and the wheels of the carriage resounded on
the cobblestone street. Together with the swish of the
coachman's whip cutting the air, the sound made Se-yŏng
cringe.
"This place is creepy. Perhaps we should better go back
towards the railroad station and have some pastries at some
place like the Armenia." Se-yŏng shrugged his shoulders.
"But it's not creepy at all. It's perfectly safe here. There's an
apartment full of Koreans down the street. More than seven or
eight families in fact."
"How do you know?"
"We used to live here before we moved into company housing."

"Where do you live now?"

"In the newspaper compound."

"Shall I take you there?"

"I've got to go back to the hospital."

The carriage passed the apartment she had mentioned. Se-yŏng could see a sign saying Tonghwayŏsa.

"I want to go back. I'm cold," said Yuriko turning to him, her voice frozen.

"I'm sorry." Se-yŏng put his arm around her. Her hand held his tightly. It was a warm hand.

'But she's Japanese,' Se-yŏng told himself.

The carriage stopped in front of an inn. Se-yŏng helped Yuriko out.

2

Se-yŏng was making rounds with Head Nurse Mida Akiko. Although he had promised to meet her in private, he had not kept his word the next day nor the next. He was afraid she might know about him and Nurse Oka. He was acutely conscious of her eyes. Maybe because of her pride, Mida had not mentioned the promise. Walking in front of her, Se-yŏng brooded about it and wondered if Mida was thinking about the same thing.

Se-yŏng pushed open a door with a nameplate saying Hwang In-ae and went into the room. Head Nurse Mida followed.

"Doctor." The hollow eyes of the patient brightened as she greeted him in a barely audible voice.

"Good day, Doctor." The patient's niece from Nanam rose from her chair. While Se-yŏng checked the patient's condition, Head Nurse Mida stood in attendance, her downcast face changing colors every minute.

"Have your bowels moved?"

"No, Doctor."

"Well, they should soon."

"Thank you very much, Doctor. This is my niece. She's a

pharmacist at the provincial hospital in Nanam. Ok-suk, introduce yourself to the doctor and thank him for me. I would be
dead if it weren't for him."

"My name's Kim Ok-suk, Doctor," the woman introduced
herself, putting a stop to the patient's enfeebled babbling.

"So you're working at the provincial hospital?"

While the nurse took the patient's temperature, Se-yŏng and
the woman talked about their hospitals. She said there should
be more Korean or Manchurian speaking nurses in Se-yŏng's
hospital. He agreed but mumbled, "I guess there will be in the
future."

The woman's enthusiasm impressed him, especially since,
preferring to be a loner, he had avoided becoming truly
involved in the hospital for the last year and a half. In many
ways, he was an isolated island much removed from the main-
land. His private hours were usually spent among stacks of
books except for those rare occasions when his Japanese colleagues pulled him away from his desk to join them at a bar or
a tea house, at which time he was constantly amazed by how
little he knew about life.

He had been like that when he studied in Tokyo as well. He
did not have enough time to enjoy his friends' company
because he had to catch up so much in the basic courses. He
felt it was a luxury he could not afford. His ideas about the
glamorous side of Tokyo life were thus only vague memories
about the neon lit Ginza and its perfumed women in extravagant dresses.

"Could you spare some time for me today, Dr. Chin?" Mida
Akiko asked in a businesslike manner when they finished making rounds.

"The devil, I completely forgot." He stopped on purpose and
Mida waited stubbornly, though she did not take her eyes off
the chart she was holding. "If no emergency surgery comes up,
I'll see you at the Armenia at seven."

"I'll be there at seven, sir."

Her voice was reverberating in his mind when Dr. Noma,

the chief of surgery, entered the room grumbling, "My knees hurt again. I really dislike walking these days." He was followed by Dr. Hayashi and Nurse Oka. They had been to see a patient Dr. Noma had operated on some time ago.

"A monk can't shave his own head and you can't heal your own arthritis, eh, Chief," commented Dr. Hayashi.

"It's the weather. When my feet get cold, my knees tingle and then my legs are all pins and needles."

"Why don't you try a hot spring? What's the name of that place that's famous for sand baths, the one that's in northern Korea?" Raising his hands, Hayashi stretched his body. He was prematurely bald. He had a beguiling way about him but he was very unpredictable. He would be very friendly one day and quite reserved the next. Se-yŏng made it a point to keep his distance from Hayashi whether he was in a good mood or not, and seldom joined in his gossipy talks. Even though he knew Chuŭl was the place Dr. Hayashi was trying to remember, he did not volunteer the information. In fact, his mind whirled with memories at the mention of the place.

"You must mean Chuŭl. It's said to be a nice place. I've heard a lot about its herbal baths. They're supposed to work wonders for a man like me. Remember that White Russian hunter by the name of Yankowski? I hear he has a deer farm there. Many of the rich White Russians in Peking and Harbin go to Chuŭl and the farm to winter or summer there."

"Have you been there, Chief?"

"No, but I've done my homework because I want to go there. I'm definitely going there this winter, no matter what happens," said the chief, warming his knees at the radiator.

"Let me join you." Dr. Hayashi sniggered, slouching down in his chair. Nurse Oka chuckled.

"Then who will take care of the patients? It would be too much work for Dr. Chin alone."

"There won't be too many patients in the winter. Look how few we've had today."

"Uhuh. How true it is that doctors become blue when the

persimmons get red. It's such an apt saying. From autumn to the middle of winter, we always have fewer patients than any time of the year."

"Let's just hope it'll be that way this year too."

Hayashi had hardly finished speaking when a couple of patients came in. Nurse Oka, trying to keep a straight face, took them to Head Nurse Mida.

Dr. Noma reluctantly left the radiator and returned to his chair. He removed his glasses and began to wipe them. With a round face and rather close-knit eyebrows, he looked like a typical family man. He replaced his glasses which made him look dignified.

The morning's patients were all Japanese and no new patients turned up in the afternoon. The chief remembered an X-ray he had in his desk and handed it to Se-yŏng. "Take a look at this. I can't decide if the dark mass behind the kneecap is a tumor or not. It belongs to a patient who came here when you were in surgery the other day."

Se-yŏng studied the film. He had been smoking in silence while the other two doctors talked. He was suffering from the depression that used to seize him from time to time.

"Both Hayashi and I would like to think it is a tumor. What do you think?"

"Well, it lacks the legs of a tumor."

"Legs?"

"I mean inflamed blood vessels."

"Then what do you think it is?"

"It might be an abscess caused by inflammation of the bone."

"An abscess? Hmm." Dr. Noma tilted his head.

"I'm positive it's a tumor." Dr. Hayashi said confidently.

"I see a light spot near the bone which makes me think it could be an abscess. I came across a similar case when I was a student," explained Se-yŏng still looking at the film.

"Then why don't you operate on him. If it's malignant, it would be better not to operate since he'll die soon anyway, but if it's an abscess, he would benefit from surgery."

"But if it is malignant, it would just hasten his death." The possibility worried Se-yŏng.

"Of course, we can look at it the other way around. If it's truly an abscess, you'll be saving his life. And if you fail, it would be a good experience from which future patients might benefit."

Encouraged by the chief, Se-yŏng operated on the patient's knee the next day. To his relief, it was an abscess and not a tumor.

"You're a lucky man. A very lucky man indeed. It's usually luck that makes a difference between a famous doctor and an ordinary one. You were lucky to have seen a similar case when you were a student." Chief Noma complimented him light-heartedly after the operation. Se-yŏng did not like the way the chief joked but he had to admit that he had been anything but positive about the identity of the mass before operating. Nonetheless, the patient and his family were greatly impress-ed. The patient's wife even said he had saved her husband's life. The patient was a Korean named Shin Pyŏng-hwan, but since his wife was Japanese and he spoke flawless Japanese, he looked and acted more like a Japanese. Because of his Japanese tendencies, Se-yŏng regarded him as a conceited snob. However, what he heard from the nurses about the way the man acted with visitors could have made him prejudiced.

Shin was an executive of the Manchurian Development Company. Most of his visitors were upper class. His wife, Fujiko, was a petite woman with a gentle, deferential disposi-tion. She told Se-yŏng that she had studied at Mejiro College in Japan, and had met and fallen in love with her husband in Sugamo Prison and that they had gotten married three years later. She seemed to want to tell Se-yŏng because he was Korean.

"We were bound together by political ideologies. We came to know each other because both of us were imprisoned for our radical ideas. One could say that Sugamo Prison was our matchmaker. We were in love with Marxism and in love with each other, weren't we dear?" Sitting at a corner of her husband's bed, Fujiko prompted her husband.

"My wife likes to glorify that period of our courtship." Shin said fondly, smiling proudly at his wife.

"But it's true. A fact's a fact."

"Yeah, I used to run to you to snatch a hug whenever I saw you, even when I was on my way to a work yard. But why do you talk about back then, instead of our life now? You could tell him how much we're still in love with each other." He chuckled.

"Oh, you're outrageous. The doctor isn't married yet. What'll he think of us."

"He's welcome to think whatever he likes. You'll understand soon enough when you get married, Doctor."

"You should understand that my husband is just a spoiled boy. Can you imagine, Doctor, I've got to shampoo his hair. And he thinks I was born to wash his feet."

The woman's face glowed with happiness, which overwhelmed Se-yŏng as he left their room.

"I envy them. They make me want to get married right away." Oka Yuriko exclaimed once during rounds, causing the entire surgery staff to laugh.

Mida Akiko, in the meantime, remained glum, and did not comment on the couple.

3

Se-yŏng arrived at the Armenia, a classy delicatessen run by an Armenian, at five minutes to seven. With a shaded light glowing over each of the red tables and low-keyed exotic music, the place was quite romantic.

Mida Akiko walked in at exactly seven o'clock and sat down very quietly across the table from Se-yŏng, her face half hidden by the upturned collar of her coat. Se-yŏng wondered what Yuriko would say if he told her he was meeting Mida Akiko. Even after tea and cake were served, they sat in silence, each immersed in thought. Se-yŏng glanced at Mida Akiko. She looked younger and vulnerable without her stiff hospital manner. He stifled a ridiculous impulse to blurt out that he used to dislike her but instead told her to drink her tea. She finally looked up after a careful sip of tea and said quite unexpectedly, "Er, I wonder when that patient Shin Pyŏng-hwan will be discharged from the hospital?"

"In about a month or two, I expect," Se-yŏng answered, quite puzzled.

Disregarding his questioning eyes, she went on, "Do you think he can be completely healed?"

"He will limp a bit."

"How long will it take for him to recuperate?"

"I guess about half a year at least, even though he doesn't have to be hospitalized more than a month or two."

Mida Akiko's eyes roamed around the shop for some time before she resumed. "Mrs. Shin is quite a woman. I think a woman could safely say her marriage is successful if she can devote herself to her husband as much as Mrs. Shin does."

"Oh?" queried Se-yŏng. Is she envious of Mrs. Shin, he asked himself. He was as surprised as he would be if he found blood circulating in a wax doll.

"Mrs. Shin says that she is happy that she could be of use to her husband, and that her family actually denounced her because of her marriage to him. Still, rumor has it that he's where he is now because her mother arranged a good position and housing for him. It seems she is from a very old, respectable family." Mida looked across at Se-yŏng with a sarcastic smile. If Mida had any special feelings for him as Oka Yuriko insisted, she certainly was showing it in a strange way. Life is certainly strange, thought Se-yŏng.

"But I think one-sided giving and devotion is pathetic. It's sick really. Emotions like longing or sympathy don't last long." She rambled on while Se-yŏng kept asking himself what she was driving at. "Don't you think one should endure such a marriage once there are children involved?"

"It depends. Each case is different."

"Or perhaps, for those who insist on receiving and never giving, children might not be of any great concern, especially when they are of different nationalities."

Now Se-yŏng was really puzzled. 'Why is she worrying about that? Of course, that is the way she is, always thinking ahead.'

Mida Akiko stifled a sigh and said wearily, "Hwang In-ae, the patient you operated on a few days ago, is my mother."

Se-yŏng put his tea cup down on the table and stared at her.

"I mean the woman lying in our hospital bed is my mother." She sighed again and stirred her tea vigorously. "I don't know why I'm telling you all this." Her shoulders drooped as if drenched with water. Se-yŏng kept silent. Akiko looked so sad that he felt he had no right to venture any comment.

"Last August my father visited me with my mother, my stepmother that is. He had come into some extra money through a construction job so they came all the way from Kirin to see me." She jabbed at her cake with a spoon as she talked. "Father said he came across Mrs. Hwang on Iwaimachi Street."

Walking down Iwaimachi Street, Mr. Mida was attracted by a sign saying "Hwang In-ae Dress Shop." It was a tiny, shabby place more like a seamstress shop than a dress shop. Inside Mr. Mida found the woman with whom he had lived in Seoul years ago. He told Akiko that they might have stayed together if both families had not objected. "We loved each other. Your mother might not have been a model of womanly virtue, but she was good enough to grow old together," he said with a sigh of regret.

It was a shattering revelation for Mida Akiko, who never doubted her pure Japanese lineage. "I hated my father for having disclosed what should have been buried in the past. I was not happy nor the least bit thrilled to learn that my mother whom I had long thought was dead was in fact alive and that I could actually meet her. I couldn't bear to think that I had Korean blood in me. My father had no right to strip me of the Japanese roots I had been so proud of when I was a child in

Kyushu and later in Kirin. I think my stepmother brought me
up to be proud of my Japanese superiority because she must
have known about my father's past and was jealous of Hwang
Inae."

Se-yŏng said nothing. He did not want to embrace her
because she was Korean nor childishly try to assure her that
Koreans were not inferior to Japanese. Neither did he want to
tell her that Japanese superiority was a myth created by
shortsighted weaklings who did not have enough strength to
hold up the sword that they had raiséd up accidentally in the
first place.

"My father's family learned that he was living with a Korean
girl only after I was born. My grandfather went to Seoul from
Kyushu and took me to a wet nurse. I was taken to Kyushu
later. I understand Hwang In-ae was also taken away by her
family." She calmly explained that Mrs. Hwang had married a
childless widower much older than she was and left him
because she could not give him a child. After a brief involvement in Korea's independence movement which ended with a
few days in jail, she lost interest in worldly affairs and drifted
to Manehuria with the perverse goal of self-degradation through
prostitution. However, she was not by nature capable of
degrading herself, so she went back home to get some money
from her family. She opened the dress shop and hired a
seamstress. As business was not good, she soon got rid of the
seamstress and did all the sewing herself. She earned barely
enough to support herself.

"My father concluded that her present unfortunate situation
was due to her uncompromising upright nature."

Se-yŏng smiled involuntarily because he could see plainly
that Akiko inherited that very nature from her mother whom
she was rejecting. "She thought I had died. She lamented to
my father that she must have become barren because her child
had died and she was somehow responsible. I think my father
was moved to tell me about my birth because of her lament."
Mida Akiko had managed to regain her usual composure and

related about herself as dispassionately as if she were talking about somebody else.

"I gather Mrs. Hwang knows nothing about you then?" Se-yŏng asked in an equally objective voice.

"No, she doesn't know anything about me. Father said it was all up to me. In other words, he wouldn't mind if one day I confront her and announce that I'm her daughter." Her shoulders sagged as she tried to keep her taut face expressionless.

"So what are you going to do now, if I may ask?"

"What good would it do to show up now to claim my mother? It would be just pointless."

Se-yŏng looked across at her, but what he saw in his mind was his own mother who had been completely devoted to him.

"Why would it be pointless?"

Akiko lifted her face and eyed Se-yŏng challengingly. Her dark eyes were luminous with tears or injured pride. "My whole world will collapse. What will happen to me after my Japanese background which I was so proud of is gone? I don't want to become like you, I mean indifferent and out of place, like you're living someone else's life. I don't want to live like that." She shook her head.

Se-yŏng lit a cigarette and looked around the shop. The Armenia was packed with customers, but there was not a single sound of laughter or loud talking. People were murmuring quietly, immersed in the subdued music and dreamy lamp lights.

"I don't want to live like a zombie. I wouldn't be able to overcome the feeling of alienation, and she wouldn't be able to help me at all in that regard. We might be mother and daughter but we know virtually nothing of each other and, given the racial differences, it would be a farce for us to try to get together now."

"Racial differences, did you say?"

"Yes, she's Korean while I'm Japanese. I don't want to lower myself."

"Suit yourself. Nobody's asking you to do so, even though

I'm not sure whether it would be lowering or raising up. I've never thought of Japanese as being a better breed than Koreans, so you mustn't blame me if I can't sympathize with you."

"That's a convenient excuse for underdogs or people with an inferiority complex."

"And your argument can hold only if those underdogs do not have any historic or cultural background. Why don't you take a look at history? You'll find that Koreans actually have a far longer history and a much finer culture than yours. Only barbarians don't have any respect for culture and history."

"And that's what I am?"

"It looks that way."

"You're already looking down at me because I've a Korean mother."

"Don't be childish. I'm really sick of this Yamato spirit and all that superiority gibberish of yours. I don't understand why you confided in me, a Korean you despise in the first place."

"I wanted to. I had to tell someone and you were the easiest." Her eyes glistened with moisture.

"I'm sorry to hear that. I don't know how to console you." Mida Akiko bit her lips and tears oozed out her downcast eyes. "Don't cry. If you don't want to, you don't need to say anything to her. Nobody will know. If you're worried about me, don't be. I won't breathe a word."

"You're a sarcastic one, aren't you?!" She muttered wiping away her tears with a handkerchief.

"Not at all. I'm just a clumsy oaf trying to find some way to console you. I guess I'm a typical Korean in that way, always hoping for the best regardless of the person or circumstances. I guess it's hard for a person as cold and reasonable as you to understand."

"I think I'm a very sensitive person."

"You're sensitive? And you have no affection for your own mother?"

"That's just a primitive instinct even animals are born with."

"So what you're trying to say is that you have some affection for your mother but what is important here is not the question of affection but whether you can remain an unblemished Japanese or not. That's the gist of it, isn't it? Since you can't deny the fact that Mrs. Hwang is your true mother, it seems the only way to solve your dilemma is to conceal it. Yes, I think that's the only way."

Mida Akiko glared at him and whispered, "You hate me."

"What does it matter? Even if I did, it wouldn't hurt you a bit."

"I told you I'm a very sensitive person."

"Then you shouldn't have told me about you at all. It was quite foolish of you."

"I know. You don't need to remind me."

4

Se-yŏng returned to the office after an early lunch to find Head Nurse Mida sitting alone. She was flipping through a magazine over a cup of tea. Se-yŏng lit a cigarette and settled in his chair with a newspaper.

"Aren't you going out for lunch?" Akiko asked putting down her magazine.

"I've just had it. How about you?"

"Me too."

"My, you're fast. I thought I was the early bird around here."

"I brought some sandwiches and had them here."

"You don't feel well?"

"Er, I'm all right."

Se-yŏng studied her quickly. He thought she looked like she had lost some weight and he guessed she was still pining over the trouble with her mother. "I got a letter from Kim Ok-suk in Nanam. She sends you her regards. You're welcome to read it if you want to." He took the letter from his drawer. "You certainly remember her, don't you?"

"Yes, I do."

"You want to read it?"

"No, I don't want to." Came her curt reply.

"Mrs. Hwang called me yesterday and complained about a pain in her stomach. So I paid a visit to her dress shop." Se-yŏng drew on his cigarette as he waited for Mida to respond. She looked at him with expressionless eyes. "It must have been caused by gas. By the time I got there, she felt all right. She said that she would like to invite you and me to a Korean style dinner when she is sufficiently recovered."

Mida turned her head and stared out the window. The door opened and Dr. Hayashi entered the room talking to Nurse Oka who was following him.

"Ah, the chief's not in. It's only the two of you." Oka Yuriko said curiously. Se-yŏng could see her eyes were laughing. She must have had a very enjoyable morning. She accompanied Dr. Hayashi on his morning rounds and helped him treat a broken arm. They were scheduled to work together the whole day.

"Aha, so you're jealous of them, are you?"

"I'll forgive you for your hypersensitiveness, Dr. Hayashi," Yuriko countered Hayashi's joking remark with a chortle.

"Where's the chief gone anyway?"

"He appeared to be heading for the medical school, Doctor." Akiko informed him.

"Aha, I've heard that our hospital is to be merged with the medical school. Did you know that, Dr. Chin?" Dr. Hayashi turned his ruddy face with a hooked nose to Se-yŏng.

"Yeah, that's what I heard, too."

"It's not a bad idea, but their staff might resent us."

"That handful of professors who teach only basic courses? I understand it doesn't have many experienced doctors as it was established not long ago."

"You have a point there. Working conditions too might improve. Someone said they'll let us teach."

"Who knows."

Se-yŏng had long given up the idea of teaching. Not only did he lack experience since he had been out of medical college for only a few years but there was always the possibility that he would be discriminated against for being Korean. However, the medical school admission was to be increased greatly next year. It had been two and a half years since the breakout of the Sino-Japanese War and most of China was occupied by the Japanese army. Naturally there was a great demand for medical doctors so medical schools were being established in every major city.

Se-yŏng was brooding over the undesirable possibility of getting involved in the war when Dr. Noma, the department chief, hurried in. He was wearing an unfamiliar mask, which his subordinates thought was probably due to the icy weather.

"We've got big trouble," Dr. Noma began breathlessly as he removed the mask. "It's turned out to be the real thing. An orderly at Sunhwa Hospital died of pestilence."

Se-yŏng shot up from his chair. Everyone else stood up, too.

"Most of the hospital staff are down with it already. By the time the carrier was pinned down, they already had it." He reported that one of the hospital's orderlies had gone to his hometown where pest was raging while the chief doctor was out of town visiting Japan.

It could have been a death sentence for the entire city. However, the municipal authorities quickly organized an anti-epidemic campaign mobilizing all the doctors and the medical students in the city. Private clinics as well as hospitals were kept open seven days a week to administer vaccinations. Health officers also organized a network of vaccination teams and stationed them at every intersection in the city to vaccinate passers-by.

Every household was urged to try to eradicate rodents. The city authorities collected and incinerated them. People were asked to wear masks when they went out. The masks were later enforced as ardently as the vaccinations. Houses in which someone died from the disease were burnt down as was the Sunhwa Hospital.

The Sunch'ŏn Hospital, designated the pest center, overflowed with patients. Even the slightest cold was reported to the authorities and a doctor was dispatched quickly. If the patient developed fever, the area was cordoned off to all traffic. The quarantined area was marked by ropes with tin plates, and policemen stood guard to ensure the area was completely isolated. Supply of staples and communication services were also undertaken by the police. Even if the patient was found to be suffering from something else, it took some time for the quarantine to be lifted.

The vaccination teams stationed at every major corner of the city allowed no one without a vaccination certificate to pass. The city was tense and agitated as though it were prepared for war.

Rumors followed anxious rumors. Lurid accounts supposedly heard from eyewitnesses described in gory detail how a Manchurian was found dead in a pool of blood he vomited at a certain street corner or how a man who looked perfectly healthy collapsed during a conversation and was rushed to the pest center. A man was considered as good as dead if he was sent to the center. Anxiety reigned throughout the city.

Nonetheless, people clung to optimistic beliefs of ethnic differences. Koreans desperately trusted that their everyday diet of immoderate amounts of hot peppers would prevent pest germs from entering their bodies, while Japanese proudly boasted that no germs could survive around them because of their hygienic way of life. Manchurians hoped that the large amounts of fat in their diet would protect them against the pest germs just as it did against cold weather. All of them trusted that luck would bring them safely through the danger. For whatever reason, very few Koreans came down with the pest even though the majority of them lived in the quarantined areas.

The surgical staff of Changchun Hospital was also included in the mobilization. Se-yŏng and Dr. Hayashi went out on street patrol, leaving only Dr. Noma and the nurses behind. Se-yŏng was positioned at an eastern corner of Taemaro Street along with three medical students and a municipal health officer. Policemen with sabres were posted with them to keep an eye on passers-by. They built a huge fire and burned charcoal by the sackful, but its odor rather than its warmth reached Se-yŏng and his team.

Se-yŏng took turns administering vaccinations with the medical students. When he was not giving shots, he studied the passers-by carefully for possible symptoms of disease. There was always the danger that a carrier might unknowingly go around the streets. The Manchurians made the situation worse with their habitual spitting. The area where he was stationed was certainly prone to contamination.

It was his second day on that street. Resuming his post after a thirty-minute rest, he looked at his watch and was relieved that he had only two more hours to go until five when they would quit work for the day.

"Here, I'll relieve you now." Se-yŏng took a syringe from a student as a Manchurian held out his bared arm. A filthy mask no larger than two fingers covered a patch of an equally filthy face.

"Make the mask large enough to cover your mouth and nose. What good is it if you hang it on your chin?"

"Er, isn't this the way to wear it?"

"Do you breathe with your chin?"

"I see, I see. I happened to have just this much white cloth at home." The man bowed to Se-yŏng apologetically. The students and policemen all burst into laughter at the tiny cloth stuck under his mouth. The man laughed, too, not knowing what they were laughing at, which made them laugh harder.

After the hearty laughter that made them forget the cold, they turned again to the group of passers-by that grew to about half a dozen. Vaccinating them one by one, Se-yŏng looked up to see the owner of one particular arm that was far too thin and frail. It was a woman whose face was hidden behind a large, dark mask, but she would have been noticed anyway because her head was covered with a blue scarf, not a pointed hat like other women were wearing. After being vaccinated, she moved to the next line to get a certificate. She had a small suitcase and a handbag in her hands. Se-yŏng's eyes opened wide as he stared at her and his hands jerked off the person he was about to vaccinate. Though most of her face was hidden by the mask and the upturned collar of her coat, he knew who she was. The delicate lids of the downcast eyes and the thick eyelashes were more than enough to identify her.

"Wait. Er... Look here, miss, er...." The words tumbled out of Se-yŏng's mouth. The woman's eyelashes came up like window shades, and her eyes filled with astonishment. Se-yŏng could barely hear her muffled whisper, "Ah, Se-yŏng!" from behind her mask. There was no doubt about it, the woman was Nam-hi.

"Wait. Wait just a few minutes."

Se-yŏng speedily injected the vaccine in his syringe into the line of arms in front of him so he could hand over an empty syringe to the medical student who was working with alcohol soaked cotton balls beside him.

Nam-hi waited a little distance away from the vaccination team. Two policemen, a Manchurian and a Japanese, were taking turns watching for stray pedestrians. Se-yŏng hurried toward her, blinking his eyes. He felt that he was in a fog. He could not see Nam-hi clearly. She stood quietly, her eyes downcast. She looked serene and mindless as though she had forgotten why she was there.

"What brought you here?" Se-yŏng asked, taking off his thick mask.

"I had to come here on an urgent errand with my mother-in-law." Nam-hi told him, glancing to the far corner of the street where a streak of wind was sweeping over pebbles, pebbles that were as porous as her heart, she thought.

"An urgent errand with your mother-in-law?" An urgent errand, an urgent errand, the words spun like a pinwheel in his mind. "What is it?"

"Oh, it's just something." Her pinched look told him that

whatever it was, it was not good.

"Let's go find someplace to sit down."

"I've got to go."

"You have to?"

"My mother-in-law is waiting for me."

He never would have expected to run into her like this let alone hear such words from her. He groped for a cigarette and stopped at the doorway of a restaurant with red jambs. "This is the only place around here we can go in and talk."

Nam-hi glanced at the door with "Pekingese Cuisine" written on it and turned to Se-yŏng hesitantly.

"It's so cold and windy here you might catch a cold. Come on, let's get inside."

Nam-hi looked up at him. Her eyes brimmed with crystal sparkles. "My mother-in-law is waiting for me with my baby.

"With your baby?"

"Yes."

Se-yŏng blinked at Nam-hi. She avoided his eyes. He nodded stiffly and muttered, "I see." Nam-hi shuddered and did not look at him. "I'm glad to see you, anyway." He said sarcastically but immediately regretted his sarcasm for he had no right to be so harsh. Abruptly, he thought of the warmth of Oka Yuriko's body that was glimmering in a far corner of his consciousness. He swept back his hair and replaced his mask. His heart pounded.

"Well?" He wanted to know where she was going. She gazed at his white gown for sometime and then turned back toward the direction from which she had come. She dared not break the silence because she was afraid of admitting that she had been fearfully looking forward to meeting him here.

"Where's she waiting for you?"

"At the place we're staying."

They were silent again. Words disappeared before they were uttered. Icy winds lapped their foreheads.

"Is it so very urgent?"

"I've got to go."

"Got to?"

Silence returned. Though he could see she did not want to tell him, he asked again, "What brought you to Changchun?"

"Sang-jun was arrested by the Military Police for smuggling."

"Sang-jun's been arrested?"

"Yes, he's now being held in the military police camp."

"On account of smuggling?" Se-yŏng looked at Nam-hi in amazement. He could not believe what she was saying. She turned her face away for awhile and then began hesitantly, "He worked in the customs office at Tumen for some time. They say he sent the opium he confiscated from smugglers to someone."

"Were you at Tumen, too?"

Nam-hi looked past him. Then she stared at the toes of her shoes and said, "I've been at my parents' house, because of health reasons."

"When did you come to Changchun?"

"The day before yesterday. I've just come from taking him some food."

"And where are you staying?"

"Over there, you can see it. Tonghwayŏsa. My mother-in-law's sister has an apartment there."

"You're staying at Tonghwayŏsa!"

"Yes. It's a kind of apartment."

Se-yŏng craned his neck to look at the square two-story building down the street. He could see the signboard. It was the same place he and Yuriko had passed in a carriage one night about a month ago. Remembering Yuriko's comment, he muttered almost to himself, "You should be in a cleaner place."

Nam-hi lifted her face and looked into Se-yŏng's eyes. She wanted to see deep into his pupils as she used to, but checked herself, mindful that now they were only casual acquaintances who were taking two different paths of life.

"I'm sorry that you have to go through all that in this bleak weather. And this commotion over the pest won't make things any easier."

"It seems you are really having a rough time."

"But it's my job. Er, I trust everything is fine with your family? Your father and Tong-jun, too? I've been meaning to write to him but I always end up doing other things."

Nam-hi looked down again at her feet and nodded, "Yes, everything is going all right." She thought she should go and stepped down onto the pavement to cross the street. Se-yŏng unconsciously followed. "When are you going to leave?"

"The Military Police is going to turn him over to the police after they finish the investigation. It seems that once the police have him, he'll be sent back. We'll probably follow him then. I'll visit you at the hospital sometime before I leave, if you don't mind."

"I'll be waiting for you. I expect I'll return to the hospital in a couple of days."

"Well, I really must be going. Take care." She nodded to him after she crossed the street. He stood on the pavement mindlessly until she disappeared into the two-story building and then turned away very slowly. A policeman stopped in front of him to ask if there was any trouble. "No, no trouble at all." He said and left quickly.

5

The snow was coming down softly. Se-yŏng was in the plaza of the Changchun Railroad Station which was almost deserted. The clock on the station building indicated six o'clock. His shift was finally over. One more day at the railroad station and his quota of field work would be done.

Though the railroad station was included in the cordoning plan, it was impossible to seal off completely. The railroad service was maintained for a limited number of lines and passengers. Most of the travellers had vaccination certificates with them but there was always a few who arrived without knowing that the city was in the throes of an epidemic.

Se-yŏng ploughed through the snow toward the carriage stop. His legs were wobbly from fatigue. He climbed up into the carriage and wearily loosened his scarf.

"Dr. Chin.."

He was so dumbfounded to find Yuriko at the door of the carriage that he just stared at her pointed cap like an idiot.

"May I get in? To think I came all the way out here to see you and I almost missed you," chirped Yuriko, happy with her luck.

"Get in." Se-yŏng muttered with a dark expression. "What made you come here in this snow? Is there an emergency at the hospital?"

"It's because of the snow. I was overwhelmed by a wish to see you. Isn't that a good enough reason?" She cuddled up to Se-yŏng, eyeing him coquettishly.

"You might get the pest going around like this."

"Never. I was vaccinated well in advance. Here, take this." She pulled a new mask from her pocket. "Please change your mask. You must have been using that one all day."

"Thank you says the mouse to the cat."

"What? Why am I a cat?"

"But such is all human relationships. One is a cat, the other, a mouse."

"That's the most absurd analogy I've ever heard. How can we be a cat and mouse?"

"Anyway, thanks for the mask, cat or no cat."

Se-yŏng replaced the old mask with the new one. Their carriage stopped in front of Taegyŏngnu, the Russian soup place they had come the other night.

"We could call this our restaurant, the way we keep coming here ever so often."

"Are you tired of the food here?"

"Not at all. I'm just marveling at your steadfastness, that's all."

"And I don't trust your willy-nilliness."

"But I'm not willy-nilly at all. You're trying to pick a quarrel tonight."

"I am?"

"Yeees." She knit her brows as she trailed a retort to his rather absentminded prodding.

"If I am, you're to blame. You would do better to ask yourself for an explanation." Se-yŏng said thinking about the time she had hung around with Dr. Hayashi, though in truth he was not particularly jealous.

They finished their meal as quickly as usual but remained at the table while Se-yŏng thought about what to do next. Yuriko had come to his apartment almost every weekend but he had never allowed her to stay. Over her repeated protests, he always insisted they spend the night in an inn. It was a stubbornness that amounted to obsession, but by keeping her out of his bed he was strangely comforted with the idea that he had not degenerated. Yuriko was no doubt expecting him to take her to an inn that night also.

"Why am I to blame? You're blaming me for nothing, just for the sake of it." She glanced reproachfully at him as she methodically wiped her fingers with a handkerchief.

"Oh, yeah?"

"I know you're being sarcastic because I went around with Dr. Hayashi. But do you know why? I wanted to see what you and Nurse Mida would do if given a chance."

"So what did we do?"

"As if you've already forgot! Come, come, there's no use playing innocent." She continued impatiently as Se-yŏng burst into laughter. "Stop laughing. What a totally unreliable man you are! No sooner had I turned my back to you, and you were out with Mida. You took her to the Armenia. Where did you go after that?"

He looked at her fondly, not the least disturbed at her accusation. "I didn't know I had such a competent tail following me." He laughed again.

"I asked you, where did you go after you left the Armenia?"

"Why don't you ask the one who tailed me?"

"I might just do that, if you don't tell me." She kept looking at him accusingly out of the corner of her eye. Her eyes gleamed. "Please marry me. I can't go on like this." She said in a strained voice.

"Marry you!" Se-yŏng's head jerked up and he stared at her in surprise.

"Yes, let's get married. Isn't it a nice idea? Then we wouldn't have to let such silly things bother us."

"You want us to get married? I'm Korean. Don't forget that."

"What's wrong with that? Haven't you heard that love knows no national borders?"

"Love! But you don't love me!"

"Good heavens! Of course I love you. If I don't love you, why do I want to see you and touch you all the time? You know what the great poet Kikuchi Kwang said? He said love is touching."

"What if I say I don't love you?"

"Let's not get too serious. You know how I hate seriousness. You must have come under the influence of our noble Mida. By now you might have learned that platonic love is nothing but a myth, just sentimental girlish stuff. If a man enjoys something and refuses to admit it, he's a hopeless hypocrite with a dark secretive mind."

Se-yŏng nodded in agreement and retorted, "That's exactly what I am. How can such a man suit you, a girl so sunny and straightforward?"

"Don't worry, I'll make myself suit you. You're so naive there won't be any trouble at all."

"Well, that's enough of this silly talk. It's about time for us to get going." Se-yŏng stood up.

"Silly talk, is it? I see a faint heart running away." Yuriko chattered amiably with a smile. Se-yŏng could not make out whether she was serious or just joking but it did not make any difference to him. He had never thought of marriage before or after Nam-hi. The only time he had ever mentioned the word was when he was with her.

Outside, the snow was still falling, though not as thickly. Se-yŏng hailed a carriage. They drove to the west, passing the rail-

road station to their right. The Changchun Hospital was about
a kilometer away from the station. In a while they passed a
quarantined area marked with ropes and tin plates. Fires
burned at a regular interval outside the boundary. Dark
shadows of policemen standing guard were etched against the
glow of the charcoal fire.

"Internal Medicine found two pest victims today. One of
them was healthy enough that he tried to sneak away when he
found out what was going on. But Nurse Chang grabbed him
and sent him to the pest center. Isn't it awful, to have walked
on your own feet right into a death trap?" Yuriko shuddered,
glancing at the glimmering fire.

"That's all the more reason why you shouldn't go around so
recklessly. Precaution is the best medicine."

"But it's not so safe in the hospital either. We've had this
many pest patients in our department too," Yuriko said,
spreading her gloved fingers. The carriage stopped in front of
the hospital.

"There, now. Get off. Don't try your luck. Wash your hands
and feet thoroughly before you go to bed, got it?"

"Heavens! Where are we? I was chattering all the way, never
suspecting where you were bringing me. I'm really flabber-
gasted." Grumbling all the while, Yuriko scrambled off the
coach obediently. Snowflakes fell on her shoulders and pointed
cap. "I'll come to the station for you tomorrow night. Think
about it, will you? You know what I mean?" She looked around
and seeing that nobody was around, waved her hand and hollered, "We're getting married, okay?"

Se-yŏng grimaced and hurried her into the hospital with a
wave of his hand. The coach had already started moving. He
was immensely relieved. He looked at his watch. It was eight
fifteen. Two hours and fifteen minutes wasted. He instructed
the coachman to drive to the old town, which was where he
had been heading in the first place. He was going to the Tonghwayŏsa. He was not sure whether he would actually try to
see Nam-hi but he had been thinking of going there all day.

Even though it had snowed, the night was mild because there was no wind. He just wanted to inquire after Tong-jun, Se-yŏng told himself as he swayed in the carriage which had already reached the boundary of the old town. A blazing fire leaped into sight at the right. The area had not been quarantined the previous day. It could have been due to a simple cold for all he knew, but an eeriness hung over the almost deserted street. Lights were gone from Taebalhap, the largest and most fashionable department store in the old town. He could not see another carriage in the entire length of the street. A rickshaw emerged from an alley. Side by side his carriage and the rickshaw turned around the corner where his vaccination team was stationed the previous day. He stopped the carriage and looked down the street toward the apartment house. Light seeped out from every window of the building and also from the porch. There was no cordoning rope or forbidding tin plates. It comforted him to think that everyone in the place was well and safe.

He had the carriage move on. It passed the front of the Tong-hwayosa. He looked around and saw the rickshaw stop to let a man off at the next house. If Nam-hi had been the person who got off that rickshaw, would he have hollered at her and gone up to her? Maybe. Then Nam-hi would have earned the displeasure of her in-laws. He had the carriage turn around, and as it passed the apartment house again, a tormenting thought leaped into his mind. What if Nam-hi had gone to the hospital looking for him during the day? She might have dropped by while she was out, and she might be expecting him to call on her.

Later, back in his apartment, Se-yŏng stood staring out the window. He had not bothered to take off his mask nor his scarf. Snowflakes clung to his hair and coat like so many flowers. He could not find a place or object in his room on which to direct his weary eyes.

The next day the vaccination team at the railroad station was kept so busy that they could not work on shifts. Though the number of travellers was about the same as the previous day, the work was tripled because they were now vaccinating against dysentery and typhoid fever in addition to the pest as a typhoid breakout had been reported the day before.

Se-yŏng worked without a moment's rest the whole day. It was worse than expected because they could not get any reinforcements. When he finally quit working about ten o'clock, he was on the verge of collapse. His ears were ringing because they were exposed to the perpetual boom of the loudspeaker the whole day. If someone punched his chest or stomach, he thought the booming noise would spill out. The dusty air of the station did not help either. Needing some fresh air, he walked toward the plaza as he had done the previous night. He felt as though a great weight was lifted from his chest when he was in the vast openness of the plaza, even though it was spotted with muddy puddles. He even found the harsh night air biting at his face quite refreshing. He picked his way along the places where snow remained and neared the station building. The hands of the clock over it were spread askew indicating ten twenty.

The station building was far less crowded than usual, but the number of coolies comfortably perched on filthy bedding rolled up and bound with rope had not decreased. Perpetual nomads subsisting on three cents a day, the coolies found the railroad station that lay deserted for a few hours between the arrival and departure of trains to be an ideal shelter for the night or until they moved onto the next place where they might earn a meal.

Sometimes there were Koreans among them, identifiable by their conspicuous white clothes. Waiting for their train to arrive, they would sprawl comfortably among the coolies and the Manchus and chatter amicably with them, never minding the clouds of dust that rose from their clothes at the lightest touch or the lice that crawled over them.

Coolies clustered in a corner would pull their clothes inside out and chew on the seams or run their fingernails hard along them to kill lice. Lice hunting was a pastime preferably done in a warm sunny place but any well lit location would do. The coolies believed that they should retrieve the blood the lice took from their bodies. Thus they chewed them up and spat out the skins with as much aplomb as they would spit out the skin of sunflower seeds.

However, the scene in the station that night was very different because each of them had a mask over his mouth. The masks were lifted often to let the wearer spit and to blow his nose between his thumb and forefinger and rub the discharge on the cement floor already caked with the stuff.

In the winter, they wore dog skin coats and dog skin caps, their only armament against the cold. They were at the same time their beds and their shelters against blizzard. However, somewhere inside those shiny sleeves glistening with grime or deep around their waist they were said to be carrying their life's savings. They prided themselves on easily outweighing the meager pockets of some genteel people of little substance.

If there was anyone of little substance, Se-yŏng thought bitterly, he was sure to be counted. What did he have that he could take pride in? Aside from the basic necessities, he had nothing. He did not have a close friend with whom he could release the stress he experienced living among Japanese. He did not have a girl to consider marrying. He did not have any hobby to indulge in, nor could he afford one, financially or mentally. He had no family or relatives to speak of. All he had was a handful of titles people called him at their whim: doctor, surgeon, physician....At least he could take some satisfaction in them, god knows they were hard earned. But why did he feel so hollow tonight? What was making him feel like he were in a vacuous cavern all alone?

A ricksha drew up in front of him invitingly. *"Nidiyo buyo, buyo ubuyo."* Muttering in Chinese, he waved it away. He rode in a ricksha the first autumn he came to Changchun. Even though the day was cool, sweat beaded the nape of the man pulling the ricksha. He never rode a ricksha again, though he was well aware that his feelings did not help the ricksha man.

He caught a carriage instead. All he had for supper was simple vinegared rice, but he felt full. He was absorbed in thoughts of Nam-hi. The street in the old town where she was staying felt friendly because she was there. His carriage drove down the wide Taedong Street and then the West Sammaro Street toward the old town. Absentmindedly listening to the coachman encouraging his horse, Se-yŏng glanced around to see if there was a newly quarantined area, hoping all the while that the area where Nam-hi was staying was not quarantined.

He had priority over Nam-hi, and he should claim it. After all, he knew her first, didn't he? So what? What was he trying to prove? He was an indecisive coward. He coughed out of disgust and spat hard out the carriage. He wanted to slap the face of the earth.

He liked Changchun when it was dark. There was something breathing in the darkness that could not be seen in the blazing sun. Once outside the hospital, he knew nobody. Passers-by were strangers and he liked that too. Above all, he liked the darkness that wrapped and separated each of them.

There was no quarantine rope near Tonghwayŏsa. He knocked at the door and a rather fat Manchu appeared. He said he did not know a woman by the name Nam-hi. Se-yŏng explained he was looking for a young Korean woman who had come there several days ago with a child and an old woman.

"Come back tomorrow morning. Everyone's gone to bed and you can't find anyone without the room number."

Se-yŏng gave the man a half *won* silver coin. He grabbed it greedily and, turning his head, said he would see what he could do and headed toward the hall.

"Wait, *Changgwe*. I changed my mind. I'll come back tomorrow. And don't tell the woman I came here."

Se-yŏng turned around and walked out, overcome by the sudden awareness of how futile and meaningless his behavior was and how it would hurt Nam-hi. He leaned against the wall for some time and then stepped down onto the sidewalk. He stared blankly at a mud puddle in the street. An image of Nam-hi when he met her at the railroad station in Pukch'on floated on it. The image followed him as he drove to his apartment.

It was only when he was turning the key to his apartment that he remembered Yuriko had not shown up at the station. He grimaced, thinking how she might have pestered him with talk about marriage.

He reported to the station again the next day because his team was reassigned there. Thoughts of Nam-hi stabbed his mind every once in a while, but he could not tear himself away from his work. It was far more chaotic than the other days because a Japanese collapsed in the plaza and a Manchu collapsed across from the carriage stop. The complexion of both men was ominously dark. They were sent away to the pest center and charcoal fires were burnt on the spots where they had laid.

As evening approached, Se-yŏng became increasingly fearful that the area where Nam-hi was might have been quarantined.

"Dr. Chin."

Se-yŏng looked up to find a masked Mida Akiko in front of him. The hem of her white uniform showed under her coat, indicating that she had left her hospital work to come out.

"Do you have much work left, Doctor?"

"I'm almost finished. What's the matter?"

"Please come with me to the hospital."

"Is something wrong there?"

"Well, not exactly."

Akiko stepped out of the way and watched the vaccination team work. The team was stationed between the entrance and exit turnstiles. They had put up a white cotton screen to shelter a few chairs and a desk. Though the entire team comprised two dozen people, only half of them were working at the moment, and they were posted at three different points in the station. Because the station personnel, guards, military police and even the policemen working with them were receiving their second vaccination between the arrivals of the trains, the booth was kept busy even when the line of travellers slackened. Also, most of the coolies were receiving their second vaccination.

Se-yŏng had been working since nine in the morning. After his shift, the other half of the team would work through the night. A new team was to take over the next day, so his street work was to end that day.

He had planned to go to Tonghwayŏsa again that night. He just wanted to see if the area was quarantined or not. It had been stupid to walk in there in the middle of the night and ask for Nam-hi. It was fortunate that a glimmer of reason had come to him at the last moment, he thought.

He drove to the hospital with Akiko. Trying to fathom her stony silence, he wondered if Mrs. Hwang In-ae had visited the hospital. Most of the twenty doctors had already gone home when they arrived at the hospital. Only a couple of interns on night duty were present.

Nurse Mida led Se-yŏng into an office and then said in a subdued voice, "Nurse Oka is not well. I gave her some medicine suspecting it might be indigestion. But there's something upsetting.... I didn't consult any other doctors."

"From when?" Se-yŏng asked, washing his hands.

"Right after supper."

"Will you bring her here."

Akiko disappeared without a word. Se-yŏng lit a cigarette and waited, lounging in his chair. The pest germs did not perish unless burnt or steamed. After one long drag, he stubbed out the cigarette and stood up. He rummaged his coat pockets. Two masks were there; the one he used the day before yesterday and the one from Yuriko which he used yesterday. If Yuriko was down with it, he might also be carrying the virus. His legs felt stiff and he seemed to have a dull pain in his armpits.

A very gloomy Yuriko arrived leaning heavily on Akiko.

"Let me see. You must have eaten your supper too quickly," commented Se-yŏng, taking her hand. "You have a little fever."

"I took a nap because I felt so tired, and when I woke up, I was overcome with nausea and dizziness."

Se-yŏng wished she was exaggerating, but there was every symptom of typhoid fever, a fatal disease for Japanese especially.

"Don't invent symptoms to get my sympathy." He examined her with a sullen face and took samples of blood to the lab and had the interns run tests. They confirmed that she definitely had typhoid fever.

"What is it, doctor?" Yuriko asked when he returned, her face flushed with fever.

"Seems like you've caught a cold." Se-yŏng felt Akiko's puzzled glances on his face.

"I feel nauseous and dizzy constantly. I mean it. I feel really awful." She forced a smile, though her brows were knit with discomfort.

"A severe attack of indigestion. What did you have for lunch?"

"I had some glutinous rice cakes because I didn't have any appetite."

"How many?" Se-yŏng signed with his eyes to Akiko that he had done all he could.

"One and then another." Yuriko smiled again, her eyes closed.

"You'd better take a rest in the isolation ward. You know how hectic the other wards are, with the epidemics and everything." Se-yŏng deliberately chatted to give Mida Akiko and the interns time to prepare the isolation ward.

"I've got the pest, don't I? You don't need to lie. I know I have it."

"Idiot! You sound as if you want to have it. Don't say such an awful thing, not even jokingly."

"But I'm dying. If I die and become ash, will my heart be left behind with you."

"Who says you're dying? If you keep talking so, you really might get the pest."

"Are you sure it's not the pest? If I get all right, will you marry me?"

"I'll think about it."

"You promise?"

"Yes, I promise."

"Liar. I'm sorry that I didn't come to you last night. I was so tired I could hardly keep my eyes open. I felt bad standing you up."

Orderlies brought in a stretcher. Yuriko jumped off the examination bed. "No. No. I'm not going. I'm all right. I mean it. I felt a bit depressed, that was all. Please examine me again, Dr. Chin. I really feel all right now. Oh, I see. Nurse Mida brought them, didn't she?" Yuriko was hoarse with despair and terror. Akiko looked at Se-yŏng for instruction.

"What you have is typhoid fever. People don't die of such a simple thing. But you should stay in bed so you don't develop fever."

"Typhoid fever. No, it's just indigestion. The cakes are just laying heavy in my stomach. I ate five of them. You saw how many I had, didn't you, Mida? You're a surgeon, Dr. Chin. You don't have any right to examine me. You're wrong. How can anyone trust the diagnosis of a Korean doctor, anyway? You're a fake. Nobody trusts a Korean doctor."

Nurse Mida and the interns forced Yuriko onto the stretcher and bound her firmly. Wailing and thrashing, she cursed Mida and Se-yŏng as she was taken away.

The next morning Se-yŏng visited Yuriko in the isolation ward. Her lips were parched from fever. The duty nurse reported a persistently high fever.

He went to her again the next day. She was awake, her eyes looked glassy because of the unabating fever.

"Ah, I've really wanted to see you, Doctor. But you shouldn't be here. You might get my germs. Promise you won't stay long. I'm going to be all right soon. In a week, they say. We're going to get married when I get all right, aren't we?"

Se-yŏng nodded mutely. That was the least he could do for

her at the moment.

"Nurse Mida told me she had a date with you. That's why I kept pretending to go around so with Dr. Hayashi. I'm sorry. Mida said that you were really heartless."

Se-yŏng shook his head reproachfully. "Shhh. We'll talk about that over Russian soup when you get better. You'll get over it soon, if you get appropriate bed rest. I'll come and see you every day." Se-yŏng rearranged the ice bag on Yuriko's forehead and gently dabbed her parched lips with a moist cotton ball. Her eyes sparkled with tears. "Don't. There's no need to cry."

"I should have listened to you. I should have been more careful."

"It's all right, Yuriko. Everything will be all right soon."

A faint smile appeared among the tears on her face.

"Come, come. Don't cry, Yuriko."

"I promise I won't cry. Er, how is Mr. Shin doing, I wonder? I haven't been around to that part for some time."

"He's doing just fine. Nurse Chang of internal medicine is in charge of him since Mida's so tied up."

"I'm causing trouble for everyone."

"Nonsense. I really must go."

Se-yŏng looked at his watch, though he did not need to know the time.

"We'll get married and live happily ever after, like the Shins, won't we?"

Se-yŏng stopped at the door and nodded. His mouth under the mask remained firmly closed out of the same stubbornness that shut her out of his bed. But his eyes glistened with tears as he left her.

He returned to her every day until she died. The day before her death, a week after she first showed the symptoms of typhoid, Se-yŏng found her so pitifully weak that she could not open her eyes to greet him. Occasional moans escaped from her parched lips. As usual he dabbed a wet cotton ball over her lips and under her nose that were cracked and blistered and coaxed a few drops of water into her dry mouth. As he was about to leave, Yuriko whispered hoarsely, "Please help me. I'm dying." Tears trickled out of her closed eyes. They felt hot to Se-yŏng's fingertip as he wiped them away.

"These days are the worst. Don't worry, you're going to be all right."

"And marry you."

"Shhhh." Se-yŏng quieted her. That was the last word he spoke to her. The next morning she was dead.

6

That night Se-yŏng took a carriage to the old town. There was no rope near Tonghwayŏsa. He had the coachman drive past it slowly. He could see men's shadows through a window of what seemed to be the front desk. A few minutes later he had the carriage turn around and was driving past the apartment again when a voice called to him from behind. It was the overweight Manchu of the other night.

"*Changgwe, Changgwe,*" the man hollered after him and waved his hand. Se-yŏng stiffened but visibly relaxed the next moment as the thought that Nam-hi must be at the apartment hit him. A warm feeling spread through him. The man peeped into his face and asked, "It's you, isn't it? The man who was looking for the woman from Korea the other night?"

"Yes, it was me."

"She's gone. She left last night." The man said with a sweeping gesture.

"Last night?" A tight rope broke somewhere in Se-yŏng's chest and his heart dropped with a thud.

"Yes. Last night. I told her a *changgwe* had been here looking for her and she blushed."

Se-yŏng's eyes gleamed. He remembered that the railroad station was not completely reopened. She could not have left Changchun because of the control.

"She couldn't have gone to Korea."

"She left in a carriage with the old woman and the child."

She might have moved to another place for some reason, but where? Se-yŏng's face darkened with frustration.

"You could've met her if you'd returned the other time. She was a real beauty." The man said with a lewd grin. He had not forgotten the half *won* tip Se-yŏng gave him that night.

"Thanks, anyway." Se-yŏng nodded to the man and told the coachman to move on. The Manchu spat behind him.

Nam-hi didn't want to see him again, he thought as he crouched into a corner of the seat. A real beauty she might be but she wasn't the only beauty in the world, was she?

The coachman wanted to know where to take him. Well, where to, indeed? He asked into the fathomless cavern in his heart. "Where to?" Pressed the coachman again.

"Take me to a bar."

"To a bar? What kind, Korean, Japanese, Chinese?" asked the coachman, turning around.

"A Korean bar."

The horsewhip swished in the air. Where could she have gone? It seemed Sang-jun's problem was not going to be settled easily. One question after another tormented him. Why did he want to see her so? He had no business with her, he told himself. In fact, he hadn't seen her since that first day on the street corner. At first he did not dare call on her at the apartment because he was afraid he might put her in an uncomfortable position with her in-laws. Then he became terrified that he might infect her with the pest since he was constantly exposed to it. After Yuriko came down with the disease, he was paranoid about causing her to catch it. If he had come across her on the street, he might have just waved his hand and dismissed her. However, he did not stop his nightly visits to the old town. Every night after work, he took a carriage as far as Tonghwayŏsa to satisfy himself that there was no forbidding rope. He would loiter there for some time and then drive back to his apartment.

"There's a bar over there." The coachman stopped at a

corner of Choiltong Road. Se-yŏng got out of the carriage. A sign saying "Golden Coach" came into view around the corner. He was familiar with the place, though he had never been there. He went inside. The dimly lit bar was giddily decorated in black, blue, red and yellow. There was not many customers. A few hostesses, clad in Korean, Japanese and Western clothes, clustered listlessly in one corner.

"Hi, there." A girl in dark Korean clothes greeted him in a bored voice. Se-yŏng took a seat across from her.

"A chilly night, huh? What d'ya have?" The girl asked with a drunken slur as she scribbled on a sheet of paper.

"Give me something strong," he said, offering her a cigarette.

"Thanks." She lit the cigarette and, after a hearty pull at it, asked again, "Would d'ya want it by the bottle or by the glass?"

Painfully aware of his lack of experience in such a place, Se-yŏng said recklessly, "I'll have a bottle."

"A bottle of vodka here." The girl called, clapping her hands.

A voice called from across the bar, "Hey, Tess. What's keeping you there?" Some clapping and laughter burst from where the voice came.

"Aren't you afraid of the pest?" the girl asked, removing what seemed to be a speck of tobacco from the tip of her tongue with the tip of her finger. She had a small, lean face with a pinched look. Her eyes were heavily made up.

"If you're afraid of the pest, you shouldn't be here." Se-yŏng puffed at his cigarette, again thinking of Nam-hi.

"I didn't come to work for several days, but it was worse, stuck at home, alone. I ached all over and felt like I'd drop dead any minute."

Se-yŏng puffed at his cigarette and watched the smoke float way.

"Dear me, I'm afraid I'm already drunk. Oh, you've got a customer. Is he your patron, Satchang?" A bespectacled hostess in a white Korean dress chattered as she swaggered towards them. The smell of whiskey wafted from her.

"Why, Satchang, you're really groggy, aren't you. Idiot, you shouldn't gulp down every drop they give you." The woman in white sat down by the girl.

"What am I to do, Sis. I think I've got the pest. I've got this terrible pain and I'm so sleepy. Ah, I must take a nap. Just let me alone so I can sleep, all right? Forgive me, Mister." The girl in the dark dress slouched on a cushion, panting breathlessly.

"Good Heavens. Go to the back room if you want to nap. What a stupid girl! Oh, dear me, we're a mess, neglecting our customer this way. I'm dreadfully sorry, Mister. Have you ordered something?" The woman in white smiled apologetically, her eyes disappearing in wrinkles.

"What is this thing, this life of mine? It's not worth living at all. I think I should better die. Yes, I'll just die. My man's not coming. I wait and wait, yet he's not coming back to me. Ah, the swallow from the south returns bringing the spring with him...." The girl called Satchang croaked a broken tune an sobbed into the shoulder of the older woman.

"Come on, Satchang. Sober up. You know how we live. Forgive us, Mister. I'm afraid we had too much to drink from the early evening on. We had to humor those customers over there. It's all because of that damned pest."

Se-yŏng kept smoking without a word.

"I warn you, Satchang. One of these days you're going to have your insides all torn up because of so much drinking. And why are those people over there calling you Tess? Who is this person, Tess, anyway? Aw, come on, Satchang. Get up and go to bed. You hear me?"

A bottle of vodka and water were brought to the table.

"No side dishes? You'll need something solid to go with it." Said the woman as solicitously as a kindly aunt, pouring the liquor into a glass.

"Do you have oranges?"

"Bring some oranges here!" the woman hollered. At the same time a chorus of a Christian hymn burst forth from somewhere.

"We shall meet on that beautiful shore. In the sweet, by and by, we shall meet on that beautiful shore...."

Se-yŏng turned around and stared at a pale young man with a beret and a dark coat and a dark man with gleaming eyes singing the hymn with the hostesses.

"Damn it! Do they think they're at a funeral or what? See that guy with the beret? He's supposed to be a poet. He says he's translated this thing called Tess. The other one is a news-paper man, a critic or something." The woman chatted as she peeled an orange for him and another for herself. The hostess called Satchang hummed and sobbed, her eyes closed because of some mysterious pain.

"Wow! Bravo! Bravo!" Loud laughter came from the table. The dark man held a kimono clad hostess in his arms and the girl began to sing a nostalgic Japanese song, "So far away from your home in this foreign land of Mauchus...."

"Aw, hell! What a sad song! Nobody asked you to come all this long way from your precious home anyway." The big, dark man who was said to be a newspaperman dumped the girl onto a couch with a grim smile. The other hostesses applauded him playfully. They were all carousing with reckless abandon.

"Liquor. Have some more liquor." The newspaperman thrust his glass to the man in a beret. The women clapped their hands to call for more liquor and sang noisily, each a different song.

"Fill your glass. Let's drink this night away, waiting for the whistler to come...."

"This wine is my tears, my sighs. In my every footprint I leave my tears as I wander aimlessly. Horns of the departing boat mourns of my love lost...."

A girl in a green dress who had been snuggling against the man with the beret staggered up and whined, "Mr. Yi, you never talk nor laugh. You're so glum and moody, caring for nothing but your liquor. You break my heart to pieces." The women burst into laughter, clapping their hands.

"Tut, tut. Look at them. Aren't they disgusting. They're bored to death because business is bad." The woman in white clicked her tongue disapprovingly and turned away from them. Se-yŏng forced down gulp after gulp of vodka, which he had seldom had before. His chest burned but his mind remained stubbornly lucid. Pretending to be as drunk as the other men in the bar, he slurred a question, "If they're a poet, a novelist and a newspaperman, what about you, what are you?"

"Me? I'm a virgin."

"A virgin?"

The woman giggled and said, "Because I'm single. Aren't single women supposed to be virgins?"

"Why do you stay single?"

"And why do you want to know? Are you a reporter, too?"

"Nope, but I might be a matchmaker."

"A matchmaker, huh?" She laughed revealing a clean row of teeth. "My husband died, that's why I'm single now. When I was only twenty-one. There was nothing a young widow could do. After the three-year mourning period, I learned silk weaving and wove silk for a couple of years. It drove me crazy, stuck in that dreary place, just weaving yard after damn yard of silk. So one day I just dashed out of the house and never went back."

Se-yŏng blinked away. Nam-hi's face that kept overlapping the face of the woman. Making an effort to keep his eyes wide open he asked how she liked it here. He wanted the conversation to go on and on to kill time.

"Oh, it's all right. Much better than weaving silk. I can't forgive myself for spending so many years poring over strands of silk until I ruined my eyes. After all, what you do or where you do it doesn't make any difference as long as you know what you're doing. You know the old saying, you can get away from a tiger in one piece if you're only alert enough. Most customers know I'm different from these kids. An old cow knows where to graze, eh? I mean, I encounter all kinds of weird freaks in this business but as long as I keep myself sober and alert, they can't do me any harm. I work for my own sake."

Se-yŏng offered a glass of liquor in a salute to her

philosophy. "Here's to you. You're quite a woman."

"Thank you, but no more liquor for me. I've had more than enough. I wouldn't be telling you all about myself if I were sober."

Se-yŏng emptied the water jug and filled it with vodka for her.

"Good heavens! Why you're a virgin in this field, aren't you? To think one could gulp down this much vodka." She had another glass brought and poured some of the liquor in it. Lifting the glass, Se-yŏng asked playfully, "Do you have a boy friend?"

"A boyfriend? Why?"

So I can be your boyfriend if you don't have one."

"Sorry, you've just missed your chance. I'm betrothed already. Too bad you showed up one beat behind." The woman giggled.

"The guy might not be right for you."

"Nope, he suits me fine. He looks as flat as a millstone but is loaded with money. If he has enough money to keep me comfortable, what more can I ask for? All I want of this life is to be comfortable."

"Then what am I to do?" Se-yŏng put his glass on the table and looked at her sadly like a lost child.

"What are you to do? Hmm, that's an interesting question. Yes, I've got a great idea. I'll make you a match. Right away. Wake up, Satchang. Sober up and be this gentleman's girlfriend." The woman chuckled as she shook Satchang. The girl was sound asleep, slouched against a dark cushion. Her breathing was strangely raspy.

The door to the bar had opened and closed quite frequently. The man with the beret and his noisy group were gone but most of the tables were taken up by new arrivals.

"If only my hand were not already promised, I'd be all over you trying to win your favor, Mister. Come on, Satchang. You'd be better off making a friend of this gentleman than getting drunk to death every night waiting for some useless guy."

The woman shook Satchang again, and asked Se-yŏng, "By the way, what do you do for a living? This girl's name is Sachiko. Her man deserted her a few days before they were to be married because of some misunderstanding between them. She followed him to Manchuria but by the time she came here he had already left for northern China. No love, no money and ashamed to return home, it all ends up in drinks and sighs. Perhaps it's because of her sad story she's called Tess. Tess or no Tess, I really feel bad for her. She's such a nice, gentle girl."

"Hmm, that sounds quite familiar. Sounds like the story of my life. It seems we will hit it off perfectly, matchmaker."

"But I should know what you do for a living if I'm to matchmake you."

"Ah, well, I'm a butcher."

"A butcher? Aw, you're the last person to be a butcher."

"Why? What's wrong with a butcher?"

"I'll have to think about it?"

A strange sound coming from the girl caught their attention. "Why, the girl's really fallen asleep." Muttering to herself, the woman looked into Satchang's wan face. She was moaning audibly. Stupefied from the unaccustomed drinks, Se-yŏng glanced at her indolently. Her face was pallid and there was bloody foam at the corner of her mouth. Se-yŏng sobered instantly as if someone had thrown a bucket of icy water over him. The word pest hammered in his mind. He put on a mask with a shaky hand. In fact, he was shaking all over and it was with great effort that he managed to raise himself and leave the table.

"What are you doing, mister? What's the matter?"

"Come away from there."

Bewildered, the woman complied with his instructions.

"Bartender, lock the door immediately and don't let anyone leave this place."

The boisterous shouts and laughter filling the bar fizzled down and the people stared at Se-yŏng. Some seemed to think he was a gangster.

"Please, everybody, put on your masks and stay where you are. We have a sick person here and we'll have to check the cause of her illness." Still shaky from the liquor, Se-yŏng telephoned his hospital. Nurse Mida answered. A heavy silence filled the bar while he spoke into the telephone. As soon as he turned away from the phone, people began producing all kinds of certificates and clamorously asking to be let out of the bar.

"I've got a terrible headache. My heels and elbows hurt too. And my neck, oh, it's so stiff. What could this be, doctor? You know I haven't been myself this evening, babbling my head off. Oh, what am I to do?"

"Heehee, you're going to spend some very pleasant days here with all of us, that's what you're going to do. And we'll die all together if we have to," said a man, mimicking her strong northern accent. The man's mimicry brought weak laughter, but it died as quickly as it came. People watched grimly as Se-yŏng examined Sachiko, who kept moaning and panting breathlessly. She did not have a fever. The sharp horn of an ambulance signaled the arrival of the medical team from the Changchun Hospital. The door swung open and a physician strode in followed by Nurse Mida. Se-yŏng could see only her sparkling eyes as an oversized mask hid most of her face.

"You shouldn't have come here." Se-yŏng scolded her in a low voice.

"You shouldn't have either," retorted Mida as she handed a stethoscope to the physician. The physician tilted his head this way and that in puzzlement as he examined Sachiko. He handed the stethoscope to Se-yŏng, who repeated what the doctor had done. Nurse Mida took the girl's temperature and reported, "No fever."

"Drugs?" Both men said simultaneously and exchanged glances meaning it did not look like pest or typhoid fever.

The girl was moved to the ambulance. Instructing the people in the bar to remain there until he called from the hospital, Se-yŏng boarded the ambulance. Several policemen were already posted outside the Golden Coach to ensure that nobody left the place. Even if the girl proved to be suffering from something other than the pest or typhoid, the people in the Golden Coach were to be isolated until they were cleared of having no latent virus. If the girl proved to have the pest, the bar would be burnt down.

However, it turned out that Sachiko had neither pest nor typhoid. Nor did she have an ulcer caused by drinking every night. She was suffering from a drug overdose. Despite the best emergency measures the hospital could offer, it was too late to save her life.

Sachiko's death was self-induced. A suicide note scribbled with pencil was found in her pocket. Se-yŏng remembered the piece of paper. She had been writing on it when he went to the bar.

> I have the pest. I've known about it for several days now but I'm too terrified to go to the pest center. I can't walk into the crematory on my own feet. So I've come to work instead. When I'm this lonely in a crowd of people, how horrible it would be to die alone at that pest center. I've swallowed quinine pills. Lots of them. I don't care what is done with me or where I'm sent after I die, because I won't know. My apologies to the proprietor of the bar and the other girls. Forgive me, Aeran.

Aeran was the hostess in white. She was close to the dead girl. Permanent domicile, Inch'ŏn; Sŏk Ok-hi; age, 20; profession, hostess; cause of death, suicide from hysteria resulting from pest paranoia. So read her death certificate.

7

As the month turned into late December, most of the quarantine ropes and the charcoal fires disappeared from the streets. The clicking sounds of the boots and the sabers of the policemen who patrolled the city also disappeared. Occasionally cases of recovery from pest were reported. The immunization network which had controlled the city so tightly became more and more flexible until the pest alert was entirely lifted. Though the pest claimed many lives, man had won an unusual victory over the formidable epidemic.

Still, the streets remained deserted for quite some time. The hawking of Manchus selling ice candies and the jangling of the scissors of Korean taffy vendors broke the silence from time to time. The taffy vendors' calls in Korean, together with the jangling of the scissors, were soothing sounds that reminded expatriate Koreans of their homeland.

Se-yŏng listened to the calls of such a taffy vendor as he rode in a carriage with Mida Akiko down Choiltong, a street predominantly inhabited by Koreans.

"I hear there are Korean taffy vendors even in Tokyo. I wonder if you had taffy there?" Akiko asked in a subdued voice.

"There seemed to be some around but I never actually came across one. I haven't had any taffy here either. I used to have it a lot when I was a kid, though."

"I haven't ever tasted it, but it seems to be a lot like caramels. Oka loved it."

"She did?" Se-yŏng felt a pang in his heart at the mention of Oka. She was found dead the morning he reported to the hospital late after having been busy until the wee hours because of Sachiko's suicide. She was the only member of the hospital staff to die during the epidemic. Her cheerful disposition had earned the affection of many of the hospital staff.

Though Se-yŏng's relationship with Oka was not a well guarded secret, Mida Akiko feigned ignorance.

"Yuriko used to bring in a ball of brown taffy in the winter. She said she first had it when she lived in the same apartment with a Korean family and found it to her liking. The way she ate it was quite unusual. She would put it on a tin plate, place it on a radiator and wait until it got soft. Then she'd pull the gooey stuff like a rubber band, roll it into a little ball, and pop it into her mouth. She called it warm candy, as opposed to the ice candy."

"Warm candy?"

"Yes, and she joked that she was going to marry a taffy vendor because she loved the warm candy so much."

"Poor girl, you must have scowled at her a lot."

"Oh, but Yuriko was willing to challenge my scowls. In fact, she detested me. Perhaps she ate so much taffy just to irritate me. She loved ice candy as much as the warm candy." Akiko said softly. "About the time she fell ill, she boasted she was in love with you. She suspected every nurse in the hospital of being after you and accused anybody who said anything against you of being jealous."

"Being outgoing and simple, she believed that everybody should think as she did."

"Nurse Chang Hi-suk told me about Yuriko several days ago, while we were talking about Mrs. Shin Pyŏng-hwan."

"What did she tell you?"

Se-yŏng immediately regretted his question, embarrassed that it made him look conceited and anxious to know what people said about him.

"Nurse Chang read what Mrs. Shin had written in her diary about a conversation she had had with Yuriko. Mr. Shin showed it to her when his wife was away."

Se-yŏng looked away but Akiko went on about what she had heard from Miss Chang. Yuriko confided to Mrs. Shin that she was dating a Korean doctor, that she had begun the whole thing rather lightheartedly without any idea of marriage, but that she was becoming more and more serious. She wanted to marry the man and asked Mrs. Shin's candid opinion as to whether it was advisable to marry a Korean since she was experienced in such things. Mrs. Shin responded enthusiastically and referred to an ancient legend about Goddess Amaterasu Ōmikami rash brother Susanono Mikodo who fled to his mother's country when he was severely scolded by his sister. Citing the popular theory that their mother country was somewhere near Kyŏngju, she explained that Koreans and Japanese might actually be brothers and sisters with the same ancestors. Regardless of the legend, she asked Yuriko if there really was much difference between the two countries, other than that their country had some useless overweight sumo wrestlers and mighty superior weapons. And it was with those weapons that their countrymen threatened and seized Korean's sovereignty, extorted their property, and took away their lives when they resisted, reducing them to an inferior breed eventually. She said the Japanese educational policy in Korea was the most eloquent evidence of how they were playing god there and that Japan was making a grave mistake, that it should learn to fear God. There had been a time when she denied the existence of God, but she became a God-fearing person through her love of her husband. Before she met him, she was a self-righteous Marxist. It was the Communist ideology that brought her and her husband together in the beginning, but that phase of their life was completely over. Now that they were one in body and soul, all she cared about was her husband, his safety and well-being and she found herself constantly praying for him. Shin was no more or no less than her faithful husband, and had long ago removed the books on Marx's concept of history and Lenin's economic theories from his bookcase. Furthermore, he became a more loyal citizen of the empire than she was while she herself thought sometimes that she were a pure Korean. Yes, they were very happy together. The only thing that was missing in their lives was a child, but perhaps it was god's will not to make their happiness complete. Nevertheless, they were complete in their own terms because each could be the child of the other. Oka Yuriko's apprehension was caused by her lack of faith in love. She concluded that the most important thing was to have steadfast faith in love.

The carriage drove past the Paeksan Park along the broad Hungan Road. It should have turned to Iwaimachi at the corner of Daiya Street to go to Mrs. Hwang In-ae's but Se-yŏng let the driver detour because he wanted to fill his chest with fresh air. They were skirting the darkened woods of the park. A bus was far ahead, its purplish lights blinking like enlarged fireflies.

Discouraged by Se-yŏng's silence, Akiko stopped talking about Yuriko. Se-yong thought about Nam-hi, how she had come all the way to Changchun and then avoided him and left. He did not want to believe that she had abandoned him. Even if she had, it would not make any difference to him anyway. Living in a limbo that felt like eternal indigestion, relating every aspect of his life with Nam-hi was already a set pattern he had long accepted. There were times when he was racked by a dull pain in the chest. There were also times when he was utterly depressed with a terrible sense of futility. It was as if there was a vast vacuity in him that nullified his very existence.

Akiko glanced at Se-yŏng who kept staring straight ahead with a tightly drawn face. She turned and looked at the arcs the coachman's whip was drawing in the air. The horses galloped as if they would never stop, their grey manes flying in the wind.

"Where are we going?"

Akiko's question flushed Se-yŏng out of the reveries in which he was immersed. He looked at his watch without seeing it in the dark. He had the carriage turn around.

"Where were you planning to go?"

"I just thought we might have a nice drive before going to Mrs. Hwang's."

"Did you plan to beforehand?"

"Oh, sort of."

A streetcar rattling past caught Akiko's attention.

"Oh, a streetcar!"

"It seems this is the first time you ever saw one."

"No, but it's been a long time since I was in this part of the city."

"Come to think of it, I haven't seen a streetcar for some time, either."

"Dr. Chin?" Akiko's tone made him turn and look at her squarely. "What were you thinking about a while ago?" There was a feeble tremor in her voice.

"What was I thinking about?"

"You've been thinking of Yuriko all this time, haven't you?"

"Yuriko? Ah, yes, poor Yuriko. If it hadn't been for the commotion over that bar girl's suicide, I could have gone to her and been with her when she passed away."

"Koreans are terribly sentimental."

Se-yŏng turned and looked at Akiko, whose pale face was turned straight ahead. "Perhaps it just proves we really do have blood in us."

"Too much."

"Yes, you're the type to be afraid of too much blood, too much feeling. But you don't need to fret, your blood is cool enough, though I'm sure your mother is already firmly ensconced in your heart."

"That's against the rules. We weren't going to touch that subject."

"But we're going to your mother. If you really want to deny her, you're welcome to get off here and now."

"I am somewhat curious."

"About your mother?"

"About how Koreans live."

"So you're sightseeing, are you? You're only curious, huh? And not even about your mother."

"She just makes me miserable."

"What a pity."

"I can't pull myself down that way. I want to remain as I am now."

"At least you're honest. Your attitude is an example of the misguided Japanese spirit of the nouveau riche who are always impatient to display their meager superiority."

"Don't Koreans swagger the same way towards Manchus? And under the acquiescence of the Japanese, too."

"Sure, you're right. That's the frailty of the human mind, the tragedy of the weak in any society. And when the weak come into possession of swords, they can be doubly dangerous, injuring a great many people."

"I believe you're a nationalist."

"Me, a nationalist? How can a mere subordinate doctor working in a Japanese community be a nationalist? Real nationalists would probably stone me to death."

"What does it have to do with one's profession? Especially when yours is a profession of humanitarian calling, and you treat five races—Mongols, White Russians, Manchus, and Koreans as well as Japanese."

"But I've done regrettably little to deserve the title nationalist. It's been hard enough just taking care of myself."

"But you can't say you're not patriotic. You love your country."

"Sure, I love my country dearly. I love it as I would love a woman, though it might sound crazy to you." Se-yŏng said, his heart rushing back to his home and to Nam-hi.

"Then you can't accuse me of loving my country. Only my patriotism lies with Japan."

"Don't confuse bigotry with patriotism. They're two different things. There's no reason for a person to be arrogant because his country is powerful."

"Thanks for pointing out that I'm nothing but a snob. The truth is I can't even be a snob anymore because I'm no longer confident of which is my country. What a screaming shame! It's so frustrating. I'm not sure of anything anymore."

"Just accept the fact and admit that you're her daughter."

"You mean tell her I'm her daughter? Never. I can't even think that."

Se-yŏng stopped the carriage in front of a glass door on which "Hwang In-ae's Dress Shop was written in gold. He swung open the door. Hwang In-ae almost ran out of the living quarters behind the shop to welcome him and Akiko. "Oh, I'm so happy to have you honor my humble house. I was worried you might not be able to find your way," she said excitedly.

To Se-yŏng's surprise, Mrs. Hwang's pharmacist niece also came out to welcome them, drying her hands on a white apron.

She seemed to have been helping in the kitchen. Together, they ushered the visitors to an inner room with a heated *ondol* floor. It was pleasantly furnished, a folding screen enhancing its coziness.

"I'm so glad you could come to my house, Miss Mida. It's the first time to see you since I was discharged from the hospital, though I've seen Dr. Chin a couple of times. You were so good to me when I was in the hospital. Please make yourself comfortable with this cushion." Mrs. Hwang apparently felt easier with Se-yŏng because they were both from the same country.

"I wish Miss Oka could be with us, too. I was sad to hear about her death. She was very nice to me," Mrs. Hwang said regretfully.

Mida Akiko sat on a corner of the cushion, but under the repeated urging of Mrs. Hwang, relented to a more comfortable position taking up more of the cushion. "You might like to sit on the bare *ondol* floor," Mrs. Hwang told Se-yŏng. "It's quite warm. We Koreans are so addicted to the sizzling warmth of the *ondol.*"

Taking her advice, Se-yŏng flopped down on the floor, ignoring the silk cushion with an embroidered orchid. Though such floors were commonplace in Korea, he had never been on one so smooth and beautifully covered with golden oil paper. Most of the houses in his village had clay floors with rush mats. Even the rooms in Nam-hi's house had mats only. He found himself again thinking of Nam-hi. Images of her came and went like a sigh, sending a tiny shudder along his spine.

"Do you have a chill, doctor? I think we should better bring in a brazier," said Mrs. Hwang, noticing Se-yŏng shudder. She had been coaxing Mida to relax instead of sitting rigidly on her knees.

"Not at all. It's too warm, in fact. How about you, Mida? I bet this is the first time you've ever been in an *ondol* room?"

"Yes, but I know well about them." She retorted quietly, still sitting on her knees.

"Most Japanese living in Korea have an *ondol* room in their houses these days," Mrs. Hwang commented, running her hand across the spotless floor.

"Are you from Korea, Miss Mida?"

"I'm from Japan."

"Oh, from Japan. From where, may I ask?"

"Kyushu."

"Kyushu?"

"Yes."

Mrs. Hwang looked hard at her as she asked, "Do you live with your family?"

"My parents are in Kyushu," Akiko lied calmly, looking squarely into Mrs. Hwang's eyes.

"I see." A sad look flickered across her face a fleeting moment before she pulled herself together. She jerked up, unconsciously revealing a glimpse of her shapely legs under her skirt, and pulled a square dining table toward them. She said proudly, "This table is made of red sandalwood. It is as dear to me as a child. You can see that the grain of the wood is as delicate as silk. This and that folding screen are my most precious possessions."

"Ugh, Auntie, you're showing off those things again," teased Kim Ok-suk coming from the kitchen through a glass door separating it from the living room. "Bring in the tray, Ch'un-ja."

A young girl came in carrying a Korean style tray loaded with food. Mrs. Hwang explained that she was her maid, her shop clerk and her adopted daughter all in one.

"Please rest, Auntie, I'll prepare the table." Kim Ok-suk told her aunt setting the dishes from the tray onto the sandalwood table.

Akiko looked around the room, straining her ears all the while not to miss the conversation. Her eyes travelled carefully over the small chest, the coffer, the wardrobe, all immaculately arranged against the flowery papered walls and shining with loving care. Akiko turned her attention to Mrs. Hwang's niece and wondered what she was doing in Manchuria this time. It wasn't hard to guess her ulterior motive, she thought.

"Come over here, Miss Mida, and make yourself at home."

Akiko glanced back and forth between Se-yŏng and Ok-suk who was setting the table, and nimbly took a seat at the table. Mrs. Hwang sat opposite her, and Ok-suk sat across from Se-yŏng.

"What an extravagant dinner. You shouldn't have gone to so much trouble to prepare so much." Se-yŏng protested, taking a bowl of rice from Ok-suk.

"My aunt's been saying she's permanently indebted to you and should treat you to her best," explained the younger woman.

"Well, I'm sure I will enjoy the meal."

Akiko was not used to silver chopsticks but found them quite easy to handle. She also found the food to her liking, with no smell of the garlic for which Korean food was famous. She was fascinated with the seaweed laced chicken soup and, the sweetened rib stew. She felt quite full before she had finished trying everything on the table such as the spiced herbs, broiled fish and kimch'i, and the main dish was yet to be served. Marveling at the great appetite of the Koreans, she tried a small piece of a dark rice dish called *yakshik* and was surprised at its unexpected sweetness. After a second helping of it, she had a bowl of sweetened cinnamon water. She was surprised at herself, realizing that she had had more than twice her usual amount. Still Mrs. Hwang insisted that she try the drumsticks. "Whew, I'm stuffed. I simply can't take another bite." Akiko refused with a giggle.

"You're going to regret not having stuffed yourself when you're back at the hospital, Mida." Se-yŏng's clumsy warning made them all laugh.

"I still have a shooting pain when I laugh. I wonder how long it's going to persist?" Asked Mrs. Hwang, grimacing. Akiko grimaced too without knowing it.

"Even a simple appendectomy takes a year to get completely over, and yours was a major operation."

"Oh, did you take out her appendix, Doctor?" Ok-suk asked.

"Yes."

"My god, I heard that things tend to stick to the intestines if you don't have an appendix to hold them in." Mrs. Hwang said worriedly.

Se-yŏng explained that it was the most useless organ in the body, created through a mistake by God, but that he personally appreciated God's mistake very much because it was a good financial gain for the doctors. The women burst into laughter again.

"By the way, that man, what was his name, er, Shin somebody, is he now out of the hospital?" Mrs. Hwang asked, holding her aching stomach.

"That's Shin Pyŏng-hwan. He's still hospitalized."

"His wife is supposed to be wonderful. I heard all about them from Miss Oka. It seems it's much better when a Korean man marries a Japanese woman than when a Japanese man marries a Korean woman," murmured Mrs. Hwang almost to herself. Offering Akiko a piece of persimmon, she noted thoughtfully, "You remind me of someone I used to know. Did you say you were from Kyushu?"

"Yes."

"You're imagining things, Auntie. To me she looks just like you. Don't you think so, Dr. Chin? Look at the line of her chin," said Ok-suk lightly touching her own chin with a fingertip. Se-yŏng looked at the woman. Her triangular eyes, sunken brows and rather protruding mouth were still there, but she looked much more comely than when he first met her in the hall of the hospital. Ok-suk said soothingly to Akiko, whose face Mrs. Hwang was still studying carefully, "You mustn't think I'm being impolite saying you look like my aunt. I mean it as a compliment. She used to be quite a beauty in her youth. She's reputed to have been fairer than a flower."

"Aw, stop it. Let bygones be bygones. I would have rather

been born horribly ugly but with lots of luck." Mrs. Hwang said wistfully.

"My aunt is a true specimen of what they call an ill-starred beauty. Beauty and luck seldom go hand in hand, they say. It's amazing how sisters can be so different. My mother is of the same blood but quite ugly, just like me."

"What do you mean you're ugly? The trouble with you is that you think too much, and know too much. The way you look at men so critically, it's no wonder you're twenty-five and still unmarried. That old saying about too much learning brings trouble is really true. Don't you agree, Dr. Chin?" Mrs. Hwang's attention was now completely diverted to her niece. "You're quite talented, Ok-suk. Of course, the more talent one has, the more one wants. That's the way humans are, but you're too much. It's about time you lower your high and mighty standards."

Se-yŏng suddenly understood Mrs. Hwang's intention, and he said, "You seem to be worrying over nothing. I'm sure your niece has her own plan."

"You know a monk can't shave his own head. So there's no hope of her finding her own husband. She says my past failure thoroughly extinguished whatever interest she had in romance. It's a screaming shame really. I know she will make a fine wife. She's so good-natured and respectable to her seniors. She came here today just to see if I'm all right. Such a thoughtful girl. Oh, by the way, are your parents well, Dr. Chin?" Mrs. Hwang asked Se-yŏng feigning casualness.

"Neither of them is alive."

"I see, that explains why you are still unmarried."

"A monk can't shave his own head?"

"Of course, of course." Mrs. Hwang nodded in satisfaction.

The hospital was as quiet as a deserted house. After checking at the staff room, Se-yŏng began to browse through the newspaper alone in the out-patient clinic. It was New Year's Day. The chief of his department had gone to Chuŭl to enjoy the hot

.springs as he had planned and Dr. Hayashi had gone to Dairen with his wife. It seemed most of the other doctors had also gone for a couple of days of vacation. Nurse Chang went to Korea to visit her uncle in Munch'on. Nurse Mida had also been out of sight the day before.

Throwing the newspaper on the desk, Se-yŏng lit a cigarette. The year was new but men never got any newer. He puffed and watched the smoke curling up in circles. The radiators hissed by the steamed up windows. Marry Kim Ok-suk? He smiled at the thought. For the second time in a row, he was invited to Mrs. Hwang's the day before and went to a movie with her and her niece after dinner at a Chinese restaurant. He had had to have tea with them before he could bid them goodnight. Mrs. Hwang insisted that Se-yŏng should come to her house the next morning and have the traditional New Year's rice-dumpling soup with them, explaining that she could not help thinking of Se-yŏng as one of her family, but he declined her invitation with the excuse that he was on duty on New Year's Day. "Then you must come in the evening. Please. We'll be waiting for you. If you don't, we might come to the hospital and bring you back with us." Mrs. Hwang told him. By now Se-yŏng was well aware why she was so persistent. Though she did not propose the idea forthright, it was quite obvious that she wanted him to get to know her niece better and marry her eventually.

He wondered if he really had to go to Mrs. Hwang's again that evening. But who would keep the hospital, then? The door opened and Nurse Mida stepped in. She looked pale and tired.

"Happy New Year, Nurse Mida."

"Same to you, doctor." Mida went to her chair and sat down.

"Were you sick yesterday? You look rather ill."

"Yes, a little."

That night two days ago, she had left Mrs. Hwang's more depressed than before. Se-yŏng thought her depression was quite understandable, since she had subjected herself to the innocent hospitality of Mrs. Hwang and shared a meal with her at the same table. In all probability that was why she did not report to the hospital yesterday, Se-yŏng guessed.

"Why don't you take another day off? We won't have any patients today anyway and I can handle everything by myself."

"Have you made rounds?"

"I'm going to a bit later with the charge nurse."

"But then don't you have somewhere else to go," said Akiko, looking down at a bulky magazine.

"Where do you mean?" Se-yŏng asked bewildered.

"Mrs. Hwang's, where else?"

"Are you invited, too?"

Akiko lifted her face triumphantly and challenged Se-yŏng with gleaming eyes. "So she invited you, didn't she?"

"Uhuh. She wants me to have New Year's soup with her."

"Well, not me. She has no reason to invite me again. Once is more than enough."

"I guess you're right." Se-yŏng agreed with her deliberately to add salt to her wound. A monk who could not shave his own head, a doctor who could not heal his own illness, and a nurse who could not handle her own trouble....Will we ever be free of our own obsessions, wondered Se-yŏng. He had to admit that he and Mida suffered from the same kind of character trait. If Mida had known how he had closed up his heart, living a lonely life forever pining over Nam-hi, she would have advised him in no uncertain terms to forget her, that she was already another man's wife and his stubbornness was sick.

"That woman Mrs. Hwang seems quite eager to matchmake you with her niece."

"Clever girl. You do have sharp eyes, but your tongue's even sharper than your eyes. How can you call your mother 'that woman Mrs. Hwang'?"

"I never asked her to get so close with my father. I despise women who make children that way. Especially the one who made me like that." Her usually subdued voice vibrated with a sudden vehemence.

"And it's not just those who make children like that but the

children as well that have to face the vengeful world." Se-yŏng
goaded her to remind her of the hopelessness of her racial
superiority.

"You seem to believe that I'm very miserable."

"That's obvious. If not being able to identify yourself to your
own mother doesn't make you miserable, I don't know what
would."

"That's what you think. I was told that my mother died right
after I was born and I still believe it."

"Don't be absurd. Can you swear that you really believe
that?"

"I try to believe that way. I'm not a sentimentalist like you."

"So you're going to be happy if you make yourself believe
that?"

"That depends on how you look at it. I'm not asking much
out of life and I work for what little I ask for. There can't be
much room for doubt or complaints."

"That's a great idea befitting a dried up spinster. Your
attitude is not one of contentment but of resignation and self-
deception." Se-yŏng taunted her, suddenly tired of the whole
thing. It made him angry that Akiko was related to Hwang In-
ae, that he had gotten involved in the private problem of a
mother and daughter and above all that, in denouncing her
mother, Mida was implicitly disparaging Oka Yuriko about her
affair with him.

Akiko jerked up and walked to the window. Her face
twitched as she stared out trying to calm herself. Se-yŏng eyed
her with grim satisfaction.

"It seems you're really going to become Mrs. Hwang's
nephew. You're being so unfair, siding up with her against
me." She protested in a shaky voice.

"Why am I to become her nephew all of a sudden? You certainly have an amazing imagination."

"As if you don't know what I mean!"

"It seems you're quite interested in Mrs. Hwang's niece.
That's quite understandable, considering you two are cousins."

"Don't be disgusting."

"Well, I won't say any more if you don't want to hear it. I just wish you and your mother would discover each other."

"And I wish you and Kim Ok-suk would get married and be done with it once and for all."

Akiko snatched up the magazine from her desk and stormed out of the room. Se-yŏng's shoulders sagged as he relaxed. "But I prefer things the way they are," he said to the door from which Akiko disappeared and turned and stared out the window without seeing anything.

CHAPTER III

1

The train rumbled heavily past Yongdam Village, its whistle wailing. As the pins and levers across its wheels chugged laboriously, another set of pins and levers leaped back and forth in Se-yŏng's mind with an equal persistence as he looked inside himself.

U-yŏng, his cousin, might be watching the northbound train at this minute from the latticed door of his house, never imagining that he was aboard it. U-yŏng's house had two latticed doors and a paneled entranceway on the front side. Outside the house was a winding path that meandered to the Yongch'ŏn River with its sandy shore and clear water. A wooden bridge that once precariously spanned the river had been widened the last time he was there.

Having left Yongdam behind, the train was now crossing the river. After the river would come the Changsumok crossing and then the little country station of Pukch'on. Beyond the station there would be a dirt road separating an orchard and wild shrubs growing up the mountain slope and there would be acacias bordering the orchard. Below the orchard would be rice patches and then the stone mound and the cluster of houses....

The villagers said that Changyŏn Basin was a dragon that could not ascend to heaven because of a mangled fin. The train was now chugging along the writhing contour of the dragon that lay in darkness. As the pins held the rails in place for the train to roll on, the pins of memories of past times held Se-yŏng's bones and muscles tightly in place. They were there for him to live by; always intact, they would never be attrited until the day he would get himself together and find a new land where he could make a new life for himself.

With a short whistle, the train slowed down. A little station with a sign reading Pukch'on came up and receded dreamily into the darkness. The train pulled to a stop. Se-yŏng peered out the window towards the northeast. Somewhere in the darkness lay the houses of Choi Ch'i-man and his sons, and Song Kun-sam and Kim Kap-il.... Having filled its water tank, the train shunted to the right track and started to pick up speed. Poplar trees with young leaves spreading out came and went like witches wrapped in dark shrouds.

The train whistled again. It was at the crossing to Tongch'on. To the right was the road that Nam-hi had fearfully said was haunted by a ghost. Further on there would be the pond and the school. With another labored whistle, the train entered the Changyŏn Tunnel.

"Aw, a tunnel. Please close the window." A middle-aged woman who had been dozing in front of Se-yŏng jerked up and told the man next to her. Se-yŏng quickly closed the window and looked at her because the woman in a white *chŏgori* over a gray skirt made him think of Nam-hi's mother-in-law who traveled with her to Changchun. She looked gratefully at Se-yŏng and waved away the smoke.

"Heavens, what a foul smell. I hate trains because of these tunnels." The woman muttered, covering her nose as smoke and nauseous fumes filled the train. It was a long tunnel and the train whistled jubilantly when it was finally out.

It passed several small stations including the one at the resort where Yankowski the Russian had a villa. The area was quite famous for lush pine groves and clear water. The middle-aged couple in front of Se-yŏng got off.

Se-yŏng took his bag down from the overhead rack. The next stop was Chuŭl, his destination for the night. The door of his coach opened and the conductor came in with a police detective to check the tickets. Se-yŏng craned his neck to look around at the passengers who held out their tickets obediently. Some smiled respectfully at or kowtowed needlessly to the two men. There were some who almost cringed as if they were helpless children expecting to be scolded by an adult. Disheartened by the servile attitude of the well-trained colonized people, Se-yŏng glumly thrust his ticket to the conductor.

"Let me see it." The detective snatched the ticket from the conductor as he was returning it to Se-yŏng.

"Are you from Seoul?"

"Yes, that's where I boarded the train."

"You don't live there?"

"No, I live in Changchun."

"Oh? Isn't it easier to come via Tumen?" The detective asked, eyeing Se-yŏng suspiciously.

"I had to visit Seoul first."

"Where's your birthplace?"

"Pukch'on."

"Pukch'on of Changyŏn?"

"Yes."

"What do you do?"

"I'm a doctor."

"Hmm. And you haven't stopped at your birthplace?" The detective squinted at him, apparently waiting for some show of anxiety that would indicate a falsehood.

"I have no family there."

"They have all moved to Changchun?"

Se-yŏng smiled ruefully. He had found his two-week home leave rather burdensome. He did not have any plan or desire to go off anywhere. He started by buying a train ticket as far as P'yŏngyang, having a vague notion that the city was worth visiting once in one's lifetime, but found it to be smaller than he had expected. Its marketplace was interesting, however, not because of its size or the richness of its goods but because it was teeming with people almost uniformly clad in white. The women all wore white head covers. He went to the famed Moranbong Hill by the Taedonggang River and there, too, people were dressed in white. He knew the phenomenon was representative of the implicit nationalistic sentiment of the city, but he felt an uncomfortable estrangement which prevented him from mingling with them.

He left P'yŏngyang the next day and went to Seoul but found he did not want to dally there after only three days. He left Seoul after a cursory sightseeing tour to the ancient palaces such as Kyŏngbokkung, Tŏksugung and the Secret Garden. He could have called on some of his classmates from medical school but did not because he did not see any reason to renew what little friendship he had had with them. In fact, he had not made many friends during his school days because he stayed away from his classmates most of the time.

He was almost happy when he finally boarded the north-bound train and viewed the landscape with the fondness of an expatriate going home after a long trip to foreign countries. And now he was to get off the train at the next stop at Chuŭl.

Se-yŏng felt strangely remorseful to have to disappoint the dogged detective as he answered truthfully, "No, I don't have any family there, either."

"You're not married yet."

"No."

"Doctors are usually quite detached, aren't they?"

"I don't know what you mean."

"They are seldom found to be members of underground organizations."

"Oh?"

"Do you teach as well?"

"No."

"But you will in the near future?"

"I have no idea."

"Then how did you get this discount ticket?"

"The staff of the university hospital are entitled to a discount."

"Ah, that explains it. How long is your home leave?"

Se-yŏng was fast losing his patience. Stifling an urge to scream, he answered, "Two weeks."

The detective sat down across from Se-yŏng, forcing a friendly smile. "Sometimes I wish somebody would invent a magic mirror that could reflect people's thoughts and beliefs. It would make my job so much simpler. Would you care to smoke?"

Se-yŏng waved away the cigarette the detective held out to him.

"You don't smoke?"

"I do."

Nodding his head understandingly, the detective went on. "But then it's quite simple to pick out a suspicious character when you have trained eyes, just like you doctors can tell who's sick and who's not. By the way, are you going to spend your whole two weeks here?"

"That depends."

"Ah, well. Enjoy your vacation. Sorry to bother you." Nodding slightly, the detective left.

It was the second time he was interrogated by the detectives from Seoul to Chuŭl. He would have been interrogated a third time if there was another shift of traveling detectives. Though it was said to be a screening to detect common thieves and smugglers, it was actually to harass anti-Japanese Koreans. It was not uncommon to see Koreans trying to catch their countrymen who were anti-Japanese. They would say that all jobs were the same, that one job was just as good as another and should be done thoroughly and faithfully. So now the guy was saying that a detective's job was to catch criminals and a doctor's job was to attend to sick people.

So I'm a doctor, a doctor attending to the needs of sick

people. But what am I really? Se-yŏng gazed straight ahead into the ochre light illuminating the coach. He could advise others about their lives, like he did Mida Akiko, and not hesitate to cajole or reprimand. But not himself. He shook his head.

A prolonged whistle sounded and a number of passengers moved towards the exit. Se-yŏng followed them lugging his bag.

"Hi, so you're leaving." The detective nodded to Se-yŏng as he stepped onto the platform.

2

"Have a good day." The maid bowed and smiled. Her voice as well as her smile was tinged with a subtle sadness. It was a girl named Misako who had been attending to Se-yŏng the past two days.

"And a good day to you, too." Returning her greeting, Se-yŏng left the hotel. The sky was hanging low, dipping into the morning mist. The sun was masked by thick fog that was not moved by a breeze. The sulfuric odor of the hot spring filled the air. He could hear the spring water burbling somewhere. He had literally soaked in the sulfuric water for two solid days.

He took a short cut and came out of the arched gate of the Kaneda Hot Spring. He was on his way to visit Tong-jun at the public school. Tong-jun had told him that he should come and enjoy Chuǔl's famous hot springs while he was there the night they ran into each other at Pukch'on Station years ago.

Tong-jun's invitation must have been behind his decision to spend the rest of his vacation in Chuǔl. He was sure that by now he could hide his emotions from Tong-jun while Tong-jun would be so happy to see him that he would be quite emotional. They had not heard from each other for some time but there was a bond of understanding between them that a long period of silence could not affect. The silence actually enhanced their friendship as it did when Tong-jun kept silent about his relationship with Nam-hi.

Se-yŏng looked around. The street was quiet with only a couple of elderly women strolling about. He looked at his watch and turned in the direction of downtown. An old bus tottered down the street and Se-yŏng got on it. It took ten minutes for the sluggish bus to reach the railroad station, and Tong-jun's school was a five-minute walk from there. The school yard was teeming with children as it was recess. Tong-jun was not there. Se-yŏng was told that his friend had been transferred to the Changyŏn School two years ago.

He left school and walked to the railroad station. He slouched absentmindedly onto a deserted bench. He felt as if someone had hit him on the head. Even though he had no specific reason to see Tong-jun, he felt lost and bitterly disappointed to find that his friend was not waiting for him. He went aimlessly to a stationery shop but bought some paper and envelopes. Returning to the bench which remained unoccupied he began to write to Tong-jun. Informing him of his plan to stay in Chuŭl for a few days, Se-yŏng invited him to join him over the weekend. He asked him to send a cable if he could not make it, scratched that out and wrote again asking to be informed whether or not he was coming. He addressed the envelope to the Changyŏn School. Since it was Wednesday, he thought Tong-jun would be able to come either on Friday evening or Saturday morning.

As soon as he dropped the letter into the mailbox, he regretted it. It seemed unbearably tedious and idiotic to be waiting for three days when there was nothing more to see Tong-jun for than to ruminate about the past. Besides, what if a cable came saying he could not make it? But there was no use to fuss over the letter that was already in the mailbox. It would be even more ridiculous to try to retrieve it. Se-yŏng turned away telling himself that even if Tong-jun was unable to visit, he had done his best.

He strolled back to the bus stop to find that he would have to wait more than fifteen minutes for the next bus. He gave up the idea of the bus and started to walk toward downtown. The streets were quite crowded. Strangers. They were all strangers to him and the familiar sense of estrangement surged into him as it did in P'yŏngyang and in Seoul. It had been the same in Tokyo at first. In the midst of the crowded street, a line from the English Bible he had read to improve his English when he was still a high school student came to mind: "Are they Hebrews? So am I! Are they Israelites? So am I! Are they the seed of Abraham? So am I!" Taking a deep breath, Se-yŏng ran his eyes over the street, the drapery shop, the grain shop, the dried fish vendor, the pharmacy, the wallpaper shop, all lying half hidden under low awnings. "Are they Koreans? So am I! Are they Hans? So am I! Are they the seed of Tan-gun? So am I!"

Chuǔl was a spa town with two hot springs about six kilometers from each other on a sprawling hillside that curved like a tightly pulled bowstring. The Kaneda Spring was nearer to the station, only about two kilometers away. The other one, called Oku, was farther towards the mountain and more famous because it had a waterfall with hot water cascading into an open stream and besides, the nearby deer farm the Russian Yankowski owned attracted many tourists. Most of the vacationers from afar favored Oku, but Se-yŏng chose Kaneda which was closer to the railroad station, and checked into the Sŏnjang which was recommended to be the best hotel in the area. The hotel was famous for its sand bath and well-groomed lotus pond and cherry garden which burst into fantastic bloom in the spring.

Se-yŏng walked slowly, groping his way. Very soon he came to the end of the town where a country road that led to Chuch'on about 24 kilometers away started. The memory of the day he lay prostrate on that road after walking the 24 kilometers came to him. It was the road to the burning shame that had consumed him.

On a windy day after his mother's funeral Se-yŏng ran away

from his cousin's house without so much as a coat. He took the mountain trail and kept running until he reached Chuch'on, but there was no one to welcome him. Leaving his mother's relative, he set off towards Chuŭl. In the nightmare of his mother's suicide and the flogging of her dead body on the day of her funeral, he had barely had a proper meal for over ten days and, succumbing to hunger, cold and fatigue, fainted on the road near Chuŭl.

It could have been the road he was taking now. When he regained consciousness, he found himself lying in a camp at a construction site under the worried gazes of some construction workers. A kindly Japanese carpenter took notice of him and eventually took him to Japan.

The construction could have been for the hotel in which he was staying. Or it could have been anywhere else. Se-yŏng looked back to those days philosophically. If he had not been rescued, in all probability he would have died on the roadside, unknown and uncared-for. He would have been forgotten by everyone, by Tong-jun, by Nam-hi and by all his neighbors in Pukch'on.

Se-yŏng thought he was in no better shape than a frost-pinched vegetable. A cock crowed somewhere. He stopped and looked at a little thatched house off to the right of the road. A little girl in a red frock came out and fed some chickens. He was already two or three hundred meters out of town. The air was fragrant and the sky, now that the fog had lifted, looked quite high. The cock crowed again. The girl flopped on the ground and clapped her hands calling after the chickens. The road was bordered by potato patches and beyond them spread barley fields in undulating velvet green waves. Over him, the jade tinged expanse of sky was specked with light cottony clouds. They were all painfully familiar scenes of his childhood. So he resumed his walk, quickening his pace, to shake off the phantoms of his youth. They seemed to be saying, "Chin Se-yŏng, the orphan. A miserable orphan. You should have married and sired five sons and five daughters to build a fortress of a home for you."

Somewhere, a cock crowed again, and the distant barking of a dog followed. A village of small thatched houses stood to his left about two hundred meters off the road. A sun bleached dirt road snaked to the village. It was no different from the road to their village which Nam-hi once trudged home wailing at the top of her voice because her brother had punched her. He wondered how she was doing now.

He tread back to the arched gate and returned to the hotel through its garden dappled by the young leaves of the cherry trees. He climbed clamorously up the stairs to his room as if to stamp out all his wistful thoughts and vain wishes.

"My, you're as boisterous as an athlete." Misako the maid scrambled up from the parapet on which she had been perching. She had changed into a green Japanese dress with red stripes and wore a tiny apron over it. Despite the brightness of her dress she remained remarkably pallid.

"Sorry if I disturbed you."

Se-yŏng went into his room and flopped down on his back. He lay there staring at the ceiling for about five minutes until, with a knock, Misako slid open the paper door to his room.

"I've brought you some tea." Misako sat down on her legs in one fluid movement. Se-yŏng sat up and watched her through the smoke of his cigarette. She was skinny with a small face which, despite the light makeup, showed she was young and vulnerable.

"Please enjoy your tea and let me know if there's anything else you want." Misako said, placing the tea on a small table.

"That will do. Thank you."

"How long are you staying?"

"Why?"

"Oh, I just want to know." Misako answered staring at a corner of the tea table. Se-yŏng savored the bitter flavor of the tea on his tongue.

"Thanks for the tea. I really needed it."

Se-yŏng stood up and took off his jacket to change into a light

sweater. The girl hung around as if she had some undone busi-
-ness and followed him as he stepped out of his room with a
towel. Leaning over the parapet to look down at the garden,
Se-yŏng asked, "Will it be all right if I go to the public bath in
the annex building?"

"Of course. It belongs to the hotel. But we don't recommend
it to our customers. It's not very clean because it is used only
by people not staying overnight."

"Like whom?"

"Koreans mostly."

"No Japanese?"

"Only very poor ones."

"It seems every Japanese in this area is doing quite well,
huh?"

"I guess so. At least well enough to maintain the good image
expected of a Japanese."

"The good image of a Japanese?"

"Yes."

"Well, I'm going to the public bath. I trust the water is of
the same quality."

"The water's the same but it's quite crowded."

"How about the herbal bath?"

"It's all the same over there. You must be very bored to want
to go to a crowded place."

"Is there anything better to do if I am bored?"

"Try boating. It's fun."

"Boating? I guess I could give it a try if you were to come
with me."

"Why not, though it won't be very comfortable."

"Why won't it be comfortable?"

"Because the boats are designed for only one person."

"That's not a boat but a toy. Surely it can hold two persons?"

"Yes, it can manage."

"Good. Then you must take me on a boat ride and row for
me. I don't know how to row."

"You don't?"

"No."

"Well, why not. But you'll have to wait until the evening. I'm not available during the day."

Birches, maples and weeping willows stood in the garden among various configurations of light and dark rocks of fantastic shapes. Beyond a wisteria arbor with a couple of benches shined a gleaming lotus pond. A number of colorfully painted tiny boats floated on it. A tender green sea of cherry trees flickered on the left bank of the pond.

"You're waiting for someone, aren't you?"

Misako, viewing the garden beside Se-yŏng, murmured questioningly.

"How did you know?"

"You look that way. I got the same feeling yesterday, and the day before yesterday, too."

"You're as uncanny as a fortuneteller."

Se-yŏng turned away and walked down the stairs toward the annex building.

The annex bathhouse was indeed swarming with bathers as Misako had warned. The smell of wet flesh and sulfur permeated the stifling steam that filled the place. He had to admit that it was boredom that made him join them. He went to the herbal bath but the smell there was even worse. The huge room with tubs of opaque herbal water was packed with people, all nude. Muttering the Koreans were herbal bath freaks, he turned away from what he thought looked like the gateway to purgatory.

He then peeped into the sand bath. One man lay buried in the black sand from the neck down. Se-yŏng undressed down to his underwear and stepped into the sand bath. The sandbox was burning hot and reeking with the smell of sulfur. An attendant with a shovel came over to cover him with sand. Se-yŏng hesitantly crouched and pinched the sand between his fingers. It might have been sterilized by constant heat, but still the sand bath was favored by people with dermatological problems. Imagining the unseen discharges and scabs in the sand, he jerked up, almost stepping on the man lying next to him. The man removed a towel revealing a long, pallid face and stared at Se-yŏng with a ghostly gaze. Se-yŏng cursed him silently and hurried out of the sand bath, half expecting a ghost to grab him from behind. Not to risk facing the man again, he barely put on his clothes properly. He had to satisfy himself with a plain bath in the hot water that gushed between the rocks.

"Whee, whirrr wheee."

The flute of a masseur sounded from the cherry grove. It came nearer the hotel. Se-yŏng asked for the masseur. It was a balding blind man.

"You have a great physique, sir." The blind man uttered, massaging Se-yŏng's shoulders.

"How do you know?"

"I can see it with my hands."

"That's enough for the shoulders. Please do my legs, will you." Se-yŏng told the masseur and stretched his legs as he leaned his back against the wall. The hands of the masseur kneaded his legs as nimbly as a musician coaxing a tune out of his instrument.

"You seem to be a runner. You have very strong legs." The masseur commented again grinning under his shaded glasses.

"You can tell many things with your hands, huh?"

"Of course, and I can discern more things than most people can see with their eyes."

"You mean you tell fortunes?"

"Sometimes."

"Are you good at it?"

"Sure," the masseur said with a grin. Se-yŏng pulled his legs away from the masseur as he began to work on his arms.

"Hmm, very skillful hands." Se-yŏng looked at the man's fat chin as he lifted his head in the way blind people do awaiting a reply. "These are the hands of a fine artisan. Do you happen to be a goldsmith?"

"How can you tell so well? You really are a great fortuneteller."

"Your hands are large, strong yet very smooth."

The masseur grinned triumphantly, revealing ugly dark gums. Se-yŏng jerked his hands away. He was not sure whether he was prompted to do so by the hideous smile on the greasy face or the soft footsteps out in the corridor. The paper door slid open quietly and Misako looked in holding a finger over her lips. She motioned with her hands for Se-yŏng to keep silent about her. The masseur's hands became still. Se-yŏng watched the man's Adam's apple bob up and down as he strained his ears to listen. Casting a hateful glance at the masseur, Misako tiptoed in and stood very still near the closet.

"You have a visitor?"

"Yes, I have. That's enough for now." Se-yŏng paid the masseur and showed him to the door.

"It's a lady visitor." The blind man sniffed and said, "Is that you, Missy? Yes, it must be you, that's your smell of lilac." His nostrils widened as he sniffed again. Misako waved impatiently to Se-yŏng to get rid of the man.

"Come on. You've no more business here."

"Of course, of course. Thank you for everything. You want me back tomorrow evening?"

"No, I don't."

"I see. Well, then. Have a good time, both of you."

"Get out. You talk too much."

"Heehee. There's no need to lose your temper. My eyesight is the only thing that's missing. I'm as well equipped as anyone in other areas, and quite superb as a nightly companion for a lonely lady in a sleepless bed in the detached pavilion."

Sensing the man was trying to pick a quarrel, Se-yŏng kept silent. The masseur finally disappeared down the corridor, his flute trailing a rather plaintive sound that was not as unpleasant as him. Se-yŏng and Misako stared at the door like two children holding their breath waiting for something terrifying to leave.

"I'm sorry about that unpleasant man." Misako knelt and

apologized. Her face was pale and looked somewhat upset.

"I should apologize to you. He was no masseur, but a hoodlum. The presumptuous wretch was trying to make fun of us as well as blackmail us." Se-yŏng grumbled.

"That one scares me." Misako sighed.

"Who did he think you were?"

"I guess he thought I was the daughter of the hotel proprietor."

"Wicked man. His big mouth is going to get him in trouble someday."

"The man is a devil. I'm sure he's right out of the underworld. His flute chills my bones. He's really driving me crazy. I'm sure he's the ghost of this place come alive. I wonder what my father would do if he knew about him." The maid said hysterically, her lips trembling.

"Your father?"

"No, I mean the hotel proprietor. I'm just... er, I've come about the date we made for the afternoon. Shall we go for the boat ride?"

"Good grief, I forgot. But it's too late now, isn't it?"

"No, not really. The pond is brightly lit at night."

"Still, I don't think we should. I don't like the idea of being embarrassed in a one man boat."

"People usually ride in pairs in the boats. It's up to you, though. I just wanted to keep my word."

"Thank you anyway."

The maid prepared Se-yŏng's bed, brought some tea and left, urging him to call her if he wanted anything.

Long after she left, the sound of the masseur's flute hovered in the back garden. Across from the front of the hotel, cars screeched to a stop as they brought more travellers. The coquettish greeting of the maids floated up to Se-yŏng as he fell into a troubled sleep.

3.

Se-yŏng stood by the fence some distance from the exit

turnstile at the Chuǔl railroad station. He had been there the day before and the day before that. His excuse was that he was waiting for Tong-jun even though he did not believe he would really come out of the train. He found the two-kilometer wilk back and forth quite refreshing and that getting himself to move around was much better than waiting at the hotel doing nothing. He bought a newspaper, glanced over the headlines and tucked it under his arm. His eyes wondered back toward the exit turnstile.

Passengers left the train and came forth in twos and threes. Se-yŏng craned his neck and scrutinized every male passenger. He had thought that he could recognize Tong-jun anytime and anywhere, but now he was overcome with doubt. He assured himself that if he missed him, Tong-jun would look for him at the hotel since he knew where he was staying. It was then that his wondering eyes came upon a woman who was carrying a child. His breath caught in his throat and his eyes gleamed. The woman put down the child and together they walked at the toddler's pace. It was a little child dressed in a dark blue sailor suit and gray cap and shoes.

Se-yŏng let out a long breath and stared disbelievingly at the white pom-pom atop the hat bobbing up and down as Nam-hi's child teetered toward the ticket collector. Nam-hi, in a light silver *chogori* and a long violet skirt, carried a baby wrapper over her arm and what appeared to be a bag stuffed with diapers in her hand. Se-yŏng backed away from the fence. Nam-hi was the only person left behind the turnstile. She picked up the child again and checked her ticket with a bowed head. She did not bother to look around even after she came out of the station.

"I'll carry you on my back, little one. You've walked far too much." Nam-hi said and turned her back to the child. She secured the child on her back with the wrapper. Se-yŏng moved to within a few steps behind her.

"After a chug-chug of a train, we'll ride on a honk-honk of a car. Right?"

"Chug-chug, honk-honk."

The child waved his hands happily on Nam-hi's back. A crippling pain shot through Se-yŏng as he was stabbed by a knife of jealousy, but he did not dare disturb the mother and child. Even though he kept telling himself that he should disappear if he cared for Nam-hi's peace of mind and happiness, he could not help following her at some distance. He had a great urge to go to her and ask what she was doing in Chuŭl.

Nam-hi stopped at the bus stop. Se-yŏng stood still behind her. He was oblivious of the unwieldy strands of hair falling over his forehead. As usual, his tall figure attracted the attention of the people around him. He was a man blessed with innocent good looks.

The bus was not to come for another fifteen minutes as one had just left with travellers who had gotten there ahead of them. Se-yŏng's eyes greedily devoured Nam-hi's slightest movement. Deep in his throat, he called her name. She stood listlessly, the diaper bag hanging from her hands that supported the child on her back. Se-yŏng hesitantly stepped toward her. He could not disappear as a hero in a tragic story might. Nam-hi's fragile peace was undisturbed for the few minutes it took him to rein in his riotous emotions.

"Nam-hi?" Se-yŏng called, stepping in front of her.

"Se-yŏng!" Namhi's eyes sparkled under her thick eyelashes. A vein pulsated on her slender alabaster white neck.

"What brought you here, Nam-hi?"

Se-yŏng remembered that he had asked the same thing at the corner of Taemaro Street in Changchun. He could not help noticing that Nam-hi's reply was also the same. As she had done in Changchun and also on the platform of the Pukch'on railroad station, she addressed him as she would a brother. After all, there was no other way for her to address him.

"I'm staying at my father's house these days, and young Tong-shik brought your letter from his school."

For a fleeting moment, a sense of exhilaration rose like smoke in Se-yŏng as he imagined Nam-hi intercepted his letter to Tong-jun and came to see him.

"So?"

"Tong-jun lives here now. He's trying to run a pottery."

"A pottery! So Tong-jun has been here in Chuŭl all this time." Se-yŏng said, shaking his head. So Nam-hi came here to deliver his letter to her brother. "Is his family with him?"

"Yes, they live in a house about one kilometer from here."

Se-yŏng remembered the little house on the roadside with the girl in the red frock feeding chickens but there was no need to confirm the exact location of Tong-jun's house for the moment.

"We'll have to wait more than ten minutes. May I call a taxi?"

"You go ahead. I'll send my brother to your hotel later."

Se-yŏng looked at the child who had fallen asleep on his mother's back. Instead of asking if the child was weighing her down, he suggested, "Let's go somewhere where you can sit and rest."

No, I'm all right. I'll wait here."

Se-yŏng realized that Nam-hi was uncomfortable being with him. But it was nothing new and he had no right to resent her for having scruples. She had been the same in Changchun as well.

"Please go ahead." Nam-hi said again. Tiny beads of sweat stood on her white forehead.

"I would like to drop by Tong-jun's house now if you're going there. Could we walk together?"

Nam-hi frowned. She opened her mouth as if to protest but said nothing. Se-yŏng began to stride ahead.

The sky was azure. Brilliant white puffs of clouds floated over the mountain range that curved like a bow. In the valleys far ahead, rosy haze evanesced into the flickers of erubescent rays. Se-yŏng and Nam-hi took the main road to the west. In silence they passed rows of whitewashed houses with tin roofs in the commercial area.

Nam-hi was overcome with anxiety. She agreed to walk with

Se-yŏng to get rid of her uneasiness but it became worse as they walked on. She was worried that they might run into Sang-jun at any minute for he was staying in Chuŭl to cure his arthritis and skin troubles. Indicted for abusing his position at the customs office by smuggling heroin, he had been sentenced to six months imprisonment. It was rumored that he managed to get away with a relatively light penalty because his family had put a lot of money into bribes, while some people said it was because the buyer of the heroin was an influential Japanese.

"I'm not going to set foot in my village again. I know everyone there regards me as a hideous crook, an opinion my father-in-law no doubt shares." Sang-jun had said and headed straight to Chuŭl the day he was released from prison. His father had acceded to such saying a rest at the hot spring for a couple of weeks would do him good, but he had been loitering in Chuŭl over a month.

Tong-jun, too, had been out of prison less then three months. He came to Chuŭl initially to recover his health but later decided to settle down in the town permanently with his family because he wanted to open a pottery utilizing the white clay in the area. He had been good at painting and calligraphy from childhood. He had impressed the women in the family by fashioning clay gourds and jars and baking them in the kitchen stove.

"I was going to take the night train if Tong-jun did not show up by tomorrow morning." Se-yŏng told Nam-hi, slowing down his pace to walk beside her as soon as they got out of the downtown area and onto a less frequented path. He offered to carry the child but she flushed and refused hurriedly, saying, "He's so shy that he doesn't take to others easily."

A pale spotted butterfly flickered across their path. Se-yŏng said with a smile, "He must take after his mother."

"Was I like that when I was little?"

The road was empty except for an occasional stroller. A bus teetered past them toward the railroad station, leaving a cloud

of dust behind. Lush clover had already matted the roadside
and the sun was dancing on the tender green leaves of the poplar trees. Nam-hi had the strange feeling that she had been
walking this road with Se-yŏng from way back. She brushed
back a strand of hair from her sweaty forehead.

Se-yŏng walked silently beside her, trudging back in time to
the days of his childhood when he and Tong-jun took turns carrying Nam-hi on their back. Together they often bullied her
to tears. One time when they were crossing a narrow log
bridge over a stream, she was stricken by fear and froze in the
middle. He took her on his back and carried her across the pre-
carious bridge, while Tong-jun hurled a colorful collection of
curse words at his "silly sister" who would never leave them
alone and tagged along wherever they went. On his back,
Nam-hi murmured into his ears how hateful her brother was
and how very loving he was. She rarely let them alone.
Whenever they went to pick wild azalea blossoms or even
when they sneaked out to snitch melons, she would somehow
manage to come with them, often at the cost of a tear-streaked
face. She usually turned to him for, being softhearted, she
could coax him into including her in their games. How many
summer days they laughed away sliding down the huge stack of
barley straw. Sometimes she would produce an ear of steamed
corn from behind her back and say proudly, "I saved it for you,
Se-yŏng." One summer when the gourd vines over the stone
wall of his house bloomed profusely, he and the other children
picked the pale blossoms and ran all over the village playing
like they were catching bats with them, and Nam-hi ran
eagerly after them to join the game.

"We turn to the left here." Nam-hi's voice broke his reverie.
They had come about a kilometer from the station. A narrow
path Se-yŏng had not noticed before stretched between the
barley fields leading to a thatched house humbly crouched
away from the view of the road. Se-yŏng walked ahead of Nam-
hi.

"When were you last here?" He asked quietly.

"About a month ago."

Se-yŏng found the house not at all as humble as it appeared when seen from afar. A lone pine tree thrived in a well tended yard and under it was a cozy wooden bench.

"They've all gone to the hill to sample the clay. They started quite late in the morning." Tong-jun's housekeeper explained apologetically. Nam-hi disappeared into a room to lay down the sleeping child. Se-yŏng sat on the narrow veranda. Sun rays sparkled and the air was sweet and warm. His heart tingled with a feeling of being at home that he had never felt before.

Nam-hi came out of the room and said, "I'll send my brother to visit you later at your hotel." Coming along after him to see him off, she pointed to what appeared to be a long stack of barley straw. "That's the kiln Tong-jun built himself."

"That's a kiln? No kidding?" Se-yŏng looked into Nam-hi's face flickering with an uneasy smile. "Well, as they say, once a thing is started, it's half done."

She kept smiling silently.

4.

Se-yŏng found Tong-jun and his wife waiting for him in the shade of a cherry tree. They had already had a sand bath and an herbal bath to wash off the sand. Though traces of the sensitive good looks of the earlier days still remained, Tong-jun looked rather rugged because of the deep tan he had acquired recently. He clasped Se-yŏng's hand firmly as he had done the day before. Thick veins bulged on his lean hand.

Looking down at his friend's coarsened hand Se-yŏng wondered what really prompted him to seek him. What he was after was the fruit that was hidden in the hard shell. Tong-jun was the shell hiding a fruit called Nam-hi. That was what made him summon Tong-jun to Chuŭl as if he had some important business and to commute to the station to see if he was coming.

Se-yŏng recalled how a tuberculosis drug was being made from apricot seeds at a research center in Changchun. The curative agent was contained in the core of the seed inside the shell. He remembered seeing people bringing in heaps of wild apricots, branches and all, to get those little cores in the fruit.

His hand still held in Tong-jun's, he thought of the apricot seeds and the branches that were broken by the impatient people to get the seeds.

He thought with a pang that all that was left between him and Tong-jun were rusted pieces of the crumbling wreckage of memories because he could not discuss his present and future with his friend.

"Let me introduce you to my brother-in-law, Se-yŏng," said Tong-jun. "This is Yi Sang-jun, Nam-hi's husband. He's of the Hadong Yi clan." Se-yŏng fought back a wry smile as he shook hands with Sang-jun who was sizing him up with narrowed eyes. He was sure Sang-jun was the ghostly figure he had encountered in the sand bath some days before. Sang-jun looked like a thin rod. His emaciated face ended with a pointed chin.

"I've heard so much about you. I understand you're quite a hero back home." Sang-jun said with a half-hearted smile that revealed two prominently large teeth.

"Isn't life full of wonderful surprises? It was a miracle that I ran into you on the street last night."

Se-yŏng sensed that Tong-jun did not want his brother-in-law to find out Nam-hi had brought the letter to him.

"And I kept hearing about you when we were in Tokyo, too," Sang-jun said, and coughed dryly several times. His eyes were feverish and his lips, parched. Se-yŏng guessed that the time he had spent in prison had caused his health to deteriorate.

"How's everything in Changchun?"

"I know very little about what's going on outside the hospital. I'm just an ordinary salary man."

"I envy you for your choice of professions. A medical doctor's the best thing to be during these troubled times. Me, I studied economics and politics and look what happened to me. I got accused of smuggling because I happened to be working in a customs office."

"Come, come. Let bygones be bygones. Even commanders make mistakes. Anybody can make an error in judgement.

"You don't understand, brother." Sang-jun protested, waving his hand vehemently.

"I understand perfectly. It's over, and that's all. Let's all go to my house and celebrate. We'll wash all the frustration out of our systems with rice wine and bean curd stew." Tong-jun said boisterously. He remembered only then to introduce his wife to Se-yŏng. Chu Kŭm-ryŏn was a so-called new woman with a Western hairstyle and a black serge skirt which made her look like a woman involved in all kinds of ideological movements.

"Are you still unmarried?"

"Yes."

"Heavens, and my eldest son is already in elementary school. It's a shame for a man to be saddled with a wife from an early stage in his life, though." Tong-jun added, grinning teasingly at his wife, who smiled back haughtily. She was a handsome woman with a long but well balanced face.

Se-yŏng invited them to lunch in the hotel restaurant over Tong-jun's vehement protest that they should all have lunch at his house. The restaurant was on the ground floor. Se-yŏng sat across from Tong-jun, and Tong-jun's wife sat across from Sang-jun at the square table. Tong-jun's wife freely joined in the men's jokes and laughed with them but did not drink any beer. Sang-jun did not drink much either, but was drunk enough to return to his favorite subject of conversation, himself.

"Those damn bastards, they framed me."

"Come on. We know all about it. It's nothing to boast about."

"That's the problem. I've got to explain it because you think it's nothing to boast about." Sang-jun looked piercingly at Tong-jun and began his story. One day on his way back from a customs inspection on a train, he ran into a Japanese classmate from college and invited him and his Japanese companion to a Chinese restaurant, purely out of good natured friendship. A few days later Uesugi Yukichi, his classmate, visited him and confided that he was engaged in a lucrative business. He ran heroin refineries quite openly in Changchun and Shenyang, relying on a network of Koreans and Chinese to get the raw materials and also to sell the products. Sang-jun asked for his name card with the intention of reporting him to the authorities and the man gave him one without even batting an eye. He left him, saying equivocally, "Don't harbor any dangerous ideas. You should be aware there are always people who think ahead of you."

Uesugi came back about a week later and handed him a one hundred yen bank note. "It's a starting fee. Bring the stuff to Changchun yourself. Nobody will suspect a customs officer and I'll be waiting outside the exit turnstile at the railroad station. All you have to do is hand the bundle to me. It's the easiest money you'll ever make in the world. Remember you can change your fate if only you want to. Don't let the lucrative chance slip by."

Sang-jun did not respond right away but experienced the most tormenting week of his life as he tried to overcome the temptation of big money. He knew the confiscated heroin was stored in the warehouse and that some of it was yet to be recorded properly. The temptation haunted his dreams and gradually overrode his fear of being caught. He contacted the Japanese in Changchun at the address on the name card, hid the raw heroin under his shirts and toilet set in a bag and boarded the Manchuria bound train amid the blessings of his unknowing colleagues. He was surprised that despite his fear he was actually able to fall asleep on the train. He did not attract the attention of the train detective either. He got off the train at Changchun the next morning without a hitch and walked with the other passengers toward the ticket collector. When there were only three or four persons remaining in front of him at the turnstile, he spotted the Japanese waiting outside.

The man nodded at him, and he heard a voice hailing him from behind. It was a military policeman. In a daze Sang-jun looked around for the Japanese but he was gone. Docilely he let the policeman take him and confessed everything he knew. He gave the name card of the Japanese to the police. A squad of investigators was dispatched to the address on the card only to find that the man had moved from there several days before. They got hold of Sang-jun's classmate at his office but he denied any close relationship with him, insisting that they were no more than casual acquaintances who happened to run into each other on the train. The heroin was of course confiscated and he ended up in prison.

"I'm sure the policeman framed me to increase his merit points. But then, there might actually be a large-scale network of heroin traffickers operating under the covert protection of the authorities. For all I know, that bastard Uesugi could be just a figurehead. My classmate pretended to be quite indignant of the injustice done to me, but then who knows, he might be the one who was behind it. His father could be the man who runs those refineries. Anyway, they are all bastards, every single one of them. I vowed that the first thing I would do when I got out of prison was to get hold of that damned classmate of mine and kill him with my own hands. You see, he ruined my life. I'd like to impale the bastard and watch his blood pour out of his dirty body. I want to watch the bastard die a slow death with my own eyes. Damn, why did I ever have to go to college? If I hadn't, I wouldn't have met those dirty bastards and I wouldn't have had a job at the customs office. Bastards!"

Sang-jun's lips snarled. His slit eyes were obviously stabbing at his unseen foes.

"Forget it. Your story just shows that it was all due to your greed. It's a nightmare you'd best forget. There's nothing you can do except mend your own weakness." Tong-jun soothed him with the exhortative tone of a senior and poured him a glass of beer.

"I wish I could forget it."

Having emptied half a dozen bottles of beer between them, Sang-jun insisted that they should all go to Oku and have another round of drinks but, sensing Se-yŏng's reluctance, Tong-jun flatly refused. Sang-jun jumped up from his seat. It seemed he had joined them in the first place with the sole intent of justifying his imprisonment.

"Well, why don't you go to Oku and enjoy yourself. You could take our friend waiting at home with you. Be sure to come and have dinner with us, though. You're expected to report to the residence of the owner of the mighty Chůůl Pottery Company." Tong-jun blabbered, shrewdly urging him to take Nam-hi with him.

"I'll think about it," Sang-jun muttered and took leave of them.

The atmosphere at their table immediately changed. The departure of Sang-jun refreshed the two friends as fresh water would a bowl of gold fish.

"Let's drink to Nam-hi, my poor sister who became a sacrificial offering to the mildewed institutions and outdated ideas of musty old men. With such a narrow-minded wretch of a husband, I know her heart will be forever filled with unrequited frustration." Tong-jun sighed and clinked his glass savagely against Se-yŏng's. Foam streaked down the overflowing glasses.

"You shoudn't say such absurd things," Tong-jun's wife said reproachfully.

"I can't fathom how much it hurts her, but I know she suffers terribly. She has completely forgotten how to laugh. Every time I see that unhappy girl, I can't help hating my father, even though I'm sure he must regret what he did to her."

"You do have a lot to hate in your life. You hate that detective Kimura because he sent you to jail, you hate me because I'm guilty of dragging you into an early marriage, and now you hate your own father."

"How right you are. That bastard Kimura is a real reptile. You can never tell when that snake will crawl to you and surprise

you with his venomous bite. My great dream to be an educator
was trampled by him. In fact, I moved out here because I
couldn't bear living under the constant surveillance of his type.
It'll be nice to earn my living with pots. I'm going to start with
earthenware. I've already designed some great patterns."

"You're boasting so much but I can hardly believe you can
succeed in it. I think I should better get out and find a job
myself." Tong-jun's wife complained.

"Ha, you haven't drunk any liquor and how come you babble
like a stupid drunk?"

The husband and wife kept exchanging lighthearted banter.

Back in his hotel room, Se-yŏng sat absentmindedly. Tuberculosis medicine was being made out of apricots. The apricots
were boiled in a pan on a fire made with the branches from
which they had been picked, and Se-yŏng wondered what the
apricot branches would think of their sacrificial act of burning
themselves to boil the fruit if they could think.

He was a conscious apricot branch that could not help but
feel a perverted sense of satisfaction at Nam-hi's unhappy marriage. He could not be a polite hypocrite and wish her happiness in her marriage.

Se-yŏng shook his head and summoned Misako the maid.
"When is the train to Changchun?" he asked her.

"If you mean the night train, the one you came on the other
day leaves at eleven thirty. By the way, that lady you had lunch
with today, was she your girlfriend? Didn't I say you looked
like you were waiting for someone?"

He nodded and walked out into the garden, irritated at Misako's curiosity. The sun hung over the annex building. He
strolled to the pond where misty haze was rising into a gentle
breeze. Dark, ancient looking moss-covered rocks were clustered around the pond and wildflowers and vines laced be
tween them. A small islet was in the middle of the pond which
looked like a disfigured gourd. A narrow bridge to it started
from a point south of the pond. A small, colorfully painted boat

floated by the bridge and two more floated near the shore way down on the busier side of the pond.

Se-yŏng went over to the bridge and looked into the water. The reflection of the azure sky was superimposed over the reflection of his face in the water. His face, half hidden by unruly hair hanging over his forehead, flickered on the water. He tensed and glared fiercely into the water. There was another face beside his in the water. With the giddiness of a man whose blood had just draind out, he turned around.

Nam-hi was there beside him. Se-yŏng's face darkened. They gazed at each other for a long time until Nam-hi, as if startled at herself, quickly turned her head and looked into the pond again.

"Where's your child?"

"He's with Sang-jun's nurse."

"You have a nurse?"

"My husband hired a nurse for himself."

"He did seem to be in poor health."

"He's become much better lately."

"Where are you staying?"

"There is a little village about two or three hundred meters to the south of here. We rented some rooms in a house there."

"What brought you here now?"

Nam-hi looked at her watch and said rather sheepishly, "Sang-jun told me to meet him here. He said he'd like to have a boat ride for a change."

"So he's coming here?" Se-yŏng asked and, as Nam-hi nodded almost imperceptibly, said "About when?" and looked at his watch.

"He's already over an hour late."

"Over an hour late?" He guessed that Sang-jun made the arrangement with Nam-hi when he went back to his place after lunch. "He must have forgotten. You'd better get back to your place."

Nam-hi nodded but did not move. She was so listless that it seemed her soul had left her.

"Won't your child miss you? Bring him with you to Tong-jun's. It seems I'm going to get to hold a child in my arms for the first time in my life tonight."

"Hold a child in your arms? What for? Do you think you can understand a child by holding it? How wrong you are. It's wrong to try to understand. It's futile." Nam-hi murmured more or less to herself.

"Nam-hi? Look at me, Nam-hi."

"I am looking at you. You're the only one that I ever see." Nam-hi said without lifting her face, her brows delicately knitted.

"Nam-hi, please look at me, I tell you. Look into my eyes."

"But I am looking at you. I've always been looking at you. I can see you even in the darkness of a moonless night. See, look into the water. I can see you here and there, and over there, too. But I don't see you when I'm at my home. Think how terrible it would be if I saw you at my home. I shouldn't see you there. As it is, Sang-jun says I've been struck by a spirit." Nam-hi babbled into the water of the pond.

"Nam-hi, how can you be here and not look at me. Now, Nam-hi, look at me." Se-yŏng grabbed her frail shoulders and shook her.

Nam-hi's eyes widened and she sighed. "What was I talking about? You didn't even answer me. I asked you if it was the soul that was given to us first or if it was the body. Which do you think came to us first when this world began? I want to know."

Se-yŏng stared into Nam-hi's eyes. He detected a slight derangement behind them.

"Which do you think came first, Nam-hi?"

"Me?" Nam-hi grinned widely. "I think the soul came first."

"Why the soul?"

"You don't agree with me?" The grin disappeared from her face immediately and she frowned at Se-yŏng. Her thin eyelids trembled almost imperceptibly.

"I've never thought about it."

"How could you not have thought about it? You and me, we had souls even before our bodies came into this world. That's how we came to know each other. We've known each other from eons ago." Nam-hi sighed and looked back into the pond.

"If that's what you mean, I guess you're right. We've known each other from eons...." Se-yŏng grabbed Nam-hi's hand as she suddenly broke away from him and moved toward the bridge.

"What is it, Nam-hi?"

Se-yŏng pulled her violently toward him but she tried to shake him off and droned, "I've got to go. Sang-jun's there in the boat."

Se-yŏng followed her eyes to the island at the other end of the bridge and let go of her hand with a groan. She crossed the bridge with reckless steps. Sang-jun was waiting for her in a boat by the island. He must have brought it from the other side, for the one that had been moored near the bridge was still idling there unoccupied.

Se-yŏng stared at the boat with hollow eyes. Their anguished relationship which made Nam-hi insist that they had souls before bodies brought moisture to his eyes. Without blinking, he watched Nam-hi approach the boat and Sang-jun give her a hand as she stepped into it. The boat rolled precariously. Sang-jun steadied it with the oars and paddled toward Se-yŏng.

"I'm sorry I lost my manners this morning." Sang-jun said and waved when the boat was a few meters from shore. He grinned his toothy smile. Nam-hi was facing the other side, gazing into the pond.

Se-yŏng was lounging on a bench in the wisteria arbor. A little boy was exploring the rocks of the garden and a shaggy brown and white dog was playfully dashing back and forth around him. The boy reminded Se-yŏng of Nam-hi's son.

"Oh, here you are. I was wondering if you'd gone out for a walk." Misako chirped with a smile, and Se-yŏng glared at her without a word.

"Waiting for someone again?" She asked and, at Se-yŏng's

silent nod, added, "Supposed to come here?"

"Maybe."

"Oh."

"I want to ride a boat. Like them out there in the boat." The boy begged Misako.

"Oh, really?" Misako glanced over the formation of the rocks to the pond and clicked her tongue in disgust. She complained that they were using the boat without permission, that the hotel kept the boats for its clients only but Koreans often took the liberty of helping themselves to them.

"They're my friends. I told them to use the boat. I'll pay for it."

"They're your friends? Good gracious, They're really making a scene. They row so awkwardly. I wouldn't be surprised if they tip over in the water any minute. Some nerve. Isn't it embarrassing?"

"Nonsense. They're a married couple. Why should it be embarrassing? Besides, you were willing to ride in a boat with me."

"But not in the broad daylight. Besides, I didn't mean it."

"So you were teasing me, huh?"

"No, I wasn't. Oh, what a nuisance anyway. Father will be so upset if he finds out they're using the boat without permission."

"Your father?"

"Uhuh." Misako nodded.

"Is he the manager of the hotel?"

"Oh, no. He's not the manager."

"Then what?"

"He's actually the owner of the hotel and I'm his successor."

Se-yŏng tilted his head and looked at her.

"Yes, I'm the real owner of this hotel, though I'm working as a maid. It's all a make-believe game to assuage my father's fear."

Se-yŏng listened to Misako, disbelieving but fascinated.

One night after Misako's father Murai began building the foundation for the hotel, he dreamed of an ancient man with a silvery beard who warned him not to build a house there. He had the exact same dream the next night. Instead of heeding the old man's warning, he galloped all over the plot of land on a horse, poured petroleum on it, set it on fire, sprinkled salt the length and breadth of the land and then resumed the construction work.

Murai became a rich man in a few years. Then his wife died of dysentery and he became so absorbed in amassing a fortune that he did not bother to get another wife. He doted blindly on his three daughters and provided them luxuries befitting a princess.

Time passed uneventfully until the eldest of the three girls died of consumption at the age of nineteen. The second daughter turned nineteen and she too came down with consumption. All medicines proved useless and the girl died.

Murai sent Misako, his last daughter, to Tokyo to get her away from the ghost. She finished her schooling there, spending much of her time in a doctor's office getting checkups. Murai did not permit her to come home, not even during school vacation, but instead visited her in Tokyo from time to time.

Misako enrolled in a college in Japan and studied home management. The dreaded age of nineteen came and went and she became twenty years old. Though he did not dare breathe it, Murai was sure that the white-bearded ghost of his dream had finally retreated from their life. He had no sooner entertained the optimistic thought, however, when he himself came down with a crippling illness. A slight injury he had sustained years before from falling off a horse developed into spinal caries, and he was bound to bed helplessly paralyzed.

Murai's greedy brother who ran the hotel for him grabbed the chance to cheat him blind, always reporting that business was bad. Murai called Misako home from Tokyo. He trusted the ghost would spare her since he was suffering a disease instead, but he insisted that she disguise herself and work as a maid to deceive the ghost.

"I can still see that white-bearded old man as clearly as I see you now. I'm sure he's the ghost of some Korean who used to live here. I haven't given him any offerings and I'm not going to, either. I regard a live Korean no better than scum and I see no reason to treat a dead one any better. I'm not even going to offer that ghost a bone, but be careful. We should deceive the wretch. Change your clothes and pretend you are a maid, at least until I get well and can take care of the business. He won't take away a maid. I've at least negotiated that much with him. I promised to offer him a glass of wine later."

"How can anybody negotiate with a ghost? I've never heard of such a thing."

"That's none of your business. You just do as you're told. Be sure you never mistakenly set foot in the hall of ghosts "

"For the first few days I was on my hands and knees working my head off. I couldn't take off my apron lest the ghost see me and discover our scheme. But I soon decided that Father was exaggerating just to make me more careful about my health and to be more wary of my uncle. I never really believed there was a very portent curse of a ghost on those who live in this house but now I'm sure I've definitely got a foot in the hall of ghosts."

Misako sighed. Her tale was more like a legend than a true story. Even though he had no idea about what kind of dire situation she was in, Se-yŏng theorized that Murai had dreams like he himself had because he was anxious over the prospect of settling in an unfamiliar land. Terror embedded in his subconsciousness manifested itself in his dreams. It was quite possible that Murai, being a member of the people who exploited Korea, harbored some guilt toward the people who used to live in the land he was exploiting so ambitiously.

Se-yŏng was not so hardheaded as to deny there were mysteries that defy reason but he could in no way see deaths from tuberculosis as some vengeful act of a ghost.

"The way you talk, it sounds like a legend. Your sisters' sickness could have been hereditary or contracted from someone else. I presume you went to a doctor because you were aware of the danger yourself. And your father's illness is actually due to an injury he suffered by falling off a horse. I see no reason why a ghost should be credited with causing them. It's all in your father's imagination and you got caught up in his imaginings. Try to see things more rationally. Anyway, I must apologize if I mistreated you in any way during the past few days."

"No, there's nothing to apologize for. If anyone should apologize, I should for misleading you. Your explanation does have some valid points, but I still believe it's all the work of the ghost."

The boy whom Se-yŏng had been told was Misako's cousin came toward them and she kept quiet until he went away.

"I do have a foot stuck in the hall of ghosts," Misako muttered again with a sigh. But at that moment Tong-jun came toward them brushing his hair back with his hand. Se-yŏng looked at his watch.

"Is he the person you've been waiting for?" At his affirmative nod, Misako left, letting her glance linger on him.

"Remember about the boat, will you?" Se-yŏng said to her back.

"All right."

Tong-jun grabbed Se-yŏng's hand, his face, darkened by the spring sun, beaming.

"Come on, buddy. I feel as young as my son today. Being with a childhood pal is like returning to one's childhood. Pukch'on wasn't the same without you there. By the way, do you know who that woman is?"

"You mean the hotel maid?" Se-yŏng asked innocently.

"She's no such thing. She's the richest woman around here. Only no one knows how long she's going to be alive. Both her sisters died young and everyone says it's her turn now. A spiteful ghost of this land is taking his revenge or something, they say."

"Can a dead ghost win over a live person?"

"Who knows? This country is teeming with nationalistic ghosts. Haven't you heard that a bamboo shoots from the ground where a patriot meets his death?"

"Just imagine a legion of those ghosts in the underworld!"

"Believe it or not, it's rumored that the Japs hammered iron posts into some seven spots in the mountain behind Pukch'on from Changsuam Rock up to the peak. They're supposedly to cut the spirit of the mountain."

"Japs are just a wretched, superstitious people. But then who knows, it might really work. I heard the rumor myself."

"I'd say it's due to mysticism rather than blind superstition."

"Some mysticism. Sit down, anyway. It's much too early to begin a drinking bout. The sun's still up."

"What has the blasted sun to do with our drinking, pal? I wouldn't have enough time to wash all my discontent out of my system if I started from morning. I've been waiting for you ever since I saw you at the Pukch'on station. My wife used to say I looked like a lovesick person the way I waited for you to visit me at that time."

"You think I didn't want to come? But I wasn't over the trauma and was in no frame of mind to enjoy a visit. Not that I'm in much better shape now. I knew all along that you would understand."

"Yeah, I did understand you. After all, we're friends."

They smiled at each other. Se-yŏng let Tong-jun pull him up from the bench. There was no trace of Nam-hi and Sang-jun on the pond where a lone boat was floating. Se-yŏng was reluctant to leave his place by the pond. He wanted to be there in case Nam-hi came back.

"I still think it's too early. I'd be imposing on your wife. Let's start a little later."

"Nonsense. What's imposing is being too polite to your friend. Do you think that you're such a big shot that a couple of hours spent together is more than enough for a simple person like me. Nope, you're not going to get away from me so easily. Never."

Because Tong-jun talked almost nonstop, Se-yŏng could not find a chance to bring up Nam-hi's health. They arrived at what Tong-jun said was the site of his pottery factory in about twenty minutes. It was a field of corn and barley.

"That's my kiln," Tong-jun pointed to an adobe structure that looked more like a pit house with a door and a chimney in the middle of the barley field. "You should see the inside. It's more interesting than it looks from here."

Tong-jun opened the sod door. The interior of the kiln was covered with earth entirely and divided by shelves of different sizes and different heights. Clay pots, jars and bowls hardened in the shade were on the shelves ready to be fired. Tong-jun explained that after they were properly fired, they would be glazed and fired again to make them finished products.

"I'm begnning with this earthen kiln but plan to build a brick one later on. It will be interesting to see from which kiln my masterpieces come," Tong-jun told Se-yŏng who was studying the thick shelves and open flues with great interest. "I've no ambition to build a big pottery factory. I want to produce choice pieces as good as Koryŏ celadons or white porcelains, but I may just end up being a mediocre potter."

Tong-jun explained his plans all the way back to the house. Two mounds of clay, one ochre and the other white, which were not there the previous day, stood at a corner of the yard.

"We were out getting that clay over there when you came here yesterday. I knew you came with Nam-hi because she told me but for her sake I told Sang-jun I met you on the street. No use risking an unnecessary misunderstanding."

They went into the house where a table was already set with dishes native to Se-yŏng's hometown which he had almost forgotten.

The house was brighter and more comfortable than one would expect from its exterior. The walls were adorned with photographs and sketches. Tong-jun explained that the latter were designs he made for pottery and his wife framed and hung them.

"Ki-jun, where are you? Come here and greet your uncle, your father's best friend." Tong-jun hollered to his eldest son and poured some wine in Se-yŏng's glass.

"Please enjoy yourself. I can see my husband is going to be terribly garrulous tonight," said Tong-jun's wife bringing in a steaming bowl of chicken.

"Aw, not again, please. Leave us alone just this once, all right? Here, Ki-jun, come and greet your uncle."

Tong-jun was intoxicated with excitement even before he had any alcohol. As he was petulantly asking his wife why Ki-jun was not coming, an exact copy of what he looked like when he was a boy came into the room and bowed deeply to Se-yŏng.

"My god, you're a spit image of your dad. It's just amazing."

"I've learned that life is nothing more than losing and gaining. I've lost quite a lot but then I've gained much more. You'll understand what I mean when you get married. Get married and make a home for yourself. You'll be free of doubts and idle thoughts." Tong-jun told Se-yŏng when his wife and son left them. They exchanged glasses with each other. Tong-jun emptied his rapidly, exclaiming again and again how happy he was to be with his old friend.

"You're a real stubborn ass, you know that? I kept writing letters to you and every single one of them came back marked 'Return to sender.' There was no way for me to know if you were alive or dead. I was so worried about you and hurt, too. Though I'm seeing you in person, I still can't believe I'm not dreaming."

As the evening turned into night and they drank more and more wine, dark depression crept into Se-yŏng. He laughed but not whole-heartedly and listened to his friend with the politeness of an outsider. He returned to his old self that mistakenly exuded an air of arrogant aloofness. He was a diseased man whose body was being foraged deep down inside by some unknown germs and he knit his brows from some inexplicable pain. Tong-jun was so absorbed in relating news about his life that he did not notice the change that came over him.

"And now I see how you've made it. You were a clever kid so the old carpenter took you to Japan, huh? Well, collecting garbage for your meals must have been some fun. At least it's more interesting than a paper route or shining shoes. And do you know what, that's all child's play compared to doing a stint in a jail where devils of all colors pop up around you. That's the fastest way to learn about life and the ways of the world. You learn a human's life is no better than an animal's. The only difference is men can communicate. In that damn place you forget you ever lived in a human community and you find one day you've turned into a hairy beast yourself and not surprised at all either. After a year in there I was on the verge of becoming a lunatic."

Tong-jun's wife interrupted and urged Se-yŏng to eat more. "We lead such a solitary life that he can't help becoming garrulous when he has company. I'm sure he's not aware he's dominating the conversation." She took away their soup and instructed the maid to reheat it.

"Aw, there you go again. Kindly keep your big mouth shut for this one night please." Grumbling half jokingly at his wife, Tong-jun offered some more wine to Se-yŏng. "I once planned to run away to Tokyo because I knew you were there. If only that little sister of mine had not insisted so strongly on coming with me, my life may have become something very different. Then I met this lady here and married her and all my dreams were shattered. I was a good school teacher, though, before I became such a rundown failure."

Tong-jun glanced at his wife reassuringly with a gentle smile. His prison experience seemed to have tamed his temper. He not only tolerated his wife's interruptions but seemed to enjoy them.

"I wonder why Miss Nam-hi's not coming? I asked her to come with her husband tonight." Tong-jun's wife changed the subject and asked if she should send the maid for them.

"Oh, forget it. The man is such an odd fish I think we should best leave him alone," Tong-jun said carelessly, winking his bloodshot eyes.

"Nam-hi seemed extremely weak. I wonder if her health is bad?" Se-yŏng asked casually. Ever since she left him by the pond, thoughts about her health had been churning in a corner of his mind.

"Nam-hi's all right. It's Sang-jun who's sick. That guy has a bad case of rheumatism and it seems he doesn't have a single organ that's sound and healthy. That's why he keeps a private nurse and gets all kinds of injections every day. He claims that he's become almost all right, though."

"Miss Nam-hi's still staying with her parents, nevertheless."

"Father brought her home to build up her strength with tonics. I guess he felt sorry for her."

"But there's no reason he should feel sorry for her."

"There is when that husband of hers is such a sickly, whining creature."

"And you were in prison longer than he was."

"Prison didn't harm me. You can see I'm quite healthy."

"Oh, yeah? Looks can be deceiving. What about the injuries to your mind? And you were deprived of your work."

"It doesn't matter. It's like losing your shoes. You always get some later. Isn't that right, Se-yŏng?"

"The trouble with you is that you're so terribly optimistic about everything. You accept things too easily. You should be aware that living in a time such as ours, when history is reversing its course...."

"Oh, no. You give me a headache with your big theories about history. I encountered some cold, hard facts about the world in prison. I should thank the Japs for that. I've tasted every foul thing of life—hunger, mortification, resentment over injustice, frustration over the inefficacy of protests, prison life and violence, the shame of being born and living in a country without sovereignty. And what I've learned is that you can't beat the law of natural selection. The weak are bound to succumb to the strong, and as the period of submission gets longer, a general paralysis sets in. I'd rather have the paralysis as soon as possible. If there's no alternative to living under submission as we do now, then I want to live it out peacefully even if I have to give up my guts. I know it's very sad but I'm ready to comply with the law of the survival of the fittest. It'd be better for our children, too, for they wouldn't know and wouldn't have to go through what we've experienced. They can worship the Japanese emperor and become his precious imperial subjects for all I care."

"My husband is just a blank page when it comes to ideology. His time in prison took away his spirit and he hasn't recovered yet. You have to admit that the world is moving, maybe not as steadily and regularly as the tides of the sea, but it is moving."

"Come on, Madam Chu. Save your breath. I don't give a shit about the world and ideologies. True to the saying a schoolmaster's dog quotes Mencius, my wife talks like that because her brother is a shaggy haired diehard socialist."

Se-yŏng again became the audience as Tong-jun and his wife became absorbed in abstract arguments between themselves.

5

It was almost midnight when Se-yŏng returned to his hotel. He was more giddy from the volubility of Tong-jun and his wife than the wine.

"You're late." Misako followed him to his room with a tea tray. There was a calling card on the tray. It was Sang-jun's with a scribbled invitation to lunch the next day.

"The man came here about nine."

"Did he come alone?" Se-yŏng asked, speaking more politely than he had before.

"Yes, alone. Please speak like you would to a maid. For the sake of my safety."

"Nonsense."

He drank the tea with relish. His head was pounding. He

felt a great emptiness as if he had dumped out things he had hoarded for a long time.

"Would you like to bathe?"

"No, thank you."

"Good night, then." Misako rose and back-stepped out of the room.

Whether she was the owner of the hotel or not, she seemed ready to hop into his bed at the slightest invitation. Se-yŏng caught his runaway thoughts and began to brush his teeth vigorously. He had to redeem his mother's misdeed.

Scenes of Tong-jun's house and the talks they had in the family room swayed in his mind as he lay in bed. Given Tong-jun's compromising nature and the radical ideas of his modern wife, they made quite a compatible pair. Perhaps that was the way a man should live, eating his meals with his wife at the same table, entertaining friends together and raising kids like they were doing. And didn't he have as much right to lead that kind of life as any other man? He sighed at the thought.

Sang-jun's name card was moving up and down on a scale in his mind. He hated to think about it but the scale kept moving. Wondering how he should decline Sang-jun's invitation, he lit a cigarette.

Was it the soul or the body that came first, Nam-hi had asked. Se-yŏng thought he could understand what made her ask such a question. She must have tried to sort out the nature of her relationship with her husband and turned to the issue of soul and mind rather than body for assuagement of the emotional conflicts she suffered.

The sound of the blind masseur's flute came from afar. It hovered near the hotel while Se-yŏng finished his cigarette. He lay listening to it. It stopped and the nervous yelping of a dog, muffled as if it were coming from inside a cavern, followed. Perhaps it was the same dog the little boy had played with in the afternoon. The hotel was quieter than other nights because it was Sunday and most of the weekend tourists had left.

Se-yŏng listened intently. Someone was coming toward his room.

"Are you asleep?" A woman's hushed voice came from outside the paper door.

"Who is it?"

"It's me."

The door slid open and Misako stepped in. Se-yŏng sat up slowly in bed.

"Forgive me for disturbing you. Please let me hide here for a few minutes," Misako begged, pale and trembling. Se-yŏng offered her a cushion and wondered what kind of mischief she was up to.

"I'm really sorry to impose on you. But I can't bear it anymore. The devil came into my room again and I didn't have anywhere to hide." Babbling incoherently Misako knelt down on the cushion. "I'm really so embarrassed and ashamed I wish I could die. I have no one to confide in." She lowered her reddened face. "That man is the ghost come alive. I'm sure of it. You see, I was next in line after my two sisters but the land ghost somehow missed the timing so he sent the devil to me. I think there's no way I can get rid of him because he's a Korean ghost and I'm Japanese. I've tried everything, but nothing worked. I can't possibly confess to my father or disgrace my family's name by turning to my fellow countrymen for advice. I simply don't know what to do and it's slowly killing me."

Se-yŏng guessed that she was talking about the blind masseur. She continued and explained that her father was being massaged by the blind man every night when she came home from Tokyo, and arranging his coming and going naturally became one of her chores. One night when she suffered from a cold and exhaustion, she called the masseur to her room for a massage. She called him again the next night. She suspected him of massaging her in some mysterious way for, before she knew what was happening, she became so aroused that she gave her body to him. Since that night he had caused her to

burn with carnal desires, and had frequented her bed more
and more often with the passing months. She had to comply
with his persistent demands because she was afraid he would
talk. She had become a slave to him and he wanted her to
marry him.

In the meantime, her father arranged to match-make her
with a captain of an infantry division in the nearby city of
Nanam, insisting that he wished to see her get married while
he was alive. She became engaged with the officer and the family was now pressing for a wedding in the near future. No one
knew about the blind man who was sticking to her like a leech.
Misako cajoled, pleaded and threatened to no avail. The devil
insisted that he was her rightful husband. He did not come to
her openly, however, afraid that she might kill herself in des
peration or report him to the authorities, but continued to come
to her as a masseur. Her predicament became even more dire
after her engagement because the blind man began to ask for
money as well as her body. Even though she was the owner of
the hotel, its management was still in the hands of her uncle
and she was actually short of even spending money. She did
not know what to do if the man kept demanding a large sum of
money. She dared not consult about her problem with any
Japanese or even report to the authorities because they were
also Japanese.

"The only way for me to get out of this is to die, but I'm
afraid even death wouldn't be the solution because he's the
land ghost and death himself."

Strangely, Misako's story brought Oka Yuriko to Se-yŏng's
mind. It reminded him of how he had been unable to keep
Yuriko away from him. If she had lived and demanded he
marry her, what would he have done? In all probability he
would have been condemned for having ruined and deserted
her.

Se-yŏng scrutinized Misako candidly. If the man had no
physical handicap, she might have tried to keep him herself. It
was inexcusable that a woman with two good eyes had been

unable to avoid a sightless man. She walked into the trap herself but was completely helpless when she wanted to walk out
of it. Everything which would normally be advantages, such as
being Japanese, a rich, educated woman and an owner of a
hotel, worked against her. They were priceless advantages for
the masseur rather than for Misako. All he had to do was bite
down on them and his physical and financial needs were satis-
fied instantly. The lucky masseur had found the legendary To-
kkaebi's magic mallet that produced whatever he wanted at a
tap. It was quite natural that the ghost of the land got the cred-
it, Se-yŏng thought, holding back a wry smile.

"Do you want me to talk with the man? Is that what you
want?"

"No, just give me some advice. I thought I could confide in
you because you're Korean and live in Manchuria very far from
here. Also, you have a good impression. You were so quiet and
patient when you waited for your friends."

"I'm really sorry about your situation but I'm afraid I don't
have any good idea. I'm also sorry because that guy is a Korean
like me."

"It's all the work of the land ghost. He hates us because
we're Japanese."

"Oh? Under the circumstances, I think the guy would plague
you and exploit you all the same if he were Japanese."

"Don't you think if the guy were Japanese, the ghost could
work through him, too?"

"We get so superstitious and gullible when misfortunes visit
us. It has nothing to do with nationality. Stop blaming the
ghost and report the man to the police. How about seeking a
high-ranking Korean police officer and ask for his help? And
you can rest assured that I'll keep this to myself."

Misako sat motionless for some time scrutinizing the plies of
the tatami mat and finally, with hands held together in a humble gesture, said, "Thank you. I think that's a good idea. I've
been taught that there's always a way out if only you try hard
to find one, but that never occurred to me." She sat quietly for

some time with her head lowered in deep thought. The dog began to yelp. Misako lifted her face, her eyes gleaming. "It seems the land ghost is tired of waiting for me and is leaving. With that devil around me, I can't say that I'm really alive. I'm going to get rid of him at all costs. Your advice has given me an idea. I think I can find a man capable of repelling a ghost or two. Thank you very much."

Misako humbly bowed to Se-yŏng and retreated. Se-yŏng smiled grimly, recalling how his cousin's wife used to grumble maliciously that every family had some dark spot if only you look hard enough.

6

The next morning when Se-yŏng returned to his room from the bathhouse he found Tong-jun waiting for him. Tong-jun wanted to take him to Oku. Se-yŏng handed him the name card Sang-jun left the previous night.

"Hmm, wanting to treat you, it seems the guy is in a rare mood. Even though I'm not invited, I must go with you. Since there's plenty of time before lunch, we can have a look at the Oku resort."

At Tong-jun's insistence, they boarded the bus for Oku even though Se-yŏng did not feel like going. Listening to Tong-jun expounding about the inexhaustible amount of quality pottery clay stored in the rolling hills they were passing, Se-yŏng looked out at the vaguely familiar landscape. To their right flowed a little stream with a bed of small pebbles. The clear water was just deep enough for children to frolic. The scenery immediately brought Nam-hi to mind.

"Let's not stay too long," said Se-yŏng, suddenly thinking that Nam-hi might come to see him.

"Why the hurry? If I were still living in Pukch'on and came here to see you, then you'd be playing host, not me. If you're so busy, why did you even write and invite me to come visit you?" Tong-jun chuckled and added, "Are you itching to befriend that female owner of your hotel? We can go back right away, if that's what you have in mind." He laughed at his own joke.

The bus stopped at Oku. The resort town sprawled on the skirt of the hills embracing it like a folding screen. A narrow, pebbled stream of warm water burbled near the village and there was a waterfall a little upstream. Se-yŏng crouched and dipped his hands into the warm water. A woman washing clothes nearby told them that it was even warm when it was covered with ice in winter.

"I bet you've never seen anything like this, have you?" asked Tong-jun, going over to a water pump by the stream. He pumped it and steaming hot water gushed out.

"Wow, this is wonderful." Se-yŏng stretched and cupped his hands to catch the water, eyeing it disbelievingly.

"Now let's go see the deer. It seems neither the hot spring nor the landscape is good enough to hold your interest very long. I should have known better than to drag you all the way out here in the first place."

Se-yŏng climbed up a large boulder by the stream and looked around at the two-story buildings and tile-and slate-roofed houses in the southeast section of the village. They were quite a contrast to the thatch-roofed houses dotting the other part. He was sure that he had passed the village years ago on his way to Chuŭl, but could recall no two-story buildings or slate-roofed houses. He shook his head slightly.

"Come on. Yankowski's deer farm is over there." Tong-jun pointed to a hill to the northwest of them.

"I'd rather not go there. I'm afraid I drank too much last night and I have an awful hangover."

"Damn, it's so difficult to spend money on you. Well, it's up to you. As they say, there's always some dumb idiot who would turn down the job of mayor of P'yŏngyang. It's all my fault anyway since I dragged you here against your will."

Tong-jun gave up and the two of them returned to the hotel. Chatting back in Se-yŏng's room, Tong-jun said as he had done several times the previous day, "Se-yŏng, find you a girl and get married and come here again on your honeymoon. Bachelorhood may guarantee you freedom but marriage gives you a purpose in life."

"Well, I'm considering it. Perhaps you can introduce me to some nice girls."

"You mean it? It'll be my pleasure. Wait, let me think of someone you can meet while you're still here."

Tong-jun was searching his mind, his eyes sparkling, when a girl in a light sweater and skirt came to them.

"Hi, Nurse Kong. Have you come to say lunch is ready? I'm not looking forward to Nam-hi's cooking, though." Tong-jun beamed at the girl and introduced her to Se-yŏng. Kong Sun-bun was a registered nurse from the provincial hospital in Nanam who was now working for Sang-jun.

"No, that's not it. Miss Nam-hi has gone home, and Mr. Sang-jun has a slight fever so he says he will come visit you tomorrow around lunch time."

"Nam-hi's gone?" asked Tong-jun frowning.

"She was gone when I got up this morning. She left a note saying that she was going back to Pukch'on."

Tong-jun clicked his tongue and asked, "How's my brother-in-law? Is the fever serious?"

"Mr. Sang-jun's much better now. I'm sure he'll be all right by tomorrow."

"Why did Nam-hi leave so early? They probably had a quarrel, huh?"

"I've no idea." The nurse replied in a businesslike tone and left.

"Let's go have some beer." Se-yŏng suggested and took Tong-jun to the hotel restaurant.

"How many bottles can you down?" He asked Tong-jun, filling his glass.

"About a dozen. I guess."

"Me too."

They had a box of beer brought to them and began to drink.

As if they had made a pact, they kept drinking in silence. When they were emptying about the seventeenth bottle, Tong-jun exclaimed suddenly, "Hey, I know how I can get you married! I've just remembered the perfect girl for you. Wait a minute. When's your train tonight? I've got a great idea." Tong-jun set down his glass and clapped for the waiter. A young man in a black and white uniform materialized promptly. "Call us a taxi, right away."

Tong-jun hastened Se-yŏng back to his room and called for the bill. Tong-jun told Misako who hurried in that Se-yŏng was checking out immediately and handed her some bank notes to settle his bill. As an appalled Se-yŏng jumped up to protest, he took out some more notes and, brandishing them at Se-yŏng, said, "It's to redeem myself for having had a privileged childhood. I've come into a lot of these because I sold the land father gave me. Let me do something for you for a change. I felt bad enough not being able to help you when we were kids."

"But you still think I'm a deprived underdog of a boy."

Tong-jun laughed sheepishly and took back the money, muttering, "An old bachelor is as sensitive as an old maid." He picked up Se-yŏng's travelling bag and, to avoid his indignation, told Misako teasingly, "We're going to Nanam to have some fun. Why not give yourself a break and join us?"

"Oh, really? You're going to Nanam?" Misako responded brightly.

"Yes, you heard me. We're going to Nanam."

"That's great. Could you wait a few minutes? I have some business to attend to in Nanam." She rushed along the corridor to the downstairs.

"It's strange, really strange. I wonder if that female's fallen for you?"

"Nonsense! What kind of girl are you fussing about matchmaking me to anyway?" Se-yŏng asked, unenthusiastically.

"Wait and see. Yon can trust me. My only worry is you might fall in love with her at first sight and want to marry her right then and there." Tong-jun said and added more seriously, "Really, I don't know why I didn't think about it earlier. But no matter, this marriage is as good as made, unless one of you is neuter. This is what we call a marriage made in heaven. But then there's that woman. Why do you suppose she's going to Nanam with us? Are you sure she hasn't fallen in love with you? I don't want to lose my matchmaking job before I even get started."

Their taxi arrived at the hilly path to Nanam about three in the afternoon and, after passing a number of orchards, turned into a cluttered suburban area. The center of the city was also disorganized and cluttered, but immediately after they crossed a stone bridge a neatly arranged community of Japanese houses, all with tarred walls and roofs, came into view.

"That's housing for the officers of the 20th Division. This part is really infested with damn Japanese soldiers." Tong-jun said in rapid Korean as he turned and looked back at Se-yŏng in the back seat with Misako.

"It's a nice, sunny location," Se-yŏng said in Japanese not to arouse Misako's curiosity and asked her, "I suppose you'd like to visit your fiance?"

"I don't have the nerve to do so until I've settled this other business." She answered under her breath lest Tong-jun hear her, and asked to be let off at a Japanese inn. As she handed money to the driver, Tong-jun grabbed it and, hurling it out the window to her, lashed out, "What do you take us for, a couple of your hotel servants?"

Because Tong-jun ordered the driver to start immediately, Se-yŏng did not have time to bid farewell to Misako properly. He waved his hand to the figure that stood on the street looking as forlorn as an orphaned child. He could not help pitying her for stupidly believing her misconduct was the work of a ghost.

"Come on. No need to be sentimental. She's no better than any other of her breed. She's just another of the pack that are outwardly friendly to us but take all kinds of advantage of us behind our backs. I really wonder what prompted her to honor us with her presence today."

"She has a fiance here," said Se-yŏng in an attempt to explain as he glanced at the sign of the building they were approaching. "Nanam Provincial Hospital? Are we going there?"

A strange premonition assailed him. He had overheard Tong-jun giving directions to the driver while he was waving to Misako, but he had not paid much attention. The car pulled past the entrance and stopped at the porch.

"Come on. You just sit here and wait." Tong-jun seated Se-yŏng on a bench in the hall filled with the odor of disinfectant, and took a seat next to him.

"Is she a nurse?" Se-yŏng asked curiously.

"No."

"A doctor?"

"Wrong again."

"She's not a pharmacist, is she?"

"Hmm, a good guess."

"I know someone who's a pharmacist here. Her name's Kim Ok-suk."

"What, you know her?"

"Uhuh. She's the niece of one of my patients."

"Heavens! It's a miracle. Since you know her already, I wonder what we should do?"

"Go to the railroad station, that's what we're going to do. There's no need to see her. How do you happen to know her anyway?"

"She's one of Nam-hi's school seniors. She came to her wedding."

"To Nam-hi's wedding?"

"Yes, and visited her last spring, too."

Se-yŏng crushed out his cigarette and stood up. "Come on, let's get moving. I don't want her to see me."

CHAPTER IV

1

"Tong-shik, tell your sister to come have dinner with us. She must be famished since she skipped lunch," said Mrs. Hyŏn, bringing in a round dinner table for the women and children from the kitchen. She had already taken one to her husband.

"She doesn't feel like eating. She told me so just now." Tong-shik said flopping down by the table. Tong-su followed his brother.

"Go ask her one more time. Tell her to hurry up."

Tong-shik rose and trudged to Nam-hi who was trying to get Yong-gun to sleep in her room. "Mom wants you to come to dinner. Come on, please. Come quickly."

Nam-hi glanced briefly at him scratching the door jamb impatiently with his nails but immediately went back to the task of getting her child to sleep.

"What are you doing there? The soup's getting cold. Why don't you come on?" Mrs. Hyŏn hollered, poking her head out the door.

"She's trying to get Yŏng-gŭn to sleep, Mom."

Mrs. Hyŏn scowled and, slipping her feet into the rubber shoes on the stepping stone outside, walked to Nam-hi's room and asked, "Is Yŏng-gŭn sick? We're going to have a cold meal."

Nam-hi withdrew her hand from the child's stomach reluctantly and came out of her room slowly.

"It seems you're the one who's sick. You look much too disheveled." Mrs. Hyŏn said to Nam-hi as she fumbled with her rubber shoes. Without saying a word, Nam-hi headed to the main room. They finally sat down around the table. Noticing the bowls heaped with rice, Mrs. Hyŏn lauded Tong-su encouragingly, "Isn't our Tong-su a nice boy to put rice in his sister's bowl."

There was no response from Nam-hi, who was scowling intently at her spoon.

"This is dirty. I need a dishcloth."

"Oh, is it? I just dried it with a clean cloth." Mrs. Hyŏn got up from her seat and handed Nam-hi a cloth.

"Ugh! This dishcloth is dirty, too. Oh, no. The chopsticks are dirty, too." Nam-hi frowned at the washcloth and chopsticks.

"I've never heard anything so preposterous. You've just come from a fairy palace, huh? I don't see any dirt at all."

"They're so filthy I feel like throwing up." Nam-hi rushed off to the kitchen and began scrubbing her spoon and chopsticks. "Ugh! The dishwater's filthy." She pulled them out of the water and emptied the washbowl to fill it with fresh water.

"Heavens, what's come over you today. Why are you behaving so strangely? You're really peculiar tonight."

Ignoring Mrs. Hyŏn's protest, Nam-hi kept washing and scrubbing, muttering all the time about how filthy they all were. "My word, aren't you a peculiar one today. Do you think I dipped them in manure or what? What can be so filthy about a simple spoon and chopsticks?" Mrs. Hyŏn lashed out indignantly. Nam-hi looked at her with wide wide eyes for some time and then broke into a broad grin.

"So you think it's funny, huh? Well, I guess it's better than getting mad. Come on, stop grinning like an idiot and eat your meal."

Still grinning, Nam-hi returned to the table but exclaimed, "Ugh, the rice is dirty. I can't eat this!"

"How peculiar! Perhaps you're suffering from morning sickness? After all, you have been with your husband." Mrs. Hyŏn emptied Nam-hi's bowl of rice and filled it again from the other part of the rice pot.

"Ugh, I can't eat it. This is filthy, too." The smile disappeared from Nam-hi's face which was turning sickly green. Mrs. Hyŏn was alarmed.

"Are you all right, Nam-hi?"

Nam-hi got up from the table and said, "I'm going out to the station with Tong-shik, Mother. Please don't tell Father. Come, Tong-shik. We'd better hurry up. There's the whistle. The train's coming."

"I didn't know Yŏng-gŭn's father was coming."

Ignoring Mrs. Hyŏn's remark, Nam-hi shook Tong-shik by the shoulder. "Listen, you can hear it, can't you? Hurry."

"No, I don't hear a train whistle." Tong-shik said, looking bewilderedly at his sister and then at his mother.

Nam-hi straightened her back and said haughtily, "You really can't hear that? There, listen. Chug, chug, sell the rice paddy, sell the barley field. Chug, chug, Japs are eating anything and everything and they're still hungry."

"My god, Nam-hi, what's come over you? Tong-shik, go ask Father to please come here. The girl's gone mad. Oh, god. What are we going to do!" She took Nam-hi in her arms and felt her cold, wet brow. Mrs. Hyŏn's eyes were moist.

"Hey, let go of me. What's the matter with you, Mom? I didn't say anything wrong. Tong-shik, you told me that the train chugged that way, didn't you?"

"Yeah, he did and he said the train is as dark as the insides of the Japs, too," said Tong-su helpfully.

Groping for his shoes outside the room, Tong-shik turned around and asked, "Why do you want to go to the station? Is brother-in-law coming tonight?"

"Your brother-in-law? Oh, him!" Nam-hi shook her head

vehemently, upon which Tong-shik hurried to his father's room to report.

"Nam-hi, come here and try to eat something. I'm sure it's all because you've been practically starving yourself these past few days that you're hallucinating. Come, Nam-hi. I beg you."

"Please, Mom, it hurts, it hurts. Don't." Nam-hi shook off Mrs. Hyŏn's hands and fled to the farthest corner of the room.

"Do you hurt somewhere? Let me see, I'll make you feel better." Tong-su took Nam-hi's hand and rubbed it gently. He was almost ten and Tong-shik was thirteen.

"Tong-su, did you know you've got such a big head you look real funny?" Chortled Nam-hi, pulling Tong-su's hair playfully, when Mr. Ch'oe, coughing dryly as was his habit, appeared at the stepping stone of the hall outside the room.

"I hear Nam-hi's sick?"

Mrs. Hyŏn whispered urgently, "It's no small matter, Father. I think you should better call the doctor."

"Is something wrong with you, Nam-hi?" Mr. Ch'oe questioned gently. Nam-hi shrank back to the wall and shook her head.

"You just said you hurt. If you're ill, you should say so. An illness should be dealt with at the beginning." Mrs. Hyŏn could not bring herself to say what she feared, that Nam-hi had lost her mind.

"Sit down here. Let me feel your pulse," said Mr. Ch'oe stepping into the room. Nam-hi knelt down obediently in front of her father and he felt the pulse in her right wrist for a long time and then in her left, muttering that her pulse was indeed very feeble. Declaring that her condition was caused by a lack of energy, he instructed his wife to brew some slices of deer antler for her.

"You said that you wanted to go to the station a while ago, Nam-hi. Is someone coming tonight?" Mrs. Hyŏn persisted.

"Oh, it must have already arrived," Nam-hi said beaming happily.

"So what?"

"Oh, god. I forgot. Yŏng-gŭn must be up and crying!" Nam-hi jumped up and rushed out of the room by the back door.

Mr. Ch'oe stood up to go back to his quarters, but was detained by his wife.

"It's no simple matter, Father. I'm afraid a ghost has stuck to her."

"What rubbish!"

"You just mark my words, Father. Tong-shik, tell your father what your sister said about the train."

"Oh, that. That's nothing, Mom. All the guys say that."

"See? You're fussing over nothing. And I thought it was only big-eyed women who get so easily scared."

"Please don't try to close your eyes to the glaring truth. Why would a normal grown-up person singsong that kind of children's rhyme out of the blue? In fact, I want to tell you that girl has been acting strange for quite some time."

"What does that mean?"

"You remember when Nam-hi went to Manchuria to fetch her husband with her mother-in-law. I could sense something strange after she returned. Sometimes she would babble incessantly from morning till night and other times she would clam up for days in a row."

"You're not suggesting that she's suffering an illness that's never befallen our family, are you? I'm sure it's a temporary thing caused by a lack of energy. She's only a child and is overcome by fatigue from child rearing."

"If only it were something that would go away if you just keep saying it will! But mind you, Nam-hi's no more a child than I am."

"Keep quiet, woman, and start brewing the deer antler."

"You know I'm willing to brew any amount of medicine if it'll only cure her."

Mr. Ch'oe slid open the paper door of his room and stepped into the garden. A waning moon clung in the sky. Worries over his daughter hung heavy in his heart and he had long given up any hope of sleeping. He turned to the back garden toward Nam-hi's room telling himself that she would be all right after a good night's sleep. He stood outside her room and listened intently, but he could hear only the regular breathing of her sleeping child. Deciding that nothing could have gone wrong with anyone, especially not his own daughter, who was sleeping so quietly, he turned away quite relieved.

Nurŏngi, their brown dog, emerged from nowhere and greeted him with a wag of his tail. "Good dog. You know who I am, don't you. Bless you and live all the years Heaven alloted you, dog," Mr. Ch'oe said. He was thinking again about the Widow Chŏng who had had to die before living out her alloted years. The more he tried to get rid of them, the more his head filled with images of her. Lamenting that he too had no energy and had to have some deer antler brewed for him, he returned to his room. Tong-shik was fast asleep on a pallet beside his. He lit his pipe. An early cock was already heralding the dawn, and a dog was barking somewhere. He lay on his pallet and waited for daybreak.

He must have dozed off because his wife's frightened voice reached him only in a dream. "Wake up, Father. Please wake up."

He bolted up and hurriedly opened his door. He thrust his feet into his shoes and stepped down beside his wife. Some pale stars shone over them.

"It's so awful I don't know what to do. I took the brewed deer antler to Nam-hi just now and there she was giggling and babbling to herself and the bedding was piled up on Yong-gun. The child could have suffocated if I hadn't...."

"Calm down and tell me more coherently what happened,' demanded Mr. Ch'oe.

Mrs. Hyŏn exhaled a long, shuddering breath and reiterated from the beginning. She had gone into Nam-hi's room and found her straddling a pile of bedding. Her eyes were gleaming with such a strange light that she was taken aback. She realized that she could not see Yŏng-gŭn and asked Nam-hi about his whereabouts. Nam-hi did not say a word but jumped up off the pile of bedding and retreated to the corner of the room. Mrs. Hyŏn turned over the pile and there was the child, soaked with sweat and prostrate with no sign of breathing. She did everything she knew to revive him. She held him upside down and slapped his bottom and then 'she breathed into his nose and mouth and massaged his body all over until he started breathing, gurgling and foaming at the mouth. Nam-hi did nothing the whole time except mutter incoherently and look around absentmindedly. Mrs. Hyŏn slapped her hard on the face, at which she looked at her rather normally and asked what she was doing there. She gave her the bowl of tonic. She drank it obediently and, saying that it was about time she helped Yŏng-gŭn pee, she picked up the child with all the innocence in the world. It took some time for Mrs. Hyŏn to calm her down and get the two of them back in bed.

"We must take Yŏng-gŭn away from her," said Mr. Ch'oe before opening the door to his daughter's room. Nam-hi lay on a pallet, nursing the child. She sat up as her father opened her door.

"No, don't bother to get up. Is Yŏng-gŭn all right?"

"Yes, he's all right."

"How about you?"

"I'm all right, too."

"I thought I heard Yŏng-gŭn cry and wondered if anything was wrong with either of you."

"He didn't cry. And I drank that bowlful of medicine Mom made for me."

Mr. Ch'oe thought a devil was playing a trick on him. Nam-hi looked to him as sane as anybody in the world.

Back in the hall, he flopped down on the floor and worried what he should do about his grandchild's safety.

"I'm afraid her condition might get worse if she's deprived of the child."

"You have a point there," conceded Mr. Ch'oe to his wife.

2

From that day on, Nam-hi's mind gradually deteriorated. Yŏng-gŭn was sent to her parents-in-law and Nam-hi was put on all kinds of medicine that were believed would help her but to no avail. In some rare moments of lucidity, she trudged all over the house and garden in search of her son, begging everybody to go find him. Those moments did not last long, however, and she would soon study the sky distractedly and follow the clouds with vacant eyes or draw houses and figures on the ground.

It was one of those days that Sang-jun came from Chuŭl to visit her. She had not budged out of her room the whole day, having closed and locked the door and window, even though the early summer day was quite warm.

"Nam-hi, open this door." Mrs. Hyŏn banged on the door but received no response from the other side. She poked a hole in the paper and peeped into the room. Peering into a mirror, Nam-hi was snipping off her eyelashes with scissors. Mrs. Hyŏn forced the door open, breaking some lattices in the process. Sang-jun pushed her aside and called to his wife from the doorway.

Nam-hi started like a child caught in a forbidden game and hid the scissors behind her. Her lashes were completely gone. Sang-jun stepped into the room and heading toward her inquired, "What's the matter with you? What on earth is going on here?"

Nam-hi dropped the scissors and stammered, "If you mean Yŏng-gŭn, he's out there playing. I'll go and get him for you." She stood still, her eyes half closed because the stubs of the lashes pricked uncomfortably.

"You must come with me to Chuŭl. I think you need to rest at the health resort." Sang-jun suggested, pulling her hand down to make her sit on the floor.

"No, no. Let go of my hand. I've got to wash my hands. Your hands stink. Oh, how filthy!" Shaking her husband off, Nam-hi rushed out of the room to the courtyard, hardly seeing anything. Blood clots encircled her eyes just like in her childhood when, afraid that long lashes might bring her bad luck, she had cut off her lashes.

A shaman *kut,* much quieter than usual, was underway in the back garden of the house. It was being held at the insistence of Mrs. Hyŏn. Mr. Ch'oe had been in his room all day and the boys were at school. The only person who had been told the exorcising ritual would be held was Nam-hi's oldest sister-in-law, because she had to help Mrs. Hyŏn prepare rice cakes and build a fire for the food offerings.

The shaman carefully set the altar near the wall surrounding the back garden and solemnly arranged the steamer with the rice cakes, a boiled pig's leg, ten dried pollacks, a bowl of water, a pack of candles and a roll of clean paper to burn to the spirit on it. Having finished displaying the offerings, the shaman bowed deeply hundreds of times, each time raising both her hands high above her and rubbing them together all the way down until her face touched the ground.

She then proceeded to the room in which Nam-hi had locked herself in. Nam-hi was flopped on the center of the floor drawing pictures, altogether oblivious of the hubbub going on outside.

The shaman began to sing and dance in the room. The skirt of her ritual gown billowed and flapped but Nam-hi appeared unaware of everything going on about her. The shaman handed Nam-hi a pine branch, asking her to hold it with both hands. The branch was to tremble when the spirit descended into her and speak through her.

The shaman chanted on and on.

Where have you come from?
Who could you be?
If you gave birth to her,
This is no place to linger.
Leave her alone, leave her well and alone.
The child who's been cherished like jade, like gold,

Leave her alone, leave her well and alone.
If you feel sorry for leaving her behind too soon,
Rest in peace, you need not worry.
If you're her mother,
Let the pine branch speak and leave her,
Leave her well and alone.

The shaman danced and chanted beating a gong in her hand, but Nam-hi did not move nor did the pine branch.

Long is the journey to the other world,
But never so long as the one in this world.
You who bid farewell to this world
with loose hair still black with youth,
Was the road to the other world closed to you,
Embittered spirit of the one with unfinished
years in this life?
Your sorrow's no fault of the daughter of the
Ch'oe house.
It's no fault of the one who became an Yi woman.
If you are the spirit of the rancorous widow,
Tell us, tell us, tell us with the pine branch.

Nam-hi dropped the pine branch and stared at the shaman dancing with her skirt flying. Her sister-in-law quickly grabbed the pine branch and began to chant the words of the spirit.

My poor child, my poor child,
With so many worries, so many sorrows in this life,
How will you fare in this sad, sad world,
With so many worries, so many sorrows.

The shaman left the room triumphantly with a clamorous beat of the gong. She returned with a whip made of ash branches, and started lashing Nam-hi's sister-in-law dancing the shaman dance and Nam-hi staring ahead absentmindedly.

Why haven't you gone to the Hall of Ghosts?
Because I was hungry.
Eat this cake, this meat and begone this very minute.
Why haven't you gone to the Hall of Ghosts?
Because it was too dark.
Take this candle, this burning paper and begone
this very minute.
Drink this water and begone this very minute.
One lash of this ash branch will surely bring
death upon death.
No spirit, no ghost will survive this lash.
Take this, take this.

Nam-hi's sister-in-law fell down and Nam-hi cringed meekly under the lashing.

"Stop it. That's enough." Mrs. Hyŏn interrupted, grabbing the shaman's whip. The shaman let go of it and, waving her arms to expel the unseen spirits, danced out of the room.

It was a good thing that her daughter-in-law did not know anything about the Widow Chŏng, Mrs. Hyŏn thought as she collected Nam-hi into her arms. "Poor girl, it hurt you terribly, didn't it? I wish it would really clear up your mind," she said tearfully.

Nam-hi stumbled up and shrank into a corner of the room, her eyes glowing with a strange light.

"Nam-hi, it's all right now. Sit down and relax. No one's going to harm you anymore."

"No, Se-yŏng, it wasn't my father's doing. Please don't cry. I don't want you to cry. It wasn't my father who made them do it."

Nam-hi shook her head violently, her eyes brimming with tears.

Afraid that Nam-hi was hallucinating, Mrs. Hyŏn rushed to the kitchen and returned with a bowl of *soju* liquor and blew some over her face with her mouth. Nam-hi shuddered and slumped down, drops of the liquor streaking down her face to her skirt.

The shaman, having taken off her ritual gown, returned to the room and massaged Nam-hi's sister-in-law who was still prostrate from exhaustion. Mrs. Hyŏn also started to massage her.

"Seems the ghost of her real mother is in her," ventured the shaman.

"If so, she's become a mighty thoughtless ghost," grumbled Mrs. Hyŏn rather uncertainly because she was quite sure that had she taken the pine branch instead of her daughter-in-law, the ghost of the Widow Chŏng would have descended on them.

A few days after the *kut*, Nam-hi boarded the southbound train with her brother Tong-jun. He took her to a university hospital in Seoul.

3

"Dr. Hada, a patient of yours is here," Mida Akiko reported to Se-yŏng, who was now known as Hada Se-yŏng. Even though he had not taken a Japanese name as Koreans were ordered to do by the governor-general, people called him by the Japanese pronunciation of his name. It was the third spring since Japan bombed Pearl Harbor.

"Hello, Mrs. Hwang. What brought you here today?" Se-yŏng welcomed Mrs. Hwang In-ae.

"I have a familiar pain in my stomach. I'm afraid it's a recurrence of what I had years ago."

Se-yŏng took her to Dr. Noma, who was still the head of his department. The diagnosis was acute peritonitis requiring immediate hospitalization.

"Get her admitted, will you?" Se-yŏng instructed Akiko.

"I know I'm being foolish, but I have an eerie feeling. Can't you treat me without operating?" Mrs. Hwang, settled into a bed with Akiko's assistance, looked up at Se-yŏng with the face of a pleading child.

"I would prefer not to operate, but if we can't clear it up, we won't have any choice. But there's no reason whatsoever for you to fear an operation."

"Try not to open me up again, please."

"Yes, ma'am. We'll try not to."

Mida Akiko gave her an injection. Mrs. Hwang glanced around the room and said, "This is too good for me. I didn't know a second class ward was this nice."

"Sure," Akiko said, rubbing her where she had given the injection and left the room briskly. Se-yŏng followed.

"I wonder if we have the right blood in stock?"

"I'll go and check. Oh, by the way, I'm going to volunteer for service in a field hospital in South China one of these days, though I'm sure there won't be any serious work until the Kwantung troops are put into action."

"An act of patriotism?"

"I don't know how to explain it."

"Maybe it's the presence of Mrs. Hwang here?"

"No, certainly not. I've been considering it for months now. I haven't thought about her for a long time."

"What a dreadful way of thinking you have!"

"Oh?"

"What are you going to do if she dies? Will you be able to live with the guilt?"

"I don't see why I should feel any guilt at all. I haven't any special relationship with her. I told you time and again that all that'll come my way if I reveal our mother-daughter relationship is bound to be a lot of gossip and contempt, the last things I need at this time."

"You really think you can get anymore respectable by not admitting she's your mother?"

"Not by your standard, I know. But I don't care so much about that."

"If you mean you don't care for the respect of a decent Korean, my dear half-Korean friend, I must tell you that your self-conceit is reducing you to a despicable wretch."

"That's what you think."

"This is just a hypothesis, but if Japan were to lose the war, what would you do?"

Mida Akiko leered at him as she retorted hotly, "Of all the crazy ideas, that has got to be the craziest. I've never heard such a dreadful prediction. I assume it's not the first time for you to make such a ridiculous hypothesis?"

"Of course. And it would be really unnatural if I hadn't."

"If you were anybody else, I'd report you, doctor," Akiko said without smiling.

"Big deal. What a great patriot you are!"

"But Japanese are all like me."

"You think so? Oh, well, let's leave it at that. By the way, why did you put Mrs. Hwang in that ward? It's first class, not second."

"That one happened to be available. And I did it for you. I thought you would be pleased to have her think you did her a favor."

Se-yŏng did not say anything. After all, he had no reason to make her accept her mother. Moreover, he was not sure how Mrs. Hwang would take finding her daughter after having become reconciled a long time ago to not having her.

"Have they given you any classes at the medical school?" Akiko asked abruptly.

"Nope. I don't deserve any anyway. It's been barely four years since I finished school."

"But you graduated the same year Dr. Hayashi did, didn't you?"

"Uhuh."

"See? You should mind your own business instead of worrying about other people's. I heard Dr. Hayashi was assigned quite a number of classes."

"But he's in a much better position than I am."

"Like how?"

"Like being Japanese. What better qualification can you think of?"

"Do I smell an inferiority complex here?"

"If I can't afford that luxury, I wouldn't be able to survive this suffocating situation. I think it's the same as you denying a normal mother-daughter relationship. There seems to be quite a lot of inferiority involved there too."

"You're back to that subject again!"

"I'm sorry but I can't help it. It's the only way to make you realize you're no better than I am in any blessed way."

They returned to the out-patient clinic side by side through the long maze of hospital corridors. Dr. Noma and Dr. Hayashi were already gone home and Nurse Chang was keeping the place alone. She was knitting a woolen sock. Obviously thinking some pleasant thought, she beamed peacefully even after the two settled in the office.

The mice in the cage squealed loudly. It was well past their feeding time. Se-yŏng always fed them as soon as he returned to his apartment. The clamor in the cage became louder as the mice saw the feed which was a mixture of grains and vegetables. Some tried to pick up the feed with their paws. Mimicking their squeaking, Se-yŏng poured some milk in their pan, and drinking the rest himself, watched the plump white creatures eating eagerly. They were to become victims of his experiments in a few days. He had been raising them for some time now for his doctoral thesis. Imported from the south, they appeared not to thrive in the northern climate as quite a few had died since he got them.

"I hate to see you fellows die, even though I'll have to do away with you soon enough. In the meantime, try to stay alive, all right?" Se-yŏng muttered to the mice which were licking the last drop of milk. He had become quite attached to the small, helpless creatures during the past few days. Perhaps I need a wife, he told himself turning away from the cage and took off his clothes.

As he brushed his teeth vigorously, the sound of a masseur's flute floated by his window. The blind man passed by his apartment about that time almost every night, and every time he heard the flute, Se-yŏng was reminded of the balding masseur in Chuŭl with the greasy face. Toothbrush still in hand, Se-yŏng raised the window and peered out to where the sound of the flute was disappearing around the corner of the alley. The sound dragged behind like the moanful sigh of a ghost. Turning away from the window, Se-yŏng thought he too was a ghost, unreal and mournful, haunting this alley and that restlessly. The flute also sounded to him like Nam-hi's sigh.

He sat at his desk with every intention of reading medical books, but the words only floated in front of his eyes. In his mind he was calling Nam-hi, Nam-hi, Nam-hi.

Several months after he returned from Chuŭl, he received a wedding invitation from Misako with a simple note that the ghost of the land had been expelled far away once and for all. Tong-jun also wrote several times around that time but their correspondence, sporadic at best, was cut off altogether for no obvious reason after the bombing of Pearl Harbor. Tong-jun never mentioned Nam-hi or her husband in his letters, he only expounded about the bright prospects for his kiln. Se-yŏng had been bitterly disappointed each time, but he could understand his friend's tacit message that Nam-hi was another man's woman. It was only his childish obsession that kept him from becoming reconciled to the glaring fact.

The next morning Se-yŏng sent a telegram to Kim Ok-suk informing her of Mrs. Hwang's condition. The second operation involved considerable risk and he had to undertake it without Ok-suk's consent because of the seriousness of her condition. Dr. Noma was present at the operation. The patient's intestine was in worse shape than it had been the first time.

Kim Ok-suk came the morning after the surgery, apologizing that it was the best she could do even though she had taken the first available train upon receiving the cable. The prognosis was quite good.

"I really thought I wouldn't survive this operation. It's great to be alive and see you again," a tearful Mrs. Hwang said holding Ok-suk's hand. "I owe my life to Dr. Chin again. You look like you've lost some weight," she studied her niece for a long time as if she wanted to engrave her image in her mind.

Mrs. Hwang was put on a diet of thick porridge four days after the surgery. She said happily it was much more invigorating than the watery gruel they had had her on before and waited for Se-yŏng to make rounds with a bright face. Accompanied by Mida Akiko, Se-yŏng visited her and, after a few words of greeting, began to examine her.

"You're doing very well, Mrs. Hwang." He told her, moving over for Akiko to give her a shot. He noticed that Akiko's hands trembled as she administered the injection.

"Doctor, I would like to have a word with you. Could you spare some time?" Mrs. Hwang looked up at Se-yŏng, flexing the arm in which she had received the shot.

"You shouldn't bother the doctor, Auntie." Ok-suk cautioned but Mrs. Hwang gestured for her to leave the room.

"Well, I'll see you later." Akiko left the room, followed by Ok-suk.

"I'm sure the nurse must think it's mighty funny for me to want to see you alone. But it can't be helped. I've got a very serious matter to discuss with you." Mrs. Hwang stuck out her hand toward Se-yŏng. He was not sure but thought she might be reaching for his hand. He thought it looked quite young though very veiny. "Would you please marry Ok-suk? If only you had married her the first time I proposed the idea, you could have had a child or two of your own already. I really want to kick that girl for her stubborn pride. I'm sure you know the old saying that if one is too picky, one always ends up with the worst pick. I mean, you could do much worse than Ok-suk. In fact, it's not such an unfair match for you. Her only drawback is her age but after all you're older than her. I think it was by karma that we came to know each other in the first place. It's not the result of a casual thing." Mrs. Hwang heaved a strenuous sigh.

"I see what you mean, Mrs. Hwang, but you shouldn't tire

yourself with matters other than your health at the moment."
Se-yŏng commented evasively so as not to upset her.

"I just can't help thinking of you as a member of the family."

"Thank you. But first things first. You should first get well
and healthy before you worry over others."

It was with great relief that he finally took leave of Mrs.
Hwang.

4

The next morning Se-yŏng went to Mrs. Hwang with Nurse
Mida as he made his usual rounds. Ok-suk was not in sight.
Ch'un-ja, Mrs. Hwang's maid, was attending her instead.

"Ok-suk's gone home to take some rest," explained Ch'un-ja,
but Se-yŏng guessed she was trying to avoid him because of
Mrs. Hwang's proposal of the previous day.

"I don't understand, doctor. I've had a burning pain since
last night and I'm afraid I'm running fever as well," Mrs. Hwang
reported in a weak voice.

Her temperature was indeed much higher than expected.
When he removed the dressing, Se-yŏng found the gauze
soiled with dark blood and pus. He and the nurse exchanged
knowing glances. He could not decide right away if he had not
removed enough of the infected intestine or if a new infection
had developed. He left Mrs. Hwang's room greatly depressed.

"Damn it! It seems another operation is in order," exclaimed
Se-yŏng breaking a long silence at the corner of the corridor.

Akiko, who must have been mulling over the same idea,
replied, "Do you think it would turn out all right? I don't think
she can make it this time."

Se-yŏng nodded in mute agreement.

There was no one in the out-patient clinic except Se-yŏng
and Akiko. It was about ten minutes past twelve o'clock noon.
Smoking a cigarette, Se-yŏng watched Akiko sorting the charts.
He had stayed behind to talk with her.

"You're not going to lunch, doctor?"

"I guess I should, but first I want to have a talk with you, Mida. I feel this is your last chance to remove your mask. You can't afford to wait any longer. Tell her today and get it over with. I know you'll feel much better."

Akiko kept working with the charts, but both of them knew she was not getting any work done, only shuffling the papers inanely.

"It's too late now." She put the charts in the chart box and walked out of the room.

Nurse Chang sauntered in as if she had been waiting outside and said, "Aren't you going to lunch, doctor?"

"Yes, I'm going now."

"Oh, Mr. Shin. Shin Pyŏng-hwan asked me to say hello to you," she said amiably.

"I trust he's all right except for a slight limp that can't be helped."

Se-yŏng rarely chatted with Nurse Chang. She purposely ignored him in the presence of the hospital staff and disappeared promptly after work in the evening.

"Oh, yes. He was limping a little bit. I ran into him a few days ago on my way home."

"It's a good thing he didn't have a recurrence. It seems I have to operate on Mrs. Hwang again."

"Aw, that doesn't sound very good."

At that moment, Ch'un-ja burst in looking for Se-yŏng. She reported that her mistress was groaning with severe pain. Se-yŏng went to her with a sedative and found her flushed with fever.

"Please, doctor, help me. I think I'm dying." Her lips were parched and there was a grey hue under her nose. There was nothing he could do to reverse her condition. It was too late. "Doctor, I know I don't have any chance. I'm dying. Please take care of my Ok-suk." Mrs. Hwang pleaded tearfully. Ok-suk's eyes were bright with tears. Se-yŏng gave Mrs. Hwang a sedative without a word.

Akiko, worn and worried, appeared at the door. Se-yŏng glared at her, his eyes shouting an urgent message.

"You tell her, please," whispered Akiko.

"Me?"

"Yes, please."

Se-yŏng turned to Mrs. Hwang, who was looking at him with a terrified expression, expecting him to advise her to go home so that she could die in her own house as Koreans always preferred. Ok-suk watched Akiko whose lean face was a stony mask. The uneven light of the afternoon sun filtered through the window and hovered in the air taut with tension.

Are they finally going to reveal their clandestine relationship? Wondered Ok-suk who had always sensed there was something between the doctor and the nurse. It was why she had always taken a cool attitude toward her aunt's scheme of marrying her to Se-yŏng. She had no intention of competing with the Japanese nurse.

Se-yŏng cleared his throat. A lump held his words back in his chest.

"Please don't spare the truth," whispered Akiko, now rigid with nervousness.

"Mrs. Hwang, Mida Akiko is your daughter. Her father's name is Mida Hiroshi."

Se-yŏng's words fell like a soundless bomb and all four of them froze as they watched in fascination the silent dance of its myriad broken pieces.

"Mida Hiroshi?" whispered Mrs. Hwang. Her gaze turned with the minutest movement of a clock and came to rest. "So this is my daughter?" She fumbled under the covers to raise herself.

"No, you should stay in bed." Se-yŏng forced her down with a firm hand.

"But you've just said this is my daughter! I've got a daughter! My daughter has been alive!" She murmured in a trembling voice, savoring the strange word "daughter" every time she pronounced it. Fluttering her hands in the air to grab hold of the all too elusive truth, she repeated the word again and again, her dry lips twitching all the time.

"Yes, that's right. Akiko is your daughter. Her name is Myŏng-ja in our language."

"Akiko... Myŏng-ja... let me have your hand. Ah, you've been alive all this time. They lied to me! Ah, how they lied to me! You must have thought I deserted you all this time and hated me for it."

Akiko bit her bottom lip and placed her hand gently on the outstretched hand of the older woman, who clutched it desperately because she was too shocked to talk. Feverish tears flooded from her eyes. Akiko's shoulders heaved violently as she finally unleashed long stifled tears. Se-yŏng left the room quietly, leaving the three weeping women to themselves. Akiko threw herself on Mrs. Hwang's breast and repeated "Mother" over and over.

"My daughter, my daughter. Oh, god, I've got my daughter here!" Mrs. Hwang wept into the neck of her daughter, holding her tightly in her arms, oblivious to the fact that she was dying. Akiko's tears gushed forth like the water of a thawing river after a prolonged winter.

Mrs. Hwang's condition deteriorated irrevocably as evening approached. Nevertheless, she was scheduled for surgery the next morning.

"You've got to help me, doctor. May God in heaven have pity on me! I can't die now when I have just found my daughter after twenty-five long years! Oh, God, you can't let me die now!" Her pain dulled by a heavy sedative, Mrs. Hwang's eyes gleamed with futile hope.

"Ok-suk, Myŏng-ja here is your cousin. My daughter, the only daughter God gave me. Take care of her. I beg you, take care of her."

Very conscious of the meaning of the unfamiliar word, Mrs. Hwang dragged the word "daughter" every time she uttered it.

"Be kind to my Akiko, doctor. I entrust her to you. Ok-suk, promise you'll take good care of Myŏng-ja. Be good to her.

Promise you'll be good to her."

Mrs. Hwang was delirious with joy at having found her daughter but it did not last long. She died in the hospital the next day.

5

Nam-hi was moved to the spare room of her eldest brother Tong-ho's house. She had been there half a year, ever since her six month treatment at the university hospital. The house was chosen not only because Nam-hi had always been deferential to Tong-ho but also because being somewhat of a recluse, he seldom ventured out of the house, making him the perfect guardian for her.

Nam-hi developed a knack for sneaking out of the house at the first chance. Sometimes she was found near the railroad station watching the trains come and go or leaning against some fence post simply looking down at her feet listlessly. Once she was spotted in the middle of the lotus pond, clothes and all, standing like a spirit post, not even picking the lotus blossoms. Her eyes roamed all over the murky water even after she was pulled out by the villagers. She did not even seem to mind the leeches stuck to her thighs.

"Hey, there's the crazy woman! Look at her! Look at the crazy woman!" Children would call flocking behind her whenever she showed up on the street, her hair loose and as disheveled as corn floss. They would taunt her and throw stones and dirt at her.

Tong-ho's children, who would sneak into Nam-hi's room and have a peep from time to time, alerted the family when she was missing. Every member of the two houses would then rush out in twos and threes to search for her, some in the direction of Yongdam some to the new road and some to the pond. On a good day they would catch her with no trouble but more often than not she would outwit them by hiding as quietly as a kitten in a most improbable place. True to the old saying that

a prolonged illness exhausts the patience of even the most loving son, all of the family except the recluse Tong-ho were completely fed up with Nam-hi. Even Mr. Ch'oe, who had doted
on her so blindly, grumbled he would rather have her dead.

Nam-hi's in-laws were in a constant state of trepidation lest
she return to their house. To prevent such from happening,
they decided to cut off any ties with her so that the Ch'oes
could not demand them to take her back, which they could do
since a married woman, whether dead or alive, belonged to her
husband's family. Yi Yŏng-t'ae, Sang-jun's father, visited the
Ch'oe house one day on that account.

"My dear relative, I'm sure you agree that we can't let Sang-
jun go on living forever in the manner he does now," ventured
Yi pompously, challenging Mr. Ch'oe to respond, Feeling trap-
ped and ill used, Mr. Ch'oe had no choice but to nod in agreement. He could not bring himself to throw his helpless daughter to them when he was fully aware of their intention.

"You should do whatever you think is fit. I'm perfectly capable of taking care of my own daughter," he said, deliberately
omitting to call Yi his relative.

Not long after that, the news of Sang-jun's marriage to a
school teacher made its way to the Ch'oe house, followed by
rumors that his nurse in Chuŭl had barged into the Yi house
with a child she claimed was Sang-jun's. She was driven out of
the gate, it was said, but not before losing the child to the family. Sang-jun seemed to have finally become healthy enough to
open a branch of a large department store in Chŏngjin.

"Pigs, dirty pigs. I'll wait and see how Heaven punishes you
dirty pigs!" Mr. Ch'oe beat his chest choked with resentment
the day Nam-hi's divorce was formally processed and the marriage registration cancelled. "My daughter fell ill in your house,
you damn pigs. My daughter who had the clearest, sanest mind
fell ill after she married into your pigsty!" He fumed through
the night, unable to sleep a wink. He was going to cure her and
show those wretched people. He would sell his land and cure
her at any cost. But then which land should he sell? Suddenly

there seemed to be no land to spare at all.

Mr. Ch'oe headed to his son's house instead, hoping against hope perhaps his daughter might have improved on her own overnight. Though his thread-thin hope was always torn, his heart always pounded with excitement every time he opened the door to his son's house.

"Welcome, Father," Tong-ho greeted him with a wet brush in his hand as he stepped into the room and promptly returned to the calligraphy he was doing.

Mr. Ch'oe sat down rather uncomfortably near the door between Tong-ho's and Nam-hi's adjoining rooms and inquired to the back of his son, "How's she doing?"

"Do you think her illness is something that can be cured?" It was the same old comment to the same old question. Mr. Ch'oe scowled and, clearing his throat, slid open the thick paper door to the adjacent room. Nam-hi was drawing pictures with crayons, her back hunched over like a shrimp.

"Nam-hi, turn around and let me see you. How do you feel this morning?" Nam-hi stopped painting and straightened her neck at her father's voice. "You could at least say 'Good morning' to your father!"

"Nam-hi swept the stubs of broken crayons recklessly into her skirt and turned her face to him impatiently. Her eyes were pools of white light.

"Have you had your medicine, Nam-hi?" Mr. Ch'oe asked uneasily. Her eyes widened as she cringed like a cornered animal.

"No, no. Please don't do that. Don't do that. It hurts me." Nam-hi buried her face in her arms moaning pitifully. The muscles in Mr. Ch'oe's neck bulged as he glared at the woman in front of him. It was the Widow Chŏng, not his daughter, that he was seeing. "The presumptuous bitch...." With a stifled groan, he slapped her face. He had become convinced of late that Nam-hi was possessed by the ghost of the Widow Chŏng.

Tong-ho worked on his calligraphy, showing no signs of noticing his father's outburst.

"You too have lost your mind. What is this thing you're doing from morning? A man in his right mind should be attending to business and supervising his workers by now, not dancing to the tune of a crazy girl as you do day in and day out!"

He jerked up in anger. Nam-hi backed farther into a corner of her room and buried her head under a quilt. Mr. Ch'oe glared at the picture Nam-hi was coloring with crayons. It was a picture of two boys with shaven heads colored green. Three girls clad in blue skirts and crimson tops were painted opposite them. All three girls had their hair knotted in the front and wore black ribbons.

Mr. Ch'oe went straight from his son's house to the village blacksmith and bought two iron clasps. When he returned home, his wife brought him a breakfast table nervously, sensing his black mood. Mr. Ch'oe heaved a great sigh and sat at the table as usual but did not touch the food.

He went to the tool shed and, selecting some sturdy logs from the timber he stockpiled for roof rafters, built a rectangular frame.

That night, he brought Nam-hi home. She returned to her room after a long absence but only to be confined by the clasps and the wood frame. Her bedding was placed inside the frame and her emaciated wrists were put in the iron manacles fastened to the frame by long ropes. Mr. Ch'oe imagined that, being possessed by the vengeful ghost of the Widow Chŏng, Nam-hi might grab a dagger and take away his life. The fear that the ghost of the dead woman might exact revenge through the medium of his daughter weighed heavily on his oppressed heart. Nevertheless, he unclasped the manacles when one of the family could keep an eye on Nam-hi.

6

Mr. Ch'oe looked critically at the nameplate on the gate of his house. It read "Yamada Ch'iman." "What a ridiculous name. Yamada, ha! So I am a 'rice paddy on top of a mountain,' huh?

No wonder I feel so deprived these days." He spat vehemently, sending the sputum well into the garlic patch in front of the house but it did nothing to alleviate the stifling feeling in his chest.

Muttering to himself that he might as well have a look at how his son was doing, he strolled to Tong-ho's house. There was no nameplate at the entrance.

"Is your dad home?" he pushed open the gate, addressing the children who were not present as was his habit.

"Welcome, Father." Tong-ho stood up to greet him. Name-plates were strewn on the floor of his room. Having complied with the Japanese demand to change their surnames to Japanese ones, the villagers flocked to Tong-ho, the best callig-rapher in the village, to make new nameplates.

At the moment, however, Tong-ho seemed more interested in the map spread wide on the floor than in calligraphy. The map was marked with red circles and countless dots that looked like birds in flight. A sudden attack of nausea made Mr. Ch'oe wrench. Positive that his son had finally become demented, he demanded to know what the map was about and what business Tong-ho had studying such a thing. Tong-ho kept studying the map without responding. Impatient that his laconic son would not easily open his mouth, Mr. Ch'oe sighed deeply and flop-ped down beside him. Tong-ho placed a circle over one that was already there and, straightening his back, began to ex-plain to his father.

"This is a map of what the Japanese call the Greater East Asian Co-Prosperity Sphere which lay under their control until very recently."

"Huh? All this is Japan's territory?" Mr. Ch'oe grunted quite impressed. He wondered if it had anything to do with the recent turn of things which forced the entire population to adopt preposterous new names which, like his of Yamada, were so unfamiliar that they could not remember them.

"Not anymore. Much of it is gone now and they keep losing control of more and more of the co-prosperity sphere, like here and here." Tong-ho drew new lines beside the old ones.

"What difference does that make? I saw a trainload of young recruits for military service at the station only the day before yesterday."

"Japan is doomed when this red line retreats to the main islands."

"And who draws that line?"

"I do with this pencil."

"You? But what do you know about the war to do such a thing?"

"I read newspapers. All I need to do is eliminate the area from which the Japanese army is reported to have pulled out."

"So you expect the Japanese army to go out and get defeated over and over to oblige you and your lines and circles, huh?"

"But that's exactly what they're doing. They're being defeated time and again. It's a losing war as far as the Japs are concerned."

"You've gone plain mad. Don't ever repeat that to anybody, son, and burn this map in the fire this very minute. The Japs defeated! What a preposterous idea. If only those damn scoundrels would be! But they're too strong to be beaten at all."

"Not anymore, Father. They're going to be done in very soon, if they keep losing at this rate. They won't be able to retrieve the areas they've lost."

Mr. Ch'oe noticed an excited gleam he had not seen in his son's eyes in many years.

"Why is that so?"

"How can they when they can't keep the present defense line as it is? They don't have a chance." A grim smile flickered on his somber face.

Mr. Ch'oe recalled that Tong-ho had been an intelligent child who knew much more than his quiet appearance showed. He became an incommunicable recluse from... from... when was it? Yes, it was about that time, the time the Widow Chŏng committed suicide, wasn't it?

Tong-ho had been a reticent boy with a strong sense of righteousness. Young and ambitious, Mr. Ch'oe had been a stern father to his first born. More often than not the disciplinary techniques he had used in bringing up his sons had worked against the introvert boy, and the behavior of adults, such as flogging a corpse, surely did nothing but increase his desire to detach himself from mixing with the village elders.

"So what happens to us if Japan loses the war?"

"We will be liberated."

"What about these ridiculous names we have to put up with?"

"We'll get back our old names."

"You really think that's possible?" Mr. Ch'oe whispered in a tense voice. His eyes too were gleaming with excitement.

"Yamada, Yamada, hah!"

The wrinkles in his face convulsed as Mr. Ch'oe left his son's house deep in thought.

CHAPTER V

1

"I think I should go after all. I simply can't stand to stay here another day."

It was almost two years since Mrs. Hwang's death. Idly dissecting with a fork a piece of cake she was having with tea, Akiko repeated again that she was going to the front line to work as a military nurse. Se-yŏng was at a loss for words to dissuade her. He was well aware that the hospital, like a treadmill to a hamster, promised her nothing but a boring routine, the only change in a nurse's life being circulating from one department to another.

He surveyed her wearily, resigned to the fact there was no more he could do for her. It was a long time since he last visited the Cafe Armenia and he let himself enjoy its dreamy atmosphere. Tea sets were shining on the dark red, glass topped tables as before and violet light from the lamps flickered over travellers who drifted into the city in flight from the war.

"Ever since I learned about my birth, I have felt somewhat estranged from my father, not to say anything about my stepmother," Akiko resumed.

Se-yŏng nodded and said, "Why not get married? It seems

much more practical than endangering yourself in a battlefield as a military nurse."

"A great idea, but where do I get the man? Shall I put myself up for sale?"

"You've changed quite a bit, Mida."

"I guess that means I'm not young anymore."

"Could be."

"Why don't you get married, doctor?"

A shy smile spread across Akiko's face. Delicate lines were around her eyes. She certainly looked much older than a couple of years ago. Se-yŏng smiled ruefully, thinking of the creases the years must have etched in his own face.

"It's all because of a blind obsession," Se-yŏng blurted more to himself than to Akiko.

"A blind obsession for what?"

Was it for an inferiority complex? A helpless orphan was wailing inside him. Again with a rueful smile Se-yŏng said, "Ever heard the old saying, the fish you didn't catch looks bigger?"

Akiko's eyes widened. After scrutinizing Se-yŏng with twinkling eyes, she shook her head, "Dear me, you must have some illustrious past."

"Illustrious, huh?"

"Nurse Chang once commented that you looked like a lost child. I quite agree with her. You know, you don't look happy even when you laugh. Some of us think you must have been betrayed by a woman you loved very much or perhaps you married quite young and the marriage didn't work out."

"Aren't you a bunch of wise guys?" Se-yŏng commented agreeably.

"By the way, Nurse Chang wrote that she's getting married."

"Good for her."

"I came across Mrs. Shin Pyŏng-hwan the other day. She said that her husband was away visiting his family in Korea and came down with an illness there. He's from Puryŏng, Hamgyŏngbuk-do Province, you know." Akiko was pondering the coincidence of Mr. Shin and Nurse Chang being on a visit to their hometown about the same time. "Don't you think it's strange that Mrs. Shin is still here when her husband is ill somewhere else?"

"I understand she is not well herself."

"You've seen her?"

"You're not the only one who comes across people from time to time."

"Oh, you sound upset."

"But I am, because you're going away."

"Come, come. You're fussing over nothing, doctor."

"But what am I to do after you're gone? I guess I should come here and brood over music."

"Aw, I don't believe you have that kind of romantic streak in you at all," Akiko retorted over a plaintive melody that floated in the violet illumination.

That night the city was bombed. It was August 8, around midnight. Though morning was far away, a new day was already near at hand as bombs fell from unidentified airplanes.

The planes belonged to the Soviet Union. At daybreak, bombing victims were brought to Se-yŏng's hospital. There were four of them, a Manchurian prostitute, two coolies and an errand boy of a tofu shop. Except the tofu boy, all of them were from the slums near the red light district. About twenty persons were killed in that area alone. They were hit by the bombing because they lingered behind to pack their meager belongings even after the warning siren. All but the prostitute were dead on arrival at the hospital. It was a tragic comedy of life that they should lose their lives not because of the poverty they so dreaded but because of their efforts to avoid it.

Amid the mounting disorder and agitation, the municipal offices were almost non-functioning by the next day. Even in the hospital, no one seemed to work properly. The railroad station was completely overtaken by Japanese soldiers. No civilians, Korean or Japanese, were allowed to board a train to get out of the country. Bombing, though sporadic, continued every night. People organized civil defense teams and patrolled the streets at night, but their efforts were of course no more effective than shaking their fists toward heaven.

Se-yŏng stayed at the hospital from the time 'the bombing started. He thought the Red Cross flag above the hospital might ensure its safety. Besides, the shelter at the hospital was actually much better than his apartment.

Ironically, most of the staff who had never doubted the safety of the city as long as the million-strong Kwantung Army remained intact would make only a cursory appearance during the day and never dared come out of their houses after dark.

By August 12 the city was almost deserted as most of the downtown residents had fled to the suburbs and nearby farms. More than 80 percent of those who remained in the city were Manchurians.

Chaos broke out on the evening of the 14th. The streets were dominated by Manchurians, and Japanese held their breath behind the firmly locked doors of the bomb shelters.

On the 15th of August came the radio announcement of the unconditional surrender of the Japanese emperor. Documents of any importance were all piled up and set on fire at the hospital. The blazing flames burnt to ashes not only the documents but also the Japanese dominion over Manchuria.

Most of the major buildings in the city were burning by that time and vandalism by refugees was rampant.

"The Kwantung Army must have decided to burn up all their supplies," Japanese would whisper resignedly to each other at the sight of blazing flames engulfing military storehouses.

Japanese farmers from settlements in the remote border areas kept flowing into the city carrying whatever valuables they had on hand-carts or on backpacks. They were even more shabby and uncertain than when they had immigrated earlier. Most of them carried vivid images of their houses afire as they left them. It was not known whether the fires were set by them or by Manchurians. People talked about a Japanese who was so dazed at the sight of his house of so many years turning into a blazing torch that he was unaware he was being robbed by Chinese refugees.

On the night of August 15, Se-yŏng packed some medicine and surgical equipment and bid farewell to the hospital. It was a good thing he did so. The Russians advanced into the city the next day.

Se-yŏng borrowed a Chinese newspaper from his landlord the next evening and read the news of a bloody murder of two Koreans at the Tonghwayŏsa Apartments. It said that the victims were heroin dealers much hated by their neighbors and some Chinese refugees were responsible for the killing. Recalling that Nam-hi had stayed there during the pest, he wondered absently if one of them could be Sang-jun's uncle.

Heavy footsteps of soldiers on patrol and shots could be heard from out on the street occasionally. A small commotion sometimes erupted as someone actually got hit by a stray bullet.

A few days later, August 22, Se-yŏng decided to visit the Korean community and changed into street clothes. As he was leaving his apartment, he ran into Mida Akiko who was trying to get into the building to visit him. It was the first time ever for her to visit him.

"What a wonderful surprise! Come on in." Se-yŏng welcomed her, genuinely pleased to see her. She wore no makeup and in a gray blouse and dark baggy pants she looked quite haggard.

She looked around the room uncertainly, without taking the seat Se-yŏng offered. "So this is the place where you live with your mice."

Se-yŏng nodded looking her over carefully. She was trying to avoid looking him in the eye. A memory of Oka Yuriko leaped into Se-yŏng's mind as he followed Akiko's glance to the bed that he had guarded from her so stubbornly.

"Come, have a seat, Mida," he said.

He prepared tea and sat across from her. It seemed they were centuries away from their days at the hospital.

"Where have you been?"

"I've been staying at Dr. Noma's."

"And how's he doing?"

"He's been working at the hospital all these days because the Russians asked him to. But since yesterday he's been hiding somewhere because he heard they arrested Dr. Hayashi without warning." Tears glistened in her eyes.

"Does he think he can be safe hiding?"

"Well, he wants to remain hidden for the time being."

"Mida, why don't you go to Kim Ok-suk? After all, she is a relative and I'm sure she would be kind to you."

Akiko gazed at her tea cup without a word and shook her head slowly. "She suspected there was something between you and me."

He lifted his face as if trying to remember something he had long forgotten. He stood up restlessly.

Shall I have her? Better still, shall I marry her? We are two lonely souls, he thought. But the next moment, he was counting the age of Nam-hi's boy as was written in Tong-jun's letter informing him that Nam-hi was back at her parents' house because of an illness. Even though they felt as remote and vague as if they were from another world, he was unable to raise so much as a finger to touch Akiko. Nam-hi's face overlapped Akiko's for in his mind he was tracing the contour of Nam-hi's features with his eyes. Nam-hi. Was it because of her that his warm feelings toward Akiko were again waning? That he feigned ignorance of Akiko's but patient advances to him?

"Can you help us get some rice? With rationed rice gone, we don't know what to do." Akiko revealed the reason for her visit.

"Maybe I can. I'll ask my landlord."

They smiled at each other for no apparent reason, but Akiko's smile made Se-yŏng think of the human bombs and the Japanese habit of stitching *senninbari* charms for soldiers, and the ridiculousness of the war.

"Mrs. Noma says she's lost more than 10 kilograms during these past days."

"And she'll keep losing, too."

Se-yŏng took some money from Akiko and went to the landlord to ask him to get rice for them.

"We moved to a new place a few days ago. For Dr. Noma.
And we'll be moving again soon," Akiko told Se-yŏng when he
returned from his errand.

"To where?"

"I guess we'll end up in a refugee camp."

The landlord brought less than a bushel of rice apologizing
that it was all he could get. Manchurians had formerly been
lucky to get rationed millet but they could now buy rice freely
even though it was not yet harvest time. The tides had indeed
reversed in their favor. Akiko rose to leave as soon as the rice
arrived.

"Akiko?"

"Yes, doctor?"

"Come back here if you don't find any place to go. I'm sure
we could manage somehow."

She thanked him with a tearful smile. Se-yŏng was stung by
pity for the woman who looked like a crestfallen bird.

"I'll carry it for you. Going around alone is dangerous even
without rice, to say nothing about being a woman."

They disguised the rice sack with a wrapping cloth and set
forth together, Se-yŏng carrying the rice. When they reached
the road, they saw Russian soldiers herding a group of Japanese
civilians down the street amid the catcalls of Manchurians who
were watching them.

"One thing I can tell for sure is that one should never be out
in a foreign land when you lose a war. Where do you think they
are taking them?"

"Who knows. This is no time for you to worry about them.
Come this way. It's too risky over there. Those Russians have
hawk eyes." Se-yŏng moved so that Akiko walked under the
shelter of the buildings. He walked very close to her, chilled
by the menacing eyes of the soldiers.

"Where is Dr. Noma hiding?"

"I had him move into that house of my mother's."

"You mean the old dress shop?"

"Yes. Since Ch'un-ja ran away, it has been rented to a Korean family. That is, it was until the end of the war." Either out of pride or embarrassment, or simply out of disorientation, Akiko did not say "the liberation" as Koreans and other non-Japanese referred to Japan's defeat.

"Does he know about Mrs. Hwang and you?"

"No, I just told him that it was the house of some Koreans I used to know. That it was empty because the owners returned to their country."

"Of course there's no point in saying anything about her now."

"Let me carry that bundle. You're going to too much trouble for me."

"It's no trouble at all. Let's see if we can get a carriage."

"No, that's too dangerous."

"You've a point there."

They walked as far as Chimaro Street with Se-yŏng almost hugging Akiko. As they turned the corner, Se-yŏng heard a swishing, almost hurtful sound. He froze to a stop at a sharp scream, and saw Akiko slump to the ground clutching her breast. A stray bullet from the direction they were heading had hit her solidly on the breast. Se-yŏng threw away the bundle of rice and took her in his arms. She grasped his sleeve and whispered, "Thank you, doctor."

"Keep quiet. I'll take you to the hospital and remove the bullet." Se-yŏng told her even though he was despairing at the blood gushing over her.

"No, doctor. I know it's my heart."

Se-yŏng found a carriage and carried her into it, but he could not decide where to go because he knew there were no hospitals nearby. He ordered the coachman to go to his apartment.

"This is the way I've been dreaming to end my life, doctor. Dying like this in your arms. There's no more I want. I'm so happy, doctor." Akiko whispered in a barely audible voice, gritting her teeth in pain. A single tear formed in Se-yŏng's eyes and dropped on her forehead.

"Please don't cry for me, doctor."

At last the carriage arrived at his apartment. Se-yŏng laid Akiko on his bed and put the sterilizing pan on the stove.

"Doctor, let me hold your hand." Akiko stretched a shaking hand toward Se-yŏng. He grasped it with both hands. It was cold at the fingertips already. The sound of the surgical instruments rattling in the sterilizer filled the room. They rattled long after life deserted Akiko.

2

The flag of the medical team Se-yŏng was to report to was fluttering in the wind next to a train car with a No. 8 marked in chalk on it. Se-yŏng craned his neck to see what was happening at the head of the queue in which he was standing to pass the ticket checker. It was not moving forward.

"Say in Korean. Where in Korea are you from?" "Don't you have any companion?" Came the voices of young men with armbands emblazoned with "Korea." They were exchanging questioning glances. "Are you deaf?" "Deaf my ass. Here, get out of the way." The young men were speaking to a little woman huddled in a dark coat and deep, dark pointed cap. A dark skirt hung below the coat over white cotton-stockinged feet which were stuck in dark canvas shoes. She was carrying a school child's satchel on her back and a small black handbag.

"Tell them your birthplace in Korea. Tell them in Korean. Korean language is better than a ticket here." A man behind her tried to help, but it only made the pointed hat of the woman slide further down.

One of the young men said brusquely, "Get out of the line. Do you hear me?"

"I think she's deaf."

One of the men came out and pushed the woman from the line. The woman kept looking down at her feet but would not go away.

"Japanese?" "She could be just deaf." "Naah, she's no more deaf than you or me." People in the line said casting pitiful glances at the woman.

Se-yŏng stepped out of the line. He was at the Changchun railroad station where check-in for the last refugee train for Koreans was taking place with the permission of the Russo-Chinese allied army headquarters. The arrangement was made through negotiations by the representatives of the Korean settlement in Changchun. The plaza of the railroad station was packed from early morning with thousands of refugees from nearby farms and from the border areas of the Amur River, Harbin and Chichibar. Wrapped in thick padded outfits against cold, the refugees carried bundles or sacks of belongings on their backs, secured with an array of cotton belts and ropes of strange colors. Pots and pans dangled from above their backpacks like clusters of fruit, and among them were almost always one or two Korean gourds. The gourds had been there when they climbed up the mountains and crossed the rivers to come to Manchuria after the Korean independence movement of 1919 and subsequent years.

Occasionally men in more decent attire and women in fashionable fur coats and pointed hats were sighted, but were quickly lost in the turbid mass of blue bundles and padded cotton coats that were refugees. Thus, when the check-in started and the anxious people rushed toward the ticket checkers, the whole plaza took on the look of a fluctuating sea of sacks and aluminum pans and of course the ubiquitous gourds which were a mark of their nationality.

The bundles the refugees were lugging with them today as they headed back to their homeland were no larger or better than those they had brought with them ten or twenty years ago. They had come to Manchuria with empty hands and it was with empty hands they were leaving the land where they had toiled for years to eke out a life for themselves. For these people whose lives were endless repetitions of starting all over again from nothing, to get past the ticket checker because they spoke Korean was a privilege of a lifetime. It made them intensely proud of their nationality.

A single Korean word was worth a ticket to board the train, but the woman had been unable to say one and had to be pushed from the line. Se-yŏng went over to her.

"Mrs. Shin? Aren't you Mrs. Shin Pyŏng-hwan? I'm Chin Se-yŏng."

"Oh, Dr. Chin!" Mrs. Shin made an abject bow, stooping way down near Se-yŏng's knees.

"Are you going to Korea?"

"Yes, please," she said, clasping her hands.

"Mr. Shin is still in Korea?"

"All I know is that he was in the provincial hospital in Nanam before August 15. That was in his last letter." Mrs. Shin lifted her haggard face and Se-yŏng's eyes took in the damage the past few months had wrought on her.

"We must do something, then. Please come with me."

The weather wavered between clouds and sun, and the cold bit into the skin. The refugee line moved ahead at a sluggish speed. After a lapse of time, however, the young men from the Korean settlement stopped checking so meticulously and refugees rushed forward. Se-yŏng trailed at the end of the queue with Mrs. Shin. They were almost past the turnstile when one of the young men stopped the two with a shout.

"Where's your hometown?"

Mrs. Shin hung her head.

"Er, this is my sister. She's mute," Se-yŏng said, at the same time taking an arm band for the medical team from his coat pocket.

"Oh, it's too bad you came so late. I'm afraid there isn't a decent seat left. The train's overflowing with people." Giving Se-yŏng's armband a look of respect, the man advised him with a friendly smile to hurry up.

Se-yŏng nudged Mrs. Shin and whispered into her ear, "Behave like a mute from now on."

The boarding process was completed only late in the evening, and the few people who had come out to see their acquaintances off had long gone home, defeated by the bitter cold.

Nevertheless, there was no sign of the train moving. Some people went out and bought candles. Thick layers of frost began to settle on the windows. Suddenly, with a crash, the window near Se-yŏng broke and a stone landed at his feet. The shards of frosty glass sparkled like snowflakes over Mrs. Shin. The slurred sounds of a Chinese dialect came through the broken window and with them, gusts of icy winds.

Se-yŏng took off his scarf and stuck it in the broken window. He had put on as many clothes as he thought was possible but the coldness gripped him and his body began to ache all over. He kept flexing his legs to keep his blood circulating. A woman across from him continued to rave hysterically about the broken window and the stone.

A security man nudged Se-yŏng past midnight and said that there was a seat for him in the No. 8 car. It was the car he had been assigned to from the beginning as a member of the medical team. He took Mrs. Shin with him and gave the seat to her.

It was past eight the next morning that the train finally started to move. People became vivacious and chatted and laughed boisterously. They took rice balls and chunks of rice cake from their bundles and began to eat them with relish even though they had turned to balls of ice. Women fussed to borrow gourds to urinate in them. Among them was the woman called Ae-ran who worked as a hostess at the Golden Coach Bar. She was travelling with a child and a middle-aged man with a flat, complacent face.

Glasses were broken out of most of the windows but they managed to shut out the Manchurian wind with women's skirts and rags. With the heat coming from the bodies packing the coach, the unheated train was rather warm.

The train stopped every hour or half an hour because the locomotive was requisitioned at almost every station. Every time, the settlement representatives and the security people brought out money and ran from one place to another to negotiate for a new locomotive. When at one place two of the security people were held by Russian soldiers, the refugees raised money to ransom them. Whether because of the money or sheer luck, one of them was released after a day and the other managed to escape. Both were welcomed back to the train with great cheering.

In the meantime, the number of passengers increased as the train traveled south. The refugees from the settlements on the way had been camped by the railroad waiting vigilantly for the train for days. They forced themselves on the train with such desperation that they could not be prevented from boarding and there was no one who wanted to do so.

On the third day the train finally pulled into Shenyang station. It was December 3. The wind was much gentler than the biting gust that whipped them out of Changchun. Se-yŏng was kept busy attending patients aboard the train but he did find time to look into the car where Mrs. Shin was seated.

"Have you had anything to eat?" he inquired, running his eyes over her haggard face and dull eyes.

"I brought some rice balls with me," she said in a shaky voice.

Se-yŏng got off the car to look for a chicken vendor. Chinese farmers were hawking roasted chicken and ducks, boiled eggs and meats to the refugees. He bought a fat chicken and was trying to get some bread when a blind man guided by an old woman caught his eye. He recognized him. It was the blind masseur from Chuŭl. He recalled having heard that he had been driven out of Chuŭl because of his affair with Misako. Perhaps he was taking a walk to get fresh air or to find some food. His face was still as greasy as before.

"The wind is balmy like in spring."

"We've come quite far south. Watch your step, son."

"Aw, you watch your step, Mother."

Arm in arm, they went toward the meat vendor. Watching

their receding backs, Se-yŏng was amazed at the preposterous encounter. He wondered what happened to the hotel in Chuŭl. The thought naturally brought memories of Nam-hi. Still brooding about her, he returned to Mrs. Shin. She was the only one in the car, most of the passengers having gone out on the platform for fresh air.

"Here, let's share this." Se-yŏng tore a leg from the chicken and handed the rest to Mrs. Shin.

"You're very kind."

"I hope you don't mind dyed chicken."

"But it's their way of cooking."

They placed the salt on her bag and ate the chicken in silence.

"Are there many sick people?"

"They're increasing every day. We've buried two persons already."

"How awful!"

"One was a little baby. The mother held it all night, knowing it was dead."

Mrs. Shin said with tearful eyes, "I'm sure the playground of the Japanese elementary school back in Changchun has been turned into a public burial ground by now. There was only a little patch of land left when I left. It's really true that having no child is the best blessing in life. It was really awful to see children dying every day. And we couldn't do anything for them. There were doctors but no medicine. Most of the children died of malnutrition."

"It's unfair that innocent children should have to pay for the idiocy of the politicians and militants."

"But it's not just children. Every healthy Japanese male with four limbs intact was taken away. Those left behind for confinement in the elementary school were all useless old people and women and children."

Se-yŏng nodded recalling Chimaro Street where Chinese vendors swarmed to sell meat. There were a lot of Korean customers but no Japanese at all. No wonder the Japanese children were dying of malnutrition.

Having finished his part of the chicken, he glanced at her Korean dress, which looked awkward even to his eyes, and asked curiously, "Where did you get that *hanbok?*"

"I made it myself. And I made one for my husband, too. That's what I have in my satchel. I threw away all my valuables and I didn't cast so much as a lingering glance at them. My husband's clothes and the diary I have in this bag are all the possessions I have now. I've kept the diary so I can tell him everything that's happened during his absence, every day from the end of July until the morning I left Changchun. I also have some photographs we took together." With a forlorn smile, Mrs. Shin patted her dark little handbag.

"You miss him very much, don't you?"

"It's the first time we've been separated so long."

"Oh, I see."

"I don't know when I would've been allowed to leave the city if it weren't for you."

"Forget it. It was by chance I happened to spot you. It could have helped a lot if you had learned some Korean from your husband, though."

"Yes, I've been regretting it a lot. In fact, I did ask him several times to teach me Korean but he wouldn't, saying that there were better ways to use time than wasting it on a dying language.

Se-yŏng responded with a grim smile.

The train began to move again many hours later. Se-yŏng resumed his duties. He visited each of the ears assigned to him and took care of the sick people, giving them what meager medicine he could find in his bag. The refugees had long given up any attempt to wash their grimy faces but were very diligent in filling their stomachs. When the train was held for hours, they would venture to the nearby villages to buy kimch'i and rice. Sometimes, the train left before they returned but no one got very upset because they knew they could catch up with it if they walked briskly along the railroad since the locomotive was requisitioned at every other station.

The day after they left Shenyang the train was checked by the Eighth Route Army, the Communist Chinese freedom fighters that had battled the Japanese. Se-yŏng was at Mrs. Shin's side when the soldiers came aboard to inspect. She handed him her black handbag whispering, "Please keep this."

By then the passengers near her had sensed that she was not a mute but a Japanese. However, her shabby, harassed appearance more or less inspired their pity. As soon as the soldiers left the car, she eagerly retrieved her bag and ensconced it back on her lap. She then told Se-yŏng apologetically, "My husband too was a Communist fighter . He griped so much that he couldn't be very active recently because of his knee." She showed Se-yŏng an old photograph of them in Korean costumes.

"You're very pretty," Se-yŏng commented but grimaced inwardly comparing the image in the photograph with the wrinkled old woman in front of him.

"He's three years older than me. Forty-one."

In the meantime, the number of patients kept increasing. There were four more doctors on the train besides Se-yŏng and all of them were kept quite busy. Another death occurred. It was an old man. After having dreamed of going home for such a long time, he could not survive the few more days he needed to set foot on the soil of his country. Like the others who had died, he was buried in an unknown spot in Manchuria where the train happened to stop.

The train finally arrived at Antung, a border city on the Manchurian shore of the Amnokkang River. That was about one in the afternoon of December 6, but the refugees were allowed to alight from the train only after five o'clock because the Chinese station master was disgruntled for not having been notified about the increase in the number of refugees aboard the train. The Koreans were accused of reporting it to the Russian army only.

Se-yŏng got off the train with Mrs. Shin. She lost her watch in the process but could not tell how she lost it.

"Hey!" Someone slapped Se-yŏng on the shoulder. As he looked around, he came face to face with Chu Tal-ho of Harbin University.

"Why, where have you been all this time?"

"We were in the car right next to the locomotive. Here, meet my wife. This is Ho-ryŏn."

Se-yŏng was nonplussed at the sight of a Russian woman, but bowed automatically. A boy and a girl, both with blue eyes and dark hair and within a year or two of each other, were tugging at her from behind.

"Say hello, Chun. This is my oldest son. He's six years old. Po-bong, you too. Say hello to your father's friend. She's five." Se-yŏng hugged them and smoothed their hair as Chu Tal-ho continued, "My wife's the daughter of my landlord in Harbin. Her father used to be a viscount in Czarist Russia. Aristocratic blood or not, she's a very nice woman, though I know a man shouldn't boast about his wife."

Se-yŏng was aware that Chu Tal-ho was blabbering about his wife to justify his marriage to a foreigner. He had to admit that the woman certainly had an elegant air about her.

Carrying their luggage on a cart, they walked to the Amnok-kang River ferry. The sight of the river touched the hearts of the refugees. Across the river was their country, finally liberated from the colonial rule of Japan. All they had to do now was cross the river. However, since diplomatic relations were yet to be established, they had to cross it in an unauthorized manner.

They hired a boat. Midway across the river the Chinese sailors stopped and asked to be paid in full then and there. They resumed rowing at the vehement protest of Chu Tal-ho, who gave them half of what was promised them.

The last glow of the setting sun was glimmering in the north-western horizon where the vast Manchurian plain met the darkening sky. Se-yŏng looked toward the sky over Shinuiju across the river. It was the sky of his homeland. On the dark water of the Amnokkang, he tried to calm his throbbing heart.

When they arrived at the Shinuiju dock, some young local men came forward and guided them to where they could stay over night. It turned out to be a number of private houses.

"I never imagined Japs were such a blundéring bunch of fools. If only they had not bragged so much about their million-strong Kwantung Army. Why, they weren't even decently armed. Soldiers were no more than human bullets. Armed with only bamboo sticks, they fought in hand to hand combat with Russians. Can you believe that? They didn't even have those stupid Japanese swords they used to brandish everywhere. The furrows of millet fields were filled with the bodies of Jap soldiers. I saw them myself. The bloody fools didn't know about the armistice and kept fighting for two more days this side of Harbin. Talk about a dog's death. Why, they died even worse deaths than dogs." Chu Tal-ho made a face as he recalled the horrible scenes he had witnessed on the way from Harbin. Unable to get on the train, he and his family had driven part of the way in a carriage.

Even more wretched than Chu Tal-ho's report, however, was the news of the student riot in Shinuiju they heard about from the family whose house they stayed in that night. The city was still in turmoil from the repercussions of the tragic incident of half a month before.

The next morning, Se-yŏng's group joined other refugees and boarded a train at the Shinuiju Station. The journey of the refugees was thus resumed. Everywhere in the train heated talk about the student riot could be heard.

"We're going to Seoul. What's your plan?" Chu Tal-ho asked Se-yŏng as the train picked up speed.

"I think I'll eventually go to Seoul, but first I want to go to my hometown. How about you, Mrs. Shin?"

"I'm going to Nanam. That's where my husband last wrote from."

She wanted to show them her husband's letter but realized she did not have her little dark bag. Blood drained from her face.

"That's really too much. There was nothing but my diary. It was a letter to my husband in the form of a diary. That was all there was in that bag. How could anyone be so heartless as to take that away from me!" The woman lamented, tears streaming down her face. She had chosen the shabby little bag on purpose to safeguard her diary, but her precaution did little to keep her from being robbed. All that was left to her now was the little satchel she carried on her back.

"You should be more careful from now on. I'll come with you to Nanam, however."

3

"Remember you are mute," Se-yŏng cautioned Mrs. Shin again as they alighted from the train on the Nanam station platform which was covered with snow drifts. After storing his trunk and backpack in the checkroom of the station, Se-yŏng took Mrs. Shin straight to the Nanam provincial hospital. It was about four o'clock in the afternoon. He looked for Kim Ok-suk. She was in the pharmacy as he had expected.

"Goodness! What a surprise!" exclaimed a shocked Ok-suk but she welcomed him with genuine delight. Unknown to Se-yŏng, she was a leading member of the local Communist party and a well known figure in the township. She was as cool as ever, and the only change in her that Se-yŏng noticed was that she had become more extroverted than in the old days.

"Mrs. Hwang's daughter died accidentally," Se-yŏng reported dutifully.

"Mrs. Hwang's daughter? Oh, you mean Myŏng-ja. Really, we had no idea what happened to her. What a miserable end for a miserable girl. Poor thing. But then, she might be better off dead." Stiff faced, Ok-suk commented indifferently.

Se-yŏng was appalled. While he did not expect Ok-suk to lose her mind in grieving over Akiko, the cool way she brushed aside the death of the daughter of her aunt who had doted on her so seemed much too cold-blooded. At least, no one could accuse her of insincere pretension.

"I still can't forgive the girl for not having revealed herself sooner. What a hardhearted woman to admit who she was only when her mother was on her deathbed. I've never heard of such selfishness."

"I understand your feelings. Let's hope they are rejoined in the hereafter. Well, anyway, I want to introduce Mrs. Shin Pyŏng-hwan to you."

Kim Ok-suk's eyes widened in disbelief. "Why, really. I'm sorry I didn't recognize you. You were so kind to come to my aunt's funeral." Taking hold of her hand, Ok-suk suggested, "Let's go to the dining hall where we can sit down."

"Before doing that... I wonder if Mr. Shin is still in the hospital?"

"Comrade Shin Pyŏng-hwan? He was discharged a long time ago."

"He was?" Mrs. Shin lifted her shriveled face, showing eyes sunk deep from tiredness. With her hair bundled carelessly at the back of her head and the ridiculous *hanbok* peeping out from under her coat, she looked quite shabby.

"That's right. He was discharged when we were still in the building in front of the railroad station. That was quite some time ago. However...."

Both Se-yŏng and Mrs. Shin sensed something ominous in the hesitant words of Ok-suk.

"Come this way, the dining hall will be much warmer than here. The plumbing is not working properly because we were bombed before liberation. The whole place is still in a mess."

"There was bombing here, too?"

"But of course. We thought we were all going to die."

"That explains why the hospital looks so disorganized."

"We expect to be able to open the wards from New Year's."

"Er, I wonder if a nurse named Chang ever happened to come here? She used to work in the Changchun Hospital but returned to her hometown right before liberation," Mrs. Shin inquired anxiously.

"You mean Nurse Chang? I heard she got married with a medical student from the same town whom she had been dating in Changchun."

"A medical student?" Mrs. Shin repeated disbelievingly.

"Hey, I didn't know that girl was so full of secret plans!" exclaimed Se-yŏng. He recalled having seen Nurse Chang knitting a man's sweater. She had been an easygoing girl with a nice expression, never minding other people's business nor letting them pry into hers. Her acute sense of privacy caused the other nurses to talk about her. Akiko for one had believed that she had an affair with Shin Pyŏng-hwan, and Se-yŏng was under the same impression.

"Is it so strange that Nurse Chang got married?" Ok-suk asked curiously as they took seats in the dining hall.

"I was just surprised because none of us had any idea about it," Se-yŏng explained after lighting a cigarette.

"I understand the man wanted to keep it that way. That he's rather shy and didn't want his professors to know he was marrying one of their nurses."

"You know very well about her," blurted Mrs. Shin.

"She visited Comrade Shin while he was still hospitalized."

A deep blush spread over Mrs. Shin's face.

"I understand they're both from Puryŏng."

"Yes, it's near here."

A girl brought their food. Setting the dishes on the table, the girl suddenly exclaimed, "Doctor!" Her face was familiar but Se-yŏng could not remember where he had met her.

"Remember Ch'un-ja? She was like my aunt's adopted daughter."

"Oh, of course. Yes, I remember seeing you many times in Mrs. Hwang's ward."

"She came to me after liberation. It seems she had been wandering around a great deal. I trusted Myŏng-ja was taking good care of her."

Sensing Ok-suk's mute accusation of the dead woman, Se-yŏng barely stifled an impulse to protest that Akiko could do nothing since the girl ran away.

"Here, please enjoy your meal. You'll find it's not so bad, though the rice is mixed with other grains," urged Ok-suk. Se-yŏng unwrapped his chopsticks. A brooding Mrs. Shin followed suit.

"Er, I wonder if you know where Mr. Shin is? Mrs. Shin would like to go to him as soon as she learns his whereabouts. Even tonight." Se-yŏng resumed the subject of Shin Pyŏng-hwan even though he had not finished his meal.

"I know, I know, I've been thinking about it," Ok-suk snapped with her eyes averted and continued eating. Se-yŏng and Mrs. Shin could do nothing but continue eating.

Ch'un-ja waited at the table, smiling happily at Se-yŏng. Putting down her spoon as she finished her meal, Ok-suk told her, "Dr. Chin says your sister was killed by a stray bullet," and continued to instruct the girl who was stifling a cry with her hand, "Bring some scalding hot tea."

Ch'un-ja turned towards the kitchen, wiping tears from her eyes. As it was still rather early for the dinner time, there were only a couple of other diners in the hall.

"So you've not heard anything about Mr. Shin at all?" Kim Ok-suk began after their table was cleaned and steaming tea was brought.

"No, nothing at all."

"Would you believe it if I said he had married someone else?"

Turning deathly pale, Mrs. Shin stammered, "Did he?"

"No, it's just a thought. Wouldn't you prefer that to his dying? He got engaged to a girl from Puryŏng. At least that much I know as a fact."

Mrs. Shin drew a deep breath and said to Ok-suk, eyes brimming with tears, "Then he's working at Hamhung, isn't he? He's a Communist fighter. We met in the Sugamo Prison to begin with."

"Working? Even if he were, I tell you, it wouldn't help you. What I'm trying to say is, it wouldn't help you at all."

"I don't know what you're talking about." Mrs. Shin shook her head obstinately.

"Comrade Shin was a traitor."

"What?"

"He was a traitor and a renegade. That's why you won't be able to see him."

Blood draining out of her, Mrs. Shin insisted, "No, you're wrong! Wrong!" Tears dropped on the table as she shook her head in vehement denial. She grabbed Ok-suk's hand and begged her, "Please tell me. Please tell me everything. What has really happened to my husband?"

"Comrade Shin sold his country and his party to the Japanese imperialists. He connived with a female comrade and tried to flee to the south when his betrayal was found out."

"No, it can't be true!"

"He shot a policeman who was trying to detain him. There seems to have been quite an exchange of shots before he got shot down. It happened near his hometown. We learned of it from the newspaper."

"Newspaper?"

"Yes, it was in the newspaper."

The incisive tone of Ok-suk's last words caused Mrs. Shin to keel over.

"You seem to have a knack for picking up odd people. Of all the people to escort here!" Ok-suk grumbled aloud. She nevertheless offered to take her to a doctor to get treatment. Se-yŏng looked into Mrs. Shin's eyes and asked Ok-suk to bring some liquor and dribbled some between the lips of the unconscious woman. Then he explained to the people who gathered around them, "It's just fatigue and malnutrition."

Ok-suk snorted, "It befits an affluent person. I expected her to be better than that, the way she bragged about having been a fighter. She's just a weakling both in mind and body. Even if Mr. Shin were alive, he'd be married to a Korean girl by now. His parents couldn't wait to have grandchildren. The first thing they did after liberation was get him engaged to a village girl."

"I wasn't aware her health was in such a poor state. I think it was only her determination to see her husband that got her through everything."

Exasperation at Ok-suk was surging up in Se-yŏng. He had intended to ask her if she knew anything about Tong-jun and Nam-hi, but pushed the idea out of his mind. As soon as Mrs. Shin regained some strength, he took her with him and left the hospital. Ok-suk tugged along, however, saying that it was time for her to leave.

"I think I should take her to Chuŭl. There seems to be no place here for her to stay."

"Is there anyone waiting at Chuŭl?"

"I've got a friend there."

"But it won't do her any good. You should send her to the internment camp for Japanese."

"To the internment camp?" Se-yŏng glared at her indignantly.

"Where else? There's no reason to be so shocked."

"But her husband is Korean."

"Was. If he were alive, things might be different."

Snow had been falling steadily while they were in the hospital. The road was covered with a soft, thick layer. They arrived at the station where a couple of Russian soldiers were standing guard. They found that they had a full three hours to wait for the night train to Chuŭl and it would take the whole night for the train to chug to their destination, albeit it was a distance that could be reached on foot in that many hours.

Se-yŏng retrieved his baggage from the checkroom and sat down on a bench beside Mrs. Shin. Ok-suk also took a seat.

"You don't have to stay with us. We'll wait here until the train pulls in."

"I was going, anyway." After lingering for some time, Ok-suk suggested, "Would you like to come and work at the Nanam Hospital? I can arrange it if you want me to. Doctors are in short supply here and I understand there isn't any good surgeon at all." Without waiting for Se-yŏng to respond, she stood up, consulting her watch, and said, "Please let me know. I have to rush because I have to attend a meeting."

With Ok-suk gone, Mrs. Shin burst into tears which she had been stifling perhaps because of the critical eyes of the other woman.

"Please calm down, lest you attract their attention. You can cry all you want when we get to Chuŭl," Se-yŏng cautioned under his breath as he lit a cigarette.

A little after nine o'clock a man in a black coat and a charcoal gray cap approached their bench and grabbed Mrs. Shin.

"Arat!" A terrified shriek escaped her and she sought Se-yŏng frantically with sunken eyes. She could no longer pretend to be mute.

Se-yŏng demanded an explanation from the man, who simply said, "Instructions from a higher up."

Se-yŏng eyed him carefully. His face looked familiar but he could not decide whether he was a former patient of his or someone he encountered on a street in Changchun.

"Come with me," the man with the cap pulled Mrs. Shin by the arm.

Mrs. Shin bowed deeply to Se-yŏng and said between sobs, "I'm so indebted to you, Dr. Chin."

"What on earth do you mean by instructions from a higher up? This lady has been travelling with me all along."

"Aw, come on. Do you want to be accused of being a Japanese sympathizer? Let's go, woman." The man snorted and pressed her forward.

"But she's the wife of a Korean. She has undergone all kinds of hardship to come home."

"Home my ass. Don't make trouble, man, I'm not taking you. My order is to take her. You just go your way and let me do my job, all right?"

The man dragged her impatiently. Se-yŏng stared at Mrs. Shin's receding back with its forlorn satchel. It contained the *hanbok* she made for her husband. Even though the man no longer belonged to this world, the woman was carrying it with her. And it was the only possession she had in this world. Was it a cross left to bind her to her husband?

As she was stepping out of the station door, Mrs. Shin looked back toward Se-yŏng. Her eyes were those of a helpless calf being herded to the stock market. A lump in his throat, Se-yŏng hurriedly entrusted his baggage to the checkroom again and began to follow them at a distance.

They were heading east. Bright lights were streaming from the snow-covered houses by the street. There was a time when most of them were homes of Japanese who enjoyed life by measuring their prowess by the injustiees they inflicted on Koreans and relating such feats at the dinner table. Tonight Mrs. Shin was being shuffled past those houses, not for anything she had done herself, but as payment for those Japanese. Granted she too had harbored a secret sense of superiority over Koreans, though she had never overtly expressed it in her daily life. She and her fellow countrymen were not the only ones guilty of such arrogance. Koreans, too, had regarded Japanese with contempt, condemning them as a scheming lot backed by nothing but military power.

They turned to the left at an intersection. Snow settled on the narrow shoulders of Mrs. Shin, who looked as desolate as a stranded bird. Soon they came to an open field. A large building that looked like a temple stood where the field met the snow-covered hills which did not have a single tree. Bare lightbulbs hung high around the building, making it as bright as day.

The man with the cap took Mrs. Shin behind the building. Se-yŏng followed them. The man gestured for Mrs. Shin to go up the steps to a door. Se-yŏng stopped at the bottom of the steps while the man took her up the steps and pushed the door open. He shoved her in, saying brusquely, "Get in."

It was dark compared to the brightness outside. Se-yŏng caught sight of half a dozen old men prostrate like heaps of luggage in the dim light. Several women were huddied in a corner with children. "Be good to each other, you hear me?" The man addressed them all rather playfully before closing the door. He turned to Se-yŏng, who was standing at the bottom of the steps, and grumbled, "Who said you could follow us? Come, let's go. Yesterday's princes and aristocrats, today's paupers. Look what miserable lots they've become. They're no better than rats in a jar. And lice infested, too. I've seen them hunting lice every time I've come here."

"They all looked like invalids to me."

"Well, they are. Which is quite natural, too, considering they've come all the way down from the Russian-Manchurian border on foot. They wouldn't be stranded here like that if they were strong enough."

"Are they to be relocated to their country?"

"How should I know?"

"They wouldn't send someone whose husband is Korean, would they?"

"Is he alive?"

"No, he died."

"That's a different story, then."

"What a pity. She's a poor woman."

"Pity? You pity them, huh? What about all the wrong they've done?" The man snorted. He removed his cap, shook snow off of it and placed it back on his head. Se-yŏng jolted to a stop and stared at him. It was the detective who questioned him on the train years ago when he was visiting Chuŭl on vacation.

"Why do you begrudge a little pity? They are losers now and surely deserve some pity," Se-yŏng repeated insistently.

"You've got to get over it. Once you get used to such things, you'll find that those kind of cases are as common as pebbles on a country road."

"There isn't anyway for me to take the woman to Chuŭl?"

"Nope, and even if you took her there, she would end up the same." The man almost pushed Se-yŏng on the back and directed him solicitously to the railroad station.

"How did you know she was Japanese?" Se-yŏng asked when they reached the station. A suspicion about Kim Ok-suk had been nagging at him.

"Some wise person informed us," the man grinned and turned away. Se-yŏng wondered if the man was working with his past hidden or was being used because of it.

4

Se-yŏng got off at Chuŭl. Here too a couple of Russian soldiers in khaki coats and boots were standing guard under the eaves of the station master's office. The snow-covered platform sparkled in the morning sun. Se-yŏng walked past the turnstile. The streets lay quiet under a blanket of last night's snow.

Having deposited his baggage at the checkroom, Se-yŏng headed to Tong-jun's house. He found it deserted. Slouching on the veranda, he smoked a cigarette. He felt lost. His home, Pukch'on, was 40 kilometers to the south.

It was eight years since he had left his village with a small travelling bag in hand. Now he was here again, with a backpack and a trunk. Why did he come here? He had no premeditated plan to come back to his homeplace or to his friend, but here he was at Tong-jun's. Perhaps it was Tong-jun's friendship that beckoned him here, or was it? Wasn't it really some unrequited feeling that refused to disappear into oblivion? His mother and Nam-hi were like a constant pain he could not get out of his system.

A snow-covered field spread in front of him. Wandering over it, his eyes came upon a well to the right. He was thirsty. He put down his backpack and stood up. At the well, he noticed footprints in the snow. They led to the east to the kiln which hulked like a dugout in a mound of earth. He followed the footprints and came to the sod door of the kiln. He knocked on it but there was no answer. He pounded on it noisily but still there was no response. He pulled the doorknob but it did not budge. He kept pounding for a while but to no avail. It seemed the door was either locked or someone was pulling it from inside.

"Tong-jun? Hello? Is anybody there?"

Only a profound silence came from inside the kiln. He went around to the other side to a small push-up window. It was pasted over with weather-bleached paper. He poked a finger into the paper, and when there was no response, made the hole larger so he could peep in. It was too dark to see anything. He tore away all the paper. He saw a man lying on the floor.

For all he knew, the man could be a leper, but Se-yŏng hollered to him, "I'm a refugee from Manchuria. I'm a doctor. If anything's wrong, I can help you. Open the door."

The man on the floor looked to the other side. Se-yŏng realized there was another person crouched against the wall. Dark eyes gleamed at him under dark brows.

"You must be Japanese. Want a cigarette? I've come to see my friend who used to make ceramics here some time ago."

At Se-yŏng's friendly explanation, the man stretched a mud-colored hand and almost snatched the pack of cigarettes Se-yŏng held towards him.

"Give me one," mumbled the one on the floor making an effort to lift his head. The voice and the face were those of an old man. His arm stretching for the cigarette was as emaciated as a dried stick.

"Are you looking for Mr. Ch'oe Tong-jun?" The one against the wall asked after lighting a cigarette for himself and one for the old man.

"Yes. You know him?"

"He went to his homeplace a few days ago. It seems there was some family business he had to tend to. But I think his wife and children are still in Chuŭl. The lady seems to be working at the Women's Union."

"Women's Union!" Se-yŏng exclaimed and recalled his first impression of Tong-jun's wife.

"That's right. Anyhow, come around the other way. I'll unlock the door."

The heavy mud door opened as Se-yŏng went around to it. Inside, he waited for his eyes to get used to the darkness of the earthen pit. He could gradually make out the bony face of the old man lying on a straw mat. He was covered with a ragged blanket.

Pest were piled carelessly in a corner of the kiln and some grocery bags made of newspaper were on them. Earthenware pots and jars stood on the shelves.

"Light the lamp," the old man told the other man and breathed a long, shuddering sigh.

The small, kerosene lamp was lit. Sallow faces half hidden under coarse gray beards emerged from the darkness. Se-yŏng thought the Count of Monte Cristo must have looked like them when he was in the dungeon.

"Difficult times, huh?"

At Se-yŏng's sympathetic tone, they blinked their bleary eyes. The younger man said, "I know we deserve it, still it's hard to swallow. We've survived the past few months because of Mr. Ch'oe's generosity. He has let us stay here and given us things to eat." Placing a page of newspaper on the torn window, the man said, "We're Murais. That's my older brother. We used to run the Sŏnjang Hotel at Kaneda Resort."

"The Sŏnjang Hotel!" Se-yŏng exclaimed. He wondered what had happened to Misako.

"You've been to our hotel?"

"Yes, it was some years back."

"Ah!"

"How's Miss Misako?"

At this the old man jerked and stammered tearfully, "You, you know my daughter?"

"Yes, I do. My name is Chin Se-yŏng."

"Oh, you're Mr. Chin. My niece talked about you many times," ventured the younger Murai.

"My daughter was taken away by the conquerors. A long time ago. She must have been killed. If not, she must have become their plaything by now," the older Murai spit out the words.

Eyes fixed on the ceiling, he sighed, "What a tenacious thing life is! I should have quit living long ago!"

"We shouldn't have waited around trying to sell our property," faltered Misako's uncle, his voice hoarse with compunction. He too stared hard at the ceiling. His face was covered with layers of dirt. He did not wash his face on purpose.

He said that he had entrusted his young son Toshio to a friend who had plans to sneak out of the country from the port of Ch'ŏngjin the day after liberation. They returned in two days, however, without even making it as far as Ch'ŏngjin, because they learned from Japanese refugees coming south from there that the coast had already been blocked. He sent the boy with another group who were going down south. The last news he had of them was that they came to a roadblock and everyone in the group dispersed. He had no idea where his son was now roaming or even if he were dead or alive.

"My brother's here because of me," Misako's father said apologetically.

"The hell I am. It's just because I couldn't wrench myself away because some damn guy seemed interested in buying our hotel," the younger man said wearily with a bitter, self-derisive smile.

"How have you been managing?"

"I go over to the hotel and clean the place. They didn't ask me to, but they give me left over food. I make porridge with the stuff. And Mr. Ch'oe's been helping us a lot."

"They don't know you're here? I mean the Russians?"

"No, at least up until now they haven't."

Se-yŏng left his backpack with them and went to town. Frozen in silence broken only by the occasional crunching of the feet of the patrolling Russian soldiers, the downtown was a far sight from the hustle bustle of its heyday. Hardly any buses or automobiles were on the streets. Se-yŏng went to the butcher shop to buy a kilogram of meat and to the grocery store to buy eggs, sugar, onions and some other vegetables for the Murais. He also bought them two packs of cigarettes.

"We won't be able to forget your kindness even after we become heaps of bones." Misako's father thanked him with clasped hands and his brother prostrated himself in a deep bow.

Se-yŏng returned to town and checked into an inn near the railroad station. He decided to wait and see how things developed before making any plans for himself. The next day he went to the Women's Union to look for Tong-jun's wife. It was in a house confiscated from a Japanese family not far from the elementary school where Tong-jun had taught.

Se-yŏng almost did not recognize the large woman with short hair and a short skirt that appeared at the foyer at his request.

"You're looking for Chu Kŭm-ryŏn? I'm she."

"My name's Chin Se-yŏng. Er, I'm your...."

"Comrade Chin! Why, indeed!" She exclaimed delightedly, but Se-yŏng winced at the unfamiliar way she addressed him. The woman, however, seemed perfectly at ease calling people "comrade."

"How did you ever find out I was here?"

"I learned it from the Murais in the kiln."

"You've seen them?" She knit her brows and invited Se-yŏng to an office which was floored with Japanese tatami mats. "We've had a lot of arguments over those people. I keep telling my husband that he should get the healthy one to go wherever he should and the sick one over to an internment camp. We would be in a real difficult position if we were found to be sheltering the Japs who were so unjust and abominable to our people."

Her argument was well founded and had good reason. Nevertheless, she had been unable to put her ideas into practice herself. Instead of nagging her husband, she could very easily kick them out of the kiln or simply report them. She was kept from doing so less by compassion or Buddhistic beliefs than a simple lack of ruthlessness. And Se-yŏng thought the compassion he had shown the Murais was due to no better motivation than hers.

The last day of the year, Se-yŏng hung a signboard "Chin Se-yŏng, Surgeon" on an outer section of a house near the station. Chu Kŭm-ryŏn worked as hard as if it were her own business to help him prepare the clinic.

That evening, on the way to take a hot bath at the Kaneda Resort, which was renamed Morae, Se-yŏng dropped by the kiln to visit with the Murais. The kiln was deserted. He went inside and lit the lamp. The glass globe of the lamp was freshly cleaned and there was little kerosene left. He lifted the lamp high above him and looked around. Everything was the same as the first time he found it except the blankets were nowhere to be seen. No groceries were in the corner other than a handful of uncooked barley. They have finally been taken away to the internment camp at Mrs. Chu's report, he thought. After all, it was the best for everyone. Se-yŏng felt relieved, unlike the time he left Mrs. Shin in the camp. Their life here had been much too unstable and hopeless. He even congratulated himself for thinking realistically for a change.

He returned the lamp to its place and was going to blow the light out when a white envelope caught his eye. With an uneasy premonition he tore it open and pulled out a note.

> I woke up this morning to find my brother had killed himself. I waited until it got dark and buried him the best I could on a frozen slope about 100 meters south of here. I wish I could wait until the land thaws so I could give him a decent burial, but what's the use?
>
> I'm going to head south on foot. My brother has been urging me to hurry up because he saw the land ghost of the hotel in his dream. Not that I'm afraid of that, but I don't want to lose a minute now that I've decided to leave.
>
> Thank you for everything.
>
> Murai Nobusuke
> December 28, 1945

Se-yŏng thrust the letter into his pocket and went to the Sŏnjang Hotel as he had first intended.

The name Sŏnjang had given way to a new one and the interior of the hotel was greatly changed. He liked the change, especially the absence of the flapping sound of Japanese slippers. The man who had pitied the death of Murai the former owner of the hotel, stood motionlessly, overwhelmed by a surge of emotion. It was as sweet as the rain that caressed the leaves after a drought. He could feel it filtering into every pore of his skin and joy spread throughout him. It was the first time for him to experience his country's liberation realistically with his mind and body.

5

It had been almost a month since Se-yŏng opened his clinic. He was yet to see Tong-jun, about whom he heard only through his wife. He also heard from her that Nam-hi was still not very well.

One day, Tong-jun visited Se-yŏng at the clinic. He explained that the trouble over his family's land at Pukch'on was more or less settled.

"I trust all your family is well? Beginning with your father?"

"He's far from being well. That's what worries me," said Tong-jun bitterly. Because of Mr. Ch'oe's obsessive attachment to his land, he literally took to his bed when he lost most of it under the new land reform. In fact, it was because of his illness that Tong-jun had been detained at Pukch'on.

Se-yŏng looked at Tong-jun, hoping to hear some news about Nam-hi.

"That house is a mess. It's bad enough not having a source of income, but it's even worse to have three invalids."

"Three invalids?"

"My brother's locked himself up in his house saying he doesn't want to lay eyes on the world again, and Nam-hi is as good as dead. Everyone is just waiting for the day her life comes to an end."

"Tell me about Nam-hi."

"I've never known anybody so pitiful. She rarely speaks and then she only mumbles to herself. She just turns away if anyone tries to come near her. My father loves her so dearly in spite of all that."

Se-yŏng stared at Tong-jun vapidly for a long time. A sense of futility swept through him like a bleak wind.

"Ah, well, so much for my wretched family back home." Tong-jun heaved his shoulders in a deep sigh and changed the subject. "Say, what's the matter with you? Why aren't you married yet?"

"Why, indeed?" Se-yŏng stood up and walked around the room restlessly, his arms folded. "In fact, I was thinking about it just now. I'm not even sure if something's wrong with me or if my mother's responsible for it all."

"I think it's because you and Miss Kim Ok-suk are so terribly obstinate. You two are both waiting for the other to make the first move." Tong-jun went on as Se-yŏng came back to his seat and lit up a cigarette. "Or perhaps the woman you were in love with died?"

"Yeah, I might have surrendered if a woman approached me aggressively. I've been wary of women as long as I can remember."

"I simply can't imagine life without my wife. It'd be too inconvenient. Who'd fix my meals? And take care of my handkerchiefs, socks and shirts? Not to say anything about being lonesome and all that stuff." Tong-jun was his usual pragmatic self.

"You're a lucky guy. Having had no luck with parents, I don't think I'd have much luck with a wife either."

"Yeah, you've done really well considering you had to manage all by yourself. You're a self-made man, worthy of mention in a textbook."

"Aw, you and your exaggerations." Se-yŏng opened his mouth to say something, but swallowed the words.

"How's business? Many patients?"

"Just so-so. About half of them can't pay."

"So you're doing social work?"

"No, I'm just watching time go by."

"By practicing medicine?"

"Why not? Isn't that what living is all about? Watching time go by?"

"Yes, I guess you have a point there."

"Er, I've been thinking about treating Nam-hi myself. Do you think you can bring her here and let her stay with you?"

"But you're a surgeon."

"I've been studying neurology these days."

Tong-jun looked hard at Se-yŏng for a long time before he stood up. "I'll talk about it with Father."

Tong-jun clasped Se-yŏng's hand and left. Was Se-yŏng unable to get over Nam-hi? Tong-jun shook his head disbelievingly, telling himself it did not make any sense. All the way home, Tong-jun's head hung low as he was deep in thought.

There was no one at home except his youngest son who was playing with neighborhood kids. His wife was getting more and more involved with the Women's Union and the hours she was away from home were getting longer and longer. He went into the house with his four-year-old son on his shoulders. With the older boys at school and his wife not around, his house felt deserted. He set off for his wife's office with the child.

"Oh, you know I would come home in good time. What am I to do if you keep coming here like this?" Mrs. Chu was flustered at her husband.

"But you left the house unlocked without anyone to keep an eye on it. And it's lunch time, too."

"You could fix your own lunch. And our next-door neighbor promised she would keep an eye on the house. She always did, when you were away."

"It seems our country's liberation has only liberated women from tending their husbands and children and set them loose in the streets."

"I don't understand why you've become so sarcastic these days. I thought you of all people would be more understanding than other men."

"Do you know what day tomorrow is?"

"Sure, the last day of the year by the lunar calendar."

"I'm going to Pukch'on to say New Year's greetings to Father."

"New Year's greetings? But you've barely been back from there. Besides, we don't observe lunar New Year's anymore."

"But there will be the ancestral rites and New Year's greetings at home as usual."

"Ah, well, all that will be over as of this year. They won't be able to afford them next year," Mrs. Chu commented in a cool, indifferent voice.

"All the more reason for me to participate in this year's ceremony, then."

Tong-jun left the child with his wife and returned home. He was not sure whether she deserved his angry accusations or not but it was quite clear that ever since liberation she had become so wrapped up in her new job at the Union that she neglected to take care of her family. Muttering that he was going to make her behave once and for all, Tong-jun went to the station to catch the train.

Mr. Ch'oe Ch'i-man had confined himself to his bed, not because he was physically ailing anywhere, but he felt more comfortable in bed.

"Bloody thieves!" Whenever his mind returned to the crops that had been usurped by his tenants right after the harvest, anger flared up in him and he thrashed in bed turning his face to the wall. It was his way of condemning the "two-faced scoundrels who betrayed him by alternating between the liver and the gall bladder" but his satisfaction at doing so lasted no longer than the time it took him to turn to the wall.

"May thunderbolts strike those wretches!" So cursing, he would bolt up from his pallet. All his cursing and swearing did nothing to appease his anger and injured feelings but only led the family to fear him.

Only Nam-hi stayed with him. Like a child she played house alone without a word, drew things with crayons or pasted and unpasted patches of cloth on paper. Her hair was unkempt unless someone combed it for her. She ate only when she was spoon-fed. She seemed to have no sense of day and night and would shuffle and squirm while others were sound asleep and huddle like a shrimp and fall asleep in the broad daylight.

"Tut, tut, if you're not the reincarnation of my enemy in the former life, I don't know what is!" Mr. Ch'oe grumbled at Nam-hi. Nevertheless, he tended her with care as he would a suckling baby.

His worries did not end with Nam-hi. Tong-ho, his eldest son, was even more of a burden. As he had alienated himself from worldly things completely, never caring about daily needs, his family was totally dependent on Mr. Ch'oe. Even in the days he was able to take good care of them with the farm rent that flowed in abundance, Mr. Ch'oe had been far from happy about his son and could not wait until his grandson T'ae-yŏn would come of age and take control of the family. Things had become much worse now that he was deprived of farm rents. The source of livelihood for both his and his son's family was completely gone.

Clinging to the old saying that there was a way out even when heaven caved in, he was hoping for one little miracle. Tong-jun, who had been imprisoned for his anti-Japanese activity, was the only known independence fighter in the village. Mr. Ch'oe consoled himself saying, "Wait until Tong-jun becomes the principal of the school here and let's see if you scoundrels still can claim my land!" His hope was not entirely groundless. Some of Tong-jun's friends in the village told him that they heard rumors of his appointment and Mr. Ch'oe simply expanded the idea to his benefit.

It was already four years since the new high school was established near Yongch'ŏn on the other side of the railroad. Mr. Ch'oe was one of the most generous donors at the time of

its founding, a fact which played considerably in getting T'ae-
yŏn and Tong-shik in the school regardless of their age. Both
were now in fourth grade and Tong-shik's brother Tong-su was
in second grade.

The younger brothers of Nam-hi's friends Ae-sun and T'an-
shil were also going to the school. Both of them had children
of their own old enough to go to elementary school. How true
it was, Mr. Ch'oe mused, that time could turn mulberry
forests into blue sea and sunny places into the darkest shade.
But then, such was the way with human life. It was so
unfathomable that something one thought was propitious one
moment might turn out to be the cause of misfortune the next,
and what seemed to be a great disaster might bring a wonderful
turn of luck.

"Nam-hi, don't you miss your son at all? It's about time
Yŏng-gŭn entered elementary school, huh?" Mr. Ch'oe muttered almost to himself rather than to his daughter who sat
mindlessly.

"Father, your second son is here," Mrs. Hyŏn announced
the arrival of Tong-jun to her husband who was still in bed.

"What brought him here?" Mr. Ch'oe jumped up, hoping
that his son had finally become the school principal.

"Why, it's obvious. He's here to do New Year's greetings and
memorial services for the ancestors."

"Memorial services, pah! What are we going to hold memorial services with? We don't have any decent offerings."

"We should do our duty nevertheless."

"If only someone would do his duty these days!"

"Tell Tong-ho he should do the memorial services and everything else from now on as any other eldest son in the world
would do. I'm sick of taking care of everything."

"I've already prepared all the offerings. We can let Tong-ho
do them from next year."

"How on earth have you prepared offerings? With what?"

"Well, we're not exactly starving. Though we don't have any
income, we do have a stock of things and I reckon they'll last

for some time. Don't worry so much, Father. As they say, there'll be no cobweb over the mouth of a living person."

"Hm, you think we're living in the good old days when no one had any worries at all? No land, not even a palm-sized piece, no servants, no farmers! All I have is a lot of mouths to feed. You talk as if it's only a special breed who gets poverty stricken, but anyone who has nothing to eat is going to starve and that's what we are going to do."

"But we have boys. You have T'ae-yŏn and Tong-shik."

"They'll have to go into the military right after they finish school. There'll be no precious time for them to tend to the family."

"Come, come. There's no need to fret so. We'll manage all right. We could even become wage earners if worse comes to worse."

"Wage earners!"

While Mr. Ch'oe was bandying words with his wife, Tong-jun washed his face and combed his hair. Looking into the mirror, he thought he looked too haggard to see his father.

"How have you been doing, Father?" asked Tong-jun coming to his father and lowering himself in a great bow. Squatting with his long bamboo pipe in his mouth, Mr. Ch'oe glanced at his son's crouched back with lackluster eyes.

"What brought you back so soon?"

"I've come to say New Year's greetings to you and...."

"And what?"

"Oh, it's nothing important. We can talk about it some other time."

Mr. Ch'oe removed the pipe from his mouth and looked at Tong-jun, his eyes swirls of hope, anxiety, and frustration.

"What is it?"

"It's just about Nam-hi. Nothing important. I've been thinking about taking Nam-hi with me and getting her treated at my home. There's a doctor who's good in that sort of thing and he has opened a clinic recently."

"Where did he work before?"

"In Manchuria."

"I don't think a doctor from Manchuria can be any good."

"But he was in Changchun and there were good hospitals there."

"Where's he from?"

"Er, from Chuŭl."

"From Chuŭl? Of what clan of Chuŭl?"

At a loss as to what to say, Tong-jun lifted his face and looked up at his father.

"It's Chin Se-yŏng, isn't it? That wretch Chin Saengwon has been bragging about him. Se-yŏng wrote him that he set up a clinic in Chuŭl."

"It really doesn't matter who the doctor is. Why should it matter if it is Se-yŏng? What matters is for Nam-hi to get proper treatment."

"Shut up. I won't hear anymore. No doctor in the world can cure her illness, especially not Chin Se-yŏng. He's the last person I'd entrust her to. You don't have to worry about Nam-hi. I'll take her with me when I die," Mr. Ch'oe said eyeing the back of Nam-hi who was scribbling with crayons on a sheet of paper and resumed smoking his pipe.

"Let me take her and just have her examined."

"Don't say anymore. I don't want another word from you. Don't trouble yourself. Why don't you worry about yourself, instead."

Tong-jun tried to understand his father and wondered if he wanted to keep his mindless daughter beside him as he would a bird, a gold fish or even a potted plant. Mindless and word-less, she was like a very calm and peaceful moving picture. Her eyes, curtained by her long lashes, were as beautiful as ever even though they had lost their luster.

Mr. Ch'oe went out of the room in an obvious gesture of dis-pleasure at his son's scrutiny.

"Nam-hi, look at me," Tong-jun called to his sister.

Nam-hi went on drawing. Tong-jun grabbed the paper and tore it to pieces. Nam-hi remained motionless a long time with her head hung low, and then turned away and began to unknot a tangled bunch of embroidery threads one by one. Tong-jun snatched the gaudy bunch from her hands. She lowered her hands slowly to her skirt and started fingering the hem quietly, without looking up at her brother.

6

One day in early April Tong-jun got an express letter and a telegram at the same time. The telegram was from his home telling him to come because his father was in critical condition, and the express letter contained his appointment as the principal of the Chuŭl No. 3 Elementary School. He went to the Women's Union with both the letter and the telegram. He suspected that his wife was behind the appointment to the principal's position.

"I'll go and see about Fahter for you. You must report to the school immediately since you're a public servant as of today."

"Will you send a telegram to the school in my name saying I'm away and will be delayed a day? I'll be off and back overnight."

"So you want to report tomorrow. All right, shall I notify them by special delivery?"

"That's a good idea."

Out of the blue. Tong-jun suddenly thought of Detective Kimura. He had heard that he was found dead a few days after liberation, his body badly beaten.

"Good, consider it done."

After seeing his wife, Tong-jun hurried to Se-yŏng, fearing that his father might be mortally ill. Explaining to Se-yŏng, he said, "The telegram just says he's in critical condition. I've no idea what ails him but can you come with me with a surgical kit, just in case it's his appendix or something like that? Will it be all right with your schedule?"

Tong-jun was thinking it was a good excuse to have Nam-hi examined as well. Se-yŏng accepted his request instantly.

It was totally unexpected news that Tong-jun found when he arrived at Pukch'on that night. His stepmother Mrs. Hyŏn reported that the people of Pukch'on were holding a people's court regarding one of the villagers the next day at the courtyard of the Changyŏn county office. She said that only the Ch'oe house was kept in the dark while all the rest of the village had known about it for many days. She had only learned about it the day before and even then from only rumors her children brought home.

"Your father doesn't know anything yet. Please keep quiet until the notice arrives from the county office."

Tong-jun thus reported to his father that he was appointed the principal of the Chuŭl No. 3. Elementary School, saying nothing about the telegram.

"Humm, Chuŭl No. 3. Changyŏn would be better, still...." A triumphant smile lit up Mr. Ch'oe's face for the first time in months as he vowed silently, "The damn bastards all think I'm completely done for, but I'll show them, just wait...."

Early the next day people began to congregate at the county office. About nine o'clock a messenger came to the Ch'oe house asking Ch'oe Ch'i-man and his sons to report to the county office.

"They want us to come there? What for? Do they want to hear all the curses they deserve?" Mr. Ch'oe sneered at the messenger.

"I'm here just to convey the message I was told to deliver. I don't know anything."

Kun-sam, the messenger, had been one of Ch'oe's tenants before the year's harvest.

"That's quite obvious. All you know in the world is how to pocket someone else's rice."

"Heck, you're out of your mind, old man. You don't know the time of day! Talk about rice! You're in for a surprise, old man. We'll see if you can talk about your precious rice afterwards." Kun-sam scoffed.

Mr. Ch'oe was prevented from charging after Kun-sam by

Tong-jun and Mrs. Hyŏn who held him back forcefully. He gulped down a bowlful of boiled water and flopped back on his bed. The day was dark and cloudy from morning.

"Let's go, Father. Tong-ho's here with me," Tong-jun said. On his way back from the railroad station where he went to send a telegram to the school saying that he would be further detained a couple of days, he stopped at Tong-ho's house and brought him home with him.

"I'm not going anywhere. You two go ahead and do whatever you please. I don't care whether there's a trial or a crazy *kut*." Ch'oe grunted from his bed.

At five minutes past ten, he had not budged from his room. Kun-sam came again bearing a warning from the People's Committee of Pukch'on that he would face grave consequences if he did not appear at the court.

"Grave consequences, pah! Are they going to kill me or what? All right, all right. Let's go. Let them do whatever they want with me. I don't care a bit." Grumbling, Mr. Ch'oe put on his coat and hat and headed to the county office with a son on each side supporting him.

The yard in front of the office was packed with people. Not only Pukch'on residents but also people from Tongch'on, Yongdam and even some from Sŏch'on were gathered to watch what was going to happen. A high wood platform stood near the office with a plain table on it.

"This way. Come this way." Kim Sŏndal stepped aside to make way for Mr. Ch'oe and his sons. Beside him was his daughter Ae-sun with her daughter on her back. She was obviously not doing very well as her face was splotched and freckled and the wrapper holding the child on her back was ragged.

Se-yŏng looked on from the far side of the crowd. A man came up on the platform. Several people, looking very solemn, were already seated on chairs at one side of the platform. Mr. Ch'oe and his sons were led to them by Kun-sam. Sun-shil, Kun-sam's daughter, was in the front row nearest the platform with her aged grandmother beside her. Her good-natured face pinched with worry, she was following her father and the three Ch'oe men with uneasy eyes.

The man on the platform cleared his throat and bellowed, "Comrades!" Everyone became attentive to him. "Now you've seen, Comrades, how slow Ch'oe Ch'i-man and Ch'oe Tong-ho, the two defendants, are in making themselves available for their own trial, haven't you? They obviously haven't gotten over their old habit of exploiting the farmers, have they?"

The crowd applauded.

"Good heavens! I know him. He's the guy who dug ditches in my field, isn't he? His name is Hwang Chin-su, I think. And what grudge does that blasted man have against me to be so rude?" Mr. Ch'oe asked Tong-jun, his white beard jerking up and down. Tong-jun's face was crimson. He realized that the purpose of this gathering was none other than to publicly accuse his father and elicit the people's verdict right on the spot. He wished he had brought his wife.

"Just what the hell's going on here, huh?" Mr. Ch'oe grunted.

"Don't say anything, Father. We'll have to wait and see what they're up to," Tong-jun quieted his father, holding him firmly by the arm.

Hwang Chin-su turned out to be the secretary of the People's Committee of the county and was playing the moderator and judge of the trial.

"Comrades, we are here to indict Ch'oe Ch'i-man and his son, the most vicious landlords in the Changyŏn Basin, and to bring them to justice for the crimes they committed. Isn't that right?"

"Aye, aye," the people responded in unison.

"So it is. Then, comrade Chin U-yŏng, come forth and make your charges."

Chin U-yŏng, Se-yŏng's cousin, scrambled up the platform and, placing his hands on the table, blinked his eyes over the crowd.

"Now, what on earth is Chin Saengwon doing up there?" Mr.

Ch'oe muttered. He seemed unable to believe that they were out to condemn him in public.

"Comrades, I know until a while ago all of you looked upon this man Ch'oe Ch'i-man with great respect. Well, you did so because you didn't know all about him," said Chin dramatically. "Comrades! I'm sure you can still remember, though it was years ago. I had a cousin named Chin Sŏk-chae. I want to tell you the man who got his widow pregnant was none other than this man here, Ch'oe Ch'i-man."

Chin U-yŏng pointed his finger at Mr. Ch'oe. As if struck by hailstones, the people gasped and groaned at his words.

"What's more, his oldest son Tong-ho also violated the poor widow. Now you can see, Comrades, why the man has been stuck in his house like a cripple, why he has been withdrawn from the world. The widow was driven to kill herself because she was caught between him and his father!"

The yard was boiling like porridge, everyone exclaiming and swearing.

"You scoundrel! Shut your foul mouth! How dare you say such a lie!" Mr. Ch'oe screamed at the bottom of the platform, stamping his feet.

"Now, Comrades, perhaps we could forgive him if he'd finished then and there. We would understand because a man can err once or twice in his life. But what is truly unforgivable is that he had the village butcher flog the dead woman. Nine times, no less. He was the one who sinned and he had the woman pay for his sin. He was the one who deserved those nine flogs and many more, but he had the dead widow flogged instead. How could a human being commit such an atrocious act! His son Ch'oe Tong-ho is better than him. At least he became a recluse after the incident."

"How do you happen to know so well?" Came a voice from the crowd.

"Well, I'm one of the family, aren't I? She was my cousin's widow and she confided in me."

"You sure you're telling the truth?" Another voice hollered.

"Would I dare tell a lie here of all places? I swear, Comrades, it's the truth, nothing but the truth." Chin U-yŏng beat his chest and descended from the platform.

Hwang Chin-su came up and hollered, "Comrade Kim Kapil, come forward and testify."

Kim Sŏndal ascended the platform and spoke. "I was a tenant of Mr. Ch'oe. I didn't get along very well with him, him being very stingy and unbending. I'm sure glad I'm farming for myself."

The crowd laughed.

"Just confine yourself to the part relating to the injustices done by the Ch'oes."

"Yes, yes, you're right. Mrs. ch'oe used to give us glutinous rice for New Year's Day but never Mrs. Ch'oe. A mighty stingy man he was."

The crowd burst into laughter again.

"Now, it's Comrade Song Kun-sam's turn."

Song Kun-sam got on the platform. Ae-sun blushed and looked around for her mother but looked at her father as he began to speak.

"Old Man Ch'oe dealt with us harshly all the time. He accused me of cheating him on the crops and wouldn't listen to reason. Even at the time of the Widow Chŏng thing, I had to do as I was told because he was a fearful man and I was afraid."

After Song Kun-sam, Hwang Chin-su urged the people to come out and testify about the vices of the Ch'oe family. Mr. Ch'oe suddenly raised his hand and, vehemently shaking off the restraining hands of his sons, scrambled up onto the platform. With his white beard flowing down over his gray robed chest, he still cut an impressive figure.

"Take off your hat, old man!" Someone in the crowd shouted.

Mr. Ch'oe removed his hat and placed it on the table. The crowd calmed down. Mr. Ch'oe's lips, half hidden by the beard, were unusually red. Though he was close to seventy, he could have passed as a man in his fifties if it were not for his white beard. His long, slit eyes gleamed as they had not done in a long time. His gray hair, however, was in such disarray it resembled an overgrown mugwort.

"Vi... Vi... Villagers," Mr. Ch'oe began with a hoarse stammer and rubbed one of his eyes. "I'm... I'm... a... a sin... sin... sinner." He rubbed the other eye. "Yes... yes... I... I sinned against the Wi... Wi... Widow Chŏng. But only against the Wi.. Wi... Widow Chŏng. Chi... Chi... Chin Saengwon is evil. He... He's a liar. A molester. He for... for... forced himself on his cousin's widow in the mi... middle of the night. The vi... villain is now accusing my son, my innocent gentle son, of an... an act he never dreamed of. He... He blackmailed me into letting him farm my land without paying any tenant fee. While my son Tong-ho has been be... be... behaving wretchedly believing that I was the one who had the Wi... Wi... Widow Chong's bo... bo... body flogged. It was Chi... Chin Saengwon and no one else who insisted on the flo... flo... flogging.

"As... As you all know, my dau... dau... daughter's been suffering an incurable illness of mind for over six years now. I've accepted it as pu... pu... punishment for the sin I committed against the Wi... Wi... Widow Chŏng. I'm paying for my sin by keeping my in... insane daughter in my own room. Yes, I'm paying dearly for my sin, and I invite you to go ahead and pu... pu... punish me more. Please pu... pu... punish this old man. And punish that wicked Chi... Chin Saengwon also. The poo... poor woman won't feel vindicated even in death if you don't."

Mr. Ch'oe choked back sobs and pounded his chest with his fists, probably in an effort to pound the remorse and guilt that had been oppressing his heart for so long.

"You crafty old serpent! Let's get it over with once and for all! You and your lot've been living comfortably off the blood of us farmers and laborers and now you're accusing an innocent man. Everyone, Old Man Ch'oe is dragging me into this because I revealed his secret!" Chin U-yŏng ran up screaming onto the platform and kicked and hit Mr. Ch'oe who was still sobbing.

"Get that one first! Get that villain who beats an old man!" An old man in the front row bellowed, stamping his feet.

Angry shouts burst from here and there among the older people. One of them was the old man who had been beaten miserably by the Japanese detective Kimura because he was riding an ox cart. It was on his account that Tong-jun was imprisoned and got the reputation as Changyŏn's first and only anti-Japanese activist.

"Scoundrels! Have you forgotten that this is the land of courteous people! Regardless of who did what, how dare a young man beat his senior! You unlearned upstart!"

Older villagers who had been seething with discontent for the way things were being done recently saw a chance to vent their frustration. Soon neither Ch'oe Ch'i-man nor Chin Saengwon could be seen on the platform. Only Hwang Chin-su was on it pounding the table in an effort to restore order.

Se-yŏng left the crowd. His vague suspicion about the relationship between his mother and Mr. Ch'oe was confirmed finally and the reason for his cousin's strange behavior was brought out into the open. Distrust, deceit and hate were sprouting everywhere like poisonous mushrooms. And that was the nature of the world he had to live in, Se-yŏng thought.

The broad road seemed deserted until he noticed a strange, dishevelled woman under a tree. Colored threads hung from her unkempt hair and there was a straw rope bound around the waist of her dark coat. Brown rubber men's shoes stuck out from under her dark purplish skirt.

Se-yŏng went toward her, realizing she must be Nam-hi. She did not look at him. She kept looking at a clump of clouds at the end of a lean, leafless branch of a poplar tree, or perhaps she was looking at a sliver of blue sky that suddenly glimmered between the dark clouds.

'I'm paying for the sin I committed against the Widow Chŏng by keeping my insane daughter in my room.' Mr. Ch'oe's words churned sluggishly in Se-yŏng's head like a watermill in a time of drought.

"Nam-hi, Nam-hi," he said in a determined tone of voice.

She appeared not to hear him but turned slightly toward him and, with eyes cast downward, began to dig the dirt with the point of her shoe until the tender sprouts of grass hidden underground came into view. Her lashes were as long and thick as ever. The pale whiteness of her face was tinged with darkness, perhaps because she had lost a lot of weight, and her pale beautifully sculptured lips were firmly closed.

Se-yŏng shuddered. Pity, resentment and desire flamed up in him.

"Nam-hi, look at me! It's me, Se-yŏng. Please, Nam-hi!"

His arms trembled with the desire to embrace the ragged woman who was unfeeling of everything, even her confusion. His arms trembled as his veins throbbed with pent-up emotions.

'Now I know, Nam-hi. Yes, I can see it clearly now. You're my destiny, Nam-hi, a destiny that I can never deny. Forgive me, Mother.'

Gently he took her hand in his. She looked up at him with expressionless eyes. A train whistle came from the direction of the railroad station. The train began to chug slowly to the south. Nam-hi started toward the station but stopped short after a few steps. Looking up at the sky, her lips parted slightly in a smile that was barely visible.

"Nam-hi, let me take you home."

Dirty and ragged, she still had something that dazzled Se-yŏng like a diamond. His eyes glued on her face, he stretched his hand to her, but she kept looking at the sky mindlessly.

"Heavens, Nam-hi! How you managed to sneak out here I'll never know!"

It was Mrs. Hyŏn. She hurried to Nam-hi and, glancing around with eyes bloodshot from crying, untied the rope from her waist. "Come. I've been away just awhile but you can sneak away so fast. Oh, Nam-hi, how I wish you'd get your mind back!" said Mrs. Hyŏn and headed to her house pushing and pulling Nam-hi.

Back in his room at the inn, Se-yŏng sprawled against a pile of bedding, his head resting on his arms. Tong-jun came about two in the afternoon.

"I don't know how I can even face you," a totally enervated Tong-jun said flopping down on the floor.

"It's nothing for which either of us is responsible. Please don't ever mention it again. By the way, I saw Nam-hi today."

"Nam-hi?"

"Yes, I saw her."

Tong-jun's face was furrowed with pain. "It seems we should leave Pukch'on. They say Tong-ho should labor two years in a coal mine in Hoeryŏng and Father, being too old for that, is to do ground-levelling work at the hill west of here. For half a year, at least. And the family has to be out of the house tomorrow. We're not to take anything with us but some clothes. So we have no choice but to leave the village. I don't know what I should do with my nephew and my little brothers. They're only middle school students."

Tong-jun rubbed his face with his hands.

It began to rain in the evening. For Mrs. Hyŏn and Tong-ho's wife who were packing bundles of clothes dejectedly, it was as dark and gloomy as the last day of the world.

"Look here, son," Mrs. Hyŏn said to Tong-jun. "Obviously, it's a disgrace. We can't do anything about it. And I just can't pick up and leave Pukch'on. I'll rent a room. At least that way the boys will be able to continue their schooling."

"Please do whatever you think is best, Mother."

The next morning when Tong-jun went to his father's room to say good morning to him, he was not there. Nam-hi was up and was gazing at the drizzle that was darkening the window.

"I wonder where Father is?"

"I don't know. I guess he's gone to T'ae-yŏn's," answered Mrs. Hyŏn sniffling as she packed.

Someone called from outside. It was the voice of Kim Sŏn-dal. When Tong-jun went to the gate, Kim wiped his eyes on his sleeve and said, "A bad thing happened to your old man out in the orchard."

They ran on the muddy ridgeway between the rice paddies.
Black waves of fear were surging in Tong-jun as he ran past the
fields turned tender green with sprouts of dropwort and clover
that last night's rain had brought out.

Raindrops dripped from the fruit trees in the orchard. And
they dripped from the face and body of Mr. Ch'oe dangling
from a pear tree.

A note they found under his pallet after they brought his
body home read: "I am leaving Nam-hi behind in this world. I
believe, after all, it will be best for all of you to let her live out
her destiny."

7

Surrounded by toys, Nam-hi played with a pinwheel in the
middle of the room. There was a little toy house with tiny windows and tiny kitchenware. Se-yŏng watched her as he wound
his wrist watch. She stopped fingering the pinwheel and turned
to him, her eyes expressionless.

He kept winding the watch, looking back into her eyes. She
looked at the watch on his wrist. He removed it and fastened
it around her wrist. After gazing at him for a long time, she
began to finger the watch.

For sometime now she had been living in a room Se-yŏng
designed specially for her. Immediately following his father's
death, Tong-jun brought her to his house in Chuŭl and, not
long after, to Se-yŏng's.

The watch was taken apart within the day.

Despite Nam-hi's condition, Se-yŏng married her. The wedding took place one fine day soon after they observed the first
anniversary of Mr. Ch'oe's death. At Se-yŏng's insistence,
Nam-hi was dressed in pure white and a sparkling coronet
woven with flowers and she held a bouquet of white roses and
green asparagus leaves. Her face shined with the lucid sheen of
a marble sculpture. Her lips were painted a bright color and a

pearl dangled from each of her ears.

Se-yŏng too was dressed formally with a bow tie and even white gloves. Tong-jun officiated at the ceremony. It was held in Se-yŏng's small living room which was also his study and bedroom. All Nam-hi's family except Tong-ho were there, including Mrs. Hyŏn, Tong-ho's wife, and Nam-hi's younger brothers and nephews. The face of every grown-up was clouded with mixed emotions.

8

The procession of refugees stretched endlessly to the south. Though it was October, the air was already like winter. The frost on the stubble in the rice paddies sparkled white under the sun.

Many of the refugees pushed carts loaded with their belongings and sometimes with their children. Most men carried packs on their backs and women carried bundles on their heads so they could hold the little hands of their children.

Se-yŏng clutched Nam-hi's hand firmly as he walked. He was traveling light, carrying only a backpack of some medical instruments that might come in handy. It was about four months after the war broke out.

Squadrons of airplanes tore across the sky high above them occasionally. Pressed by the Korean army, the Communist forces were retreating to the north at the time. People who had been hiding in deep valleys during the worst of the air raids were out on the road to seek safer places.

They were heading south. The 38th parallel that divided the country being no longer effective, the road was crammed with southbound refugees. There was no one trying to halt the surge of refugees that included Se-yŏng and Nam-hi as well as Tong-jun and his second son. They traveled the 40 kilometers to Pukch'on on foot in two days.

"How far do you intend to go?" Tong-jun asked Se-yŏng.

"I'm going all the way down and cross the 38th parallel."

"What for?"

"To get good treatment for my wife, of course."

"Do you think there's a chance for her to get all right?"

"That's what I hope. And how about you?"

"I don't know. All the boys are in the military. Tong-shik, Tong-su, T'ae-yŏn and even my oldest one are gone. I doubt if they'll survive this beastly war. I think after all I should better cross the 38th and at least save this kid."

Se-yŏng turned to him in surprise. "What about your wife?"

"She's fortunate in a way. She loves her Communist friends more than her family. At least that's how she feels right now."

"Don't you think it's a tragedy? The way things are turning out."

"That's life, huh? Who knows, maybe there'll come a day when the 38th parallel really disappears.... Remember that White Russian named Yankowski? The one that raised deer at Oup'o?"

"Uhuh."

"I don't know whether it's a rumor or fact but they say the old guy was arrested by the Russian army and his son ran away to the south. I thought that was a real tragedy when I heard it."

"And you don't think it's a tragedy now?"

"I've become numb. I don't feel anything anymore."

"But you've been managing quite well, compared to others. You've been quite decently treated, being a school principal."

"Yeah, I guess you could look at it that way. Keeping that position has been a real struggle and I'm completely worn out. Perhaps it's a sign I'm getting old."

"How's your brother doing?"

"Well and healthy, I hear. He's now working in an armory somewhere in the mountains. Earning his own meals at last."

That night they stayed at Tong-ho's house over the railroad track in Pukch'on. As her two sons were in the military, Mrs. Hyŏn was living with his family. Stroking Nam-hi's hands and knees tearfully, she did not leave her until late in the night.

The four travellers, Se-yŏng, Nam-hi, Tong-jun and Tong-jun's son, started on the road early the next morning. They had with them a bundle of rice balls Mrs. Hyŏn and Tong-ho's wife rolled carefully in oak leaves, which was the best they could do for them.

"I'll walk Nam-hi across the bridge. Why don't you say good-by here," Mrs. Hyŏn told Tong-ho's wife.

The sun was already high above Changnŭngsan Mountain. The bright sun rays highlighted the maze of wrinkles etched in Mrs. Hyŏn's face. Her gray hair was lackluster like dusty cotton threads.

"Miss Nam-hi, Miss Nam-hi, may you get well and live well and long," said Tong-ho's wife stifling a sob and told Se-yŏng, "Please take good care of my poor sister, I pray you." Her face too was lined with wrinkles and her hair was streaked with gray.

They crossed the bridge. To their left, the steel Yongch'ŏn railway bridge loomed against the sky like a magnificent fortress. The Yongch'ŏn River flowed under it, reflecting the blue sky.

The road on the other side of the bridge was sandy as it stretched through an expanse of dazzling sand. At the end of the sand, an embankment bordered a dense growth of willows. The rice paddies on the other side of the embankment to the east of the sand were once potato patches and corn fields. Se-yŏng could still remember Nam-hi coming to him by that field to bring Tong-jun's letter with her little brother. Her image, fresh and fragile like a white azalea, was a memento of the happier life he cherished.

The field also made him think of Yun Sŏbang, the butcher who lived near his cousin Chin U-yŏng. The village butcher with an absurdly large topknot and cotton pants crammed into gaiters on the day of his mother's funeral was another image deeply etched in his memory.

The last time he saw him, he was without the topknot. He might be working in some gold mine with Chin Saengwon.

The road ahead of them was already quite crowded with refugees. They reminded him of the refugees that converged on the railroad station in Changchun. He also thought the Israelis crossing the Red Sea under the guidance of Moses might have looked like them.

Suddenly the crowd stopped and looked up at the sky. With a thundering roar, silvery planes flashing in the sun zoomed overhead toward the bridge and endless bombs fell from the sky. The crowd dispersed over the sand and embankment with terrified shrieks and clung flat to the ground like spiders. Se-yŏng covered Nam-hi with his body. Tong-jun crouched likewise over his son. Mrs. Hyŏn was prostrate somewhere between them.

With an ear-splitting explosion, the likes of which they had never heard before, something crumbled down. Everyone held their hands over their ears long after the bombing ceased. Se-yŏng covered Nam-hi's ears with his hands.

Se-yŏng did not hear anything after the explosion. He turned his head in the direction from which they had come. The middle of the steel bridge over the Yongch'ŏn was caving in silently. Nam-hi too was looking at the bridge. Her eyes began to move back and forth quickly. She looked dazed like someone waking up from a deep sleep.

"Nam-hi, Nam-hi, Nam-hi," Se-yŏng called but he could not hear his own voice.

"Se-yŏng!"

"He knew her lips were forming his name but no sound reached him. Almost instantaneously he realized he had lost his hearing to the explosion and Mrs. Hyŏn was dead. Blood was oozing from her head where shrapnel had hit. Tong-jun's hip was bleeding.

A man brushing his pants said to Se-yŏng, "Hey, I know you. You're from Nanam, aren't you?" It was the man who had taken Mrs. Shin custody at the Nanam Station that snowy night. Se-yŏng, however, did not hear him nor anyone else.

"Everyone who's not injured please get up," someone hollered. "We need your help."

Tong-jun scrambled up and Nam-hi followed suit.

Tong-jun helped carry the injured and the dead to near the embankment. On his last trip, he reeled with surprise to find the body of Yi Sang-jun there. His wife was wailing beside him.

Not far from them Nam-hi was sobbing, her face buried in Mrs. Hyŏn's chest. Her moans were so painful that, if held in a bowl, they would be dripping blood.

No one but Tong-jun knew of the death of Yi Sang-jun.

It was some days later that they set forth on the road again. The wind had become more cold and cutting. Nam-hi wore a hemp mourning ribbon in her hair and Tong-jun and Se-yŏng wore hemp arm bands for Mrs. Hyŏn.

They passed Yongdam and headed up the slope of Norumok Hill. An eagle, its wings spread wide, glided over their heads to the east. The cold wind swept the uphill path rolling the dry leaves. Nam-hi noticed three army trucks driving up the hill heading to the south. If they were lucky, they might be able to get a ride on one of them. She stopped and looked around at Se-yŏng, who kept walking straight ahead, unable to hear the trucks.

Ah, your hearing is so much, so much more important than my mind I regained, she whispered to herself with an aching heart. She halted suddenly as the image of her son Yŏng-gŭn came into her mind. Ah, my poor baby, she whispered again desperately. But she knew that he was being well taken care of by his grandparents who doted on him.

The trucks drove past them. They would have to keep walking, hoping for better luck with the next ones. If no trucks came their way, they would walk until the train or boat services reopened. If there were no trains or boats, they would keep walking, walking to freedom. To the south, to the land of sunshine and freedom.... After all, that was what life was, an unceasing journey through sorrows and misfortunes in search of sunshine and freedom.

Se-yŏng trudged on, firmly clutching Nam-hi's hand. Someday his hearing would be restored. The wind swept under their feet again, but overhead the sun was bright and the sky was blue.